THE EVERLASTING WHISPER

A Tale of the California Wilderness

JACKSON GREGORY

1st WORLD
LIBRARY
Literary Society

The Everlasting Whisper

Jackson Gregory

© 1st World Library, 2007
PO Box 2211
Fairfield, IA 52556
www.1stworldlibrary.com
First Edition

LCCN: 2007924141

Softcover ISBN: 978-1-4218-4280-6
Hardcover ISBN: 978-1-4218-4182-3
eBook ISBN: 978-1-4218-4378-0

Purchase *"The Everlasting Whisper"*
as a traditional bound book at:
www.1stWorldLibrary.com/purchase.asp?ISBN=978-1-4218-4280-6

1st World Library is a literary, educational organization
dedicated to:

- Creating a free internet library of downloadable ebooks

- Hosting writing competitions and offering book
  publishing scholarships.

Interested in more 1st World Library books?
contact: literacy@1stworldlibrary.com
Check us out at: www.1stworldlibrary.com

1ˢᵗ World Library Literary Society

Giving Back to the World

"If you want to work on the core problem, it's early school literacy."

- James Barksdale, former CEO of Netscape

"No skill is more crucial to the future of a child, or to a democratic and prosperous society, than literacy."

- Los Angeles Times

Literacy... means far more than learning how to read and write... The aim is to transmit... knowledge and promote social participation."

- UNESCO

"Literacy is not a luxury, it is a right and a responsibility. If our world is to meet the challenges of the twenty-first century we must harness the energy and creativity of all our citizens."

- President Bill Clinton

"Parents should be encouraged to read to their children, and teachers should be equipped with all available techniques for teaching literacy, so the varying needs and capacities of individual kids can be taken into account."

- Hugh Mackay

To Maxwell E. Perkins

With The Author'S Grateful Recognition Of His
Countless Sympathetic Criticisms And Suggestions

CHAPTER I

It was springtime in the California Sierra. Never were skies bluer, never did the golden sun-flood steep the endless forest lands in richer life-giving glory. Ridge after ridge the mountains swept on and fell away upon one side until in the vague distances they sank to the monotonous level of the Sacramento Valley; down there it was already summer, and fields were hot and brown. Ridge after ridge the mountains stretched on the other side, rising steadily, growing ever more august and mighty and rocky; on their crests across the blue gorges the snow was dazzling white and winter held stubbornly on at altitudes of seven thousand feet. Thus winter, springtime, and ripe, fruit-dropping summer coexisted, touching fingers across the seventy miles that lie between the icy top of the Sierra and the burning lowlands.

Here, in a region lifted a mile into the rare atmosphere, was a ridge all naked boulder and spire along its crest, its sides studded with pine and incense cedar. The afternoon sunlight streaked the big bronze tree trunks, making bright gay spots and patches of light, casting cool black shadows across the open spaces where the brown dead needles lay in thick carpets. It was early June, and thus far only had the springtime advanced in its vernal progress upward through the timbered solitudes. Some few small patches of snow still lingered on in spots sheltered from the sun, but now they were ebbing away in thin trickles. Down in a hollow at the base of the sunny slope was a round alpine lake no bigger than a pond in a city park. It was of the same deep, perfect blue as the sky, whose colour it seemed not to reflect but to absorb.

A tiny fragment of this same heavenly azure drifted downward among the trees like a bit of sky falling. A second bit of blue that had skimmed across the lake and was visible now only as it rose and winged across the contrasting coloured meadow rimming the pool was like a bit of the lake itself. Two bluebirds. They swerved before the meeting, their wings fluttered, they lighted on branches of the same tree and shyly eyed each other. Did a man need to have the still message of all the woods summed up in final emphasis, this it was: spring is here.

The man himself, as the birds had done before him, had the appearance of materializing spontaneously from some distilled essence of his environment. A moment ago the spaces between the wide-set cedar-trees were empty. Yet he had been there a long time. It was only because he had moved that he attracted attention even of the sharp-eyed forest folk who were returning to tree and thicket. As the bluebirds had been viewless when merged into the backgrounds of their own colour, so he, while sitting with his back against a tawny cedar, had been drawn into the entity of the wilderness to which, obviously, he belonged. Here he blended, harmonized, disappeared when he held motionless. The well-worn, tall, laced boots were of brown leather, much scuffed, one in colour with the soil dusting them. The khaki trousers gathered into the boot-tops, the soft flannel shirt, were the brown of the tree trunks; skin of hands and face and muscular throat were the bronze of ripe pine-cones and burnished pine-needles. And, in a landscape spotted with light and shadow, the head of black hair might have passed for a bit of such pitch-black shadow as a tuft of thick foliage casts upon the light-smitten ground.

Beyond this outward harmony there was something at once more intangible and yet more vital and positive that made the man a piece with the natural world about him. Perhaps it was that he had lived so many months of so many years in the open that he had grown to be true brother of the wild; that he had shed coat after coat of artificial veneer as he took on the layers of tan; that in doing so he shed from his mind many of the artificialities of the twentieth century and remembered ancient instincts. His deep chest knew the tricks of proper breathing; he would come to the top of a steep climb with unlaboured breath. He stood tall and stalwart, filled with vigorous strength in repose like the straight valiant cedars. His eyes were black and piercing, as keen as those of the hawk which, circling in the deeper sky, had seen him when he moved; he, too, had seen the hawk. All about him was a lustily masculine phase of the world, giant trees dominating giant slopes, rugged boulders upheaved, iron cliffs defying time and battling the years; he, like them, was virile, his sex clothing him magnificently. He had not shaved for three days and yet, instead of looking untidy, was but clothed in the greater vitality. While his eyes sped swiftly hither and thither, now busied with wide groupings, now catching small details, his face was impassive. In keeping both with his own magnificent physique and the rugged note of the forest, it was the face of a man who had defied and battled.

Beyond the lake a peak upthrust its rocky front into the sky. It frowned across the ridges, darkened by the shadows which its own irregularities cast athwart its massive features. But the sun, slowly as it rolled, sought out those shadows; they moved, crept to other hiding-places, and the golden light coaxed a subdued, soft gentleness across the massive boulders. This, too, the man saw.

He stood looking out across the ridges and so to the final bulwark against the sky still white with last December. He sought landmarks and measured distance, not in miles but in hours. Then he glanced briefly at the sun. But now, before starting on again, he turned from the more distant landscape and, remembering the immediate scene about him as he had viewed it last, drowsing in the Indian summer of last October, he noted everywhere the handiwork of young June. The eyes which had been keen and alert filled suddenly with a shining brightness.

The springtime, eternally youthful coquette, had come with a great outward display of timidity and shyness into the sternly solemn forest land of the high Sierra. To the last fine detail and exquisite touch was she, more here than elsewhere, softly, prettily, daintily feminine, her light heart idly set on wooing from its calm and abstracted aloofness this region of granite and lava, of rugged chasms and august ancient trees. She filled the air with fragrances, lightly shaken; she scattered bright fragile flowers to brighten the earth and clear bird-notes to sparkle through the air. Hesitant always in the seeming, she came with that shy step of hers to the feet of glooming precipices; under crests where the snow clung on she played at indifference, loitering with a new flower, knowing that little by little the thaw would answer her veiled efforts, that in the end the monarch of all the brooding mountain tops would discard the white mantle of aloofness and thrill to her embrace; knowing, too, that with each successive conquest made secure she would only laugh in that singing voice of hers and turn her back and pass on. On and on, over ridges and ranges, and so around the world.

The woods lay steeped in sunshine, enwrapped in characteristic quietude. There was no wind to ruffle the man's hair, no sound of a falling cone or of dead leaves crackling under a squirrel's foot. And yet the man had the air now of one listening, hearkening to the silence itself. For silence among the pines is not the dead void of desert lands, but a great hush like the finger-to-lip command in a sleeper's room, or the still message of a sea-shell held to the ear. The countless millions of cedar and pine needles seemed as motionless as the very mountains themselves, yet it was they who laid the gently audible command upon the balmy afternoon and whispered the great hush. That whisper the man heard, it seemed to him, less with his ears than with his soul.

He went back to the tree against which he had rested and picked up his hat and a small canvas roll. And yet again, with his hat in his hand, he stood motionless, his eyes lingering along the cliff tops across the little lake, his attitude that of a man listening to an invitation which he would like to accept but in the end meant to refuse. Already he had marked out the way he planned to go, and still the nearer peaks with the sunshine upon them called to him. One would have hazarded that they were familiar from oft-repeated visits, and that among his plans to the contrary a desire to climb them insisted. He glanced at the sun again, shook his head, and took the first step slantingly downward along the slope. But only once more to grow as still as the big trees about him. Slowly he drew back into the shadows to watch and not be seen.

For abruptly two figures had appeared upon the rocky head of the mountain across the lake. They had come up from the further side, and when he saw them first stood clear-cut against the sky. They might have been hunters since each carried a rifle. And yet the watcher's brows gathered in a frown and his eyes glinted angrily.

The two figures separated, one going along the crest of the ridge, the other climbing downward cautiously until he stood at the edge of the cliffs. He craned his body to look down as though seeking a way to the lake; he straightened and stared for a long time toward the snow tops of the more distant altitudes. The sun lay in pools all about him, and across the distance separating him and his companion from the man who watched them so intently, his gestures could be followed readily. He turned and must have said something to his companion, who leaped down from a boulder and came to his side. The second man towered over him, head and shoulder. This the eyes upon the other slope were quick to note; they cleared briefly as though with a new understanding, only to grow harder than before.

They talked together, and yet the only sound to carry across the lake and meadow was the rush of air through innumerable tree-tops. The blue water glinted softly under the westering sun; in the blue void of the sky the hawk wheeled, silent and graceful and watchful. The smaller man pointed, his arm outheld steadily. The other drew nearer, towering above him.

He, too, pointed or seemed about to point. They stood so close together that the two figures merged. From a distance they looked like one man now.

It was with startling abruptness that the two figures were torn apart, each resolved again into an individual. One, the towering man, had drawn suddenly back; the other was falling. And yet the silence was unbroken. There was never a cry to echo through the gorges from a horror-clutched throat. The falling man plunged straight down a dozen feet, struck against a ragged rock, writhed free, fell again a few feet, and began to roll. There had been the flash of the sun on the rifle in his hand; he had clutched wildly at that as though it could save him. Now it flew from his grasp as he rolled over and over, plunging down the steep flank of the mountain.

The man who had watched from across the lake had not stirred. The big man on the cliffs came back slowly to the brink and crouched there, looking down, motionless so long that it was hard for the eye to be sure of him, to know if it were really a human being or a poised boulder squatting there. There came no call from below; the hawk wheeled and wheeled, lost interest, drifting away. In the little hollow where the lake glinted it was very still with the soft perfection of the first spring days.

The man on the cliff stood up, holding his rifle. He had done with looking down; now he pivoted slowly, looking off in all other directions. Presently he began climbing back up the few feet to the knife-like crest from which he had descended not five minutes ago. He paused there for hardly more than an instant and then went on, down the further side, out of sight.

The man who had seen all this from his own slope caught up his canvas roll again and hurried down toward the lake. For the first time he spoke aloud, saying:

"Swen Brodie. There's not another man in the mountains brute enough for that."

He hastened on, taking the shortest way, making nothing of the steepest slopes. He was going straight toward the nearer end of the lake, which he must skirt to come up the further mountain and to the man who had fallen; and, by the way, straight toward the peak, still bright in the sunlight, which he had wanted to revisit all along.

CHAPTER II

Much of the descent of the long slope was taken at a run, on ploughing heels. He crossed the springy meadow at a jog-trot. But the climb to the fallen man was another matter. The sun was appreciably lower, the shadows already made dusky tangles among the trees, when the man carrying the canvas roll came at last under the cliffs. From out these shadows, before his keen eyes found the man they sought, he heard a voice calling faintly:

"That you, Brodie?"

"No. Brodie's gone."

The voice, though very weak, sharpened perceptibly:

"You, who are you?"

"What difference does it make?—if you need help."

"Who said I wanted help? Not Brodie!"

"No. Not Brodie."

He dropped his roll and began working his way through the bushes. Presently he came to a spot from which he could see a figure propped up against a tree. There was a rifle across the man's knees, gripped in both hands. And yet surely the rifle had been whirled out of his hands in his fall. Then he was not

Jackson Gregory

hurt badly, after all, since he had managed to work his way back up to it.

"Oh! It's you, is it, King?" The man against the tree did not seem overjoyed; there was a sullen note in his voice.

King came on, breaking his way through the brush.

"Hello," he said, a little taken aback. "It's you, is it? I thought it would be—" But he did not say who. He came on and stood over the man on the ground, stooping for an instant to peer close into his face. "Hurt much?" he asked.

The answer was a long time coming. The face was bloodlessly grey. From it a pair of close-set, shallow brown eyes looked shiftily. A tongue ran back and forth between the colourless lips.

"It's my leg," he said. "I don't know if it's broke. And I'm sort of bunged up." He looked up sharply. "Oh, I'll be all right," he grunted, "and don't you fool yourself."

"Did Brodie—?"

The man began to tremble; the hands on his gun shook so that the weapon veered and wavered uncertainly.

"Yes, rot his soul." He began to curse, at first softly, then with a strained voice rising into a storm of windy incoherence. Suddenly he broke off, eyeing King with suspicion upon the surface of his shallow eyes. "What are you after?"

"I didn't know how badly you were hurt. I came to see if I could lend you a hand."

"You know I don't mean that. What are you after, here in the mountains?" His voice was surly with truculence.

King grew angry and burst out bluntly:

"The devil take you, Andy Parker. I wanted to help you. If you don't take my interference kindly, I'll be on my way."

He turned to be off. Why the man was not already dead from that fall he did not know. But if the fellow was able to shift for himself, it suited King well enough. He had business of his own and no desire to step to one side or another to deal with Swen Brodie or Andy Parker, or with any man who trailed his luck with such as these. But now Parker called to him, and in an altered voice, a whine running through the words.

"Hold on, King. I'm hung up here for the night, anyhow. And I ain't got a bite of grub, and already I'm burning up with thirst. Get me a drink, will you?"

Without answer, King went to his canvas roll, and Parker, thinking himself deserted, began to plead noisily. On his knees King opened his roll, got out a cup, and began to search for water. Above him there were patches of snow; he found where a trickle of clear cold water ran in a narrow rivulet, and presently returned to the injured man with a brimming cup. Parker drank thirstily, demanded more, and sank back with a long sigh.

"The thing's unlucky, you know, King," he said queerly.

"Is it?" said King coolly. It was like him not to pretend that he did not know to what Andy Parker's thoughts had flown.

Parker nodded, pursing his lips, and kept on nodding like a broken automatic toy. At the end he jerked his head up and muttered:

"There's been the devil's luck on it for more'n sixty years and maybe a thousand years before that! Oh, *you* know! Look how it went with those old-timers. The last one of the Seven got it. Look how it happens with old man Loony Honeycutt, clucking and chuckling and stepping up and down in his shadow all the time; gone nuts from just *smelling* of it! Look what happens to me, all stove up here." He paused and then spat out venomously: "Oh, it'll get Swen Brodie and it'll get you, too, Mark King. You'll see."

"Another drink before I go?" demanded King.

Parker put his fingers to his scalp and examined them for traces of blood.

"I got a terrible headache," he said. "Aching and singing and sort of dizzy."

King went for more water, this time filling his one cook-pot. When he returned Parker was trying to stand. He had drawn himself up, holding to the tree with both shaking hands, putting his weight gingerly on one leg. Suddenly his weak hands gave way, he swayed and fell. King, standing over him, thought at first he was dead, so white and still was he. But Parker had only fainted.

The sun sank lower; the shadows down about the lake shores thickened and began to run, more and more swiftly, up the surrounding slopes. The tall peaks caught the last of the fading light, and like so many watch-towers blazed across the wilderness. Upward, about their bases, surged the flooding shadows like a dark tide rising swiftly; the light on the tallest spire winked and went out; and all of a sudden the rush of air through the pine tops strengthened and a growing murmur like the voice of a distant surf made it seem that one could hear the flood of the night sweeping through gorge and canon and inundating the world. And, despite all that Mark King could do, the sunset glow had gone and the first big star was shining before Andy Parker stirred.

His first call was for water. Then he complained of a terrible pain in his vitals, a pain that stabbed him through from chest to abdomen. Thereafter he was never coherent again, though for the most part he babbled like a noisy brook. He spoke of Swen Brodie and old Loony Honeycutt and Gus Ingle all in one breath, and King knew that Gus Ingle was sixty years dead; he dwelt hectically on the "luck of the unlucky Seven." And when, far on in the night, he at length grew silent and King went to peer into his face by the light of his camp-fire, Andy Parker was dead.

*   *   *   *   *

Mark King made the grave in the dawn. In his roll, the handle slipped out so that it might lie snug against the steel head, was a short miner's pick. A little below where Parker lay in his last wide-eyed vigil under the stars, King found a fairly level space free of rock and carpeted in young grass. Here with a pine-tree to mark head and foot, he worked at the shallow grave. He put his own blanket down, laid the quiet figure gently upon it, bringing the ends over to cover him. He marked the spot with a pile of rocks; he blazed the two trees. It was all that he could do; far more than Andy Parker would have done for him or for any other man.

The sun was rising when, he made his way to the top of the ridge and came to stand where he had seen Parker and Swen Brodie side by side. He clambered on until he came to the very crest over which Swen Brodie had disappeared. Just where had Brodie gone? He wondered. The answer came before the question could have been put into words. Though it was full day across the heights where King stood, it would be an hour and longer before the sun got down into the canons and meadows. He saw the flare of a camp-fire shining bright through the dark of a low-lying flat two miles or more from his vantage-point. Brodie would be cooking his breakfast now.

After that King did not again climb up where his body would stand out against the sky which was filling so brightly with the new morning. He moved along the ridge steadily and swiftly like a man with a definite objective who did not care to be spied on. In twenty minutes, after many a hazardous passage along a steep bare surface, he came to a spot where the knife edge of the ridge was broken down and blunted into a fairly level space a hundred yards across. Here was an accumulation of soil worn down from the granite above, and here, an odd, isolated tuft of scrawny verdure, grew a small grove of trees, stunted pine and scraggling brush.

Toward the far end of this upland flat was the disintegrating ruin of a cabin. The walls had disappeared long ago, save for two or three rotting logs, but a small rectangle of slightly raised ground indicated how they had extended. Even the rock chimney had fallen away, but something of the fireplace, black with burning, stood where labouring hands had placed it more than half a century before.

Here he made his own breakfast from what was ready cooked in his pack, dispensing with the fire, which would inevitably tell Brodie of his presence. For Brodie, callously brutish as he was, must be something less than human not to turn his chill blue Icelandic eyes toward the spot where he had abandoned his fallen companion.

King's first interest was centred on the ground underfoot. He went back and forth and about the ruin of the cabin several times seeking any sign that would tell him if Brodie and Andy Parker had been here before him. But there were no tracks in the softer soil, no trodden-down grass. It was very likely that no foot had come here since King's own last October. A look of satisfaction shone for an instant in his eyes. Then, done with this keen examination, they went with curious eagerness to the more distant landscape. He passed through the storm-broken trees and to the far rim of the flat, where he stood a long time staring frowningly at one after another of the spires and ridges lifted against the sky, probing into the mystery of the night still slumbering in the ravines. Now his look had to do, in intent concentration, with a slope not five hundred yards off; now with a blue-and-white summit toward which a man might toil all day and all night before reaching.

He might have been the figure of the "Explorer," grim and hard and determined; silent and solitary in a land of silence and solitude, brooding over a region where "the trails run out and stop." Something urged, something called, and his blood responded. About him rose the voice of the endless leagues of pines in a hushed utterance which might have been the whisper:

"Something hidden. Go and find it. Go and look behind the Ranges—Something lost behind the Ranges. Lost and waiting for you. Go!"

He made sure that he had left no sign of his visit here, not so much as a fallen crust of bread, caught up his pack and found the familiar way down the cliffs, striking off toward the higher mountains and the high pass through which he would travel to-night.

CHAPTER III

To have followed the pace which he set that day would have broken the heart of any but a seasoned mountaineer. No man in these mountains could have so much as kept him in sight, saving alone Swen Brodie, and he was left far back yonder, miles on the other, lower, side of the ridge. By mid-forenoon King had outstripped the springtime and was among snow patches which grew in frequency and extent; at noon he built his little fire on a snow crust. He crossed a raging tributary of the American, travelling upward along the rock-bound, spray-wet gorge a full mile before he came to the possible precarious ford. At six o'clock he made a second fire in a bleak windy pass, surrounded by a glimmering ghostly waste. Trees were stiff with frost; the wind whistled and jeered through them and about sharp crags, filling the crisp air with eerie, shuddersome music. He set his coffee to boil while meditating that down in the Sacramento Valley, which one could glimpse from here by day, it was stifling hot, like midsummer. He rested by his fire with his canvas drawn up about his shoulders, smoked his pipe, remade his pack, and went on. He counted on the moon presently and a bed at a slightly lower altitude among the trees; to-night Andy Parker was sleeping in his army blanket.

He crunched along over the snow crust which rarely failed him, and though the daylight passed swiftly, the dead-white surface seemed to hold an absorbed radiance and shed it softly. By the time he got down to the timber-line again the moon was up. He left the country of Five Lakes well to his left, ignoring the invitation of the trail beyond down the tall walls of Squaw Creek cañon. He went straight down the long pitch of the mountain, heading tenaciously toward the tiny lakelet which, so far as he knew, had been nameless until his old friend Ben Gaynor had built a summer home there two years ago and had christened the pond among the trees. Lake Gloria! Mark King liked the appellation little enough, telling himself with thorough-going unreason that there was a silly name to fit to perfection a silly girl, but altogether out of place to tie on to an unspoiled Sierra lake. Ben would have done a better job in naming it Lake Vanity. Or Self-Regard. King could think of a score of designations more to the point. For though he had never so much as set his eyes on either Gloria or her mother, he had his own opinion of both of them. Nor did he in the least realize that that opinion was based rather less on actual knowledge than moulded by his own peculiar form of jealousy, that jealousy which one time-tried friend feels when the other allows love of women to occupy a higher place than friendship.

He made his camp at eight o'clock in a sheltered spot among the firs. He built a fire, made a mat of boughs, wrapped himself up in his canvas, and went promptly to sleep. He awoke cold, got his blood running by stamping about, put on fresh fuel and went to sleep again, his feet toward the blaze. Half a dozen times he was up during the night; before dawn he had his coffee boiling; before the sun was up he was well on his way again, driving the cramped chill out of him by walking vigorously. And at nine o'clock that morning he stood on the bench of a timbered slope whence, looking downward through the trees, he got his first glimpse of Lake Gloria and of the rambling log house which Ben Gaynor had been prevailed on to build here in the wild, a dozen miles from the Lake Tahoe road.

He noted, as he came nearer, swinging along down the slope and seeing the little valley with its green meadow and azure lake, how Ben had had a log dam thrown across the pond's lower end, backing up the water and making it widen out; he saw a couple of graceful canoes resting tranquilly on their own reflections; a pretty bathing-house already green with lusty hop-vines. Ben Gaynor had been spending money, a good deal of money. And no one knew better than Mark King that Ben had been close-hauled these latter years. He shrugged, telling himself to pull up short, and not find fault with his friend, or what his friend did, or with those whom his friend loved.

An hour later he came to the grove of sugar-pines back of the house. Here he paused a moment, though he was all eagerness for his meeting with Gaynor. He had seen a number of persons coming out of the house, a dozen or more, pouring out brightly, as gay as butterflies, men and women. Their laughter floated out to him through the still sunny morning, the deeper notes of men, a cluster of rippling notes from a girl. He wanted to see Gaynor, not a lot of Gaynor's San Francisco guests. No, not Gaynor's; rather the friends of Gaynor's womenfolk. It was King's hope that they were going down toward the lake; thus he would avoid meeting them. He'd come in at the back, have his talk with Ben, and be on his way without the bore of shaking a lot of flabby hands and listening to a lot of gushing exclamations.

He stood very still where he was, unseen as he leaned against a light-and-shadow-dappled pine. A girl broke away from the knot of summer-clad figures, ran a few steps down the path toward the lake, poised gracefully, executed a stagy little pose with head back and arms outflung as though in an ecstasy of delight that the world was so fair. She was a bright spot of colour with her pink dress and white shoes and stockings, and lacy parasol and brown hair, and for a little his eyes went after her quite as they would have followed the flight of a brilliant bird. Then, as in sheer youth, as one who during a night of refreshing sleep has been steeped body and soul in the elixir that is youth's own, she yielded her young body up to an extravagant dance, whirling away as light as thistledown across the meadow. Hands clapped after her; voices, men's voices, filled her ears with a clamour of praise as extravagant as her own dancing; the guests went trooping gaily after her. King seized his chance and went swiftly toward the house. As he went he noted that the girl alone was watching him; she was facing him, while the others had turned their backs upon the house. She had abandoned her dance and was standing very still, obviously interested in the rough-clad, booted figure which had seemed so abruptly to materialize from the forest land.

Ben Gaynor had seen him through a window and met him at the door. Their hands met in the way of old friendship, gripping hard. Further, Ben beat the dust out of his shoulders with a hard-falling open palm as he led the way inside.

"My wife has been saying for years that you're a myth," said Gaynor, the gleam in his eyes as youthful as it had ever been; "that you are no more flesh and blood than the unicorn or the dodo bird. To-day I'll show her. They were up half the night dancing and fussing around; she will be down in two shakes, though."

"In the meantime we can talk," said King. "I've got something to tell you, Ben."

Gaynor led the way through a room where were piano and victrola and from the floor of which the rugs were still rolled; through a dining-room and into what was at once a small library and Gaynor's study; King noted that even a telephone had found its way hither. A chair pulled forward, a box of cigars offered, and the two friends took stock in each other's eyes of what the last year had done for each.

"You look more fit than ever, Mark—and younger."

King wanted to say the same thing of his friend, but the words did not come. Gaynor was by far the older man, King's senior by a score of years, and obviously had begun to feel the burden of the latter greying days. Or of cares flocking along with them; they generally come together. His were seriously accepted responsibilities, where Mark gathered unto himself fresh hopes and eager joys; the responsibilities which come in the wake of wife and daughter; a home to be maintained in the city, the necessity to adapt himself, even if stiffly, to unfamiliar conditions. This big log house itself, it seemed to King, was carried on the back of old Ben.

They had been friends together since King could remember, since Ben had big-brothered him, carried him on his back, taught him to swim and shoot. Then one year while King was off at school his friend took unto himself a wife. This with no permission from Mark King; not even after a conference with him; in fact, to his utter bewilderment. King did not so much as know of the event until Gaynor, after a month of honey-mooning, remembered to drop him a brief note. The bald fact jarred; King was hurt and grew angry and resentful with all of that unreason of a boy. He went off to Alaska without a word to Gaynor.

With the passage of time the friends had again grown intimate, had been partners in more than one deal, and the youthful relationship had been cemented by the years. But it had happened, seemingly purely through chance, although King knew better, that he had never met Gaynor's wife or daughter. When Gloria was little, Mrs. Gaynor had been impressed by the desirability of a city environment, had urged the larger schools, music teachers, proper young companions, and a host of somewhat vague advantages. Hence a large part of the year Gaynor kept bachelor's quarters in his own little lumber town in the mountains where his business interests held him and where his wife and daughter came during a few weeks in the summer to visit him. At such periods King always managed to be away. This year the wife and daughter, drawn by the new summer home, had come early in the season, and King's business was urgent. Besides, he had told himself a dozen times, there really existed no sane reason in the world why he should avoid Ben Gaynor's family as though they were leprous.

... What King said in answer to his friend's approval was by way of a bantering:

"Miracles do happen! Here's Ben Gaynor playing he's a bird of paradise. Or emulating Beau Brummel. Which is it, Ben? And whence the fine idea?"

Gaynor, with a strange sort of smile, King thought, half sheepish and the other half tender, cast a downward glance along the encasement of the outer man. Silk shirt, a very pure white; bright tie, very new; white flannels, very spick and span; silken hose and low white ties. This garb for Ben Gaynor the lumberman, who felt not entirely at his ease, hence the sheepish grin; a fond father decked out by his daughter as King well guessed; hence that gleam of tenderness.

"Gloria's doings," he chuckled. "Sent ahead from San Francisco with explicit commands. I guess I'd wear a monkey-jacket if she said so, Mark." But none the less his eyes, as they appraised the rough garb of his guest, were envious. "I can breathe better, just the same, in boots like yours," he concluded. He stretched his long arms high above his head. "I wish I could get out into the woods for a spell with you, Mark."

And he did not know, did not in the least suspect, that he was failing the minutest iota in his loyalty to Gloria and her mother. He was thinking only of their guests, whom he could not quite consider his own.

"The very thing," said King eagerly. "That's just what I want."

But Gaynor shook his head and his thin, aristocratic face was briefly overcast, and for an instant shadows crept into his eyes.

"No can do, Mark," he said quietly. "Not this time. I've got both hands full and then some."

King leaned forward in his chair, his hand gripping Gaynor's knee.

"Ben, it's there. I've always known it, always been willing to bet my last dollar. Now I'd gamble my life on it."

Gaynor's mouth tightened and his eyes flashed.

"Between you and me, Mark," he said in a voice which dropped confidentially, "I'd like mighty well to have my share right now. I've gone in pretty deep here of late, a little over my head, it begins to look. I've branched out where I would have better played my own game and been content with things as they were going. I—" But he broke off suddenly; he was close to the edge of disloyalty now. "What makes you so sure?" he asked.

"I came up this time from Georgetown. You remember the old trail, up by Gerle's, Red Cliff and Hell Hole, leaving French Meadows and Heaven's Gate and Mount Mildred 'way off to the left. I had it all pretty much my own way until I came to Lookout Ridge. And who do you suppose I found poking around there?"

"Not old Loony Honeycutt!" cried Gaynor. Then he laughed at himself for allowing an association of ideas to lead to so absurd a thought. "Of course not Honeycutt; I saw him last week, as you wanted me to, and he is cabin-bound down in Coloma as usual. Can't drag his wicked old feet out of his yard. Who, then, Mark?"

"Swen Brodie then. And Andy Parker."

Gaynor frowned, impressed as King had been before him.

"But," he objected as he pondered, "he might have been there for some other reason. Brodie, I mean. Remember that the ancient and time-honoured pastimes of the Kentucky mountains have come into vogue in the West. Everybody knows, and that includes even the government agents in San Francisco, that there is a lot of moonshine being made in out-of-the-way places of the California mountains. There's a job for Swen Brodie and his crowd. There's talk of it, Mark."

"Maybe," King admitted. "But Brodie was looking for

something, and not revenue men, at that. He and Parker were up on the cliffs not a quarter-mile from the old cabin. They stood close together, right at the edge. Parker fell. Brodie looked down, turned on his heel and went off, smoking his stinking pipe, most likely. I buried Parker the next morning."

"Poor devil," said Gaynor. Then his brows shot up and he demanded:

"You mean Brodie did for him? Shoved him over?"

"That's exactly what I mean. But I can't tie it to Brodie, not so that he couldn't shake himself free of it. Parker didn't say so in so many words; I saw the whole thing from the mountain across the lake, too far to swear to anything like that. But this I can swear to: Brodie was in there for the same thing we've been after for ten years. And what is more, it's open and shut that he was of a mind to play whole-hog and pushed Andy Parker over to simplify matters. In my mind, even though I can't hope to ram that down a jury."

"How do you *know* what Brodie and Parker were after?"

"Andy Parker. He was sullen and tight-mouthed for the most part until delirium got him. Then he babbled by the hour. And all his talk was of Gus Ingle and the devil's luck of the unlucky Seven, with every now and then a word for Loony Honeycutt and Swen Brodie."

"If there is such a thing as devil's luck," said Gaynor with a sober look to his face, "this thing seems plastered thick with it."

King grunted his derision.

"We'll take a chance, Ben," he said. "And, after all, one man's bane is another man's bread, you know. Now I've told you my tale, let's have yours. You saw Honeycutt; could you get anything out of him?"

"Only this, that you are dead right about his knowing or thinking that he knows. He is feebler than he was last fall, a great deal feebler both in body and mind. All day he sits on his steps in the sun and peers through his bleary eyes across the mountains, and chuckles to himself like an old hen. 'Oh, I know what you're after,' he cackles at me, shrewd enough to hit the nail square, too, Mark. 'And,' he rambles on, 'you've come to the right man. But am I goin' to blab now, havin' kept a shut mouth all these years?' And then he goes on, his rheumy-red eyes blinking, to proclaim that he is feeling a whole lot stronger these days, that he is getting his second wind, so to speak; that come mid-spring he'll be as frisky as a colt, and that then he means to have what is his own! And that is as close as he ever comes to saying anything. About this one thing, I mean. He'll chatter like a magpie about anything else, even his own youthful evil deeds. He seems to know somehow that no longer has the law any interest in his old carcass, and begins to brag a bit of the wild days up and down the forks of the American and of his own share in it all; half lies and the other half blood-dripping truth, I'd swear. It makes a man shiver to listen to the old cut-throat."

"He can't live a thousand years," mused King. "He is eighty now, if he's a day."

"Eighty-four by his own estimate. But when it's a question of that, he sits there and sucks at his toothless old gums and giggles that it's the first hundred years that are the hardest to get through with and he's gettin' away with 'em."

"He knows something, Ben."

"So do we, or think we do. So does Brodie, it would seem. Does old Honeycutt know any more than the rest of us?"

"We are all young men compared with Loony Honeycutt, all Johnny-come-lately youngsters. Gus Ingle and his crowd, as near as we can figure, came to grief in the winter of 1853. By old Honeycutt's own count he would have been a wild young devil of seventeen then. And remember he was one of the roaring crowd that made the country what it was after '49. He knows where the old cabin was on Lookout; he swears he knows who built it in that same winter of '53. And—"

"And," cut in Gaynor, "if you believe the murderous old rascal, he knows with sly, intimate knowledge how and why the man in the lone cabin was killed. All in that same winter of '53!"

King pricked up his ears.

"I didn't know that. What does he say?"

"He talks on most subjects pretty much at random. He knows that the sheriff only laughs at him, since who would want to snatch the old derelict away from his mountains after all these years and try to fix a crime of more than half a century ago on him? But as the law laughs and at least pretends to disbelieve, his pride is hurt. So he has grown into the way of wild boasting. You ought to hear him talk about the affair at Murderer's Bar! It makes a man shiver to stand there in the sunshine and hear him. And, with the rest of his drivelling braggadocio, to hear him tell it, hinting broadly it was a boy of seventeen who, carrying nothing but an axe, did for the poor devil in the cabin."

"And I, for one, believe him! What is more, I am dead certain—call it a hunch, if you like—that if he had had the use of his legs all these years, he'd have gone straight as a string where we are trying to get." He began to pace up and down, frowning. "Brodie has been hanging around him lately, hasn't he?"

"Yes. Brodie and Steve Jarrold and Andy Parker and the rest of Brodie's worthless crowd of illicit booze-runners. They hang out in the old McQuarry shack, cheek by jowl with Honeycutt. I saw them, thick as flies, while I was there last week. Brodie, it seems, has even been cooking the old man's meals for him."

"There you are!" burst out King. "What more do you want? Imagine Swen Brodie turning over his hand for anybody on earth if there isn't something in it all for Swen Brodie. And I'll go bond he's giving Honeycutt the best, most nourishing meals that have come his way since his mother suckled him— Swen Brodie bound on keeping him alive until he gets what he's after. When he'd kick old Honeycutt in the side and leave him to die like a dog with a broken back."

"Well," demanded Gaynor, "what's to be done? With all his jabberings, Honeycutt is sly and furtive and is obsessed with the idea that there is one thing he won't tell."

"Will you go and see him one more time?"

"What's the good, Mark? If he does know, he gets lockjaw at the first word. I've tried—"

"There's one thing we haven't tried. Old Honeycutt is as greedy a miser as ever gloated over a pile of hoardings. We'll get a thousand dollars—five thousand, if necessary—in hard gold coin, if we have to rob the mint for it. You'll spread it on the table in his kitchen. You'll let it chink and you'll let some of it drop and roll. If that won't buy the knowledge we want— But it will!"

"I've known the time when five thousand wasn't as much money as it is right now, Mark—"

"I've got it, if I scrape deep. And I'll dig down to the bottom."

"And if we draw a blank?"

But there was a step at the door, the knob was turning. Mark King turned, utterly unconscious of the quick stiffening of his body as he awaited the introduction to Ben's wife.

CHAPTER IV

At first, King was taken aback by Mrs. Ben's youthfulness. Or look of youth, as he understood presently. He knew that she was within a few years of Ben's age, and yet certainly she showed no signs of it to his eyes, which, though keen enough, were, after a male fashion, unsophisticated. She was a very pretty woman, *petite*, alert, and decidedly winsome. He understood in a flash why Ben should have been attracted to her; how she had held him to her own policies all these years, largely because they were hers. She was dressed daintily; her glossy brown hair was becomingly arranged about the bright, smiling face. She chose to be very gracious to her husband's life-long friend, giving him a small, plump hand in a welcoming grip, establishing him in an instant, by some sleight of femininity which King did not plumb, as a hearthside intimate most affectionately regarded. His first two impressions of her, arriving almost but not quite simultaneously, were of youthful prettiness and cleverness.

She slipped to a place on the arm of Gaynor's chair, her hand, whose well-kept beauty caught and held King's eyes for a moment, toying with her husband's greying hair.

"She loves old Ben," thought King. "That's right."

Mrs. Ben Gaynor was what is known as a born hostess very charming. Hostess to her husband, of whom she saw somewhat less each year than of a number of other friends. She had always the exactly proper meed of intimacy to offer each guest in accordance with the position he had come to occupy, or which she meant him to occupy, in her household. Akin to her in instinct were those distinguished ladies of the colourful past of whom romantic history has it that in the salons of their doting lords and masters they gave direction, together with impetus or retardation, to muddy political currents. Clever women.

Not that cleverness necessarily connotes heartlessness. She adored Ben; you could see that in her quick dark eyes, which were always animated with expression. If she was not more at his side, the matter was simply explained; she adored their daughter Gloria no less, and probably somewhat more, and Gloria needed her. Surely Gaynor's needs, those of a grown man, were less than those of a young girl whose budding youth must be perfected in flower. And if Mrs. Ben was indefatigable in keeping herself young while Ben quietly accepted the gathering years, it was with no thought of coquetting with other men, but only that she might remain an older sister to her daughter, maintain the closer contact, and see that Gloria made the most of life. Any small misstep which she herself had made in life her daughter must be saved from making; all of her unsatisfied yearnings must be fulfilled for Gloria. She constituted herself cup-bearer, wine-taster and handmaiden for their daughter. If it were necessary to engrave another fine line in old Ben's forehead in order to add a softer tint to Gloria's rose petals, she was sincerely sorry for Ben, but the desirable rose tints were selected with none the less steady hand.

Ben Gaynor's eyes followed his wife pridefully when, at the end of fifteen pleasant, sunny minutes, she left them, and then went swiftly to his friend's face, seeking approbation. And he found it. King had risen as she went out, holding himself with a hint of stiffness, as was his unconscious way when infrequently in the presence of women; now he turned to Ben with an odd smile.

"Pretty tardy date to congratulate you, old man," he said with a laugh. "Don't believe I ever remembered it before, did I?"

Ben glowed and rubbed his long hands together in rich contentment.

"She's a wonder, Mark," he said heartily.

Mark nodded an emphatic approval. Words, which Ben perhaps looked for, he did not add. Everything had been said in the one word "congratulate."

"Sprang from good old pioneer stock, too, Mark," said Gaynor. "Wouldn't think now, to look at her, that she was born at Gold Run in a family as rugged as yours and mine, would you? With precious few advantages until she was a girl grown, look at what she has made of herself! While you and I and the likes of us have been content to stay pretty much in the rough, she hasn't. There's not a more accomplished, cultured little woman this or the other side Boston, even if she did hail from Gold Run. And as for Gloria, all her doing; why," and he chuckled, "she hasn't the slightest idea, I suppose, that she ever had a grandfather who sweated and went about in shirt-sleeves and chewed tobacco and swore!"

"Have to go all the way back to a grandfather?" laughed King.

"Look at me!" challenged Gaynor, thrusting into notice his immaculate attire. He chuckled. "One must live down his disgraceful past for his daughter, you know."

From without came a gust of shouts and laughter from the Gaynor guests skylarking along the lake shore.

"Come," said Ben. "You'll have to meet the crowd, Mark. And I want you to see my little girl; I've told her so many yarns about you that she's dying of curiosity."

King, though he would have preferred to tramp ten miles over rough trails, gleaning small joy from meeting strangers not of his sort who would never be anything but strangers to him, accepted the inevitable without demur and followed his host.

He would shake hands, say a dozen stupid words, and escape for a good long talk with Ben. Then, before the lunch-hour, he would be off.

Gaynor led the way toward a side door, passing through a hallway and a wide sun-room. Thus they came abreast of a wide stairway leading to the second storey. Down the glistening treads, making her entrance like the heroine in a play, just at the proper instant, in answer to her cue, came Gloria.

"Gloria," called Gaynor.

"Papa," said Miss Gloria, "I wanted—Oh! You are not alone!"

Instinctively King frowned. "Now, why did she say that?" he asked within himself. For she had seen him coming to the house. Straight-dealing himself, circuitous ways, even in trifles, awoke his distrust.

"Come here, my dear," said Ben. "Mark, this is my little girl. Gloria, you know all about this wild man. He is Mark King."

"Indeed, yes!" cried Gloria. She came smiling down the stairway, a fluffy pink puffball floating fairy-wise. Her two hands were out, ingenuously, pretty little pink-nailed hands which had done little in this world beyond adorn charmingly the extremities of two soft round arms. For an instant King felt the genial current within him frozen as he stiffened to meet the girl he had watched in the extravagant dance down to the lake.

Then, getting his first near view of her, his eyes widened. He had never seen anything just like her; with that he began realizing dully that he was straying into strange pastures. He took her two hands because there was nothing else to do, feeling just a trifle awkward in the unaccustomed act. He looked down into Gloria's face, which was lifted so artlessly up to his. Hers were the softest, tenderest grey eyes he had ever looked into. He had the uneasy fear that his hard rough hands were rasping the fine soft skin of hers. Yet there was a warm pleasurable thrill in the contact. Gloria was very much alive and warm-bodied and beautiful. She was like those flowers which King knew so well, fragrant dainty blossoms which lift their little faces from the highest of the old mountains into the rarest of skies, growths seeming to partake of some celestial perfection; hardy, though they clothed themselves in an outward seeming of fragile delicacy. *Physically*—he emphasized the word and barricaded himself behind it as though he were on the defence against her!—she came nearer perfection than he had thought a girl could come, and nowhere did he find a conflicting detail from the tendril of sunny brown hair touching the curve of the sweet young face to the little feet in their clicking high-heeled shoes. Thus from the beginning he thought of her in superlatives. And thus did Gloria, like the springtime coquetting with an aloof and silent wilderness, make her bright entry into Mark King's life.

"I have been acting-up like a Comanche Indian outside," laughed Gloria. It was she who withdrew her hands; King started inwardly, wondering how long he had been holding them, how long he would have held them if she had not been so serenely mistress of the moment. "My hair was all tumbling down and I had to run upstairs to fight it back where it belongs. Isn't a girl's hair a terrible affliction, Mr. King? One of these days, when papa's back is turned, I'm going to cut it off short, like a boy's."

An explanation of her presence in the house while her guests were still in the yard; why explain so trifling a matter? A suggestion that she retained that lustrous crown of hair just to please her papa, whereas one who had not been told might have been mistaken in his belief that this should be one of her greatest prides. Two little fibs for Miss Gloria; yet, certainly, very small fibs which hurt no one.

Gloria's eyes, despite their soft tenderness, were every whit as quick as Mark King's when they were, as now, intrigued. Of course both she and King had heard countless references, one of the other, from Ben Gaynor, but neither had been greatly interested. King had known that there was a baby girl, long ago; that fact had been impressed on him with such rare eloquence that it had created a mental picture which, until now, had been vivid and like an indelible drawing; he had known, had he ever paused for reflection, which he had not, that a baby would not stay such during a period of eighteen years. She had heard a thousand tales of "my good friend, Mark." Mark, thus, had been in her mind a man of her father's age, and about such a young girl's romantic ideas do not flock. But from the first glimpse of the booted figure among the trees she had sensed other things. King would have blushed had he known how picturesque he bulked in her eyes; how now, while she smiled at him so ingenuously, she was doing his thorough-going masculinity full tribute; how the ruggedness of him, the very scent of the resinous pines he bore along with him, the clear manlike look of his eyes and the warm dusky tan of face and hands—even the effect of the careless, worn boots and the muscular throat showing through an open shirt-collar—put a delicious little shiver of excitement into her.

Miss Gloria had a pretty way of commanding, half beseeching and yet altogether tyrannical. King, having agreed to stay to luncheon, was in the bathroom off Gaynor's room, shaving. Gloria had caught her father and dragged him off into a corner. "Oh, papa, he is simply magnificent! Why didn't you *tell* me? Why, he isn't a bit old and—" And she made him repaint for her the high lights of an episode of Mark King making a name for himself and a fortune at the same time in the Klondike country. She danced away, singing, to her abandoned friends, who were returning to the house. "It's *the* Mark King, my dears!" she told them triumphantly, not unconscious of the depressing result of her disclosures upon a couple of boys of the college age who adored openly and with frequent lapses from glorious hope to bleak despair. "The man who made history in the Klondike. The man who fought his way alone across fifteen hundred miles of snow and ice and won—oh—I don't know *what* kind of a fight. Against all kinds of odds. The very Mark King! He's papa's best friend, you know."

"Let him be your dad's friend, then," said the young fellow with the pampered pompadour, his eyes showing a glint of sullen jealousy. "That's no reason—"

"Why, Archie!" cried Gloria. "You are making yourself just horrid. You don't want to make me sorry I ever invited you here, do you?" And a brief half-hour ago Archie had flattered himself that Gloria's dancing had been chiefly for him.

They were all of Gloria's "set" with one noteworthy exception. Him she called "Mr. Gratton" while the others were Archie and Teddy and Georgia and Evelyn and Connie. It was to this "Mr. Gratton" that she turned, having made a piquant face at the dejected college youth.

"*You* will like him immensely, I know," she said, while the ears of poor Archie reddened even as he was being led away by the not very pretty but extremely comforting Georgia. "He's a real man, every inch of him." ["Every inch a King!" she thought quickly, unashamed of the pun.] "A big man who does big things in a big way," she ran on, indicating that she, too, after that brief meeting had been lured into superlatives.

"Mr. Gratton," smiled urbanely. For his own part he might have been called every inch a concrete expression of suavity. He was clad in the conventional city-dweller's "outdoor rig." Shining puttees lying bravely about the shape of his leg; brown outing breeches, creased, laced at their abbreviated ends; shirt of the sport effect; a shrewd-eyed man of thirty-five with ambitions, a chalky complexion, and a very weak mouth with full red lips.

"Miss Gloria," he whispered as he managed to have her all to himself a moment, "you'll make me jealous."

She was used to him saying stupid things. Yet she laughed and seemed pleased. Gratton egotistically supposed her thought was of him; King would have been amazed to know that she was already watching the house for his coming. And he would have been no end amazed and bristling with defence had he glimpsed the astonishing fact that Gloria already fully and clearly meant to parade him before her summer friends as her latest and most virile admirer. Gratton's heavy-lidded pale eyes trailed over her speculatively.

That forenoon King shook hands with Archie, Teddy, Gratton, and the rest, made his formal bows to Gloria's girl friends, and felt relief when the inept banalities languished and he was free to draw apart. Gratton, with slender finger to his shadowy moustache, bore down upon him. King did not like this suave individual; he had the habit of judging a man by first impressions and sticking stubbornly to his snap judgment until circumstance showed him to be in error. He liked neither the way Gratton walked nor talked; he had no love for the cut of his eye; now he resented being approached when there was no call for it. Never was there a more friendly man anywhere than Mark King when he found a soul-brother; never a more aloof at times like this one.

"I have been tremendously interested," Gratton led off ingratiatingly, "in the things I have heard of you, Mr. King. By George, men like you live the real life."

The wild fancy came booming upon King to kick him over the verandah railing.

"Think so?" he said coolly, wondering despite himself what "things" Gratton had heard of him. And from whom? His spirit groaned within him at the thought that old Ben Gaynor had been lured into paths along which he should come to hobnob with men like Gratton. He was sorry that he had promised to stay to lunch. His thoughts all of a sudden were restive, flying off to Swen Brodie, to Loony Honeycutt, to what he must get done without too much delay. Gratton startled him by speaking, bringing his thoughts back from across the ridges to the sunny verandah overlooking Lake Gloria.

Gratton was nobody's fool, save his own, and both marked and resented King's attitude. His heavy lids had a fluttering way at times during which his prominent eyes seemed to flicker.

"What's the chance with Gus Ingle's 'Secret' this year, Mr. King?" he demanded silkily.

King wheeled on him.

"What do you know about it?" he said sharply. "And who has been talking to you?"

Gratton laughed, looked wise and amused, and strolled away.

At luncheon Mrs. Gaynor placed her guests at table out on the porch, conscious of her daughter's watchful eye. When all were seated, Mark King found himself with Miss Gloria at his right and an unusually plain and unattractive girl named Georgia on his left. Everybody talked, King alone contenting himself with brevities. Over dessert he found himself drifting into *tete-a-tete* with Miss Gloria. They pushed back their chairs; he found himself still drifting, this time physically and still with Gloria as they two strolled out through the grove at the back of the log house. There was a splendid pool there, boulder-surrounded; a thoroughly romantic sort of spot in Gloria Gaynor's fancies, a most charming background for springtime loitering. The gush and babble of the bright water tumbling in, rushing out, filled the air singingly. Gloria wanted to ask Mr. King about a certain little bird which she had seen here, a little fellow who might have been the embodiment of the stream's joy; she knew from her father that King was an intimate friend of wild things and could tell her all about it. They sat in Gloria's favourite nook, very silent, now and then with a whisper from Gloria, awaiting the coming of the bird.

CHAPTER V

"But, my darling daughter," gasped Mrs. Gaynor, "you don't in the least understand what you are about!"

"But, my darling mother," mimicked Miss Gloria, light of tone but with all of the calm assurance of her years, "I do know exactly what I am about! I always do. And anyway," with a Frenchy little shrug which she had adopted and adapted last season, "I am going."

"But," exclaimed her mother, already routed, as was inevitable, and now looking toward the essential considerations, "what in the world will every one say? And think?"

In the tall mirror before her Gloria regarded her boots and riding-breeches critically. Then her little hat and the blue flannel short. Too mannish? Never, with Gloria in them, an expression in very charming curves of triumphant girlhood.

"What in the world was Mark King thinking of?" demanded her mother.

"What do you suppose?" said Gloria tranquilly "He would have been very rude if he hadn't been thinking of your little daughter. Besides, he had very little to do with the matter."

"Gloria!"

"And, what is more, there was a moon. Remember that,

mamma." She tied the big scarlet silk handkerchief about her throat and turned to be kissed. Mrs. Gaynor looked distressed; there were actually tears trying to invade her troubled eyes, and her hands were nervous.

"But you will be gone all day!"

"Oh, mamma!" Gloria began to grow impatient. "What if I am? Mr. King is a gentleman, isn't he? He isn't going to eat me, is he? Why do you make such a fuss over it all? Do you want to spoil everything for me?"

"You know I don't! But—"

"We've had nothing but 'buts' since I told you. I should have left you a note and slipped out." She bestowed upon the worried face a pecking little kiss and tiptoed to the door.

"Wait, Gloria! What shall I tell every one? They're your *guests*, after all—"

"Tell them I asked to be excused for the day. Beyond that you are rather good at smoothing out things. I'll trust you."

"But—I mean *and*—and Mr. Gratton?"

"Oh, tell him to go to the devil!" cried Gloria. "It will do him no end of good." And while Mrs. Gaynor stared after her she closed the door softly and went tiptoeing downstairs and out into the brightening dawn, where Mark King awaited her with the horses.

From behind a window-curtain Gloria's mother watched the girl tripping away through the meadow to the stable, set back among the trees. King was leading the saddled horses to meet her; Gloria gave him her gauntleted hand in a greeting the degree of friendliness of which was gauged by the clever eyes at the window; friendliness already arrived at a stage of intimacy. King lifted Gloria into her saddle; Gloria's little laugh had in it a flutter of excitement as her cavalier's strength took her by delighted surprise and off her feet. They rode away through the thinning shadows. Mrs. Gaynor, despite the earliness of the hour, went straight to her husband, awoke him mercilessly, and told him everything.

"Oh," he said when she had done and he had turned over for another hour or so of sleep, "that's all right. Mark told me about it last night."

"And you didn't say a word to me!"

"Forgot," said Ben. "But don't worry. Mark'll take care of her."

She left him to his innocent slumbers and began dressing. Already she was busied with planning just what to say and how to say it; Gloria knew, she thought with some complacency, that her mother could be depended upon in any situation demanding the delicate touch. She would be about, cool and smiling, when the first guest appeared; it would be supposed that she and Gloria and Mr. King had been quite a merry trio as the morning adventure was being arranged. That first guest stirring would be Mr. Gratton on hand to pounce on Gloria and get her out of the house for a run down to the lake, a dash in a canoe, or a brief stroll across the meadow before the breakfast-gong. Instead of Gloria's terse message for him, she had quite an elaborate and laughing tale to tell. After all, Gloria usually did know what she was about, and if Mr. Gratton meant all that he looked—Mrs. Gaynor had cast up a rough draft of everything she would say that morning before she opened the door to go downstairs. And for reasons very clear to her and which she had no doubt would be viewed with equal clarity by Gloria after this "escapade" of hers was done with, she meant to be very tactful indeed with Mr. Gratton.

* * * * *

Never had Mark King known pleasanter companionship than

Gloria Gaynor afforded this bright morning. They passed up the trail, over the first ridge, dropped down into a tiny wild little valley, and had the world all alone to themselves. Only now was the sun up, and there in the mountains, blazing forth cheerily, it seemed to shine for them alone. When they rode side by side Gloria chatted brightly, athrill with animation, vivid with her rioting youth. When the narrow trail demanded and she rode ahead, bright little snatches of lilting song or broken exclamations floated back to the man whose eyes shone with his enjoyment of her. On every hand this was all a bright new world to her; she had never run wild in the hills as her mother had done through her girlhood; she had never been particularly interested in all of this sprawling ruggedness. Now she had a hundred eager questions; she saw the shining splendour of the solitudes through King's eyes; she turned to him with full confidence for the name of a flower, the habit of a bird, even though the latter, unseen among the trees, had only announced himself by a half-dozen enraptured notes.

Yesterday, surrendering her volatile self to a very natural and quite innocent feminine instinct, Gloria had fully determined to parade Mark King before her envious friends as very much her own property. It was merely a bit of the game, the old, old game at which she, being richly favoured by nature, was as skilful as a girl of eighteen or nineteen could possibly be. In the eternal skirmish she was an enterprising young savage with many scalps dangling from her triumphant belt. The petted pompadour of poor Archie, the curly locks of Teddy, the stiff black brush of Mr. Gratton were to have an added fellow in King's trophy. Then she had caught a word between her father and his friend; had heard Honeycutt mentioned and a ride to Coloma, and on the break of the instant had determined with a young will which invariably went unthwarted, that high adventure was beckoning her. A ride on horseback through the mountains with a man who had stirred her more than a little, who filled her romantic fancies with picturesque glamour, who was on a quest of which she knew ten times more than he had any idea she knew. And that quest itself! Pure golden glamour everywhere.

Hence, some few minutes afterward, in a cosy nook of the verandah while the others danced, the moon and Gloria were serenely victorious. King, once assured that the long ride was not too hard for her, saw no slightest reason for objecting to her coming; he did not think of all of that which would mean so much to Ben's wife—the conventions and what would people say. Conventions do not thrive in such regions as the high Sierra. Ben, to whom King mentioned the thing, looked at it quite as did his friend. Gloria would be in good hands and ought to have a corking good time; he wished he could get away to go along. So King telephoned to San Francisco, arranged to have three thousand dollars—in cash—sent immediately to him at Coloma, and to-day fancied himself strictly attending to business with an undivided mind.

"I know now where the original Garden of Eden was!" Gloria, turning to look back at him as he came on through a delightful flowery upland meadow, sat her horse gracefully upon a slight hillock, herself and her restless mount bathed in sunshine, her cheeks warm with the flush upon them, her lips red with coursing life, her eyes dancing. "It's perfectly lovely. It's pure heavenly!"

King nodded and smiled. He was not given to many words, grown taciturn as are mountaineers inevitably, trained in long habit to approve in silence of that which pleased him most. So, while Gloria's eager tongue tripped along as busily as the brooks they forded, he was for the most part silent. An extended arm to point out a big snow-plant, blood-red against a little heap of snow, was as eloquent as the spoken word. Thus he indicated much that might have passed unnoticed by Gloria, keenly enjoying her lively admiration.

To-day he chose always the easier trails, since with the good horses under them they had ample time to come to Loony Honeycutt's place well before midday. Also they stopped frequently, King making an excuse of showing her points of interest; the tiny valley where one could be sure of a glimpse of a brown bear, the grazing-lands of mountain deer, the pass into the cliff-bound hiding-place of the picturesque highway-men of an earlier day whence they drove stolen horses into Nevada, where they secreted other horses stolen in Nevada and to be disposed of down in the Sacramento Valley. There lasted until this very day the ruins of their rock house, snuggled into the mountains under their lookout-point.

"It would be fun," said Gloria, the spell of the wilderness mysteries upon her, her eyes half wistful and altogether serious, "to be lost out here. Just to get far, far away from people and ever so close to the big old mountains. Wouldn't it?" And a few minutes later she drew in her horse and cried out softly: "Listen!" She herself was listening breathlessly. "It sounds like the ocean ever so far off. Or—or like shouting voices a million miles away. Or like the mountains themselves whispering. It is hard to believe, isn't it? that it is just the wind in the pines."

Another time, while, under the pretext of letting their horses blow, King had suggested a short halt to give the girl a chance to rest, she said with abruptness:

"What do you think of Mr. Gratton?"

Already she knew Mark King well enough to realize that he would either refuse to answer or would speak his mind without beating about the bush.

"I don't like him," said King.

Gloria looked thoughtful.

"Neither do I," she said. "Not up here in the mountains. And down in San Francisco I thought him rather splendid. What is more, if we were whisked back to San Francisco this minute, I'd probably think him fine again."

She appeared interested in the consideration, and when they rode on was silent, obviously turning the matter over and over in mind.

* * * * *

To-day were three mysteries tremblingly close to revealing themselves one to another: the great green mystery of the woodlands; the mystery of a man clothed in his masculinity as in an outer garment; the tender mystery of a young girl athrill with romance, effervescent with youth, her own thoughts half veiled from herself, her instincts alive and urgent, and often all in confusion. How could a man like Mark King quite understand a girl like Gloria? How could a girl like Gloria, with all of her surety of her own decisions, understand a man like King? Each glimpsed that day much of the other's true character, and yet all the while the mainsprings were just out of sight, unguessed, undreamed of.

At Gloria's age, if one be a girl and very pretty and made much of by adoring parents and a host of boys and men, the world is an extremely nice place inhabited exclusively by individuals pressing forward to do her reverence. She is beautiful, she is vivacious, filled with delight; she is a sparkling fountainhead of joy. She is so superabundantly supplied with eager happiness that she radiates happiness. If she thinks a very great deal of herself, so for that matter does every other individual in the world; it is merely that with all of her sophistication she remains much more naive than she would ever believe; she is a coquette because she is female; she is pleased with herself and with the high excuse that every one else is pleased with her. Hence she demands adoration as a right. If she rides on a street-car she fully expects that the conductor will regard her admiringly and that the motorman will turn his head after her. She doesn't expect to marry either of these gentlemen; she does not particularly require their flattering attentions.... Gloria did not expect to marry Archie or Teddy or Mr. Gratton; she had no thought of being any one's wife; that term, after all, at Gloria's age, is a drab and humdrum thing. She did not dream of Mark King as a possible husband; another unromantic title. She merely hungered for male admiration. It was the wine of life, the breath in her nostrils. As it happens to be to some countless millions of other girls.... All of which is so clearly a pretty nearly universal condition that it would seem that if Mark King had had his wits about him he must have realized it. And yet had he glimpsed that which should have been so obvious he would have been startled, somewhat shocked, and would have grieved over his friend's empty-headed daughter, holding her unmaidenly—when she was but dallying with dreams which mean so much to all maidens.

But Gloria did not say to him: "Mark King, I am determined that you shall adore me, pretty face, pretty figure, pretty ways and all." Nor yet to herself did she put things so baldly. She did, however, yield herself luxuriously to the springtime, the romance of the hour, the appeal of her latest cavalier, and preen herself like a mating bird. King saw, admired, and in his own fashion played his own part. It was not clear to him that there had been a new pleasure in his own strength when he had lifted her into her saddle, and yet her little breathless laugh had rung musically in his ears. Had a man arisen to announce, jibingly, that Mark King was "showing off" before a girl like a boy of ten, though within bounds, he would have called the man a liar and forthwith have kicked him out of the landscape ... They rode on, side by side, each content with seeing only that which lay on the surface—both of his companion and of himself. In a word, they were living life naturally, without demanding of the great theatrical manager to know exactly what parts they were to play in the human comedy. Externals sufficed just now; the fragrant still forests, the pulse-stirring sunshine, the warm, fruitful earth below and the blue sky above.

From the first he called her Gloria quite naturally; to her he was Mr. King. But the "Mark" slipped out before they came into sight of the roofs of picturesque Coloma.

CHAPTER VI

"You are sure you won't be gone more than an hour?" Gloria asked.

Never, it seemed to her, had she seen a lonelier-looking place than old Coloma drowsing on the fringe of the wilderness. The street into which they had ridden was deserted save for a couple of dogs making each other's acquaintance suspiciously. Why was it more lonesome here than it had been back there in the mountains? she wondered.

"Less than an hour," he assured her. "What business I have can be done in fifteen minutes if it can be done at all. But, in the meantime, what will you do?"

"Oh," said Gloria, "I'll just poke around. It will be fun to see what kind of people live here."

He put the horses in the stable, watered and fed them himself, and came back to her outside the front double doors. She had dropped down on a box in the sun; he thought that there was a little droop to her shoulders. And small wonder, he admitted, with a tardy sense of guilt. All these hours in the saddle—

"Tired much?" he asked solicitously.

The shoulders straightened like a soldier's; she jumped up and whirled smilingly.

"Not a bit tired," she told him brightly.

"That's good. But I could get a room for you at the hotel; you could lie down and rest a couple of hours—"

Gloria would not hear to it; if she did want to lie down she'd go out under one of the trees and rest there. She trudged along with him to the post-office; she watched as Mark called for and got a registered parcel. Further, she marked that the postmaster appeared curious about the package so heavily insured until over Mark's shoulder he caught a glimpse of her, and that thereafter, craning his neck as they went out, he evidenced a greater interest in her than in a bundle insured for three thousand dollars. She was smiling brightly when Mark King hurried off to his meeting with old Loony Honeycutt.

Honeycutt's shanty, ancient, twisted, warped, and ugly like himself, stood well apart from the flock of houses, as though, like himself even in this, it were suspicious and meant to keep its own business to itself. Only one other building had approached it in neighbourly fashion, and this originally had been Honeycutt's barn. Now it had a couple of crazy windows cut crookedly into its sides and a stovepipe thrust up, also crookedly, through the shake roof, and was known as the McQuarry place. Here one might count on finding Swen Brodie at such times as he favoured Coloma with his hulking presence; here foregathered his hangers-on. An idle crowd for the most part, save when the devil found mischief for them to do, they might be expected to be represented by one or two of their number loafing about headquarters, and King realized that his visit to Loony Honeycutt was not likely to pass unnoticed. What he had not counted on was finding Swen Brodie himself before him in Honeycutt's shanty.

King, seeing no one, walked through the weeds to Honeycutt's door. The door was closed, the windows down—dirty windows, every corner of every pane with its dirty cobweb trap and skeletons of flies. As he lifted his foot to the first of the three front steps he heard voices. Nor would any man who had once listened to the deep, sullen bass of Swen Brodie have forgotten or have failed now in quick recognition. Brodie's mouth, when he spoke, dripped the vilest of vocabularies that had ever been known in these mountains, very much as old Honeycutt's toothless mouth, ever screwed up in rotary chewing and sucking movements, drooled tobacco juice upon his unclean shirt. Brodie at moments when he desired to be utterly inoffensive could not purge his utterance of oaths; he was one of those men who could not remark that it was a fine morning without first damning the thing, qualifying it with an epithet of vileness, and turning it out of his big, loose mouth sullied with syllables which do not get themselves into print.

What King heard, as though Brodie had held his speech for the moment and hurled it like a challenge to the man he did not know had come, was, when stripped of its cargo of verbal filth:

"You old fool, you're dying right now. It's for me or Mark King to get it, and it ain't going to be King."

Honeycutt all the time was whining like a feeble spirit in pain, his utterances like the final dwindlings of a mean-spirited dog. King had never heard him whine like that; Honeycutt was more given to chucklings and clackings of defiance and derision. Perhaps Brodie as the ultimate argument had man-handled him. King threw open the door.

There stood old Honeycutt, tremblingly upheld upon his sawed-off broom-handle. Beyond him, facing the door, was Swen Brodie, his immense body towering over Honeycutt's spindling one, his bestial face hideous in its contortions as at once he gloated and threatened. In Brodie's hands, which were twice the size of an ordinary man's, was a little wooden box, to which Honeycutt's rheumy eyes were glued with frantic despair. Evidently the box had only now been taken from its hiding-place under a loose board in the floor; the board lay tossed to one side, and Brodie's legs straddled the opening.

Honeycutt did not know immediately that any one had

entered; either his old ears had not heard, or his excited mind was concentrated so excludingly on Brodie that he had no thought of aught else. Brodie, however, turned his small, restless eyes, that were like two shiny bright-blue buttons, upon the intruder. His great mouth stood open showing his teeth. On that lower, deformed, undershot jaw of Swen Brodie were those monstrous teeth which were his pride, a misshapen double row which he kept clean while his body went unwashed, and between which the man could bend a nail.

Swen Brodie was the biggest man who had ever come to the mountains, men said, unless that honour went to one of the Seven who more than a half-century ago had perished with Gus Ingle. And even so Brodie kept the honour in his own blood, boasting that Ingle's giant companion, the worst of a bad lot, was his own father's father. The elder Brodie had come from Iceland, had lived with a squaw, had sired the first "Swen" Brodie. And this last scion of a house of outlawry and depravity, the Blue Devil, as many called him, stood six or eight clear inches above Mark King, who was well above six feet. Whatever pride was in him went first to his teeth, next to his enormous stature; he denied that his father had been so big a man; he flew into a towering rage at the suggestion; he cursed his father's memory as a fabric of lies. His head was all face, flattening off an inch above the hairless brows; his face was all enormous, double-toothed mouth.

Slowly the big mouth closed. The shiny blue eyes narrowed and glinted; the coarse face reddened. Brodie's throat corded, the Adam's apple moved repeatedly up and down as he swallowed inarticulately. This old Honeycutt saw. He jerked about and quick lights sprang up in his despairing eyes. He began to sputter but Brodie's loud voice had come back to him and drowned out the old man's shrillings. Brodie ripped out a string of oaths, demanding:

"Who told *you* to come in? You—you—"

"He was aiming to kill me," cried old Honeycutt, dragging and pulling at King's sleeve. "He was for doin' for me—like that!"

He pointed to the floor. There lay a heavy iron poker bent double.

"He done it. Brodie done it. He was for doin' me—"

"You old fool, I'll do you yet," growled Brodie. "And you, King, what are you after?"

Always truculent, to-day Brodie was plainly spoiling for trouble. King had stepped in at a moment when Brodie was in no mood to brook any interruption or interference.

"I came for a word with Honeycutt, not with you," King flashed back at him. "And from the look of things Honeycutt is thanking his stars that I did come."

"If you mean anything by that," shouted Brodie threateningly, "put a name to it."

"If it's a fight you want," said King sharply, "I'm ready to take you on, any time, and without a lot of palaver."

Old Honeycutt began sidling off toward the back door, neither of his two visitors noticing him now as their eyes clashed.

"What I come for I'm going to have," announced Brodie. "It's mine, anyhow, more than any other man's; I could prove it by law if I gave the snap of a finger for what the law deals out, hit or miss. Was there a King with Gus Ingle's crowd? Or a Honeycutt? No, but there was a Brodie! And I'm his heir, by thunder. It's mine more'n any man's."

King laughed at him.

"Since when have you been studying law, Brodie? Since you got back this last trip, figuring you might have a word with the sheriff?"

"Sheriff? What do you mean, sheriff?"

"I happened to see you and Andy Parker standing together on the cliffs. I saw Andy go overboard. What is more, I had a talk with him before I buried him."

Again Brodie's big mouth dropped open; his little blue eyes rounded, and he put one hand at his throat nervously.

"Andy's a liar; always a liar," he said thickly. But he seemed annoyed. Then his face cleared, and he too laughed, derision in his tone. "Anyway, he's dead and can't lie no more, and your word against mine ain't more'n an even break. So if your nosing sheriff gets gay with me I'll twist his cursed neck for him."

"Suit yourself. I've told you already I came for a talk with Honeycutt and not with you."

"Then you'll wait until I'm done with him," roared Brodie, all of his first baffled rage sweeping back through his blood. "And now you'll clear out!"

King stooped forward just a little, gathering himself and ready as he saw Brodie crouch for a spring. It was just then that both remembered old Honeycutt. For the old man, tottering in the opening of the rear door, was muttering in a wicked sort of glee:

"Up with them hands of your'n, Swen Brodie. High up an' right quick, or I'll blow your ugly head off'n your shoulders!"

In his trembling hands was a double-barrelled shotgun, sawed off and doubtless loaded to the muzzle with buckshot. Though the thing wavered considerably, its end was not six feet from Brodie's head, and both hammers were back, while the ancient nervous fingers were playing as with palsy about the triggers. King expected the discharge each second.

Brodie whirled and drew back, his face turning grey.

"Put it down, you old fool; put it down!" he cried raspingly. "I'll go."

The old man cackled in his delight.

"I'll put nothin' down," he announced triumphantly. "You set down that box."

Hastily Brodie put it on the table. He drew further away, backing toward the front door.

"Git!" cried old Honeycutt.

They could hear the air rushing back into Brodie's lungs as he came to the door and his fear left him.

"I'll be back, Honeycutt, don't you fear," he growled savagely. "As for you, King, you and me ain't done. I'll get you where there's no old fool to butt in, and I'll break every bone in your body."

"I'll be ready, Brodie," said King. He watched the great hulking figure as it went out; two hundred and fifty pounds of brawn there, every ounce of it packed with power and the cunning of brutish battle. If he ever fought Swen Brodie, just man to man, with only the weapons nature gave them, what would the end be?

But Brodie was gone, his shadow withdrawn from the doorstep, and he had his business with Honeycutt. He left the door wide open so that no one might come suddenly upon them and turned to the old man.

"Put your gun down, Honeycutt," he said quietly. "I want to talk with you."

"I got the big stiff on the run!" mumbled the old man. "He

cain't come an' bulldoze me. Not me, he cain't. No, nor if
Swen Brodie cain't git the best of me, no other man can," he
added meaningly, glaring at King.

"There's that box on the table," said King. "Maybe you'll want
to put it away before he makes you another visit."

Honeycutt hastily set his gun down, leaning it against the wall
with both hammers still back, and shambled to the table. He
caught the box up and hugged it to his thin old breast,
breathing hard.

"If there's money in it—" said King, knowing well that the old
miser had money secreted somewhere.

"Who said there was money? Who said so?"

He went to his tumbled bunk in a corner, sat down on it,
thrusting the box out of sight under the untidy heap of dirty
bedding.

"I ain't talkin'," he said. He glanced at his gun. "You *git*, too."

King felt that he could not have selected a more inopportune
moment for his visit, and already began to fear that he would
have no success to-day. But it began to look as though it were a
question of now or never; Brodie would return despite the
shotgun, and Brodie might now be looked to for rough-shod
methods. So, in face of the bristling hostility, he was set in his
determination to see the thing through to one end or another.
To catch an interest which he knew was always readily
awakened, he said:

"Brodie and Parker were on Lookout Ridge day before
yesterday. Brodie shoved Parker over. *At Lookout Ridge*,
Honeycutt." He stressed the words significantly while keenly
watching for the gleam of interest in the faded eyes. It came;
Honeycutt jerked his head up.

"I wish I'd of shot him," he wailed. "I wish to God I'd of blowed his ugly head off."

"It might have saved trouble," admitted King coolly. "Also, it might have been the job to hang you, Honeycutt. Better leave well enough alone. But listen to me: Brodie told you, and he meant it, that it was going to be Brodie or King who got away with this deal."

"He lied! Like you lie!" Here was Honeycutt probed in his tenderest spot. "It'll be me! Me, I tell you. I'm the only man that knows, I'm the only man that's got the right—"

"Brodie spoke of right. No one has a right more than any other man. It's treasure-trove, Honeycutt; it's the man's who can find it and bring it in."

"That'll be me. You'll see. Think I'm old, do you?" He spoke jeeringly and clenched a pair of palsied fists. "I'm feelin' right peart this spring; by summer I'll be strong as a young feller again."

"By summer will be too late. Don't I tell you that already Brodie has gone as far as Lookout Ridge? That means he's getting hot on the trail of it, doesn't it? As hot as I am."

"Then what are you comin' pesterin' me for? If you know where it is?"

"I don't know." Honeycutt cackled and rubbed his hands at the admission. "But I'm going to find out. So, probably, is Brodie. Now, look here, Honeycutt; I haven't come to browbeat you as Brodie did. I am for making you a straight business proposition. If you know anything, I stand ready to buy your knowledge. In cold, hard cash."

"No man ain't got the money—not enough—not any Morgan or Rock'feller—"

King began opening the parcel he had brought from the post-office. As he cut the heavy cord with his pocket-knife Honeycutt looked on curiously. King stepped to the table, standing so that out of the corners of his eyes he commanded both doors, and stripped off the wrapping-paper.

"Look sharp, Honeycutt," he commanded. "Here's money enough to last you as long as you live. All yours if you can tell me what I want to know."

A golden twenty-dollar coin rolled free, shone with its virgin newness and lay on the table-top, gleaming its lure into the covetous old eyes. Another followed it and another. King regretted that there were not more, that the parcel contained banknotes for the most part. He began counting it out.

"There's one thousand dollars. Right in that pile," he said. "One thousand dollars."

"One thousand dollars. An' some of it gold. New-lookin', ain't it, Mark? Let me have the feel of one of them twenties."

King tossed it; it fell upon the bedding, and Honeycutt's fingers dived after it and held it tight. He began rubbing it, caressing it.

King went on counting.

"One more thousand in this pile," he said. "That's two thousand, Honeycutt!"

"Two thousand," repeated Honeycutt, nodding. He was sucking at his lips, his mouth puckered, his cheeks sunken in. He got up and shambled on his cane close to the table, leaning against it, thrusting his peering eyes down.

King counted out the last crisp note.

"Three thousand dollars." He stepped back a pace.

"Three thousand dollars! That's a might of money, Mark. Three thousand dollars all on my table." His thin voice was a hushed whisper now. "I never seen that much money, not all at once and spread out."

"It's likely that you'll never see that much again. Unless you and I do business."

Honeycutt did not answer, perhaps had not heard. His emaciated arms were uplifted; he had let his cane go, supporting himself by leaning hard against the table; his arms curved inward, his fingers were like claws, standing apart. Slowly the hands descended; the fingers began gathering the few gold pieces, stacking them, lingering with each separate one, smoothing at it. Gold spoke directly and eloquently to what stood for a soul in Loony Honeycutt; banknotes had a voice which he understood but which could never move him, thrill him, lift him to ecstatic heights, as pure musical, beautiful gold could.

"It's a sight of money, Mark," he whispered "It's a sight of money."

King held his silence. His whole argument was on the table.

*   *   *   *   *

Only now and then did King catch a glimpse of Honeycutt's eyes, for the most part hidden by his lowered lids and bent head. At such times, though he had counted on having to do with cupidity, he was startled by the look he saw Here was the expression of the one emotion which dwelt on in the withered, time-beaten body; here was *love* in one of its ten thousand forms. Love that is burning desire, that quenches all other spark of the spirit, that is boundless; love of a hideously grotesque and deformed sort; love defiled, twisted, misshapen as though Eros had become an ugly, malformed, leering monstrosity. That love which is the expression of the last degree of selfish greed, since it demands all and gives nothing;

that love which is like a rank weed, choking tenderer growths; or more like a poisonous snake. Now it dominated the old man utterly; the world beyond the rectangular top of the table did not exist; now its elixir poured through his arteries so that for the first time in months there came pinkish spots upon the withered cheeks, showing through the scattering soiled grey hairs of his beard.

... Suddenly King went to the door, standing in the sunshine, filling his lungs with the outside air. The sight of the gloating miser sickened him. More than that. It sickened his fancies so that for a minute he asked himself what he and Brodie were doing! The lure of gold. The thing had hypnotized him; he wished that he were out in the mountains riding among the pines and cedars; listening to the voice of the wilderness. It was clean out there. Listening to Gloria's happy voice. Living in tune with the springtime, thinking a man's thoughts, dreaming a man's dreams, doing a man's work. And all for something other than just gold at the end of it.

But the emotion, like a vertigo, passed as swiftly as it had come. For he knew within himself that never had that twisted travesty of love stirred within him; that though he had travelled on many a golden trail it was clean-heartedly; that it was the game itself that counted ever with him and no such poisonous emotions as grew within the wretched breast of Loony Honeycutt. And these golden trails, though inevitably they brought him trail fellows like Honeycutt, like Swen Brodie, were none the less paths in which a man's feet might tread without shame and in which the mire might be left to one side.

He turned back to the room. Honeycutt was near the bunk, groping for his shotgun. He started guiltily, veiled his eyes, and returned empty-handed to the table.

"If it was all in gold, now," said Honeycutt hurriedly.

King made no reference to Honeycutt's murderous intent.

"That paper is the same thing as gold," he said. "The government backs it up."

"I know, I know. But what's a gove'ment? They go busted, don't they, sometimes? Same as folks? Gold don't go busted. There ain't nothin' else like gold. You can tie to it. It won't burn on you an' it won't rust." He shook his head stubbornly. "There ain't nothin' like gold. If that was all in twenty-dollar gold pieces, now—"

"I'll get a car here," said King. "We'll drive down to Auburn and take a train to San Francisco. And there I'll undertake to get you the whole thing in gold. Three thousand dollars. That is one hundred and fifty twenty-dollar pieces."

But old Honeycutt, sucking and mouthing, shook his head.

"I couldn't leave here, an' you know it. I—I got things here," he said with a look of great cunning, "I wouldn't go away from. Not if horses was pullin' me."

"You can bring those things along—"

Honeycutt cried out sharply at that.

"You know I wouldn't durst! With the world full of robbers that would be after me like hounds runnin' down a rabbit. I won't go; you cain't make me. No man cain't."

King's patience deserted him.

"I am not going to make you do anything. Further, I am not going to put in any more time on you. I have offered to pay you three thousand dollars for what you know—and there is the very strong likelihood that you don't know a bit more than I do—"

"Don't know!" shrieked Honeycutt. "Wasn't I a boy grown when the dyin', delerious man stumbled in on the camp?

Didn't I hear him talk an' didn't I see what he had in his fist? Wasn't I settin' right side by side with Gus Ingle when that happened? Wouldn't I of been one to go, if it hadn't of been that I had a big knife-cut in my side you could of shoved a cat in—give to me by a slant-eyed cuss name of Baldy Winch. Didn't I watch 'em go, the whole seven of 'em, Baldy Winch, rot him, jeerin' at me an' me swearin' I'd get him yet, him an' Gus Ingle an' Preacher Ellson an' the first Brodie an' Jimmy Kelp an' Manny Howard an' the Italian? Wasn't I there?" He was almost incoherent.

"Were you?" said King. "And Baldy Winch, the one who knifed you—?"

The sucking old mouth emitted a dry chuckle.

"An' didn't I keep my promise? That very winter after Baldy was the only man to git back. With my side just healin' didn't I make my way through the snow out to where he was—"

"His cabin on Lookout?"

"With an axe I got there! An' him havin' a gun an' pistol an' knife. Phoo! What good did it do him? An' didn't I square with him by takin' what I wanted?"

"Gold?"

The old dry cackle answered the question; the bleary eyes were bright with cunning.

"If I don't know nothin'," jibed Honeycutt, "what're you askin' me for?"

King had learned little that he did not already know. He came back to the table and began gathering up the money.

"Wait a minute, Mark," pleaded the old man, restless as he understood that the glittering coins were to be taken away.

"Let's talk a while. You an' me ain't had a good chat like this for a year."

"I'm going," retorted King. "But I'll make you one last proposition." He thrust into his pocket everything excepting five twenty-dollar gold pieces. These he left standing in a little pile. "I'll give you just exactly one hundred dollars for a look at what is in that box of yours."

In sudden alarm the old man shambled back to his bunk, his hands on the bedding over the box.

"You'd grab it an' run," he clacked. "You'd rob me. You're worse than Brodie—"

"You know better than that," King told him sternly. "If I wanted to rob you I'd do it without all this monkey business."

In his suspicious old heart Honeycutt knew that. He battled with himself, his toothless old mouth tight clamped.

"I'll go you!" he said abruptly. "Stand back. An' give me the money first."

King gave him the money and drew back some three or four paces. Honeycutt drew out the box, held it lingeringly, fought his battle all over again, and again went down before the hundred dollars. He opened the box upon a hinged lid; he made a smooth place in the covers; he poured out the contents.

What King saw, three articles only, were these: an old leather pouch, bulging, probably with coins; a parcel; and a burnished gold nugget. The nugget, he estimated roughly, would be worth five hundred dollars were it all that it looked from a dozen feet away. The parcel, since it was enwrapped in a piece of cloth, might have been anything. It was shaped like a flat box, the size of an octavo volume.

Honeycutt leered.

"If Swen Brodie had of knowed what he had right in his hands," he gloated, "he'd never of let go! Not even for a shotgun at his head!"

"Brodie hasn't gone far. He'll come back. You have your last chance to talk business with me, Honeycutt. Brodie will get it next time."

"Ho! Will he? Not where I'm goin' to hide it, Mark King. I got another place; a better place; a place the old hell-sarpint himself couldn't find."

*   *   *   *   *

King left him gloating and placing his treasures back in his box. In his heart he knew that Brodie would come again. Soon. It began to look as though Brodie had the bulge on the situation. For that which Mark King could not come at by fair means Brodie meant to have by foul. For he had little faith in the new "hidin'-place."

But on a near-by knoll, where she sat with her back to a tree, was Gloria. He turned toward her; she waved. He saw that Brodie and two men with him were looking out of a window of the old Honeycutt barn; he heard one of them laughing. They were looking at Gloria—

King quickened his step to come to her, his blood ruffled by a new anger which he did not stop to reason over. He could imagine the look in Swen Brodie's evil little eyes.

CHAPTER VII

Gloria was genuinely glad to see King returning to her. She came to meet him, smiling her glad welcome.

"It seemed that you were gone *hours*," she explained. "I never saw such a dreary, lonesome place as this sleepy little town. It gives me the fidgets," she concluded laughingly.

"These old mining camps have atmospheres all their own," he admitted understandingly. "Once they were the busiest, most frantic spots of the whole West; thousands of men hurrying up and down, all full of great, big, golden hopes. They're gone, but I sometimes half believe their ghosts hang on; the air is full of that sort of thing. A dead town turned into a ghost town. It gets on your nerves."

She nodded soberly.

"That's what I felt, though I didn't reason it all out." Her quick smile came back as she looked up into his face and confessed: "My, it's good to have you back."

"Come," he said. "We'll go and have lunch. You've no idea how much gayer things will look then."

"We're not going to eat *here*," she announced, already gay. "I stopped in at a little funny store and ordered some things. Let's start back, take them with us, and picnic in the first pretty spot out of sight of old houses."

As side by side they went along through the sunshine King noted how Brodie and a couple of men came out to look after them. He heard the low, sullen bass of the unforgettable voice; saw that Brodie had left his companions and was going straight to old Honeycutt's shanty. King frowned and for an instant hung on his heel, drawing Gloria's curious look.

"You don't like that big man with the big voice," said Gloria.

"No," he said tersely.

"It is Swen Brodie?"

"Yes. But how do you know?"

"Oh, I know lots of things people don't think I know! All girls do. Girls are rather knowing creatures; I wonder if you realize that?"

"I don't know much about girls," he smiled at her.

She pondered the matter for a dozen steps, swinging her hat at her side and looking away across the housetops to the mountains. She did not know any other man who would have said that in just that way. The words were frank; all sincerity; that is, nothing lay behind them. Archie and Teddy, any of her boy friends in town—they knew all about girls! Or thought that they did. Mr. Gratton with his smooth way; he led her to suppose that he had been giving girls a great deal of studious thought for many years, and that only after this thorough investigation did he feel in a position to declare herself to be the most wonderful of her sex.

"Don't you like girls?" she asked. For once she wasn't "fishing"; she wanted to know.

"Of course I do," he told her heartily. "As well as a man can—under the circumstances."

"You mean not knowing them better?" When he nodded she looked up at him again, hesitated, and then demanded: "You like me, don't you?"

As the question popped out she understood even more clearly than before that Mark King was utterly different from her various "men friends." She had never asked a man that before; she was not accustomed to employing either that direct method or matter-of-fact tone. Just now there was no hint of the coquette in her; she was just a very grave-eyed girl, as serious in her *tete-a-tete* with an interesting male as she could have been were she sixty years old. And she was concerned with his answer; already she knew that he had a way of being very direct and straight from the shoulder.

"Of course I do," he said heartily, a little surprised by the abruptness of the question and yet without hesitation. "Very much."

She flushed prettily; she, Gloria Gaynor, flushed up because Mark King said in blunt, unvarnished fashion: "I like you very much." The grave sobriety went out of her eyes; they shone happily. When they reached the "funny little store" she was humming a snatch of a bright little waltz tune. And she was thinking, without putting the thought into words: "And I like you very much. You are quite the most splendid man I ever saw."

King laughed over Gloria's order. Some bars of sweetened chocolate, a bag of cookies with stale frosting in pink and white, a diminutive tin of sardines, and two bottles of soda-water.

"Fine," he chuckled, "as far as it goes. Now we'll complete the larder. A small coffee-pot, handful of coffee, a tin of condensed milk, a dime's worth of sugar, can of corned beef, block of butter, loaf of bread, two tin cups. Your marketing," he grinned at her, "we'll have for dessert."

"I didn't know," countered Gloria, making a face at him, "that I was entertaining a starved wild man for lunch."

"You'll eat your half, I'll bet, and be ready for more a long time before we get home."

Gloria, impatient to be on the homeward trail, assumed command in a way which delighted King; he glimpsed the fact that she had always had her way and was thoroughly accustomed to the issuance of orders which were to be obeyed; further, he found her little way of Princess Gloria entirely captivating: already she was bullying him as all of her life she had bullied his old friend Ben.

"I'll get all of the parcels together," was what she said, "while you go for the horses. And you'll hurry, won't you, Mark?"

"On the run, Your Majesty," he laughed.

When he had saddled and returned to her Gloria was waiting with the various purchases in a barley-sack; she made a great pretence of being weighted down by the great bulk of provisions demanded by man's appetite. He took the bag from her, lifted her into her saddle, and they rode away. Gloria flicked her horse lightly with her whip and galloped ahead; as King followed he turned in the saddle and looked back toward Honeycutt's cabin. He was pulled two ways: by the girlish figure ahead, which he must follow, since it was his responsibility to bring her back to his friend Ben; by what he fancied happening between Brodie and Honeycutt. Brodie had been in ugly mood all along; he would be in uglier mood now after King's interruption and the shotgun episode. Nor could King forget what he had seen on Lookout Ridge. If Swen Brodie were sure enough of what he was about to rid himself of Andy Parker, what would he not do with old Honeycutt?

"I ought to go back," was what King said over and over to himself as he rode steadily on after Gloria. The last roof lost to sight as they turned into the mouth of a canon, he shook off all thought of returning, overtook Gloria, and determined to forget both Honeycutt and Brodie for the rest of the day. To-morrow would be another day.

"There are hundreds of pretty places to picnic," said Gloria. "But it is so much jollier by running water."

"If you can fight down that hunger of yours for a few miles," he told her, "I'll show you the prettiest picnic spot you ever saw. And one, by the way, that precious few folks know about. It's tucked away as if the mountains had the notion to hide it from all invaders."

She was immediately all eagerness to come to it. But she was quick to see that, though King laughed with her, he retained certain serious thoughts of his own. Thoughts which, of course, had to do with his errand to-day. She wondered what had happened at Honeycutt's; if King had had any words with Swen Brodie. She had been wondering that ever since he rejoined her under the tree. But now, as then, she held back her question, since she was also wondering something else—if he would tell her without being asked.

When they came to a spring freshet which they had crossed this morning King turned off to the right, riding up-stream, his horse's hoofs splashing mightily in the water. Gloria, looking on ahead, saw only rock-bound canon walls on either hand and a tangle of alder-bushes across the creek.

"Come on," called King. "Keep your horse right in the water and in two shakes I'll show you my Hidden Place. You are going to like it."

Though she was little impressed by what she could see, she followed. Now and then an alder brushed against her; once King waited, holding back a green barrier which he had thrust to one side. The shrubbery thickened; in five minutes she could catch but broken glimpses of the slopes rising to right and left. Their horses splashed through a deep pool, and King told Gloria to let her animal have his head so that he could pick his way among submerged boulders. There came a spot where the banks sloped gently again, and here he rode out upon a bit of springy sward, ringed with alder and willow. As he dismounted Gloria looked uncertainly about her. Damp underfoot and a paradise for mosquitoes, was her thought. He caught her look and laughed.

"We get down here and leave the horses," he informed her. "They can top off their grain and hay with grass while we dine. We go only about fifty steps further but we go on foot."

She came down lightly, again all eager curiosity. King carrying their provision-bag went ahead breaking aside the shrubbery for Gloria close at his heels. They ploughed through what looked to her like an impenetrable thicket; they forded the stream where it widened out placidly, stepping on boulders. Always King went ahead, holding out his hand to her. Once she slipped, but before her boot had broken the surface of the water his arm was about her. He caught her up, holding her an instant. Gloria began to laugh. Then, as she regarded it, a thoroughly astonishing thing happened; she felt her face flushing, hotter and hotter, until it burned. She laughed again, a trifle uncertainly, and jumped unaided to the next boulder and across to the pebbly shallows, wading out through six inches of water.

"Little fool!" she chided herself, hot with vexation. "What in the world did you want to blush like that for? He will think you are about ten years old."

For his part King stood stock-still a moment, regarding the water rushing about him. He had caught her to save her from falling, he had held her for something less than a round second. And yet something of her pervaded his senses, it had been a second fraught with intimacy, her hair had blown across his face, she had thrilled through him like a sudden burst of music ... When he jerked his head up and looked at her he could not see her face; she was very busy with a white pebble she had picked up. He jumped across to land and went on, and the incident sank away into silence.

He was glad to come to what he called the door to the Hidden Place. He opened it for her; that is, he shoved aside a mass of leaves, holding the branches back with his body. Gloria went through the opening thus afforded, climbed a long, slanting whitish granite slab, and cried out ecstatically at the beauty of the spot. Before her was a tiny meadow, as green and smooth as velvet, thick with white and yellow violets. About it, rimming it in clean lines which did not invade the sward, were pines, and beyond the pines, to be seen in broken glimpses among their sturdy straight trunks, were the cliffs shutting all in. Through one of these vistas she saw a white waterfall, its wide-flung drops of spray all the colours of the rainbow as the sun caught them. The water fell into a green pool, spilled over, flowed through a rock channel of its own ancient carving, and curved away through the meadow. On the edge of this granite basin, with showers of spray breaking over it, a little bird bobbed and dipped and, lifting its head with its own inimitably bright gesture, broke into a sweet singing as liquidly musical as the falling water.

"The Water-Ouzel!" cried Gloria. "See, I remembered his name. And he is here to welcome us."

Under the pines, where the ground was dry, King made their camp-fire, a small blaze of dry twigs between two flat stones. Gloria was every bit as exultantly delighted with the moment as she could have been were she really "about ten years old."

"I want to help. What can I do? Tell me, Mark, what can I do? Oh, the coffee; you can't make coffee without water, can you?" She caught up the new tin coffee-pot and ran across the meadow to the creek. The little bird had given over singing and watched her; when she was mindful of his previous rights and did not come too near his waterfall, he gave over any foolish notion he may have had of flight and cocked his eye again at the pool. Perhaps the coffee-pot put him in mind of his own dinner. Gloria, kneeling at her task, watched him. He seemed to reflect a moment; then with a sudden flirt and flutter he had broken the surface of the water and was gone out of sight. She gasped; he had gone right under the waterfall, a little bundle of feathers no bigger than her clenched hand. She knelt with one knee getting wet and never knowing it; she began to feel positive that the hardy, headlong little fellow surely must be battered to death and drowned. Then with the abruptness of a flash of light there he was again, on the surface now, driving himself forward toward the bank. And there he sat again on his rock, the water flung from him to flash and mingle with the falling spray, his head back, his throbbing little throat pouring out his fluent melody. Gloria laughed happily and went back to King and the fire with her pot of water.

* * * * *

"I love this!" said Gloria softly.

She was drinking a tin cup of strong cheap coffee cooled with condensed milk; in her other hand was a thick man-made sandwich of bread, butter, and corned beef. King laughed.

"What?" he demanded. "What particular article of my daintily served luncheon has made the great hit with you? Is it, perhaps, the rancid butter that you adore?"

"You know. I love this." Her look embraced the universe— began with the dying fire, swept on beyond the tree-tops against the deep blue of sky. "I don't know why people live in cities, with all of this shut out."

"The call of the wild!" He spoke lightly and yet he glimpsed a soul really stirred; saw that for the moment, if for no longer, the great solitudes held her enthralled. More seriously he added: "It's the blood of your ancestors. It is just getting a chance to make itself heard. The racket of Market Street drowns it out."

She nodded thoughtfully. They did full justice to their lunch, finished with her purchases for dessert, quite as he had prophesied, and lazed through the nooning hour. Gloria lay on a yielding mat of pine-needles, her eyes grave as her spirit within her was grave, moved by influences at once vague, restless, and tremendous. This was not her first day in the woods, and yet she felt strangely that it was. He had spoken of her "ancestors." She knew little of her mother's and her father's forbears; she had never been greatly concerned with individuals whom she had never known. In a way she had been led to think, by her own mother, however so innocently, that she was "living them down." They had been of a ruder race that had lived in a ruder day. In San Francisco, to Miss Gloria Gaynor in a pretty new gown, one of a cluster of dainty girls, those grandparents had seemed further away than the one step of removal between them and her nearer blood. To-day they came near her, very near, indeed, for the hour that she lay looking up at the sky. Not many words passed between her and King; he sat, back to tree, and smoked his pipe and was quite content with the silence.

She started out of a reverie to find King standing up, his body rigid as he stood in the attitude of one who listens, his head a little to one side, his eyes narrowed.

"Wait for me," he said. "I'll be back in just a minute."

She sat up and watched him. He went back to the sloping granite slab, over it, down among the alders, and out of sight. For a moment she heard him among the bushes; then as all sound made by him died away there was only the purl of the creek and the eternal murmur of the pines. Now it seemed to her more silent than before, even when King had sat wordlessly near her. And yet, incongruously, whereas the silence was deepened by utter solitude, the voices of running water and stirring trees rose clearer, louder, more insistent. A falling pine-needle, striking all but noiselessly at her side, made her turn swiftly.

Only now did she hear that other sound, which King had detected. It was the thud of horses' hoofs; with it came men's voices faintly. King had gone that way, Gloria stood up, smothered under a sense of aloneness She resented his going; she was on the verge of calling to him; her heart began to beat faster. She wasn't afraid ... she didn't think she was afraid....

When he came up over the rock again, gone but a few moments, true to his word, she ran to meet him. She had not been afraid, but engulfed by an emotion which had seemed not born within her but a mighty emanation of the woods themselves, and which in its effect was not unlike fear. An emotion which, now that King was here, was lifted out of her and blown away like a whiff of smoke before the mountain winds. She looked at him with new curiosity, wondering at herself, wondering at him that his presence or absence could make all this world of difference. She saw him in a new, bright light, as one may see for the first time a stranger on whom much depends. He was strong, she thought; strong of body, of mind, of heart. He was like the mountains, which were not complete without him. His eyes were frank and clear and honest; and yet they were, for her, filled with mystery. For he was man, and his physical manhood was splendidly, vigorously vital. She had danced with men and boys, flirted with them, made friends of a sort with them. Yet none of them had set her wondering as King did. The repressed curl of his short, crisp hair, the warm tan of his face and hands and exposed throat, the very gleam of his perfect teeth, and the flow of the muscles under his shirt—these things by the sheer trick of opposites sent her fancies scurrying. To Gratton. How unlike the two men were. And how glad she was that now it was King coming up over the rock to her.... It had been to Gratton that she had said: "He is every inch a man!" She stopped abruptly and waited for him to come to her side.

"We must be going," he said. "You have rested?"

She nodded, and he began gathering up coffee-pot, cups, scraps of paper; bits of food he left for bird and chipmunk, but the tin cans were dropped behind an old log and covered over with leaves. She would not have thought of that; she understood the reason and was glad that their own arrival here had not been spoiled for them by finding a litter of other campers' leavings. He stamped out the few embers of their fire, and, not entirely satisfied, though there was but little danger of forest fires here in green young June, nevertheless went to the creek for water and doused the one or two black charred sticks which still emitted thin wisps of smoke.

"Those men?" queried Gloria when it was clear that he would require prompting. "Who were they?"

"Some chaps from Coloma, packing off into the woods."

"Swen Brodie?" she demanded.

"Yes. Swen Brodie and half a dozen of his ilk."

"We will overtake them? Is that why you are in a hurry now?"

"No. We won't see anything of them. That's what I went to find out. We are within a few hundred yards of the fork in the trail; they turned off to the right, as I thought they would."

"You would like to follow after them?" She gathered that from a vague something in his voice and from a look, not so vague, in his eyes. "If I were not along you would go the way they have gone?"

"Yes," he admitted. "But you are along, you know! What is more,"—as he realized that she might fear he resented her being with him,—"I am glad that you are. And now shall we start? We've a long ride ahead of us yet."

She followed him down through the alders; at the pool where she had slipped before, and he had held her in his arms, she was very careful not to slip now. Nor did they look at each other while she lightly touched his hand and they crossed over.

For an hour, until the wilderness worked its green magic upon them again, they were a very silent man and girl, he pondering on Brodie and his men pushing on into the solitudes, she wondering many things about her companion—and about herself.

CHAPTER VIII

Through the long shadows of evening they rode back to the log house. While King unsaddled, Gloria stood watching him; her eyes shone softly through the dusk.

"It has been a truly wonderful day," she said simply.

"It is you who have been wonderful," he answered stoutly. "I know you are not used to long rides like ours to-day; I know you are tired out. And you never gave a sign."

"The blood of my ancestors," she laughed happily.

In the house Gratton looked at them sharply and suspiciously; Archie and Teddy saw only Gloria through sorrowful eyes. King, with a nod to the various guests and a few words with Mrs. Gaynor, entirely given to warm praise of her daughter, drew Ben aside for a discussion of conditions as he had found them and left them to-day. He was dead sure that Brodie had gone back to Honeycutt, had gotten what he wanted, and was off in a bee-line to put to the proof the old man's tale.

Gloria was off to bed early, saying "good-night everybody" rather absently. She climbed up the stairs wearily. When her mother slipped away from the others, having started the victrola and urged them to dancing, she found Gloria ready for bed but standing before her window, looking out at the first stars. Mrs. Gaynor discovered in her little daughter a new, grave-eyed uncommunicativeness. Gloria usually had so many bright, gushing things to say after a day of pleasure, but to-night she appeared oddly preoccupied.

"Oh, I'm dead tired, mamma," she said impatiently. "Nothing happened. I'll tell you to-morrow—anything I can think of. And now, good-night; I'm so sleepy." She kissed her mother and added: "I didn't tell Mark good-night—"

"*Mark*? Already, my dear?"

"He was outside with papa," said Gloria, slipping into bed. "Will you tell him good-night for me?"

"He's gone," retorted her mother, with a certain relish.

"Gone!" Gloria sat up, a very pretty picture of consternation. "Where?"

"Back into the woods. Where he came from, of course. I actually think," and she laughed deprecatingly though with a shrewd watchful look to mark her daughter's quick play of expression, "that that man couldn't sleep two consecutive nights under a roof. His clothes smell like a pine-tree. He wouldn't understand us any more than we could understand him, I suppose."

Gloria was silent and thoughtful. Then, "Good-night, mamma," she offered again, her cheek snuggled against her pillow. "And put out the light as you go, please."

Mrs. Gaynor, accepting her dismissal though reluctantly, sighed and went out. As the door closed Gloria tossed back the covers and sprang out of bed, going again to her window. She watched the mountain ridges turn blacker and blacker; saw a second star and another and suddenly the heavens filled with a softly glimmering spray of twinkling lights; she heard the night wind rustling, tender with vague voices. A tiny shiver shook the white shoulders, a shiver not from cold, since not yet had the air chilled. Through her mind swept a dozen vivid pictures, all of King, most of them of him out there, alone with the night and the mountains. But she saw him also as she had seen him to-day; riding before her, breaking the alders aside, catching her as she fell. All day she had thrilled to him. Now, more than ever, she thrilled. She imagined she saw him striding along through the big boles of the pines; passing swiftly, silent and stern, through a faint patch of light; standing in the shadows, listening, his keen eyes drilling the obscurity; passing on again, vigorous, forceful, determined, and "splendid." She wondered if he would come up with Swen Brodie; most of all she wondered when she would see him again.

In all likelihood Miss Gloria, healthy, tired young animal, would have slept until noon next day had she been left to her own devices. But at nine o'clock her mother came up with a breakfast-tray. Gloria regarded it sleepily.

"I would have let you sleep, my dear," said Mrs. Gaynor, "but there are your guests, you know—"

"Hang my guests," was Gloria's morning greeting. "Just because I invited them up here do I have to give up every shred of my independence?" She was lying in identically the same position in which she had dropped off to sleep the night before; now she turned and emitted a sudden "Ouch!" Not only was she stiff from head to foot; her whole body ached as though it were nothing but bruises.

So began Gloria's day after her picnicking with Mark King. And in very much the same way her day continued. Long before the sun set she had quarrelled with Georgia, turned up her nose at Teddy, laughed derisively at poor Archie's dog-like devotion, and considerably perplexed and worried Mr. Gratton, who was astute enough to keep tactfully in the background, hurt her mother's feelings, and alarmed her father by a wild and for the instant perfectly heartfelt determination to go and be a "movie" actress. There was no dancing that night. Gloria, when they thought her upstairs, sat alone out in the gloaming, a wistful, drooping little girl surrendering sweepingly to youthful melancholia. She didn't know just what the matter was; she didn't seek for reasons and explanations; she merely stared at the far-off stars which swam in a blue blur, and felt miserable.

But morning came again, as bright as that first day in Eden; the birds sang and the air was crisp, and young blood ran pleasantly. She came down early, all radiant smiles; she kissed her mother on both cheeks and the lips, rumpled her father's hair affectionately, went for a stroll with Mr. Gratton before breakfast, craved Georgia's pardon abjectly, and made the world an abiding-place of joy for the college boys.

Gloria was mildly surprised that Gratton did not appear in the least to resent her day of adventuring with King. He was interested; he did shake his head with one of his suave smiles and murmur "Lucky dog!" when King was referred to. But his interest seemed to be chiefly in "that quaint little relic of past, turbulent days, Coloma." He had her tell him all about it; of the deserted houses, the store, everything. Hence his curiosity in Honeycutt and Brodie, and just what happened between King and them, did not stand out alone and made no impression on Gloria. Long ago Gratton had had from her lips what rumours had been repeated by her father to her mother and then relayed on to her own ears. Down in San Francisco, busied with her own youthful joys, this quest of Ben Gaynor and Mark King had had no serious import to the girl; she had merely chatted of it because of its colourful phases. Naturally, had she thought a great deal of it, she would have supposed that Gratton, in nowise concerned, was even more superficially interested than herself.

By the end of the week her guests began taking their leaves. Georgia and Connie Grayson were off to foregather with a crowd of friends at the Lake Tahoe "Tavern"; Evelyn returned to her mother in Oakland; Archie departed importantly to aid his father "in the business"; Teddy went away regretfully. Even Mr. Gratton, having lingered longest of all, went back to his city affairs, promising to run up again when he could, prophesying smilingly that he would see both Gloria and her mother in town within ten days. Ben, leaving his oldest and most dependable timber-jack to look out for the womenfolk, hastened back to the lumber-camp, where he returned like a fish to water to his old pipe and old clothes and roomy boots. And Gloria was plunged deep into loneliness.

She would walk up the creek back of the house, sit by the hour near the pool where the water came slithering down over a green and grey boulder, watching for the water-ouzel, entertained in an absent sort of way by his bobbings and flirtings and snatches of song. She dreamed day-dreams; she started expectantly every time a chipmunk made a scurrying racket in dead leaves. She made a hundred romantic conclusions to the story, just begun, by Mark King going in the night into the mountains where Brodie was. Her mind was rife with speculation, having ample food for thought in all the information she had extracted from her father. Thus, she knew of Andy Parker's death; of old Honeycutt's box; of Honeycutt's boastings of a wild youth; of Brodie's threats and King's interference and the old man's shotgun. If she could only *know* what was happening now out there beyond those silent blue barriers! Night after night she stood at her window, swayed through many swift moods by her live fancies.

She grew wildly homesick for town. A theatre, dance, a ride through the park. Activity. And people. It was for her mother that she consented to remain here another week. Mrs. Gaynor declared that she must have a few more days of rest; she was worn out from a year of going eternally, entertaining or being entertained. Gloria, yielding, plunged into an orgy of letter-writing. She answered letters weeks old; she scribbled countless bright and unnecessary notes. Also she succeeded in getting her mother to drive with her frequently to Tahoe, to call on those of their friends there who had come to the mountains so early in the season. Several times they remained overnight at the Tavern.

It was after one of these absences that Jim Spalding, the old timber-jack, told Mrs. Gaynor in his abashed stammer that Mark King had showed up while they were gone. Gloria, on her way to her room, whirled and came back, and extracted the tale in its entirety, pumping it out of the brief, few-worded old Spalding in jerky details. King had appeared late yesterday afternoon, coming out of the woods. Looked like he'd been roughin' it an' goin' it hard, at that. Had told Jim he wanted to telephone. Had stuck around for a while gettin' his call through; had eaten supper with Jim; had gone back into the woods just about dark. That was all Jim knowed about it.

Rather, that was all that he supposed he knew until Miss Gloria was done with him. She dragged other bits of information to the surface. King had phoned her father; they had talked ten minutes; Mr. Gaynor was to telephone to the log house again to-morrow or next day. There would be a message for King; mos' likely from Coloma. King wanted to know something; Ben was to find out; King would turn up within a few days for the message.

Mrs. Gaynor that same day said to her daughter in a way so casual that Gloria immediately was on the alert:

"You've been very sweet to stay up here in this lonely place with me, dear. I am ready to go at any time now. Shall we go to-morrow?"

"Mother thinks she is so deep!" was Gloria's unspoken comment.

"We've such a lot of packing to do," said Gloria, with an assumption of carelessness far more artistic than her mother's. "And I'm as sleepy and lazy as an owl after being up so late last night." Her yawn, softly patted by four pink-and-white fingers, was as ingenuous as a kitten's. "I'm really in no hurry, mamma. To-morrow, if we're ready. Or next day."

They were still in the log house when, twenty-four hours later, the telephone rang, and Gloria, quick to forestall her mother, heard the operator saying: "Coloma calling Ben Gaynor's residence."

"Coloma!" thought Gloria with a quickened heartbeat. Then it wouldn't be her father, after all; it would be Mark King—

But her father it was, and she was disappointed. The message, however, was for King.

"Mark will show up in a day or so," he said. "Tell him that I did as he asked; that Brodie is in and out from here, the Lord knows what about; that old Honeycutt boasts that what he has hidden nobody is going to find. I think if he ever talks to anybody it will be to me, and I'll run in and see him whenever I get a chance to get over here. And tell King that—that—Oh, I guess that's all; better let me have a word with your mother."

Ben Gaynor was never the man for successful subterfuge, especially with his daughter; she could read every look in his eye, every twitch of his mouth, and now, over many miles of country telephone lines, she knew that her beloved old humbug of a male parent was "holding out on her." Her first impulse was to face him down and demand to be told the rest. But realizing that a father at the end of a long-distance line was possessed of a certain strategic advantage presenting more difficulties than a mother at hand, she said lightly:

"All right, papa. I'll call her. Be sure you take good care of yourself. Bydie." She relinquished the telephone instrument to her mother and stood waiting.

She could hear the buzzing of her father's voice but no distinct word. Her mother said "Yes?" and "Yes," and "Yes, Ben." And then: "Oh, *Ben*! I don't understand." And then her mother's voice sharpened, and she cut into something Gaynor was saying: "I can't say anything like *that*! It is as though we suspected him of being underhanded. And—"

Such scraps of talk were baffling, and Gloria, with scant patience for the baffling, moved up and down restlessly. When her mother had clicked up the receiver, Gloria followed her and demanded to be told. Mrs. Gaynor looked worried; said it was nothing, and refused to talk. But in five minutes her daughter knew everything Gaynor had said. King was to be told that Gratton, instead of going straight to San Francisco, had gone down to Placerville, and next had turned up at Coloma; that he had spent three days there; that he had gone several times to Honeycutt's shanty, and had been seen, more than once, with Swen Brodie.

"It's an outrage," cried Mrs. Gaynor, "to retail all that to Mark King. What business of his is it if Mr. Gratton does go to Coloma, or anywhere else?"

"That's for you and papa to argue out," said Gloria serenely.

"We are going back to San Francisco to-morrow!"

"I'm not. You know I'm not ready to go yet."

"That is very undutiful, Gloria," said her mother anxiously. "When your own mother—"

"Oh, let's not get tragic! And, anyway, papa wanted us to stay until Mr. King came, so that we could tell him."

"Jim Spalding will be here; he can tell—"

"Why, mamma! After papa has trusted to *us* to see that his message is delivered!" Gloria looked shocked, incredulous. "Surely—"

So they waited for Mark King to come again out of the forest. All the next day Gloria, dressed very daintily and looking so lovely in her expectancy that even old Jim Spalding's eyes followed her everywhere, watched from the porch or a window or her place by the creek. She was sure that he would step out of the shadows into the sun with that familiar appearance of having just materialized from among the tree trunks; over and over she was prepared, with prettily simulated surprise, to greet his coming. But the day passed, night drove them indoors to a cosy fireplace and lights and fragments of music which Gloria played wistfully or crashingly in bursts of impatience, and still he did not come. Mrs. Gaynor went off to bed at nine o'clock; Gloria, suddenly absorbed in a book, elected to sit up and finish her chapter. She outwatched the log fire; at eleven o'clock the air was chill, and Gloria as she went upstairs shivered a little and felt tired and vaguely sad.

The next day she put on another pretty dress, did her hair in her favourite way, and went about the house as gay as a lark. The day dragged by; King did not come. By nightfall the look in Gloria's eyes had altered, and a stubborn expression played havoc with the tenderer curves of her mouth. She resented at this late date King's way of going; not only had he not told her good-bye, he had left no word with her father for her. She sat smiling over a letter received some days ago from Gratton— after she had retrieved the letter from a heap of crumpled papers in her bedroom waste-paper basket. She read to her mother fragments, bright, gossipy remarks in Gratton's clever way of saying them; she wrote a long, dashingly composed answer.

Two days later she said to her mother, out of a long silence over the coffee cups:

"Let's go back to San Francisco. This stupid place gets on my nerves."

"Why, of course, dear," agreed Mrs. Gaynor. "I can have everything packed this afternoon, and to-morrow—"

"Nonsense," said Gloria. "You know we can get packed in half an hour."

That day they left Jim Spalding in charge and departed for

Truckee to catch a train for San Francisco. Mrs. Gaynor dutifully entrusted to Spalding her husband's message for Mark King. That is to say, that portion of the message which she considered important. Gloria herself left no message with old Jim; not in so many words. But she did impress him with her abundant gaiety, with her eagerness for San Francisco, where all of her best and dearest friends were. If any one should ask old Jim concerning Miss Gloria, Jim would be sure to make it clear that she had no minutest regret in going but a very lively anticipation of the fullest happiness elsewhere.

CHAPTER IX

Three or four weeks passed before Mark King and Gloria met again. Weeks of busy gaiety on her part, of steady, persistent seeking on his. Now again Gloria and her mother and Ben were at the log house in the mountains, this time with a fresh set of guests. Only one of the former flock had been invited: Mr. Gratton. And this despite Ben Gaynor's uneasy "This chap Gratton, Nellie. He's cutting in pretty strong here of late, and I don't know that I like him. He's too confounded smooth somehow."

King came the day after the guests arrived for a talk with Ben. Gloria knew that he was coming and was coolly prepared to meet him. She gave him a bright little nod, friendly enough but casual, and resumed her lively chatter with her friends. King went off with Gaynor. That night there was no moon, but the stars, those great glittering stars of the Sierra, made the hour softly palpitant. King betook himself to smoke upon that particular, remembered corner of the porch; Gloria, slipping out from a dance, felt the little thrill that would not down when she found him there. In their two chairs, necessarily close together since the nook was so cosily narrow, her shoulder now and then brushing his as she moved, the faint fragrances from her gown and hair blown across his face by the night breeze— for them his pipe hastily laid aside—they sat talking softly or in a pleasant silence. The next morning—the matter seemed to arrange itself with very little help from either—they were to have a ride together This time they would take their lunch. When they said good-night Gloria impulsively gave him her two hands; he remembered how she had done that the first time he had seen her. Her face was lifted up to his; in the starlight he saw her eyes shining softly, gloriously; he saw her mouth, the lips barely apart. For an instant his hands shut down hard on hers; he felt the faint pressure of her own in return. When they heard her mother in the doorway calling, "Gloria, where are you?" they started apart. A strange and unanalysed sense of secrecy had fallen upon them; Gloria whispered, "Good-night, Mark," and then calling, "Here I am, mamma; just cooling off," she went skipping down the porch, slipped her arm about her mother, and carried her back into the house.

*　　*　　*　　*　　*

Before the new day was fairly come they met in the fringe of pines. Again they shook hands; again for an instant they stood as they had stood last night. They were tremblingly close to the first kiss. Suddenly Gloria, with her colour high and her eyes hidden under lashes which King marvelled at, lashes laid tenderly against her cheeks, pulled her hands out of his and began drawing on her gauntlets. Gravely, as though here were a rite to be approached solemnly, he lifted her into the saddle. They turned their horses and rode up the ridge among the trees.

They heard together the first sleepy twitterings of hidden birds; they saw the black shadows thinning; they watched the light come upon the peaks. Ridges shook off the shadow cloaks, seemed to quiver as they awoke to the new day, grew flushed and rosy. The chill of the early morning air was like wine, sparkling, tingling in the blood. The smell of resinous woods was insistent, the fine bouquet to the rare vintage. The day, the world, themselves—all were young together—all awakening to the full, true, and triumphant meaning of life. They rode a mile with never a spoken word but in a never-broken communion; then it was Gloria who spoke first, saying, as she had said once before: "I love it!"

They followed narrow trails through the ceanothus-bushes, riding one behind the other; they climbed steep trails among the pines; then went down steep trails among granite boulders; they rode side by side through little upland valleys and grassy meadows. They broke off sprays of resinous needles as they rode, inhaling the sharp odours; they stooped for handfuls of fragrant sage; they splashed through swampy places where the grass and stalks of lush flowers swept their stirrups, through rock-bound noisy streams where they must pick their way cautiously, and where the horses snorted and shook their heads and Gloria laughed gleefully. To-day was like the completion of that other day when they had ridden to Coloma—to both it seemed that it was only yesterday. The weeks in between did not matter; they were wiped out of life by the green magic. Unfinished topics, left over from the first ride, presented themselves now to be completed. Once Gloria, speaking of their first woodland luncheon, said "Yesterday." Once King, as they crossed a wild mountain brook, said, "There's one's nest now. On that rock down by the waterfall. Looks like a bit of the rock itself, with moss all about it," and Gloria understood that it was her water-ouzel he was talking about.

"It was springtime yesterday and to-day it's summer!" said Gloria.

"It's always springtime somewhere in the world," answered King. "To-day we'll ride from one season up into the other."

"More magic!" laughed Gloria.

It is always springtime somewhere in the world! As youth knows and remembers, as age forgets. Always a place some-where for laughter and love and light hands caressing, for bird song and bird mating and colourful flowers. And to-day they were seeking this place among the mountains, riding on expectantly through dark passes, climbing winding trails, looking across deep canons and blue ridges. Gloria thought dreamily that she would like always to be riding thus, leaving summer behind and below, questing the joyous, full-sapped springtime.

He had promised to show her his latest temporary camp. They came to it before noon at an altitude of well above seven thousand feet. In a grassy open space they left their horses; King carried their lunch bundle and they went on on foot. Along the frothing creek, along the mountain-side through a wild country of dwarfed vegetation. She began to understand a thing he had told her; that the Sierra is the land of dwarf and giant. Pine and cedar and, in one spot he knew, mighty sequoia piercing at the sky; and here pine, dwarfed, pygmied until it was but a mat of twisted, broken twigs carpeting the heights. "And I have walked among the pine tops!" cried Gloria. For up here there was scant soil; here the winds raged and the snow heaped itself high in the late fall and remained, icy-crusted, into late summer; and here, now, the springtime had just come. Never had Gloria seen more beautiful flowers, flowers half so delicate-looking. And yet how hardy they must be, to live here at all!

"You are like these flowers," King said quite gravely and with sincerity. Gloria told him, also gravely and sincerely, that that was the finest compliment she had ever received—she hoped that he meant it. At least she understood and she would like to be like them.

His camp was in a little nearly level spot, sheltered by crags and so hidden by them that one must come fairly upon it before guessing its proximity. Back of it rose cliffs so sheer that Gloria craned her neck to look up at them. Below were the headwaters of the creek; across it the steep slope of the other canon wall. On all hands bleak, naked rock with tiny blossoms here and there between in the shallow soil and the carpeting of pygmy pine and flattened cedar. Only infrequently did a tree, with roots gripping like claws, lift its ragged top above the big boulders. A wild place, savagely silent save for the hissing of the wind around the cliffs above.

King brought water from the creek. He showed her where he had hidden his few camp utensils; the one small pot, one frying-pan, one cup, one spoon. To these he added his big-bladed pocket-knife. He made a fire where already there was a little heap of charred coals against a blackened rock, and they made coffee and cooked bacon. Gloria used a stick which he had pointed for her to turn the bacon. They took turns with the one cup.

"What was it like up on the cliff tops?" King did not know; he had not yet been up there. And would it take long to climb them? Not over an hour, he estimated; if she wasn't tired? It was decided that King would have his postprandial smoke up there; where they could sit and look out "across the top of the world."

As they climbed they came into a current of rushing air. Higher up the wind strengthened. They stood poised on boulders, their shoulders thrown back, heads up, lungs filling. Gloria's hair was whipped out from under her turban; it blew across her face; a strand of it fluttered across King's eyes, brushed his lips. He gave her his hand up a steep place down which they sent a cascade of disintegrating stone. They stood side by side, shoulders brushing, resting, breathing deeply. Perceptibly the air thinned; one's lungs were taxed to capacity here; the blood clamoured for deeper drafts, for more oxygen. When they came to the top Gloria dropped down, panting, though they had stopped many times on the way. She closed her eyes and her senses swam through a vast blur. King gave her a drink from his canteen; she merely thanked him with her eyes.

But in ten minutes she had rested and was on her feet, her slim body leaning against the wind. He stood by her and they looked out across the mountains. For what seemed to Gloria a thousand miles there was the broken wilderness of mountains gashed with gorges, crowned with peaks, painted with sunlight and distance, glinting white here, veiled in purple there. She gasped at the bigness of it; it spoke of the vastness of the world and of the world's primitive savagery. And yet it did not repel; it fascinated and its message had the seeming of an old, oft-told, and half-forgotten tale. It threatened with its spires as cruel as bared fangs, and yet it beckoned and invited with its blue distances. Always, since the first man fashioned the first club and made him a knife of a jagged flint, has mankind battled with the great mother, the earth who bore him. He has striven with her for his food, warred with her for his raiment, entrenched himself against the merciless attack of the seasons, winter to stab him with icy spear, summer to consume him. And always has he loved her and honoured her, since she is his great mother. Gloria, her thoughts confused by conflicting instincts, inspired and awed, drew closer to King.

"—But to be out here alone!" The utter, utter loneliness of it. She looked at him with new, curious eyes. "Doesn't it bear down on you; don't you feel at times that the loneliness—"

He understood.

"I am used to it, you know. I have never known what it was out here to feel lonely until—"

She waited for him to finish, her eyes on his. Until—?

"Until after our first ride together," he said.

Again she understood. And now she looked away hastily and her cheeks reddened. He was about to tell her that he loved her; his eyes had told her; his lips were shaping to the words "I love you!" And she was suddenly conscious of a wild nutter in her heart; she was trembling as though terrified. Other men had told her "I love you." Many times and in many ways— smiling, with a laugh, with a sigh—whispering the words or saying them half sternly. And she had always been gay and ready; a little thrilled, perhaps, as by a chance strain of music. But now—she could hardly breathe. Now she was frightened. She did not know why; she could not understand the sense of it; she only knew that she was afraid. Of what? Nor did she know that. She only knew that here were Gloria Gaynor and Mark King, man and girl—man and woman—set apart from the world, lifted above it, clear-cut figures upon a pinnacle piercing the infinite blue of the heavens, and that a mystery was unfolding before them. She had a wild wish to stop the flight of time, to thrust it back upon itself, to have the present not the present but to avoid the Now by racing back into the serenity of Just A Little While Ago. Ten minutes ago— anything but this electric, terrifying moment when Mark King, a surge of emotion upon him, was about to say: "I love you."

"Look!" Gloria started and, forgetful of the strange conflict of emotions within her, clutched at his sleeve. "A man—here;—"

"Swen Brodie!" muttered King angrily.

Brodie had just clambered up the ridge and came into view only when his head and bulky shoulders were upthrust beyond a boulder. He came on until he topped the boulder, standing fully revealed upon its flattish top, the butt of his rifle resting on his boot. Gloria was suddenly afraid with a new sort of fear. Though this man was not near enough for her to see the dancing evil of his little eyes, she saw the brutish face in full relief against the sky, and marked the jeer on the ugly mouth. Her one wild thought was that Brodie would murder them both, shoot them both down in cold blood. She shuddered. King was unarmed; Brodie hated King as only a man of Brodie's kind, bestial and cruel, could hate. She remembered what her father had told her; of the death of Andy Parker. She began tugging at King.

"Take me away!" she gasped. And then, with a terrified look over her shoulder: "Oh, he is terrible!"

Perhaps Brodie heard. The stiff wind blew her words away from her lips, tossing them toward him.

"Steady, Gloria," said King in a low voice. "I'll take you away. But we needn't hurry. He won't hurt you." And, to further soothe her, he added: "He'd be afraid to shoot, were he minded to. The noise of the gun, you know. And he doesn't know how many there are with us, or how close they are. Come, we'll go this way."

He turned his back square on Brodie and with his hand firm on Gloria's arm led her along the ridge. They passed about a wind-worn rock, and Gloria looked back, hoping that it had hidden them already from Brodie; she saw his head over the top of it, felt upon her the eyes which she could not see, lost as they were under his hat-brim and hurried on. She ran ahead now with King hastening his step to overtake her.

CHAPTER X

That night when King and Gloria said "good-night" an odd constraint lay over them. To Gloria, King seemed stiff and preoccupied; she herself had red spots in her cheeks and was nervously tense. The abrupt approach of Brodie with his repulsive face—at a moment when the world swirled away from her underfoot and a divine madness was in her blood—the reaction and revulsion—all this and the resultant conflict of emotions had worn her out. She was sure of nothing in all the world—for once was not in the least certain of herself—when she drew her hand out of King's and hastened to her guests in the house. It was with a sense of relief that she heard the door close, shutting her in with familiar, homey objects and faces, opposing its barrier against the wilderness and a man who was a part of the wilderness. She knew that King was going back to the mountains; she knew when he left, going swiftly and silently, like a shadow among shadows; she knew that this time he went armed, carrying her father's rifle.

For Mark King knew that it was inevitable that his path and Swen Brodie's should run closer and closer; that trails made by two men like King and Brodie could never converge harmoniously; that there was too much at stake; that it was well to be ready for Brodie in an ugly mood in an encounter so far removed from the habitations of men that a deed done would pass without human commentary.

A week passed and Gloria went back to San Francisco. These had been seven days and nights of uncertainty for her, and had brought hours of confusion that mounted into bewilderment. She had sung and danced and flirted as even Gloria Gaynor had never done before; she had made Gratton sure of her and his eyes had smouldered and his chalky pale face had flushed; she had sent him off, gnawing at his nails; she had made other young laughter rise like echoes of her own; she had sighed and sat long hours at her window, wondering, wondering, wondering. In the end she had gone, leaving her little note for Mark King.

King did not return to the log house. He knew that long ago Gloria would have gone; there was nothing to draw him in her absence. He kept in touch, none too close, with Ben Gaynor; telephoned him once from Coloma, and once sent a note to him by a hunter he encountered on Five Lakes Creek, above Hell Hole, the note to be mailed in Truckee some time later, and to reach Gaynor the following day at his lumber-camp. These were strenuous days during which King penetrated the most out-of-the-way corners of the mountains. He constructed his theories and strove doggedly to set them to the proof. He held that when Baldy Winch had made him a cabin in so inaccessible and distant a spot as the crest of Lookout Ridge, it had been because Winch, the sole survivor of those hardy spirits who had been of Gus Ingle's party, was of a mind to make sure, day after day, that no other men went where he had been. Perhaps he knew that he alone remained alive; that the secret was his; that he had but to wait the winter out, to sit through the spring thaw, and then go back to claim his own. A man like Baldy Winch, as King envisioned him, would do that. Hence, from Lookout Ridge one should be able to see the very point, or a peak standing over the very point, where Gus Ingle's men had gone. But always the one difficulty: that point might be a mile away, or ten, twenty, thirty miles away. There was nothing to do but seek—and he knew that always Swen Brodie, too, was seeking, Brodie and the men of his own kind whom likeness drew to likeness. So King spent day after day in the canons and on the ridges, and yet, through Ben Gaynor, thought to keep an eye on old Loony Honeycutt.

But there were many hours, alone in the forests resting, sitting over a bubbling coffee-pot, lying in his blankets under the stars, that King thought very little of Brodie, Gus Ingle, or Honeycutt. There were times when the solitudes were empty; when a new, strange feeling of loneliness swept overpoweringly over him. At such moments he fancied that a girl came stealing through the trees to him; that she slipped her hand into his own; that she lifted to his her soft eyes; that something within the soul of him spoke to her and that she answered. His pulses quickened; a great yearning as of infinite hunger possessed him. He remembered how they had stood together upon the ridge the last time; how his arms had been opening for her; the look in her eyes. That had been a moment when the world had lain at their feet; when they had been lifted up and up, close to the gates of paradise.

He saw virtually nothing of Brodie. Now and then smoke from a camp-fire; once or twice the charred coals where Brodie's men had been before him. Upon these camp sites he looked contemptuously; carelessness and wastefulness were two things he hated in a woodsman, and always he found them in Brodie's wake. Also he found bottles. Further, he was of the opinion that he could go in the dark to the particular canon in which the illicit still made its output of bad moonshine whiskey. But, though that canon lay in the heart of the country he was combing over, it was one which he had explored from top to bottom two years ago, and now was content to leave aside.

One day he came upon signs of a killing made the day before; by one of Brodie's outfit, he assumed. Some one had baited for a bear and had killed. The mother bear, he discovered the following morning. For he came upon a little brown cub whimpering dismally. King made the rebellious little fellow an unwilling captive—and smiled as he thought of Gloria. Gloria had talked of bear cubs. If she but had one for a pet! Well, here was Gloria's pet. King that day turned toward the log house. And thus he received at last Gloria's note at Jim Spalding's hands:

"DEAR MARK,

"Mamma and I have to go back to town to-morrow. I am
so sorry that I can't stay up here always and always. Do you
realize that I have never seen you in the city? It's lots of fun,
too, in its own way, don't you think? Another kind of a
wilderness. I wonder if you would come down—if I asked
you to? I'll say it very nicely and properly, like this: 'Miss
Gloria Gaynor requests the pleasure of Mr. Mark King's
presence at her little birthday-party, on the evening of
August twelfth, at eight o'clock.' Just the four of us, Mark;
mamma and papa, you and

"GLORIA."

"August twelfth," said King. "I'll go."

He didn't write, as the necessity of an answer did not suggest
itself to him. He took it for granted that she would know that
he would come. He chuckled as he thought of the birthday gift
he would bring her. There was still a week; he remained with
Spalding at the Gaynor mountain home and devoted hour
after hour to taming the cub. On the eleventh he was in San
Francisco. Before he had taken a taxi at the Ferry Building it
had dawned on him that his best suit of clothes was somewhat
outworn. It would never do to go to the Gaynors' in that. Nor
was there time for a tailor. Therefore he went direct to a
clothing-store in Market Street and in something less than half
an hour had bought suit, hat, shoes, socks, shirt, collar, and tie.

"I can have the alterations made by to-morrow afternoon," said
the salesman.

"What alterations?" demanded King, turning before the long
glass and staring at his new finery.

"The coat is a trifle tight just here—the trousers—"

King laughed.

"As long as I'm satisfied, you are, aren't you?" he said.

The clerk watched him with admiring eyes as he went out. For the clerk, an odd thing in a man who sold clothing and therefore was prone to judge by clothes, caught a glimpse of the real man.

"Big mining man, most likely," muttered the clerk. "Don't care for clothes and is rich enough to get by with whatever he wears." He looked vaguely envious.

King was busied for an hour or so, finding quarters for his cub, registering at the St. Francis, getting a shave and hair-cut. A manicurist saw his hands and, smothering a giggle, pointed them out to the young fellow she was working on.

"Go after them," he grinned. "There's a fortune for you in them."

"Nothing doing," she returned from her higher wisdom. "He ain't the kind that knows he's got any hands unless he's got a job for them to do."

Later King telephoned to the Gaynor home. A maid answered and informed him that Mr. Gaynor had not arrived yet, though he was expected this afternoon or in the morning; that both Mrs. and Miss Gaynor were out. King hung up without leaving his name.

King sat in the lobby, musing on San Francisco. As Gloria had said, it was a wilderness of its own sort. Time was when it had appealed to him; that was in the younger collegiate days. He wondered what had happened to his one-time proud evening regalia; how he had strutted in it, dances and dinners and theatre-parties! But briefly and long, long ago. It was like a half-forgotten former incarnation; or, rather, like the unfamiliar existence of some other man. He grew restless over his paper and strolled into the bar. There he was fortunate enough to stumble on a man he knew, an old mining engineer.

The two got off into a corner and talked. Later they dined and went to the theatre together.

The next evening King got a taxi, called for his bear cub, stopped at a florist's for an armful of early violets, and growing more eager and impatient at every block was off to the Gaynor home.

"Here you are, sir," said the chauffeur, opening the door.

King fancied the man had made a mistake in the number. The house was blazing with lights, upstairs and down; there was an unmistakable air of revelry about it; faintly the music of a new dance tune, violin and piccolo and piano, crept out into the night. Above the music he could hear gay voices, muffled by door and window and wall.

King was of a mind to go back to the hotel. He had counted on the Gaynors alone, not on this sort of thing. But also, most of all, he had counted on Gloria, and his hesitation was brief. He jumped down and, leading his bear cub by its new chain, went up the steps.

A housemaid came to the door, opened it wide for him, saw the cub against his leg, and screamed.

"Why, what on earth is the matter, Frieda?" said some one.

It was Gloria passing through the front hallway with a worshipful youth. Gloria came to the door, the youth at her heels, looking over her shoulder.

"Oh!" cried Gloria. King knew then in a flash that she had not expected him, that probably because he had never answered her letter she had forgotten all about it. Unconsciously he stiffened—his old gesture before a woman.

But now Gloria came running out to him, her two hands offered, her eyes alight with pleasure.

"You did come," she said gladly.

Gloria's escort, obviously holding himself to be privileged through virtue of his briefly temporary office, thrust himself along in her wake. Him King did not notice; King saw only Gloria. As of old she set his pulse stirring restlessly with her sparkling, vivid loveliness. To-night was Gloria's night; she was eighteen and queen of the world.

"And—Oh, look!" She let her hands remain in his but her eyes were all for the little brown bundle of fur at King's feet, that began now to whine and pull back at its chain. "My birthday present!"

Just now Mark King would have given anything he could think of to have that bear cub back in the woods where it belonged. He hadn't had time to analyse impulses; he didn't know why all of a sudden his gift seemed out of place. As he let Gloria's fingers slip through his he looked at the young fellow, a boy of Gloria's own age, in the doorway. Perhaps the full evening dress had something to do with King's new attitude toward his pet. But now as Gloria, a little timid and holding her skirts back and yet clearly delighted, flashed him her look of understanding and gratitude, he was content.

Gloria remembered to make Mr. King known to Mr. Trimble. Then King suggested that they take the cub around back and lodge him for the night in the garage. But Gloria, discovering that she could pat and fondle the little creature, and that he was of friendly disposition, insisted on having him brought into the house for all to see.

"It's the most delightful present of all!" she whispered to King.

In the hallway they were surrounded by a crowd of the curious. Girls in pretty dresses, young fellows in black suits, all very exact as to the proper evening appointments. At first they were disposed to look on King as "the man who brought the cub," and it was only when Gloria began a string of introductions that they understood. One and all, they regarded Mark King curiously.

The cub was made much of, and finally led off to the kitchen for sugar and a bed in a box under the table. Mrs. Gaynor appeared and was "very glad indeed to see Mr. King again." Gratton, whom King remembered with small liking, came up and shook hands, and looked at King in a way which did nothing to increase the liking. Ben, it appeared, had been unable to come this year. King was sorry for that as he looked about him. Only now did he remember the violets he had brought for Gloria.

The evening was anything but that to which he had looked forward. From the beginning he regretted coming; before the end it was slow torture for him. He was out of place and felt more out of place than he was. Glances at his carelessly purchased clothes were veiled, and never utterly impolite, but he was conscious of them. He was conspicuous because he was different; outwardly in garb, inwardly in much else. There was no one here whom he knew; he had never felt that he knew Gloria's mother, and to-night Gloria's self, puzzling him, baffling him, was an Unknown. Not that she was not delightful to him; she was just as delightful to every other man there, and in the same way. His days with her in the forest blurred and faded.

Gloria gave him the first dance after his arrival, highhandedly commanding a fair-haired and despondent youth to surrender to King one of his numbers. King caught her into his arms hungrily—only to feel that she was very far away from him. He knew that he was dancing awkwardly; he had not danced for a dozen years. Gloria suggested sitting out the rest of the dance; she said it prettily but he understood. He understood, too, by that sixth sense of man which is so keen at certain moments of mental distress that all of Gloria's friends were wondering about him, where he came from, "what his business was." He was tanned, rugged. He was not of them. He fancied, sensitively, that among themselves they laughed at him. As he sat with Gloria and found little to say, he was conscious of her eyes probing at him when she thought that he did not see. He looked away, a shadow in his eyes, and chanced to see Gratton. Gratton, who had struck him as contemptible in the woods, a misfit and a poor sort of man at best, was here on his own heath. He carried himself well, he talked well; he bore himself with a certain distinction. Clearly he was much in favour among the girls and women, much envied by the younger men. Yes; Gloria was right: this was another sort of wilderness where Mark King was the misfit, where Gratton was as much in tone with his environment as was King among the forest and crags of the ridges.

Another dance. Gloria excused herself lightly and escaped into the arms of Gratton himself. Escaped! King understood; that was the word for it. He watched them; saw Gratton whisper something into her ear, saw Gloria toss her head, saw her cheeks flush. Then Gratton laughed and she laughed with him. They danced wonderfully together, swaying together like two reeds in the same gentle wind. Others than King noticed; there were knowing smiles. At the end of the dance King saw the look which Gloria, flushed and happy, flashed up at Gratton, and his heart contracted in a sudden spasm of pain.

When again couples were seeking each other to the jazzy invitation of the musicians, King slipped away and went outside. He stood in the shadows of the porch seeking to get a grip on himself. In a moment he would go in and say good-night to Mrs. Gaynor; he'd say good-night to Gloria; he would go and put an end to a hideous nightmare. He held himself very much of a fool, and he knew that he was fanciful. But he was of no mind to stay.

Two or three couples came out; he remained unnoticed in the darkness. He heard a girl's voice:

"But *who* is he? I think he's terribly handsome. And distinguished-looking. Superior to our kind of nonsense."

"Who are you talking about, Betty?" Her dancing partner pretended to be in doubt. "Me?"

A whirlwind of girls' laughter. Then one of them saying:

"*You* distinguished-looking! Or handsome! She means the sixty-nine-dollar serge suit."

Good God! Was there a price tag on him?

"Oh, the animal trainer!" They laughed again. Then Gloria came and they called to her, demanding:

"*Who* is he?"

"Oh," said Gloria carelessly, "he is an old friend of papa's and his name is King."

They went in, two of the girls lingering a little behind the others. Gloria and another. The other, bantering and yet curious, said:

"Georgia told me all about a Mr. King up in the mountains this spring. And that it looked like love at first sight to her. 'Fess up, Glory, my dear."

Gloria's laughter, unfettered, spontaneous, was of high amusement.

"Georgia said, just the same, that she'd bet on an elopement—"

King reddened and stirred uneasily. Gloria gasped.

"Georgia's crazy!" she said emphatically. "Why, the man is impossible!"

* * * * *

Five minutes later King went in, found his hat, and told Mrs.

Gaynor good-night. She was glad that he was going, and he knew it though she made the obvious perfunctory remark. Gloria saw and came tripping across the room.

"Not going so soon?"

"Yes," he said briefly. "Good-bye, Gloria."

"Good-night, you mean, don't you?"

"I mean good-bye," he said quietly.

Gratton thrust forward. King left abruptly, leaving them together, conscious of the quick look of pleasure on the face of Gloria's mother.

CHAPTER XI

Always Gloria, yielding to the heady impulses of youth, was ready for High Adventure. Therein lay the explanation of many things which Gloria did.

Time went scurrying on. Mark King had returned to the Sierra; no word came from him, and Gloria told herself with an exaggerated air of indifference that she had just about forgotten him. Autumn came, that finest of all seasons about San Francisco Bay, the ocean fogs were thrust back, unveiling the clear sunny skies by day, the crystalline glitter of stars by night. The city grew gayer as the season advanced; dinners and dances and theatre-parties made life a gloriously joyful affair for Gloria. She had hardly the time to ask herself: "Just where am I going?" It was so much easier to laugh and cry lightly, in the phrase of the day, "I am on my way!" She had drifted, drifted like one in a canoe trailing her fingers idly in the clear water and never noting when the little craft was caught by a steady, purposeful current. It was speeding now; but she only laughed breathlessly and drank her fill of the hour, and left to others the thoughts which carve fine lines about brow and eyes. She knew that her father was beset by some sort of financial troubles; for the first time in her life he had not come to her birthday-party, and her mother had explained, rather soberly, that it was because of a business crisis. Gloria did not know that crises lasted so long. Weeks and weeks had gone and still she knew from a look which her mother could not hide that the money troubles were still stalking her father, and coming so close that for the first time in history they cast a shadow from the top of the Sierra down into her mother's heart in San Francisco.

Now Gratton became the man of the hour. He had studied Gloria with infinite patience and he never displeased her. "He understood her," as she comfortingly assured herself. That meant, of course, that he gave in to her always; that tirelessly he exerted himself to please her. At a time when there was much financial depression, Gratton's obvious affluence was very agreeable to the pleasure-seeker. He dressed well; he entertained with due respect for the most charming accessories; he took her to dance or theatre, or for a drive in the park or down the peninsula in a new, elegantly appointed limousine. And about the same time fate had it that by two entirely unassociated trends of circumstance he should draw to the dregs of Gloria's lively and romantic interest. In the first place, he began to become a prominent figure in San Francisco. His name was in the papers with names of "men who counted." And, of far greater import to Gloria, he became what she liked to consider a "Man of Mystery!"

For, weeks ago, Gloria had noted that regularly once a week Mr. Gratton dropped out of sight, to be gone for one or two days. He was never to be seen Saturday; seldom Sunday; always any day from Monday to Friday night. During week-ends he was "out of town." And, though there were countless opportunities for an off-hand explanation, Gratton never gave it. Others than Gloria remarked the fact; a girl friend insinuatingly remarked: "Better watch out for him, Glory, dear. *Cherchez la femme*, you know."

Gloria never suspected any such condition of affairs; she was too sure of Gratton's attentions. But, being Gloria, she wondered.

One night she and Gratton were having a late supper together at the Palace. They had been to the theatre and now, yielding to the demands of her young appetite, they sat before sandwiches and coffee. Gloria saw the page as he came to the doorway; he stood, an envelope in his hand, looking up and down the room. When at last his eyes rested on her and her companion, the boy came to the table.

"Telegram, Mr. Gratton."

Gratton, more interested in what she was saying than in the yellow envelope, opened it carelessly. But in a flash his attention was whipped away from her; she stopped in the middle of a sentence and knew that he had not noticed. A quick spurt of blood flushed his dead-white skin; his eyes grew bright with excitement. He read in a sweeping glance, and before his eyes came back to her they went hurriedly to his watch.

"I've got to go, Gloria," he said nervously. "Immediately. This is important."

"Why, of course," she agreed. "I can get a bite when I get home."

He thrust the telegram into his pocket and came around to the back of her chair. He was all impatience; it seemed he could not wait until hat and coats were gotten. On the way to the street he looked again at his watch.

"I've got to go out of town," he explained. "I'll be gone a couple of days."

"But this is only Wednesday!"

"And usually I don't go before Saturday?" He was tapping at his cigarette-case as they came to their taxi. "Yes. But something has happened."

He helped her in and lifted his foot to follow.

"Gloria," he muttered, "I can't make it. If I see you home I will miss the last boat across the bay."

She was more and more interested. She had never known Gratton to show emotion as he showed it to-night; she was more and more curious about that "business" which carried him out of town. Why hadn't he tossed the telegram across the table for her to read? Here was a shut door, and from being barred a door always invites the more temptingly. Especially to a girl like Gloria.

"Why, I can go home alone—"

"I don't like it. I—" He ended abruptly and thrust his head into the car, his eyes questing hers in the half-light; the chauffeur with his engine going looked over his shoulder.

"Come with me, Gloria!"

Gloria wondered what he meant: whether the man was suggesting an elopement or just a wild bit of downright unconventionality.

"I mean it," said Gratton. "Listen. The new day has already started. By the time the ferry lands us in Oakland it will be nearly three o'clock. I've got to drive up into the country; we'll phone your mother and will start right away. We'll get there long before noon; we'll be back before night. It would mean only a day's outing and no harm done. Won't you come, Gloria? Please come!" He pulled out his watch again. "We've just got time to catch the boat comfortably." He called to the taxi-driver, "To the ferry," and jumped in.

"But—"

"You can come as far as the ferry, anyway. Even if you won't give me a day of motoring. It's wonderful out in the country this time of year. And—"

When they came to the ferry there was no time for debating the matter; the crowd was pouring toward the last boat, and Gloria, her eyes bright with the joy of her escapade, went with him through the little gate where the tickets were presented for the last boat across the bay. It was unconventional, as she saw quite clearly. But to Gloria unconventionality was a condition fairly divided into two widely separated browsing-grounds; there was the thing which was just "daring"; there was that other which was ugly because it was "compromising." This adventure promised to fall into the safer category; to be off motoring with Mr. Gratton from three o'clock in the morning until late afternoon was what she considered a "lark."

They laughed together in anticipation as they crossed the bay. They sat where they could watch the red and green lights, reflected like topazes and rubies in the shimmering water, fall away and dwindle as the silhouette of the embarcadero receded. On the electric train they were whizzed among many sleepy folk into a sleeping town, Oakland, drowsing and silent. Gratton summoned a somnolent taxi-driver and they were whisked through the cool air to a garage. He left her a moment, sitting in the taxi, while he ran in and arranged for a roadster.

Gloria, left to her own thoughts, began to regret having come. The thing, reviewed in solitude, was "crazy." She grew vaguely distressed. She wanted to go back to San Francisco—but there would be no boat now until full morning, three or four hours; she could not get home before seven or half-past seven o'clock. She tried to recall a friend on this side of the bay to whom she could go at this time of night—day, rather! Her lips shaped to a half smile.

"I've got the car." Gratton was back offering to help her down. "And I phoned your mother."

"Was she—?"

"She trusts you with me, Gloria," he said quickly.

She let him help her into the car he had hired. Gratton took the wheel and turned into San Pablo Avenue. The street was deserted and he gently pressed down the throttle; he had hired a dependable, high-priced car, and the motor sang softly. The wind blew in Gloria's face and her zest came back to her.

Gratton would not tell her where they were going; he made a great lark of their escapade, assuring her gaily that their destination was reserved as the final surprise for her. He evaded laughingly when she asked. "Maybe we'll keep right on going, always and always," he jested with her. She thought that under the jest there was a queer note; when his eyes flashed briefly toward her she tried to read their message. But the hour, mystery-filled, filled them with mystery.

Gloria began laughing.

"What will we look like to-morrow—I mean when it's full day! Me dressed like this—you in evening suit!"

"By Jove!" said Gratton. Then he laughed with her. "It's the lark of my life."

The ocean breeze smarted in their eyes, the motor thrummed merrily, trees and houses flew by, the racing car leaped to fresh speed. On the cement highway the spinning tyres whined musically.

They were far up-country when the sun rose. Gloria, very sleepy now, watched it climb above the hills. She had watched the sunrise last June—with Mark King. Later, again with Mark King, she had seen it thrust its great burning disk above the pine ridges.

She was asleep and started wide awake when the car stopped suddenly. They were in the one street of a little town; it must be eight o'clock. She was cold.

"What do you say to a cup of coffee? And toast and eggs?"

"I am hungry," she confessed.

Over their breakfast in the little wayside restaurant, with its untidy tables and greasy lunch-counter, it was Gratton who did all of the talking. Gloria by now realized that she was downright sorry she had come. He seemed eager, his eyes very bright, his voice quick and vibrant with an electrical urge dominating. She wondered vaguely what made him seem "different."

"The waiter," she said as they finished, "is staring his head off at our clothes."

"We're going to remedy that matter. Come on; the stores are open."

"Fancy shopping here!" The thought made her laugh.

"Just the place for what we want. Khaki trousers and flannel shirt and boots for me; an outing-suit for you."

He took her arm and they walked the half-dozen doors to the dry-goods store.

"I haven't a cent with me—"

"Let me be your banker," he said lightly.

Gloria hesitated. But very briefly. Hot coffee had done much for her drooping courage; the escapade, even this going at eight o'clock in the morning into a country store with a man, and on money borrowed from the man, was an experience to put the gay note of adventure back into the affair.

Gloria made her purchases in fifteen minutes and the change from theatre gown into an olive outing-suit in another fifteen. Her discarded garments were gathered up, put into a cardboard box by the clerk, and wrapped in heavy paper to be stowed away in the car. She confronted Gratton smilingly in her new garb, her hands in her pockets, her face saucy, her slim body boyish in its swagger and richly feminine in its unhidden curves. Gratton's eyes shone, quick with admiration. She laughed and a flush came into her cheeks as he gravely paid for her clothing and his own. When they went to their car both were strangely silent.

"I owe you a lot of money," she said with assumed carelessness.

"Which I hope you never repay," he returned meaningly.

At nine o'clock they were threading the streets of Sacramento. At a little after ten they were in Auburn. They drove through "Old Town," passed the courthouse and through the newer portion of the village; by the Freeman Hotel and the railroad-yards, through the "subway" under the tracks, and turned off to the right, leaving the highway for the first time and skirting the olive-orchards on the hill. Then, sweeping around a wide curve they caught the first glimpse of the American River deep down in its historic canon. On, over a narrow, red-dirt road, closer down to the gorge, across the long bridge, up and up the steep, writhing grade. They came to the top of the ridge; raced through Cool, through Lotus—

"Coloma!" gasped Gloria. "You are going to Coloma!"

He slowed the car down that he might look at her keenly.

"Well?" he said lightly.

"It is to Coloma that you have been coming every week!"

"Well?" he said a second time.

"Then you—you, too—"

He glanced at the road, cut down the speed still more, and looked back into her thoughtful eyes.

"Would you rather that it was Mark King or I who succeeded?"

She was clearly perplexed.

"Mark King is papa's partner," she said musingly.

"And I? I hope one day to be more than his partner!"

She understood but gave no sign of understanding. He did not press the point.

"Here we are," he said presently as the first of the picturesque old rock-and-mortar houses of Coloma stood forth out of the wilderness. "And you're dead tired and nearly dead for sleep. I am sorry we can't have a city hotel up here; but I'll get you a room where you can lie down. You can sleep and rest for two or three hours; then we'll start back."

Gloria had been tired and sleepy half an hour ago; not now. Gratton was playing his own hand in his own way—against her father and against Mark King. And Gratton had a way of winning. Something had happened; some one had telegraphed for him to come. Gloria was aquiver with excitement. She watched Gratton while he was watching the road; he, too, was tense and eager.

When he stopped the car she got down, not knowing just what to do or say. He led the way to the little "hotel," and she followed. Since she could not insist on following him about his "business," it was, perhaps, just as well if she lay down. And, alone, thought things out. He placed a chair for her and arranged for her room. He paid for it in advance, saying that they would be leaving in a hurry; he registered for her. Then Gloria was shown down a long hall and to her room. Here Gratton left her, impatient to be away. She went to her window and stood looking out. She heard a man call; a deep, rumbling bass voice. She saw Gratton come about the corner of the house and start across the street. A man, a very big man, came to meet him. They stood together talking in the middle of the road, their voices low, their looks earnest. They went away together. She shivered and went to her bed and sat down, her hands tight clasped, a look of trouble in her eyes. Gratton and Swen Brodie together—

"I don't understand." She said it to herself over and over. "I can't understand!"

She sprang up and left the room, going in feverish haste back to the front part of the building. The man who had given Gratton the register followed her with his speculative eyes. She went to the door and looked out, seeing neither the dusty road, the deserted house across the way, nor the mountains beyond. She was groping blindly in a mental fog; she was tired, very tired. And uncertain. Something was happening—had happened, or was about to happen, and she did not know which way to turn. Her father, poor old papa, was fighting hard against some kind of money troubles. Mark King, Gratton, Brodie—figures to race through her brain, to confuse her with their own contentions, to baffle and bewilder. Suddenly she felt utterly alone, hopelessly, helplessly alone. She wanted her mother, and with the impulse wheeled back toward the man watching her.

"I want to use the long-distance telephone," she said. "Where is it?"

"This way, miss," said the man, eager to be of service. Then, with a bashful grin, he amended: "I *beg* pardon. Mrs. Gratton, I mean!"

Gloria stared at him. Her mouth was open to correct him; she saw how naturally his mistake was made. But before she could speak a wild flutter in her heart stopped the words; she went swiftly to the register. In Gratton's own hand, set opposite the clerk's number seven indicating her room, were the words: "Gratton & Wife, S.F." She turned crimson; went white.

"I'll telephone later," she said faintly, and went again to the door and this time out into the autumn sunshine. All of the high adventure was dead ashes; the "lark" was lost in a sinister enterprise.

Gratton's wife—Mrs. Gratton—He had done that! She walked on blindly; tears gathered, tears of mortification, of blazing anger. But they did not fall; she dabbed viciously at her eyes. Why had he done that? *Why?* Never a "why" so insistent in all of the girl's lifetime. Never a moment of such blind wonder.

"Howdy, miss?" a voice was saying.

It brought her back to earth from a region of swirling vapours, back to to-day and Coloma. She stopped and looked at the man, startled. He was a stranger, yet dimly familiar. The little store, his own round face, his shirt-sleeves and boots—

"I wanted to ask," he said solicitously, "how your father was this morning."

"My father?" she repeated dully. "Oh, he's quite well, thank you."

Plainly her words puzzled him. He squinted his eyes as though to make sure of her.

"You're the young lady that stopped in here one day last spring with Mark King? June it was, wasn't it? You bought some stuff for lunch."

"Yes," she admitted. She would never have remembered him. But he, who had not seen others like her, remembered.

"Then you're Ben Gaynor's girl?"

"Yes," she said again, and was about to go on, resenting his persistent meddlesomeness.

"And you say he's *well?*"

"Quite well, I believe," she said coolly.

"But wait a minute," he called after her. "Wasn't he bad hurt last night?"

"Papa hurt?"

"I supposed that was why you was here—"

"How hurt?" she cried sharply. "When? Where? Tell me; why don't you tell me?"

He looked at her in wonder.

"All I know is just what I heard. And you know how news gets itself all twisted up travelling half a mile. I *heard* he got hurt at old Loony Honeycutt's last night. Right bad hurt, they said. But I was just asking you—"

"Where is he?" she cut in excitedly. "Now?"

"Didn't you just come out of the hotel?" He looked more puzzled than ever. "Wasn't he there?"

"How do I know? Was he taken there?"

He nodded. "Leastways I heard he was. Last night—"

Gloria did not wait for more. She turned and ran back to the building she had quitted only a moment ago, bursting into the front room, demanding earnestly and in words that came with a rush:

"Is my father here? Is he hurt?"

"Your father? Hurt—Say, you ain't Ben Gaynor's daughter, are you?"

"Yes, yes. And papa—"

"They had a doctor over from Placerville last night. He's

coming back again this morning some time."

"Take me to papa. Quick!" said Gloria imperiously. "You should have told me the minute I came."

"But I didn't know—"

"Quick!" repeated Gloria.

He showed her to the room, only three doors beyond her own. He moved to open the door but Gloria's hand was first to the knob; she opened and went in, closing the door softly. She was trembling, frightened, dreading, oppressed by fear of what might be. Though both windows were open the shades were drawn, the light was dim. She made out a man's form on the bed; there was a white bandage about his head. He stirred and turned half over.

"Papa!" cried Gloria, her voice catching.

She ran to him and went down on her knees at his bedside, her two hands finding his upon the coverlet, clasping them tight. He looked at her in wonderment; Gloria misread the look in his eyes and for a terrible moment thought that he was dying.

"Gloria!" he said in amazement. "Here—"

"Oh, papa!"

To Ben Gaynor this unannounced coming of his daughter partook of the nature of an apparition and of a miracle. At first he would not believe his senses, fearing that he had just gone off his head. Then it was that the look in his eyes frightened her. But the hands gripping his were flesh-and-blood hands, and, besides, Ben Gaynor was a very matter-of-fact man, little given to prolonged fanciful ideas, even after a night of pain and mental distress.

"By the Lord, we'll nail their hides to our barn door yet!" were his first words of greeting. He hitched himself up against his pillows.

"What in the world happened?" Gloria asked after a sigh of relief.

"How you happened to be here gets me," said Gaynor. "It's like magic. You didn't hear down in San Francisco that I was hurt, did you?"

"No. I—I just happened to be here. You see, papa—"

"That'll come later," he broke in. "You're here; that's all that counts. You're going to do something for me."

Anything, thought Gloria. And she was glad that he did not seek just now the explanation of her presence here; of course she would tell him everything—later. But she was still confused—"Mrs. Gratton "! Did she, down in the depths of her frivolous girl-heart, want to be that? Had she glimpsed, when she so gaily left San Francisco last night, that this escapade was something more than a mere "lark"?

"You are not dangerously hurt, papa?"

"Bless you, no! Not now, that you're here. Though I believe it would have near killed me if I'd been put out of the running altogether. I got a crack on the head that sickened me; but the tough old skull held out against it. And I got an arm broken and a rib cracked—"

Gloria, aghast, was once more in fear for him. But he cried impatiently:

"Don't you worry about me. I'll be on my feet in a week. Now, listen: I've got to talk fast before somebody comes in. The doctor is apt to be here any minute, and he's a stiff-necked tyrant. You know the trail through the mountains to our place; you rode it twice with King."

"Yes."

"I want you to ride it again to-day. You can get a horse at the stable. Don't let any one know where you are going. I want you to take a message to King. And it's got to get to him and into nobody's hands but his. Understand that, Gloria?"

Gloria did not answer promptly; she wanted to demur. She was tired; she was afraid of the mountains; she did not want to see Mark King. But she saw a terrible earnestness in her father's eyes and that while he awaited her answer quick fever spots glowed in his cheeks. She squeezed his hands and replied:

"Of course, papa. I'll do whatever you want."

"God bless you for that," he muttered. "This is sober, serious business, Gloria; you are the only one here I could trust. King will be at the house; at least I hope he will. I sent him word several days ago that—that something was in the wind, and to meet me there. And, Gloria, I want you to promise, by all that's good and holy, that you won't let a word or a sign or a hint slip to anybody else. Not to a soul on earth. Will you, Gloria?"

"Yes." She looked at him curiously; she had never known her father to be so tensely in earnest.

"Then," he said, "go turn the key in the lock. And hurry. Before any one comes."

She locked the door and returned to him.

"Feel under my pillow. Got it?"

She felt the cold barrel of a revolver and started back; never had she known her father to carry arms. Then, gingerly, she sought again. She found a small parcel and drew it out. It was a flattish affair and rectangular, the size and shape of an octavo volume—a flat box, if not a book. It was wrapped in a bit of soiled cloth.

"Quick," he commanded nervously. "Out of sight with it. Stick it into your blouse, if you can; tuck it away under your arm; it won't show so much there."

Catching something of his suppressed excitement, she obeyed.

"I managed a little note to Mark," he said when she had buttoned the loose shirt again and he had sunk back, white and exhausted, among his pillows. "I stuck it inside the cloth. Lord, if I was only on my feet! But you'll do it for me, my girl? With never a hint to any one?"

Gloria stooped and kissed him on the forehead.

"I promise, papa," she said assuringly.

"Unlock the door again, then. There's somebody coming. Sit down over there, across the room. And leave as soon as you can. We'll let them think you're going to the log house for— for—"

She was quicker at inventions.

"Doctor Rowell, our family physician, is at Lake Tahoe. I am going to find him. We would telephone, but he is camped out—"

"Pretty late for camping. Oh, that'll do—"

Gloria sat in her chair across the room, looking innocently the part of a daughter in a sick-room, when the door opened and the Placerville doctor came in. A moment later she slipped out.

*   *   *   *   *

She went out into the sunshine. Down the road she saw Gratton. He came quickly to meet her. She saw that he was eyeing her keenly, and her thought was that he was wondering if by chance she had seen the hotel register.

"I don't know just what to do," said Gratton. "My business is going to hold me here longer than I had thought. I—I promised to go back with you this afternoon. Would it be all right if I got a man to drive you back? I am terribly sorry, Gloria, but—"

"Business is business!" She laughed a trifle nervously. Then her inspiration: "I know! I can go to our mountain home; I'll phone mamma, and she will come up. We'll spend a few days, and—"

For an instant his eyes fairly blazed; they were bright with triumph.

"Just the thing! I'll go for the horses. I'll ride over with you and get right back here."

"But—"

But already, excusing himself hurriedly, Gratton was off for the horses.

CHAPTER XII

It was mid-afternoon when Gloria and Gratton came to the log house in the woods. Jim Spalding, coming to take their horses away to the stable, though a man of no wild flights of imagination and given to minding his own business, was plainly curious.

"We rode on ahead, Jim," Gloria told him, and Jim detected no false note in her gaiety. "Mamma is coming."

Spalding gave them a key and they went to the house. It was Gloria who unlocked the door; Gratton, his white face looking more than ever bloodless, saw her hand tremble. She hurried in, excused herself, and ran upstairs. She knew that the time had come when she would have to listen to what Gratton was going to say; she knew what the burden of his plea would be— she knew everything, she thought wildly, except what her answer would be.

She heard Gratton stirring restlessly downstairs. He walked up and down, snapping his fingers incessantly, a habit which in the man bespoke nervousness. He sat at the piano and the keys jangled under his touch; he got up and walked again. He was waiting for her to come down; he was shaping in mind the words which would greet her before she had come fairly to the bottom of the stairs.

Gloria turned into her own room, locking the door behind her. She looked at herself in her glass; she was pale, her eyes looked unnaturally big and brilliant. She bit her lips and turned away. From her blouse she brought out the parcel her father had entrusted to her, slipping it under her mattress, smoothing the counterpane when she had done. Then, with but one clear thought in the world, that of getting into immediate touch with her mother, she went to the telephone.

On this floor, in a cosy little room opening upon the upstairs sun-porch, was an extension telephone, installed for the convenience of Gloria and her mother. Gloria went tiptoeing to it rather than go down where Gratton was. She rang the necessary bell for the operator in Truckee and put in her long-distance call in low tones which demanded a repetition before the operator got it right. Then she sat with the instrument in her hand, waiting. Once she heard Gratton's step close to the stairs and jumped to her feet, thinking that he was coming up. But he passed by and the house grew silent again.

She wondered when Mark King would come! This after-noon—to-night—to-morrow? Spalding had said nothing; she had not mentioned King to Spalding, since she had not mentioned him to Gratton during the long ride—

Her telephone bell rang. After the irritating way of telephones, she was put presently into communication with Mrs. Gaynor.

"Gloria! Gloria! Is that you?" Her mother's voice sounded strange in Gloria's ears—shaken with emotion.

"Yes, mamma. I—"

"What has happened, child? Tell me, quick! I am nearly dead with worry. Are you all right?"

"Of course, mamma. I—"

"But *where* are you? Where were you all night? Are you sure everything is all right?"

Never had Gloria known her extremely clear-headed mother to be so wildly disturbed, so nervously incoherent.

"I have told you I am all right. I am up in the mountains, at our log house. Didn't Mr. Gratton tell you—?"

"Mr. Gratton?" Mrs. Gaynor was only more mystified. "He has told me nothing; I haven't seen him. I tried to phone him—oh, I have phoned everybody we know!—and he is out of town, and—"

But Gloria, panic-stricken by something her mother had said, cried:

"You have phoned *everybody!* Oh, mamma! What—*what* do you mean?"

"When you didn't come in last night—I have been crazy with worry! I thought you might be spending the night with one of your friends; I thought that maybe something had happened and it was being kept from me. I rang up Georgia Stark and Mildred Carter and the Farrilees—and even the emergency hospitals. I thought—"

The rest was only a meaningless buzzing in Gloria's ears; she sat speechless herself, bereft of all reason for a dull moment, then harbouring quick, clear thoughts, as swift, as vivid as lightning, and in the end as blinding by their very quality of blazing light. *The newspapers!*

Still, dominated subconsciously by the thought which had brought her to the telephone, Gloria managed before the connection was broken to beg her mother to come imme-diately to her at the log house; to tell every one that Gloria was with her father. Her mother promised; began asking questions, and Gloria said a bleak "good-bye" and hung up.

The newspapers. She sat there staring into space and seeing the San Francisco *Chronicle* and *Examiner*, hawked by newsboys, on stands, thrust under doors, going like spreading snowflakes of a big storm into post-offices, to racing trains, all over the land. Her mother had telephoned the emergency hospitals! Gloria could have wept in rage, screamed, thrown herself down and given over to paroxysms of weeping. But she only sat on, her face whiter and whiter, looking into emptiness and seeing headlines that towered as high as immense black cliffs. Her mother had telephoned Mildred Carter, that hateful, hateful, thrice-hateful Mildred Carter; had confessed that Gloria had gone out with Mr. Gratton; was gone all night, no one knew where; Mildred Carter who was as good as married to Bob Dwight of the *Chronicle*! And the emergency hospitals—Gloria with never a tear coming in her hour of greatest distress sat rocking back and forth on her chair, crying: "Oh, I wish I were dead!"

As one hears noises through a dream, long powerless to connect them logically with familiar happenings, so now did Gloria absently hearken to Gratton calling from the foot of the stairs. She jumped up only when she heard him start to mount them. Then, galvanized, she sprang to her feet, cried to him, "I'll be down in just a second," and ran to her room. She stood again looking at herself in her glass.

"Gloria Gaynor," she heard her own pale lips say, "you have gotten yourself into a nasty, nasty mess." The lips began to tremble; then, with a great struggle for will-power, they steadied. "And," said Gloria in a cold, harsh little voice, "it's up to you, and no one else, to get out the best you can this time."

She bathed her face and hands; she rubbed her cheeks with a towel, determined to bring some vestige of colour back; she took down her hair. Only then, so distrait to-day was Gloria, did she think of changing from her boyish suit into a house dress. Her eyes, which had harboured only bewilderment and terror, now grew speculative. She brought from her closet half a dozen dresses; chose a certain pink one without analysing the reasons of her selection, found silk stockings and pumps, and dressed from top to toe. She would have to have it out with Gratton, one way or the other—she began to know which way it would be. But always a girl should be at her best. Also, she decided, by the time that she was becomingly gowned and her hair arranged tastefully, it was as well to let Gratton wait for her a while; waiting always, to some extent, brought to the one cooling his heels a sense of disadvantage. In short, Gloria had gone through the most panicky of her moments and was getting a grip on herself again. When, after Gratton had waited and fumed for upward of an hour, she went downstairs she looked cool and pretty, and quite unembarrassed. He flashed a look at her that was eloquent of nervous excitement.

"I want to explain everything to you, Gloria—"

"It will take a good deal of explaining, won't it, Mr. Gratton?"

They went into the living-room and Gloria sat in a big chair while he stood before her, his fingers tapping and tapping at his cigarette-case.

"You listened-in while I talked with mamma, didn't you?" she said carelessly.

"No!" said Gratton, but so promptly that she knew he lied.

"Well?" she said indifferently. "Suppose we have the explanations now? I am sure that they will prove interesting."

"I am afraid," he began, talking swiftly, "that I have been instrumental in placing you in a false position. Last night I told you I had telephoned to your mother. I did try; they reported the line out of order. What could I do? I didn't want to alarm you. It was only a lark; I meant innocently, you know that, don't you, Gloria?"

"Did you?" she said, and managed to keep her lips smiling.

"It is only since coming here that I have realized how things will look; what people will think—and say, curse them. Our being out so long together; my buying clothing for you—"

"Our being registered as Mr. and Mrs. Gratton—"

His eyes burned, his lips clamped tight.

"Forgive me, Gloria! It was the mad impulse of a moment. I thought as we went in that it would look strange—a young, unmarried couple; that if I put down man and wife no one would think anything at all. And we'd be gone in a few hours; and probably you'd never go back there; and no one would know who you were."

"I see." Gloria's tone, devoid of expression, gave no clue to her racing thoughts. "You did that for my sake!"

"Yes," he said eagerly. "As I would do anything on earth for your sake. You know that, Gloria; you know, and have known for a long time—always—that I love you. I was going to ask you soon to—to marry me, Gloria. And now, now you will marry me, won't you?"

"Yes." But Gloria did not say it aloud; not yet. She merely made it perfectly clear to Miss Gloria Gaynor that she was going to marry Gratton, and that there was to be no further question of it. And, oh, God! at this fateful moment, how she hated him! How she loathed and detested him! While a week ago—yesterday—she had wondered, dreamily, if she were in love with him! But that was when he was in the city, at home in his own wilderness. But now! She was in a trap. This man had made it, cunningly using in his work all that he knew of Gloria Gaynor. There was no way out, save through the gate of matrimony. And—in her heart she laughed at him—through that other wider gate beyond, the gate of divorce. She would accept his name; the name of Gratton stood high in San Francisco. Then she would tell him how she loathed him; she would laugh at him, for physically she had no fear of him. And he would never have her for his own, despite all of his money and his position and his hideous trickery. Gratton, with all of his shrewdness, had not taken into consideration one thing: how in the city, on his native heath, he attracted Gloria; how in the woods he impressed her, in his unbecoming outdoor togs, as contemptible.

"You know how I love you," he was repeating. And he was sincere; she saw that in his eyes, in the unaccustomed colour in his face. He loved her as such an unclean animal could love. Oh, how he sickened her! "Will you marry me, Gloria? Will you forgive me for having, however unintentionally, placed you in a wrong light? Will you give me the right to protect you, to defend your good name? Oh, Gloria—"

Strange that the man had never revolted her as he did now! She wanted to get up and run from him. Meantime she was telling herself, almost calmly: "Yes, you'll marry him. The little beast!" She did get to her feet; he followed her into the hall.

"Let me be alone for a little while," she said quietly. She went to the stairway. "I am going upstairs; wait here for me—"

"You will come to me? You will marry me?"

"I—think—so. Don't!" she cried sharply as he moved to come to her. "Wait—"

He swallowed nervously. "I—I hoped you would. And I saw how terribly the events of the last few hours might be misconstrued. So, Gloria, daring to hope, I sent word for a justice of the peace. He will be here this afternoon or this evening—"

"Justice of the peace!" Gloria's nerves jangled loose in her irrepressible laughter.

"We'll have a priest later, of course," he ran on hurriedly. "But I couldn't arrange for one so soon."

Gloria went slowly upstairs, walking backward, looking down on him with unfathomable eyes.

"Tell me, Gloria. I'll promise not to come near you until you say I may. Is it *yes?*"

"Yes," said Gloria, and was gone in a flash, turning, running up and out of sight.

He stood looking after her, tapping and tapping at his cigarette-case.

CHAPTER XIII

To Gloria the sluggish moments were fraught with despondency or pulsating terror. All arrangements were made; she was powerless, in a trap; a justice was coming; she was going to marry Gratton. She lay on her bed with her door bolted and wept bitterly, moaning over and over: "Oh, I wish I were dead!" She heard Gratton stirring restlessly downstairs. She herself grew restless; she sprang up, tiptoed to her door, and slipped out as silent as a shadow. She went into the little room where the telephone was and through it to the sun-porch. For a long time she stood looking out across the mountains, her hand pressed to lips which trembled. She thought of her mother who, coming as fast as she could, no doubt by automobile, since she would not have the patience for trains, would not arrive before to-morrow morning. A night here—alone, worse than alone—

But great as was the emotional tension, lusty and now wearied youth must be served. She had danced and ridden all through the night; she had not had over an hour or so of broken sleep; she had been going all day. She dropped to sleep on the swing-couch on the porch. It was so very silent all about her; the shadows were creeping, creeping among the pines.

She awoke with a start. It was quite dark; the first stars burned with steadily growing brilliancy. Some one was standing above her, looking down at her. She could see only the vague outline—

"Gloria—"

A little cry of fear broke from her.

"Gloria," pleaded Gratton. "Don't you know I wouldn't—?"

"I'll be down in a minute," she told him, drawing as far away as she could, speaking with nervous haste. "Go down, please. Wait for me."

"The justice is downstairs," he said, his own voice agitated despite his effort for mastery. "Are you ready?"

"Yes, yes! In a minute I'll be down. Go. Please go."

He hesitated; she could have screamed at him. But presently he began withdrawing. Slowly, hideously slowly—

"When you are ready. And—he has a long ride back, Gloria. We should not keep him waiting."

She watched until he had gone. Then she crouched, staring with wide, unseeing eyes into the outside dark. The man would go right away; she would not have even him to mitigate the horrible condition of aloneness with Gratton.

"I won't marry him!" she cried out. "I won't. I hate him. He is a beast, and—I won't!"

There was, after all, nothing to force her. Nothing—save that she had been away all this time with Gratton, that he had bought clothing for her, that he had registered himself and wife. *And the newspapers!* She heard a door slam and sprang up; if the justice went away now without marrying them! She *would* marry him; why, if he had been of a notion to demur she would have made him marry her!

"I can't think clearly. I wonder if I am insane?" She went with heavy, leaden steps back to her room. A pale, weary face looked at her from her glass. She began arranging her hair. Her fingers, with wills of their own, refused to obey her own command laid upon them. She sought wildly to delay, delay to the last fragment of the last second before yielding to the inevitable; she wanted to loiter over her hair, and her fingers raced. She could hear voices downstairs. Gratton's voice, low and urgent; a thin, querulous voice; she shuddered. That would be the justice. Another voice, a man's and strange to her. He said nothing, but twice she heard him laugh, a laugh that jarred upon her nerves. She guessed who he would be; the man Gratton had sent to bring the justice.

"Gloria!" Gratton was calling from the foot of the steps.

The voice that answered for her was clear and steady and, downstairs, must have sounded untroubled:

"I'm coming. Just a minute."

* * * * *

Two hours ago, while Gloria had been watching the shadows creeping among the pines, Mark King had arrived. He had come down the ridge from the rear and thus to the outbuilding by the stable which housed the caretaker, old Jim Spalding.

"Hello, Mark," Jim had said, a trifle startled by King's sudden appearance. "Here you come again, like a Injun out'n the woods."

Jim was smoking his pipe on his bench. King paused, saying:

"Hello, Jim. Has Ben showed up yet?"

"No, he ain't showed, Mark. Expectin' him?"

"Yes. Who's in the house, then?"

"Why, some of 'em come on ahead. Ben's girl, for one, and

that city guy, Gratton, for another. She didn't say anything about Ben comin'; she did say, though, the missis would be along pretty soon."

Gloria and Gratton here? King frowned. He had had ample time during the long weeks since the twelfth of August to decide that he had nothing to say to Gloria Gaynor. And now she was here—with Gratton. He turned into Jim's quarters. He had no desire—or at least so he told himself very emphatically—to see either one of them.

"I've hit the trail hard to-day, Jim," he said as Jim followed him and King closed the door. "And I'm dead tired and as hungry as a bear. What shape's the cupboard in?"

"Fine," returned Spalding hospitably. "You know me, Mark."

So it happened that while Gloria fought her losing battle all alone, Mark King sat at Spalding's table, not a hundred yards away, and made a silent meal of coffee and bread of Jim's crude baking, and a dubious, warmed-over stew. Thereafter King threw himself down on Jim's bunk and the two smoked their pipes. With nothing in particular to be said, virtually nothing was said.

"Needn't tell anybody I'm here, Jim." King was knocking the ashes out of his pipe. "I haven't any business with the folks in there. But keep your eye peeled for Ben, will you? The minute he comes I want to see him."

"Maybe," suggested Spalding, "his girl brought word?"

"No. Ben is in Coloma. Gratton and Miss Gaynor and Mrs. Gaynor would have come up from the city, you know. That means they would have come through Placerville or Truckee."

"Guess so," agreed Spalding. "That's right. I'll set outside where I can watch for Ben. Goin' to take a snooze?"

"Yes."

And after lying ten minutes staring up at the ceiling above him King went to sleep.

"Must of been goin' some to-day," meditated the man who was once more on his bench outside the door. "King looks tuckered."

He sat through the thickening shadows watching the stars come trooping into the darkening sky, hearkening to the night breeze among the trees, and the thin singing noises of insects. An hour or so later he heard horses. "That would be Ben, now," was his first thought. His second was that it might be some one else, and that there was no sense waking a tired man for nothing. So he went down toward the house. He saw two men dismount and tie their horses; he saw the door open and Gratton come out. The horsemen went up to the porch. Neither was Ben Gaynor. One, as he passed in through the light-filled doorway, was a little grey man whom Jim had never seen before; the other man, it happened, he knew. Rather well by sight and reputation, a good-for-nothin' scalawag, as Jim catalogued him, name of Steve Jarrold. The door closed after them and Jim went back to his bench.

*   *   *   *   *

In the house they were waiting for Gloria. The little grey man whom they called "judge," and who had a way of clearing his throat before and after the most trifling remark, went up and down with his hands under his coat-tails, peering near-sightedly at pictures and books and wall-paper.

"Quite a tidy little place Ben Gaynor's got here," he said patronizingly. "Quite a tidy little place."

Gratton paced back and forth, whirling always abreast of the stairs, looking up expectantly. Steve Jarrold, the man whom Gloria had heard laugh, never budged from the spot where he had landed when entering the living-room; his wide, spraddled legs seemed rooted through the big feet into the floor. Big-framed and bony, with startlingly black restless eyes and a three or four days' growth of wiry beard no less lustrously black, he was ragged, unkempt, and unthinkably dirty. His eyes roved all about the room; they came back to Gratton, sped up the steps, came back to Gratton with a leer in them, and all the while he turned and turned his black dusty hat like a man doing a job he was being paid for.

At last, since no delay holds back for ever the rolling of the great wheels of time, Gloria came. Slowly she descended the stairs, one hand at her breast, one gripping the banister. Her pallor was so great that her lips, though pale also, looked unnaturally red in contrast. They were just a little apart; she seemed to breathe with difficulty. Her eyes, glancing wildly about the room and at the men to be seen in the hallway, were the eyes of one in a trap, seeking frantically for escape, knowing that there was no escape. Her brain, like one's in a fever, was quick to impressions, alive with broken fragments of thought like so many flashes of vari-coloured light. She noted trifles; she saw a painting over Gratton's head—a seascape her father had given her for her fourteenth birthday. She saw three pairs of eyes staring at her, men's eyes, to her the eyes of wild animals; she read as clearly as if their messages had been in large, printed letters what lay in the mind of each: in the little grey man's, the judge's, speculation; in Steve Jarrold's, the jeers of a man of Jarrold's type at such a moment when they fall upon the bride; in Gratton's, quickened desire of her and triumphant cunning.

"My dear," said Gratton, coming forward as though to meet her and then pausing abruptly and holding back, "this is Judge—Judge Summerling. He will—perform the ceremony, you know. And this is Mr. Jarrold. He brought the judge and will be a witness."

Gloria from the last step regarded the three men as a prisoner might have looked upon jailers coming to drag her to execution. Her lips moved but no sound issued. "Judge" Summerling bowed stiffly and cleared his throat. Steve Jarrold's hat ceased revolving an instant, then fairly spun as though to make up for lost time.

Suddenly Gloria began to laugh hysterically, uncontrollably. Gratton whipped back and stared at her; Summerling and Jarrold were mystified. She looked so little like laughter! And, as both had cause to regard the situation, there was so little call for laughter. But they could have no clue to Gloria's thoughts. Her wedding! With that insignificant little grey man in his cheap wrinkled clothes to officiate; with that unshaven, leering, dirty man to witness! Holy matrimony! Gloria Gaynor's wedding! She was near madness with the hideous, cruel travesty of such weddings as are dear to the hearts of San Francisco "society" girls.

The "judge" was clearing his throat again. She looked at him curiously, with the odd sensation that while Gloria Gaynor was asleep, drugged into a deep stupor, there was within her another Gloria who took a keen interest in the smallest happenings.

"This affair ain't any more regular than it ought to be," he was saying. "Now, just the matter of the licence—"

Gratton jerked about and glared at him. The "judge" broke off with a vehement clearing of his throat. In a moment he spoke again.

"Seein' as both parties *want* to get married," he said hastily, "and as circumstances is what they is—keepin' in mind how circumstances does alter cases—well then—are you ready?"

That "Are you ready?" seemed to explode like a pistol shot in Gloria's ears. Something within her shrieked: "No, no, no!" Gratton had said a quiet "Yes," and was looking at her. She heard herself saying faintly: "Yes."

Gratton put out his hand as though to help her down the last step. She made a little gesture, motioning him back. He bit at his lip and obeyed, though with a quick flash of the eyes. Gloria looked down at the step. About six inches high, and yet—and yet where she stood was as high as heaven, down there as deep as hell. She seemed powerless to achieve that last step. But Gratton was stirring restlessly; he would put out his hand again to help her. She shuddered and moved quickly. Now she stood on the same level as Gratton and the others; the physical fact was sinister as though symbolical of the psychical.

The "judge" began to grow vastly businesslike. He must have the full names correctly, ages, birthplaces. Gratton answered for himself and for Gloria, who stood now with her hand on the back of a chair just within the living-room door. Across the room was the fireplace; over it an ornamental mirror. She wondered dully what she looked like; the "bride"! But from where she stood she could see only the reflection of the window across the room, the strip of curtain at the side stirring softly in the evening breeze. That breeze came down through the pines; it wandered free; why couldn't she, Gloria, be like that? She thought poignantly of her few days among the pines with Mark King. Oh, the remembered glory of it, the clean, sweet freedom of it.

"Now, folks, if you're ready. Stand side by side—"

"Oh!" cried Gloria.

"Eh? What's that?" demanded the "judge."

She tried to smile.

"I—I think—" She saw Steve Jarrold leering. "The witness," she said wildly. "There is only one, and—"

"It's usual to have two, anyhow," admitted the "judge." "But, being as things *is* a bit irregular and everything, why we'll make one do."

"There's Jim," said Gloria. She did not look toward Gratton, but he understood that she addressed him. "Jim Spalding. I'd feel better if some one I knew—if you'd get Jim to come, please."

She knew that she did not care whether Jim Spalding came or did not come; that she was fighting for delay and could not help snatching at any straw, though she knew that in the end she would go down, overwhelmed by circumstance. Circumstance and—Gratton. Gratton also knew and frowned.

"Gloria," he said smoothly, "that isn't necessary, is it?"

"Yes, it is!" she flared out at him hotly. "Go, get him."

"It will take only a minute," Gratton said over his shoulder as he went. He would see to it that it took no great amount of time. Spalding on his bench saw Gratton running toward him.

"You're wanted in the house a minute, Spalding," he said curtly. "Step lively, will you?"

Spalding, not given to stepping lively at other men's commands, was slow in answering, and then spoke drawlingly:

"Wanted, am I? Well, that's interestin'. By who? I'm wonderin'."

"Miss Gloria. She wants you right away."

"That's different," said old Jim, getting to his feet.

Gratton turned and hastened back to the house, Jim quickening his own pace as he sensed something out of the ordinary. The house door stood open as Gratton had left it, and the two entered hastily. Jim looked from face to face with keen, shrewd eyes, ignored Jarrold, who said a mirthful

"Evenin', Jim," and turned to Gloria for explanation.

"Miss Gloria wanted—" began Gratton. But Jim Spalding lifted a big hand as though to ward off the words.

"I'm here, miss," he said when Gloria's white face only stared at him." You ain't sick, are you?"

"No, Jim, I—I am going to be married, and—"

"Married!" Jim looked incredulous and then puzzled as again his eyes went swiftly from one to the other of the three men's faces.

"Yes, Jim. And I want you to be a witness."

Jim flushed up and shifted uneasily. He had never been at a wedding; he did not know what a "witness" had to do. And to witness the wedding of Miss Gloria, who had never appeared to come down to earth long enough to know that there was such a man as Jim Spalding on the same sphere with her—He managed an uneasy "Yes'm," and backed off toward the door.

"Now, if you folks is ready," began the "judge" again.

"Right now?" muttered Jim. "You're gettin' married right now?"

"Yes," said Gloria wearily. And to Summerling: "I am ready."

"But I ain't!" cried Spalding. He got to the door and started down the hall. "Wait a minute, will you?"

Gratton hurried after him, his face hot with rage, while Steve Jarrold guffawed loudly and then, under Gloria's startled look, dropped his eyes.

"Come back here, Spalding," commanded Gratton angrily. "Whatever you've got to do can wait a minute—"

"*You* wait," growled Jim. "I'll be back quick enough."

*   *   *   *   *

Mark King was awakened by old Jim rushing into the room, lighting a lamp hastily, and making a deal of clatter. He sat up, demanding:

"Has Ben come?"

Jim began chuckling. After all, a wedding was a wedding, and therefore a matter well worth a man's allowing himself to get a bit excited. From a cupboard he began dragging forth his one and only serviceable suit of clothes, dingy black, shiny affairs, but Jim's "best." He kicked off his breeches, drew on the black trousers, and caught up the coat.

"No, Ben ain't back," he grinned at King. "Guess he'll be surprised when he does come. His girl's gettin' herself married. To that city guy, Gratton. Right now in the house!"

"What!" King had heard well enough, but that "What!" broke from him explosively.

"An' me, I'm a witness," said old Jim. "Steve Jarrold's another. They got the preacher there an' everything." He paused a moment and reflected, with puckered brows. "What do you think of her marryin' that swab, now? Think Ben's goin' to be pleased? Kind of surprising ain't it, Mark?"

King managed a laugh which escaped critical notice only because old Jim was only half listening.

"Oh, it's been open and shut all along that she'd marry Gratton," he said, keeping his head down as he drew a match across the floor as though to like a pipe whose bowl was empty. "If it suits his womenfolk, I guess Ben will stand for it."

By now Jim had drawn his coat on and was back at the door.

"Better come along, Mark," he invited. "You don't see a weddin' every day. Comin'?"

"No, thanks," said King. He broke his match between nervous fingers. He raised his head to watch Jim go.

"Lord, Mark," said Spalding, holding on his heel a moment. "You must of made one all-mighty day of it! You sure do look tuckered!"

King rose and went to the door and stood looking after the swiftly departing figure. He saw the house, the windows bright with lights, light streaming out through the door to the porch. There was Gloria. Just there. And he had slept, and Gloria was marrying. And here was the end of it—the end of everything, it dawned on him. He, who had never looked twice on a woman, had looked thrice on her and again. He, the one-woman man, had found the one woman—and had lost her. He looked out toward the house and through its thick log walls saw Gloria; Gloria as she had come down the stairs to him that first day, floating down like a pink thistledown, putting her two hands into his, looking up into his eyes with eyes which he would never forget; he saw her in the woods, riding with him; by the spring waiting eagerly for the little water-ouzel, she so like a bird herself; crossing a stream on boulders—she had slipped; he had caught her into his arms— close. Her hair had blown across his face. He stood with her on the highest crest of a ridge; the world lay below them, they were alone in the blue heavens. And he loved her. He groaned and ran his hand across his eyes as though to wipe the pictures out—pictures which would never pass away.

Gloria was marrying. Gratton. Now. He looked up into the sky bright with stars; its great message to him was "Emptiness." The world was empty, life was empty. There was nothing. Simply because Gloria had come, had laughed into his eyes, and had gone on. She was like the springtime which came dancing into the mountains which softened them and brightened them—and laughed and passed on and away. She would be laughing now—into Gratton's eyes.

He would never see her again after to-night. Other men had loved and their loves had crumbled to ashes, blown away by the winds of time. But to-night he *would* see her. The last time. While still she was Gloria Gaynor and not Gratton's wife—

He started and hurried toward the house. They were waiting for Jim and Jim had hurried. He came to the porch and, with never a board to creak under his careful tread, he made his way silently around to the living-room side of the house. There was a window there; the shade was not drawn; the curtains were blowing back and forth. He drew close and stood, watching. He would look at Gloria one last time, turning away just before the preacher said the last words; it was like looking for the last time on a beloved face before the sod fell—

He saw her. Her back was turned to him; her head was down. He watched her fingers moving nervously at her sides and his brow contracted with a sudden access of pain. Those fingers had touched his and he had thrilled to the soft, warm contact; he loved them better than he loved life. And soon they would find their way into Gratton's.

Not once did he move his eyes from her. She did not turn toward him, but as the "judge" began talking she lifted her head and King saw her throat, her cheek. How pale she was—

Though her head was up, her slim body drooped. Like a little wildwood flower wilting. So she remained for what seemed a very long time. Then suddenly he saw her body stiffen; her hands flew to her breast. The "judge," hurrying along, had asked:

"And do you take this man to be your wedded husband?"

King did not want to hear the answer; he turned to go. But hear now he must, for though until now responses had been low-voiced, hardly above a murmur, he heard Gloria crying:

"*No! No and no and no!*"

King stopped like a man paralysed. Had he gone mad? Then his pulses leaped and hammered. Gloria had cried "*No!*" A tremor shook him; he could no longer see her, but he stood where he was, his senses keyed to hear a falling pin within.

"He is a beast and I hate him!" cried Gloria wildly. "He tried to trick me and trap me. He tried to make me marry him But I won't! I won't! I'd rather die."

Her voice died chokingly away, and for five seconds it was deathly still. Still King did not move. He heard Gratton's exclamation, Gratton's hurried step. The man was excited, was expostulating. Other voices; the other men had drawn aside, amazed, leaving Gratton a clear field with his unwilling bride.

"Have you gone mad, Gloria?" King could hear the words now. "Think what you are saying—"

"I have thought. I hate you. Go away. Let me go."

Gratton's pale eyes must be ablaze with wrath now; his tone told that.

"There's no way out for you. You've got to marry me. I—"

"Take your hand off—"

Her voice broke into a scream.

"You're hurting me—"

And now Mark King moved at last. Before the last word had done vibrating through the still room he was through the window, taking the shortest way. Gratton's hand was on Gloria's shoulder; King threw it off, hurling the man backward across the room. Gloria turned to him—

"Mark!" she cried. "Oh, Mark King!"

He put his arms about her, thinking that she was going to fall.
For an instant he held her tight; he felt her heart beating as
though it would burst through her bosom.

"You won't let him—?"

He moved with her to a chair, placed her in it, and turned
toward Gratton, a look like a naked knife in his eyes.

"By jings!" muttered old Jim under his breath. "By jings!"

CHAPTER XIV

At this, the most critical moment of her life, it would appear inevitable that Gloria must bend every mental faculty to grappling with the vital issues. And yet, as she sat swallowed up in the big chair, for a space of time she was in a spell, caught up and whirled away from those about her; she forgot Gratton with the white, angry face; she had no eyes for Mark King or for Summerling, Steve Jarrold or Jim Spalding. She was thinking of another day, two years ago, when she and her mother had been alone in this room. They had been busied with the last touches of furniture arrangement; they had discussed locations for chairs and had argued over pictures. Both tired out with a day of effort, they had come near tears in a verbal battle over the best place for the sole article remaining unplaced. Gloria wanted it in the hallway; Mrs. Gaynor pleaded for it over the mantel in the living-room. Finally it was Gloria who cried with sudden laughter:

"Oh, what *difference* does it make? We're getting silly over trifles. Have it your way, mamma."

Trifles! Gloria wondered if any other act of her life had had the tremendous import of that sudden yielding to her mother's wishes. If the mirror had been placed anywhere else in the universe, even by a few inches removed from its present abiding-place, would there be a *Gloria Gaynor* in all the world right now? Or would her chair hold quite another sort of person—Mrs. Gratton? If she had not lifted her desperate eyes and seen Mark King reflected at the window, how would she have answered that one final question the "judge" propounded? Would she have said "Yes"? Or would it have been "No"? She did not know; she would never know. She had been on the verge, dizzy with profitless speculation. And now, only the extent of one little word stood between her and an unthinkable condition. That a whole life should be steered down one channel or another—oh, what immeasurably separated channels!—by one's breath in a single-syllabled word—

*   *   *   *   *

"You don't answer!" a voice was saying irritably.

She started. They were talking to her, they had been talking to her, and now she realized that she had heard voices across a great distance, and by no means as clear to her consciousness as the remembered voice of her mother two years ago arguing for a mirror over the fireplace. She turned her eyes on Gratton, since obviously it was he who insisted on an answer. But King spoke for her.

"Look here, Gratton," he said bluntly, "as far as I can see there is no reason why Miss Gaynor should pay the least attention to your effervescings if she doesn't care to. She is a free agent and under no obligations to you."

"I'll ask your opinion when I want it," snapped Gratton. "Miss Gloria—"

"You asked me something?" said Gloria. "Pardon me. I didn't hear."

Her aloof reply disconcerted him. Her attitude was spontaneous, unaffected, and hence unconsciously one of polite indifference. Suddenly Gratton, fume as he would, had become of not the least importance.

"You said that you would marry me. Not a dozen

minutes ago."

"Did I?" she demanded coolly. "Are you quite sure I said that?"

"Look here, Miss Gloria." It was Jim Spalding, who had been ill at ease all along and now had the brains and perhaps the delicacy to understand that this was no place for him. "If you don't need me after all, I'll go."

"And the rest of us with you," said King. "If Miss Gaynor cares to talk things over with Gratton—"

Gloria put out her hand impulsively, touching King's arm.

"*You* stay. Please. Until—he goes."

King inclined his head gravely, not realizing that his body stiffened under her light touch.

"What about *me*?" demanded the "judge" sharply. "Am I needed or ain't I?"

"I'd say not this evening," King's dry voice answered him. "Good-night to you."

"That's a fine way to treat a man," cried Summerling truculently. "Here I ride all this way in the dark, and without stoppin' for so much as supper; here I ain't had a bite to eat since dinner-time, and it's good-night and get out! And that hundred dollars I was to get so fast, how about that? Think I'm the man to let folks trample on me and—"

"Maybe Jim will give you a hand-out at his cabin," King told him. "As for your money, get it out of Gratton if he promised it to you—or," he added with a flash of heat, "take it out of his hide, for all I care."

"Wait for me outside, Summerling," muttered Gratton. "*I* haven't said you won't be needed, have I?"

"Just the same, I wouldn't mind takin' what's comin' to me now—"

"Man alive!" shouted Gratton, whirling on him. "Haven't I got enough on my hands without you yelping at me?"

"Just the same—"

"Jim," called King above the incoherent mouthings, "slip your arm through Summerling's and lead him off with you. Feed him if you feel like it, and let him stick around for a word with Gratton if he wants. And you, Steve Jarrold, Ben Gaynor isn't here, but just the same you can take it from me that neither you nor any other of Swen Brodie's hangdogs is wanted in Ben Gaynor's house. Out you go."

Jarrold's eyes slanted off to Gratton. Then, seeing himself ignored and forgotten, he shrugged his shoulders, pulled on his hat, and went out. Behind him, arm in arm, one smiling widely and the other pulling back and still sputtering, went Jim and the "judge."

To all this Gloria had given scant attention. The spell no longer lay over her; she was keenly awake to the demands of the present; she was thinking, thinking, thinking! It seemed that she had walked on quicksands; that a hand had drawn her up and placed her where she was now, with solid ground underfoot; but that still all about her were quicksands. What temporary sense of security was hers was due to Mark King, to his presence. As long as he stood there, where she could put out a hand and touch him, she could rest calmly, assured of safety. But when he went, there remained Gratton and his venom. Quicksands all about her in which she would be floundering at this moment but for Mark King—

* * * * *

Her heart was beating normally again, the pallor left her face, which became delicately flushed. Her eyes, large and humid, a sweet grey and once more almost childlike—eyes to remind a man that here, after all, was no woman of the world, but only a young girl—rose to King's and met his long and searchingly. Yet there was that in their expression that made him understand that she was not looking at him, the physical man, so much as through him. For the first time in her pampered life the day had come when she was face to face with vital issues; when there was no mamma and no papa to turn to; when there were no shoulders other than her own to feel the weight of events. She must do her own thinking, come to her own decisions. Here was no time for a misstep. The one great step she had already taken; she had cried "No!" That step could be reconsidered, retraced; she looked at Gratton's face and saw that. But now she would not do that; she could not. In the city, seeing the two men together, she had turned to Gratton. Now, here in her father's log house in the mountains, she wondered that she could have done so. Did men change colour like chameleons, shifted from one environment to another? Or was it she who had been unstable, she who was the chameleon? A queer sensation which had been hers before, and which she was to know more than once in days to follow, mastered her. It seemed that within her, coexistent and for ever in conflict, there were two Glorias: a girl who was very young, spoiled, vain, and selfish; a girl who was older, who looked above and beyond the confines of her own self, who was warmhearted and impulsive, and could be generous. There was the Gloria who was the product of her mother's teaching and pampering; there was that other Gloria who was the true daughter of a pioneer stock, a girl linked to the city through tradition, bound to the outdoors through instinct. There was the Gloria who was ashamed of Mark King at a formal gathering in her own home; there was the Gloria who was thrilled to the depths of her being as in the forest-lands she knew a breathless moment in the arms of Mark King.

Well, here were considerations to linger over on an idle day. Now, without seeking for hidden springs, there were on the surface certain plain facts. No matter what she had felt toward Gratton before, she detested him now; no matter what he might have appeared in San Francisco, here in his unaccustomed garb he looked to her puny, shallow, and contemptible. He was, as she had told him, a beast. He had betrayed her confidence; he had taken advantage of her headlong youth; he had displayed to her view the vileness within him. He loved her, did he? So much the better. It lay within her power, then, to repay him, if only in part, for what he had made her suffer.

* * * * *

"I repeat, Miss Gloria," Gratton was saying, a stubborn look in his eyes, "that you promised to marry me. You have had a hard day, I realize; there has been much to unnerve you. I erred in haste, perhaps; I should have waited until you had a night's rest. But you know why I did not wait. It was for your sake."

Gloria heard him through with a hard little smile.

"Nothing is further from my intention, Mr. Gratton," she told him icily, "than to marry you. Now or ever. Please let us consider the matter closed once and for all."

His fingers worked nervously at his sides. Gloria chose the moment to lift her eyes again fleetingly to King's. She wanted Gratton to see, she wanted to hurt him all that she could. She looked back to see him wince. Nor did his quick contraction of the brows result from her glance alone; he had seen the look lying unhidden in King's eyes. Mark King had to-night, for the first time, swept barriers aside and looked straight into his own heart and known that all of the love that was in him to give had been given to Gloria Gaynor; he had come from Jim's cabin to look on her for the last time; he was giving her up. And then, when he had turned away rather than hear her murmur "Yes," she had cried out ringingly: "No!" The sod had not fallen upon a beloved face; death had not entered the door; life was not extinguished—where there was life invariably there was hope—he had given Gloria up, yes; but she had come back from beyond the frontier, she had come calling to him. He was certain of nothing just now beyond the tremendous, all-excluding fact that, wise or fool, he loved her. He wanted her with a want that is greater than hunger or thirst, or love of man for man or of man for life itself. Much of this lay shining in his eyes for Gratton to read—or for Gloria.

"I am no boy to be thrown aside like an old glove," cried Gratton, beside himself, shaken with jealous fury. "You have promised; you have loved me; in your heart you love me now. Shall I stand back for a girl's nervous whim? I tell you, you shall marry me."

Gloria's laughter, cool and insolent, maddened him. He clenched his hands and was swept away by his passion to gusty vehemence:

"Think before you laugh! What if, instead of doing the gentlemanly thing, I refused to marry you? Alone with me all this time; all last night; a clerk to swear I bought clothing for you; a register to show where we engaged a room as man and wife; the San Francisco papers already bandying your name about, already nosing after scandal. You've *got* to marry me; there is nothing else for you to do!"

Gloria flushed hotly. But only in anger this time. King mystified, looking from one to the other, turned at last to Gloria and muttered:

"For God's sake let me throw him out of the door!"

"I think it might be best first," she answered quietly, "if Mr. Gratton remained long enough to understand that this is the last time I shall ever speak to him or listen to a word from him. He has tried to get me into a nasty situation; he will do all that he can to promote scandal. But I want him to know that he will, in the end of it all, have my father to reckon with—and my friends." Again she looked swiftly at King and again Gratton writhed at the look. "Papa will not be here to-night; he is hurt and in Coloma, and I'll give you his message soon. But—"

"You saw your father! In Coloma!" It was a gasp of astonishment from Gratton. "You said nothing. You brought a message to King here?"

"And you escorted me and never guessed!" Gloria taunted him. "Really it seems too bad, after all of your week-end trips to Coloma, after all of your conferences with the estimable Mr. Swen Brodie!"

His prominent eyes bulged, written large with consternation. For a moment he stood the picture of uncertainty, plucking at his lip.

"Gloria," he said shortly, "despite all you have said I shall see you again. To-morrow, when we have both rested, I'll come to you. Now, if you will pardon me, I'll have a word with King. Strictly business, you may be sure, King," he concluded sarcastically.

"There's to be no business between you and me," King told him promptly.

"But there is. If you've got two grains of common sense. Look you, Loony Honeycutt is dead at last. His secret is no longer his secret. Swen Brodie knows something—a whole lot—"

"It strikes me," frowned King, "that you know more of this than I gave you credit for. Where do you come in?"

"I know—nearly all that it is necessary to know!" His eyes flashed triumphantly. "Think I'm the man to let the crowd of you lift a fortune right under my nose? Here is my proposition, and you'll thank your stars that I make it: We are not friends, you and I, but that is no reason that we cannot be business associates until this trick is turned. You and I enter into a pact right now, purely business, you understand." He was speaking more and more rapidly in the grip of a new emotion. "Whatever we find we divide, fifty-fifty;—"

King's sudden laughter, no pleasant sound in Gratton's ears, checked the rush of words. To accept Gratton as a partner—on a fifty-fifty split of the spoils! Was the man crazy?

"I have been working with Brodie," shouted Gratton. "If I go on with him now, with him and the men with him, six or eight of them taking what he gives them either in money or in curses and orders—if, I say, I chip in with him against you, what will the inevitable end be, I ask you? Look at the odds—"

"The inevitable end," said King sternly, "will be that they'll pick your bones and kick you out."

"I demand to know what word Gaynor sent—"

"Will you have him go, Mark?" said Gloria. "He—sickens me."

King, unleashed by her words, took a quick step forward.

"Gratton," he said, "you'd better go."

Gratton, rising to fresh fury, shouted at him:

"And leave you and her here? Alone? All night—"

King bore down upon him and struck him across the mouth, hurling him back so that Gratton tripped and fell. Gloria rose and stood watching, terrified and yet fascinated. She saw Gratton crawl to his feet; his hand went out to the table to draw himself up; it found one of the heavy bronze book-ends; the fingers gripped it so that the tendons stood out like cords. She could see the faces of both men, Gratton's twitching and vindictive, King's immobile, looking at once calm and terribly stern. If there were two Glorias within her, one of them fled now; the other watched with quick bright eyes and gloried in the man who had come at her hour of direst need; one vanished, afraid, the other felt a little thrill go singing through her blood. And though that bronze block, were it hurled at

King's head, might have been the death of him, she was not once in doubt as to the end of this conflict. There before her eyes a man contended with a manikin.

"Drop that, Gratton! Do you hear me? Drop it, I say!"

He even drew closer while he spoke. In his voice was assurance that he would be obeyed; in his look was the promise of death or near-death, to be meted out swiftly and relentlessly for disobedience. Gratton, like a man in a daze, hesitated. King's hand shot out swiftly, gripping his wrist. There was a sudden jerk and the bit of bronze crashed to the floor.

"You'll go now!"

"Yes, I'll go. But—"

"On your way, then!"

"But—"

"Shut up!" A tremor not to be repressed shook King's voice. "And go before I—Just go!"

Gratton caught up his hat, stood for a moment plucking at his lip and staring at Gloria, and then turned and went out. Strangely, only now that he had gone, did Gloria shiver and look after him fearfully. The man here had seemed so futile and yet she had seen that last look, so filled with malevolence that in his wake the room seemed steeped in menace. King must have had somewhat the same sort of an impression; he went to the door and called out loudly:

"Jim! Oh, Jim."

Jim's voice answered from the cabin:

"Comin', Mark."

"Gratton's outside. I've told him to clear out. Give him about two minutes, and if he's still here throw a gun on him and run him off the place."

"Oh, I'm going fast enough." From somewhere off in the dark it was Gratton's voice calling back hatefully. "And don't you forget it, Mark King, I am going where an offer like mine to you will be accepted. We'll be there before you yet, a dozen men that won't lay down before you! And you can tell that girl in there, with my compliments, she'll be on her knees to me before she's a day older." He lifted his voice so that Gloria, shivering in the silent house, must hear every word. "You can tell her, too, that if I didn't telephone to her mother from Oakland, I did call up two of the San Francisco newspaper offices! Tell her to watch for the papers. And when they get wind of the nice little situation to-night, Gloria here all night—"

King had held the door open only to see if Gratton was going to his horse. Now, however, he slammed it suddenly and went back to Gloria. After all, Jim could be depended on to see to Gratton and to do his job thoroughly and with joy in the doing. There was still the message to be had from Ben Gaynor, who, it seemed, lay hurt somewhere in Coloma.

But he stopped dead in his tracks when he saw Gloria, and for the moment all thoughts of Gaynor or a message fled from his mind. Again she was as pale as death; she caught at the back of the chair which had served her thus before; she lifted to King eyes sick with terror.

"I haven't got the straight of things very well," King said to her, speaking very gently. For in his heart he was thinking: "Poor little kid! She's only a kid of a girl and she's pretty near the breaking-point, from the look of things, and small wonder." But aloud he continued: "Only one thing seems clear. You are tired half to death and worried the other half. I wouldn't let myself think of that snake Gratton or his poison drippings. Things will work out all right." He managed a smile of a sort, the first smile to-night, and added: "They always do, you know."

"Do they?" she asked listlessly. And she, too, forced a smile, so wan and bleak that it came close to putting a dash of tears into King's eyes.

"For one thing," he said brusquely, "I'll bet you haven't had a bite to eat since you got here; have you?" She shook her head; she hadn't thought of such a thing as eating. When had she eaten last? Not since she and Gratton, motoring up from San Francisco, had stopped at the wayside lunch-counter? Perhaps that was why this giddy faintness troubled her, why the blood drummed in her ears.

"You'll sit right down," commanded King. "Or lie down is better. In two shakes I'll have something ready for you."

"You are so good to me." That came straight from Gloria's heart; her eyes shone with a gratitude which struck him as far beyond proportion to the small deed of the moment. "I'll go upstairs a moment; papa's message—"

"It can wait ten minutes."

"Let me get it now. I—I will lie down in my room until you call me, if you want me to."

"That's good." He watched her go slowly upstairs and then hastened to the kitchen. He got a wood fire going in the range, scouted for coffee, found a glass jar of bacon, a tin of milk, all kinds of canned goods. And meantime, though occupied with much speculation concerning all that had happened to-night and must have happened before and might happen in the future, he never for an instant entirely forgot Gloria and how pitifully borne down she looked. Gratton had tricked her some way, had coerced her, had come close to breaking her utterly. And yet her indomitable spirit had in the end triumphed over Gratton's scheming; King would never forget how her voice had rung out in that fearless "No! No and no and no!"

"Just a little kid of a girl." And he had looked to her for the sanity of mature age. A mere girl, sheltered always by father and mother, spoiled to the nth degree, given no opportunity to develop her own character, to grow up to life's responsibilities. Her mother had not even told her of her grandparents, being ashamed of them, making Gloria ashamed. Grandparents of whom any one might be justly proud; folk of integrity, of stamina, of fearless hardihood, men and women of that glorious type that builds empires. And Gloria, King sensed, was like them. Deep within her, under the layers of artificiality which her mother had striven so indefatigably and lovingly to lay on, she was like them. He remembered his two days with her alone in the mountains and sought to forget the fragment of one evening in the city. "Here she was her real self; there she had been what her mother had made her over."

* * * * *

Gloria, with lagging steps, had gone to her room. Now she lay on her bed, her hands pressed tight upon her closed eyes, her will set against heeding the throbbing in her temples as she strove to think clearly. Gratton's words rang in her ears. They plunged her into panic. For scores of "friends" and hundreds of acquaintances she would furnish a topic of talk. Girls who were jealous of her would get into a warm flurry of excitement; Gloria could picture a dozen of them sitting at their telephones, calling up this, that, and the other Mabel and Ernestine, saying: "Oh, did you hear about Gloria Gaynor? Isn't it *terrible!* What *could* she have been thinking of? I knew she was—" and so forth and so on, "ringing interminable changes." Youth, though declared by the thoughtless to be a period of heedlessness, takes to heart far more seriously than does Age all happenings which touch its own interests. Pure tragedy is Youth's own realm. It feels acutely, its imaginings are fearful, it magnifies and distorts beyond all reason. Had Gloria been above thirty instead of under twenty this moment would have been far, far less deeply immersed in the gloom of despair. She suffered dry-eyed.

But Youth, condition of wedded extremes, while it holds tragedy to its bleeding heart, cannot entirely fail in time to listen to the voice of hope. Gloria clung passionately to the one straw offered her: Mark King had come; he had saved her, if only for the moment. If there were further salvation, it lay in Mark King. And so she came presently to a thought that made her sit bolt upright, that set her heart racing, that brought a new look into her eyes. Just now it had seemed so clear that only one thing could save her from clacking diatribes, from torture under the tongues of Ernestines and Mabels and daily newspapers— marriage with Gratton. But Gratton was gone and Mark King was here! If she married King! The "judge" was still here. King was her father's friend; between men like them there was nothing which would be denied when friendship asked. What if she went to King, saying to him straight-forwardly: "Thus and such is my predicament. For my sake— for the sake of papa's daughter and hence for papa's sake no less—will you go through the form of marrying me? I shall be no burden; it will make no difference in your life. For to-morrow I will go back to San Francisco and you need never see me again. You can let me have a divorce; you will have lost nothing; I shall have been saved everything. Will you many me, Mark King?"

*   *   *   *   *

"Gloria!" King was calling. "Will you come down now? Everything's ready."

"Coming," answered Gloria. "Right away."

She glanced in her glass as she went out; the colour which had played hide-and-seek all day was again tinting her cheeks a delicate rose. What were fatigue and hunger when hope attended them?

But it happened that Gloria's impulse, which was at least

honest and frank, was for a little held in abeyance, and thus it came about that she lost the opportunity to appear before Mark King at a critical moment as being straight-dealing, direct, and outspoken. She thanked him with her eyes for the lunch he had set forth for her; she gave him a quick little smile as he waited on her. He poured the coffee, gave her milk and sugar, brought the hot things from the stove. And all of the time there was in his eyes a look which he had no suspicion was there, the look of a man's adoration.

"He will do whatever I ask him to do," something sang within her.

"Won't you sit down with me, Mark?" she smiled at him.

And there, while one Gloria had determined to indulge in plain talk, the other Gloria came forward obliquely, demanding the place which had always been hers when it was a case of man and girl together. The smile was the smile of a coquette; it intoxicated; it made a man's heart beat hard; it brought him in close to her and thrust the world back. She could not have helped the smile or its message.

"I have eaten," he said a trifle harshly, she thought.

"You are so good to me." She stirred her coffee and he saw only the lashes and their black shadows on her cheeks. Then she said brightly: "This is our third little picnic together, isn't it?"

"Then you haven't forgotten? The others?" The words said themselves for him. The human comedy had begun, or the comedy begun long ago was resumed smoothly in its third act, King unconsciously answering to his cue. After that it was neither Gloria nor himself who played the part of stage-director; that time-honoured responsibility was back in the hands of the oldest of all stage-managers. The wind that drives autumn leaves scurrying, the sun that awakens spring buds were no more resistless or inevitable forces than the one now voicing its dictates.

"It would be—unmaidenly to ask him to marry you," whispered that other self within her. Oh, if she could only guess which was the *real self,* which the pretender! "And there is no need. Look at his eyes!"

King saw lying on the table the package done up in an old cloth which she had brought. Further, he knew that he had seen it before and where he had seen it. He knew that at last he had old Loony Honeycutt's secret where he could put out his hand to it, with none to gainsay him. He knew that with it was a message from his old friend Ben; that Ben, himself, lay at this moment in Coloma hurt. And yet his eyes clung to the eyes of Gloria and all of these things were swept aside in his mind. He saw that when her eyes came to a meeting with his the flush in her cheeks grew hotter. He tried to remember how he had come away from her in San Francisco; how he had given her up for all time. But that memory blurred; in its place he stood with her on a boulder in a creek, holding her in his arms; he stood with her on a mountain top, with the world lost below them. He sought to get a grip on himself; here and now was no time to talk to her of love. She was alone; it was his one job right now to take Ben's place, to protect her and efface his own madness. But was he mad? And was now no time, after all? She was alone, yes; but if some day she would marry him, was not now the time? What would he not give for the right to stop the nasty mouth of Gratton once and for all.

Fragmentary thoughts, by no means logically aligned. They came and went with other thoughts between, pro and con. But thoughts do not always sway destiny. In the crisis often enough there is no time for so slow a process as thinking; instinct leaps. Instinct compels. All of the thought in the world will not draw a steel needle to a bit of wood; all of the thought in the world will not hold back the same needle from a magnet. There are urges which must be obeyed, the urge of spinning worlds to circling suns, the urge of man to maid.

"Gloria!" he said huskily. "Gloria!"

"Yes, Mark?" she said quietly, trying to speak very calmly and as though she did not know, oh, so well, all that tumult that lay behind his calling her name. But despite her determination she was agitated; the moment had come; there was no stopping it. And did she want it? What did she want? What, exactly, did she feel?

She knew what was in his heart! His soul exulted as the certainty rushed upon him. She knew what he was going to say; words were needless between them. And the colour merely deepened in her cheeks while she hid her eyes from him.

He came to her swiftly. She rose as swiftly to her feet. He saw that a tremor shook her. He saw that she did not draw back from him; her eyes at last lifted to meet his own. They baffled him; he could not read their meaning. But they shone on him softly; they were the eyes of her whom he loved. Like magnet and steel they were swept together. He had her in his arms; he felt against his breast the wild flutter of her heart, against his face the soft brushing of her hair. He felt her body tense but unresisting in his arms; suddenly she relaxed, her head was against his breast. Gloria in his arms—Gloria's sweet face hidden from him against his rough shirt—

"Gloria!" he cried again. "Gloria!"

"The—the bacon!" gasped Gloria. "It's burning—"

She freed herself, and while he let her go he stood watching her with the new look in his eyes. Scarlet-faced she flashed her look at him from across the table. Then she fled to the stove and retrieved the burning bacon as though here were the one matter of transcendent importance. King began to laugh, his laughter as joyous as a boy's.

"Gloria—"

"That's five times you've said 'Gloria,'" she informed him hurriedly. "And—Please, Mark," as he moved toward her. "And you haven't read papa's letter yet. And—and I'm dying to know what is in that funny package. Aren't you?"

"If I'm dying at all," he told her gravely, though he found a smile to answer her own—and two very serious smiles they were—"it is of quite another complaint. And this time—"

"But *please*, Mark! I am here all alone—with you—and—"

"I know. I haven't forgotten. But, Gloria—"

They both started to a sudden sound outside, a scuffling on the porch. Involuntarily Gloria, prone to nervous alarm in her overwrought condition, moved hastily back toward him from whom just now she had escaped. They glanced toward the sound; they saw at the window the puckered and perplexed face of the "judge"; they were just in time to see a big hand grasp him by the shoulder and yank him out of sight. They heard Summerling expostulate; they heard Jim Spalding's far from gentle voice cursing him.

King understood, at least in part, what must lie under Gloria's look of distress. Surely circumstance had placed her in an equivocal position to-night. Summerling was the type to blab; he was in no charitable frame of mind; he had found her alone here with men, had come to marry her to one man, and now had seen her in the arms of another. There was but one answer, even to Mark King.

"Some time you are going to marry me, Gloria," he said gravely. "Why not now?"

"It sounds like—like an advertisement, Mark," she laughed somewhat wildly.

"Poor little kid," he muttered, seeing how she trembled. "But, Gloria, why not? Some time you are going to give yourself to me, aren't you, dear? While this man is still here, won't you let him marry us? It will give me the right to shut that fool Gratton's mouth for him and—Oh, Gloria, my dear, my dear—"

She stood staring at him with wide eyes. He pleaded with her.

"Will you, Gloria?"

And then from lips which did not smile he heard the very faint but no longer evasive "Yes."

"Now, Gloria?"

"Yes, Mark. If you are sure that you want me." She spoke humbly; at the instant she was humble. "But," she added hastily, "still you haven't read poor papa's letter. He was very anxious. Let me go a minute, Mark. I am going upstairs. I—I want to phone to mamma first. And while I am gone you can read papa's letter, and—and—" Her face was hot with blushes.

"And arrange with the judge," he said, his own voice uncertain. "Yes, Gloria."

She ran by him then. He heard her going upstairs, he heard a door closing after her. Then like a man who treads on air he went to the window and threw it up and called:

"Jim! Tell the judge not to go. I have business with him. I want him and you here in ten minutes."

And then when Jim's voice had answered him he thought to take up the parcel on the table—largely because Gloria had asked him! A hurried letter from Ben and the parcel from Honeycutt's. Something here for which he had been seeking, working, for years, remembered now only because Gloria had made the request that they be not forgotten.

*　*　*　*　*

To withdraw his racing thoughts from Gloria and her golden promise, to bend them to a letter—this was in the beginning an effort. But Ben's words caught him when he had read the first line. He had opened the packet, ripping off the old encasement of cloth. There was a book, a Bible that looked to be centuries old, battered, the covers gone; Gaynor's letter was slipped into it:

"DEAR MARK:

"Honeycutt's dead. I've got his secret. But Brodie came near doing me in. Honeycutt, dying, sent for me. I got there just in time. He gave me the Bible; it was the "parson's" and then Gus Ingle's. As I was going out of the cabin Brodie and two of his gang swooped down on me. In the dark I pitched the Bible clear and they did not see; it was just that near! They came close to killing me; when I came to I found they'd been through my pockets. I don't know how much Brodie knows. I do know he is working with Gratton, the dirty crook. I think you can beat them to it, hands down. And, for God's sake, Mark, and for my sake if not for your own, don't let the grass grow! I am on the edge of absolute bankruptcy; laid up this way I don't see a chance unless you find what we've been after so long *and find it quick*. Will you start without any delay? As soon as you get this phone to Charlie Marsh at Coloma. Leave word for me. And let that word be that nothing on earth will stop you! Then I won't go crazy here with worry. And watch out for Gratton as well as Brodie.

"BEN."

A bit of the old interest swept back over King as he read; the old excitement raced through his blood. He dropped Ben's note into the stove and eagerly took up the old Bible. There on the blank pages, written in a crabbed hand long ago, at times letters blurred out but always a trace left where the unaccustomed scribe had borne down hard in his painful labourings, was the "secret" at last—Gus Ingle's message come to him across the dead years:

"Good god I never see such gold nor no man neither and
when he come in to camp you could reed in his look he had
found it because no man could have looked at that Mother
load and not look like Jimmy. And big Brodie grabbed him
by the throat and shook him and nearly killed him until
Jimmy told. And I guess there was enough there for
everybody in all the world. We went down the gorge to the
narrow place over on the big seedar that had broke off and
that was how we come to the First Caive, and then we
come to Caive number thre and two. And good god have
mercy on my soul when Ime dead but I got the thought
right then if it was only all mine—we worked all seven until
we dropped that day and night and early in the morning
and the storm was coming but we stayed. And for two
weeks maybe thre we lost track of time until this grate big
pile of gold was dug that I am setting right on top of right
now how can a man eat gold when he is dying of hunger
and burn it when he is freezing. And it was big Brodie
killed pore Manny I seen him and the next day or maybe it
was two days Dago was gone and never come back was it
Manny's goast got him and drug him down the cliffs
screaming horrible and in the gorge—anyway that was
Two. and I am all that is left and I am going—I tride to get
out and the Big storm drov me back and all I can see is
Jimmy Kelp and the parson if I had not of killed them they
would killed me sure and big Brodie's gone he is crazy and
cant never make it back across the mountains in this storm,
and Baldy Winch he took a big nugget and went off, and
he stoled what handful of grub there was. And now I can
look down in the gorge and see the water all white and
snow and ice sickles and I am afraide to get lost in the
caives and if I write all this in the bible that was preacher
Elsons and tie it up safe in oilcloth and canvas and make a
bote out of a chunk of wood and throw it in the river
maybe it will get to one of the camps down there and a
good man will find it and Ile give him half. You come up
the old trail past where the thre Eytalians had their camp

last year and over the big mountain strate ahead and about another seven miles strate on and then there is the pass with the big black rocks on one side and streaks of white granite on the other and down into the gorge and strate up four or five miles where the old seedar broke off and fell acrost. My god here goes.

"GUS INGLE."

To any man who knew the Sierra hereabouts less intimately than did Mark King, Gus Ingle's message would have brought only stupefaction. But to King now, as to Ben Gaynor before him, the "secret" lay bare. Old names held on; the three Italians had given a name to what was now known as Italy Gulch. The caves were on a certain fork of the American River then, and King had approximately the distances and direction.

"What is more," he thought triumphantly, "I know where two caves are in there. But where the devil is 'Caive thre'?"

*   *   *   *   *

Here he started up and thrust the old Bible into his shirt. There were steps on the porch. Jim and the "judge" were coming—

CHAPTER XV

"It strikes me," said Summerling sarcastically, "that there's mighty funny goings-on here to-night. I show up to marry one man to a girl and nex' thing I know I peek in a winder and see—"

"Never mind that," cut in King hastily. "You are going to marry her after all. Only to another man."

"Meanin' you, Mark?" demanded Jim. On his honest old face was a look of utter bewilderment; for the life of him he couldn't decide whether he or every one else had gone crazy.

King flushed under the look, but nodded and managed a calm "Yes, Jim."

Summerling cleared his throat and thereafter scratched his head.

"It's irregular. I told Gratton that. But he said there was—was extenuatin' circumstances and all that. Hadn't been time for a licence. It's irregular; don't know as I mightn't get in trouble for it—"

"The marriage would be binding, wouldn't it?" demanded King.

"Sure it would; once I said 'man and wife' nary man could set *that* aside. But, if any one wanted to get *me* in bad, seeing there's no licence—well, it would make trouble with my bondsmen and they'd make trouble with me."

King silenced the man with a scowl and led him and Jim into the living-room, closing the door. It was unthinkable that Gloria should hear a lot of talk about why's and how's. For Gloria, it struck him, had undergone enough for one day. "Look here," he said to Summerling then, "either you will or you won't. If you won't, then Miss Gaynor and myself will go elsewhere. Now, which is it?"

"Gratton promised me a hundred dollars," muttered the "judge." "And he cleared out without taking the trouble to pay me."

King's face cleared. His cheque for a hundred dollars decided the "judge."

"That's a might of money to pay the old duffer for one night's work, Mark," muttered Jim. "Strikes me that way, anyhow."

A might of money! King laughed.

"Now if you folks are ready," said Summerling, grown impatient the moment the cheque was in his pocket, "I've got a long ride ahead of me."

This time Gloria did not keep them waiting. She came down the staircase to Mark King standing at the bottom. In her pink dress, like a thistledown, floating down to him. He was thinking—she, too, remembered—how for the first time they had met thus. She smiled at him; she put out her two hands to him as she had done that other time. And right there they were married—on Gus Ingle's old Bible.

"It's done!" whispered Mark, bending over her. "You are mine now; mine for all time, Gloria. And, girl of mine," he added reverently, "may God deal with me as I deal with you."

"It's done!" In an awed little voice came Gloria's response, like an echo. Mark King had seen her across the quicksands.

Jim and the "judge" had gone. They two were alone in the still house. Gloria was nervous; King could see that and thought that he understood. So he went for wood, made a cheery blaze in the fireplace, and drew two chairs up to it.

"Tell me about papa's letter," said Gloria hastily Had there not been that obvious topic she would have caught at another, any other. "He didn't tell me how badly he was hurt or what had happened."

King put out his hand for hers, and while Gloria looked into the fire and he looked into her face, he told her. At the end he brought out Gus Ingle's Bible and read to her what was written in it. All the time that his eyes were occupied she watched him eagerly, a little anxiously. But by the time he had finished she had been intrigued for the moment out of her own self-centred thoughts, her fancies caught by all that underlay this crude tale of treasure and murder, of lust for gold, of treachery and lonely death.

"And you know where it is?"

"I can go to it as straight as a string. Two days to get to it and to stake a claim; two days to come out with a couple of horses loaded to the guards. And that itself means a fortune, if it's clean, raw gold, as would seem to be the case. We need not fear the poorhouse, you and I, Mrs. King!"

"But Brodie? And Mr. Gratton?"

"They don't know where it is! They can't know, since we've got the Bible, and Honeycutt was dead before they got to him! If they knew they would have been on their way already. And I'll be striking out before dawn, leaving no such trail that they can follow it in a hurry, even if they should seek to. No; Brodie and Gratton and the rest of them have lost the game!"

"You are going so soon? Papa wanted that?"

"He wanted me to telephone as soon as I got this." He rose, lingering over her. "We mustn't forget him, even for our own happiness." He brushed her hair with his lips; he hastened the few steps to the telephone in Ben's study.

"I—I am going upstairs, Mark," called Gloria after him.

"All right, Queen of the World," he answered her. "I'm just to phone in a message for him. It won't take me five minutes to get it done; just to say: 'Tell Ben that I start at dawn and that he's got my word for it that nothing's going to stop me! And—that I've just married Gloria!'"

But he was at the telephone longer than he thought to be. The operator buzzed into his ear as he took down the receiver; San Francisco was trying to get a message through. For Gloria Gaynor. Would he take the message? Then an operator in San Francisco, droning the words: "For Miss Gloria Gaynor. Your father is hurt in Coloma. Just sent me word. Says not dangerously, but I must go to him immediately. Meet me there. Mamma."

"Got it," said King, and San Francisco rang off. Thereafter he got his own message through; he wondered how Mrs. Gaynor would take the news of her new son-in-law. Ben would be glad; he was sure of Ben.

Gloria was still upstairs. King sat in front of the fire, staring into the flames, listening to the wind in the chimney, waiting for Gloria. When time passed and she did not come, he went softly upstairs and to her door. It was closed and he knocked lightly, then dropped his hand to the knob, awaiting her voice.

His knuckles had hardly brushed the door, this door which he approached in reverence; Gloria had not even heard him. He called softly, his voice little above a whisper:

"Gloria!" He heard her move; for a moment she did not answer. He could not know how she stood, scarcely breathing, her hands at her breast; nor how, now that the great step was taken, she was again half-frightened, half-regretful, altogether bewildered and uncertain. Of herself, of him, of everything—

"Is it you, Mark?"

"Yes. May I come in, Gloria?"

"Please, Mark. It's all so new, so strange ... I intended to come right back downstairs, but I'm so tired, Mark. And I want to be alone a little; to think. I haven't had time to think of anything! You don't mind, do you, Mark?"

He answered promptly and heartily, refusing to allow himself to harbour a shadow of disappointment.

"No. No, of course not. You will go right to bed? I know you must be half-dead for sleep."

"Yes." There was a note of eagerness in the voice coming to him from beyond the shut door.

"There was a message from your mother; she has gone to your father and wanted you to meet her there. But we will talk of that later."

"Yes.... Good-night, Mark."

"Aren't you going to kiss me good-night?" he asked, hesitating a little between the words. His new privilege, a lover's, a husband's, was not an hour old; he felt strangely shy as he spoke softly to her.

"Please, Mark! I am terribly tired out, and—and I'm afraid I've mislaid the key, and—"

That hurt him; his eyes darkened with the quick pain that

came to him from her words. He had hoped that Gloria had known him better than that.

"You need never lock your door against me, my dear," he told her gently. "I don't want you to be afraid of me. Why, God bless you, I wouldn't touch the hem of your dress if you didn't want me to."

"Yes," said Gloria. "I know. You are so good, Mark. But now—"

"I am going," he returned tenderly, "to sit by the fire and think. Just to soak myself in the realization," he added with a happy laugh, "that you are mine."

"Before you go in the morning you will come to my door?"

"If you want me to...."

"Of course, Mark."

"Then—good-night, dear."

"Good-night, Mark."

CHAPTER XVI

King was astir long before dawn. He got the fire going in the kitchen and started breakfast, seeking to be very silent and succeeding in making the usual clatter of a male among pots and pans. Whilst water heated and bacon sizzled, he rummaged through the store-room at the rear of the house, gathering what he meant to put into his pack for the four or five days' trip. As he returned from the last journey to the store-room, his arms full of camp accessories, including canvas and camp blankets, he confronted Gloria, fully dressed. He dropped his arm-load and filled his eyes with her. Any shadow left overnight in his heart was sent scurrying before his new joyousness. Gloria had come down to him while he deemed her fast asleep!

"Gloria!" he cried.

A more radiantly lovely Gloria he had never looked upon. She had slept and rested; she had bathed and groomed and set herself in order. She was dressed after a fashion to bewilder a mere man in the only utterly ravishing outing costume Mark King had ever seen. He felt insanely inclined to pick up her little boots, one after the other, and go down on his knees and kiss them; her hat was a flopsy turban, from under the brim of which the most adorable of golden-brown curls half escaped to throw kiss-shadows on her rosy cheeks. And Gloria's eyes!

This time there was no door between them, nor even the memory of a door. He gathered her up into his arms so that her boot-heels swung clear of the floor.

"Do you know ... do you guess ... have you the faintest suspicion how I love you?"

"The—the coffee!" gasped Gloria. "It's boiling over!"

He laughed joyously at that, and finally, when he had set her down, Gloria, bright and flushed, laughed too.

"Burning bacon last night, boiling coffee this morning!" he chuckled. And then, there in the kitchen, they sat down to breakfast. "It's sweet of you," he told her softly, "to get up and come down and see me off."

"Oh," said Gloria, "I am going with you."

Not once had King dared think of a thing like that. He had thought that at best he would be with her again in four or five days. But that she should go with him into the mountains on this quest of his? He sat and pondered and stared at her.

"Don't you want me?" asked Gloria. "Aren't you glad, Mark?"

She was serenely prepared for objections, should they be forthcoming. For it was not on any spur of the moment, but after long deliberation, that she had decided that she would go with him. She wanted no scandal in the papers; she meant that there should be none. If it were rumoured that she had gone out of town with Gratton; if Gratton wanted to be ugly and feed rumour; then on top of that if she appeared within reach of a reporter without a husband, there would be talk. If it were answered that she was married to Mark King, there would be the question: "And where, my dear, is this Mark King?" Those girl friends in San Francisco who had met him at her birthday-party would be fairly squirming with excited curiosity to know *everything*. Among themselves they would make insinuations about the Bear Tamer or the Animal Trainer, as Gloria knew that they would variously and mirthfully designate him. They would find it unusual that King had married her one day and had gone off the next without her. They would hazard endless unpleasant explanations; they would get their heads together; they would make an astonishing patchwork of scraps of distorted rumour and bits of wild speculation.... From upstairs last night she had heard fragmentary outbursts from the "judge." "Irregular; no licence." Now Gloria meant to kill the snake outright, not to allow the scotched reptile to writhe free. She was married; she was going with her husband into the wilderness on the most romantic of all honeymoons. The papers were free to make much of that.

"Of course I want you," said King slowly. "Glad? Glad that you want to come with me? Can't you see that I am the gladdest man on earth? But—"

"I have already written a message I wanted to send to a girl friend in San Francisco...." It was to Miss Mildred Carter, who was engaged to be married to Bob Dwight of the *Chronicle*.... "I was going to have it phoned in to her. It tells her I'm— married. To you, Mark. And that we're off on the most wonderful trip together into the heart of the wild country."

"God bless you," he said heartily. But Gloria, glancing at him swiftly, saw that his eyes were clouded with perplexity.

"Of course," she said, "if you don't want a girl along—"

"Gloria!"

"Well, then? It's settled? I'm to go?"

"Only I'm afraid it isn't the sort of a trip for a girl. It's hard going, and—Oh, it's a cursed shame I can't put it off."

"You said last night that you weren't afraid of anything Brodie and his men could do? That they didn't even know where to go? That they'd never know where to find you?"

"Yes. And I meant it. But—"

He wanted her with him; she wanted to come. Further, it pained him to think that those first glorious days should be spent with the mountains between them. He was tempted, sorely tempted. Gloria knew; she smiled at him across the table; she tempted him further. ...Was there really any danger, would there be danger to her? If he thought so, that there was the faintest likelihood of harm to her, he would say no, no matter what the yearning in his heart. But if they made a quick dash in and out; two days each way, not over one day at Gus Ingle's caves? If they went on horseback nearly all the way, and travelled light? He carried a rifle nowadays, and he rather believed he might carry it ten years without ever firing a shot at any man of their hulking crowd. They could go in one way, come out another. They had at least a full day's head start of any possible followers. No, in his heart he did not believe that there would be any danger to Gloria. Further, the thought struck him that she would not be altogether safe here; there was venom in Gratton, God only knew how virulent. And there was sinister significance in the fact that Gratton was hand in glove now with Swen Brodie. Then, too, Gratton knew from Gloria's own lips that she had brought the message from her father in Coloma; hence Gratton might suspect, and Brodie after him, that Gloria was in possession of old Loony Honeycutt's secret. Instead of seeming hazardous to take Gloria with him, it began to appear that his new responsibility of guarding her from all harm had begun already, and that he could best protect her from any possible evil by having her always with him. He could not allow her to go to her parents in Coloma; he thought of that, but that was Brodie's hangout, and Ben was in no condition to send for her. Nor was it advisable for her to go alone to San Francisco; her mother was not there, and Gratton might be looked on to follow her....So with himself communed Mark King, never a man overly given to caution, but seeking now to measure chances, to set them in the scales over against the desire of his heart. A fanciful thought insisted on being heard: had Gus Ingle's treasure hidden itself all these years, awaiting the time when he and

The Everlasting Whisper   175

Gloria together came to it? Their wedding gift! How much more precious then than mere gold!

"We'd travel light," he said thoughtfully, and Gloria knew that she had won. "We'd go in quick, out quick. It's getting late in the year," he added with a smile, "and we'd have to hurry, Brodie or no Brodie. I've no notion for a prolonged honeymoon snow-bound in those mountains."

Her eyes danced.

"Wouldn't that be fun!"

His smile quickened. Her childish ignorance of what such an adventure would mean was in keeping with her vast inexperience with matters of the outdoors; she had merely begun, in his company, to glimpse the true meanings of the solitudes. She would learn further—with him. And a warm glow of pleasure came with the thought that Gloria wanted to go.

* * * * *

The pearl-grey dawn was flowering into a still pink morning when they locked the door behind them and stepped out into the crisp, sweet freshness of the autumn air. He had made two small packs, provisions rolled into the bedding and the whole wrapped in pieces of canvas; he estimated they would be gone five days, and then, making due allowance for any reasonable delay, provisioned for ten. When he saw that Gloria had noted how for the first time on a woodland jaunt with her he carried a very businesslike-looking rifle, he explained laughingly that if they developed abnormal appetites there were both deer and bear to be had. She was much interested in everything, and looked out to the mountains eagerly when King had swung her up to her saddle on Blackie, the tall, sober-faced horse, where she sat with a roll of blankets at her back and with the horn before her decorated with a miscellany of camp equipment—a frying-pan, a short-handled axe in its sheath, an overcoat done into a compact bundle. Here was another moment when thoughts were too slow processes to emphasize themselves; she was swayed by emotions provoked by the moment. Where were the trunks and suitcases and hat-boxes to accompany the young bride? In their stead, a coat tied into a tight bundle and a frying-pan before her. King looked at her and marvelled; her cheeks were roses, her eyes were Gloria's own, wonderful and big and deep beyond fathoming. From his own saddle on the buckskin he nodded his approval of her.

"You are not afraid that I can't take care of you, are you, Gloria?" he asked.

And Gloria laughed gaily, answering:

"My dear Mr. Man, I am not the least little bit afraid of anything in all the world this morning!"

So with the glorious day brightening all about them they turned away from the log house and into the trail which straightway King dubbed "Adventure Trail." And as they went he sang out joyously:

"The Lord knows what we'll find, dear heart, and the deuce knows what we'll do. But we're back once more on the old trail, our own trail, the out trail, And Life runs large on the Long Trail—the trail that is always new."

CHAPTER XVII

The magnificent wilderness into which rode Mark and Gloria
King seemed to prostrate its august self to do them honour
upon this their wedding morning. Succeeding the paler tints of
the earlier hour came the rare blue day. Last night's clouds had
vanished; the air was clear and crisp, with still a hint of frost.
On all hands had October in passing splashed the world with
colour. Along the creek the aspens danced and played and
shivered in bright golden raiment; through the bushes there
was a glimpse of vivid scarlet where the leaves of a dwarf maple
were as bright as snow-plants. A little grove of gracefully
slender poplars trembled in yellow against the azure above.
The clear, thin sunlight pricked out colours until it made the
woods a riot of them, greens dark and light, the grey of sage,
the white of a granite seam, the black of a lava rock, and in the
creek spray a brilliant vari-coloured rainbow sheen. They two,
riding side by side, while the broad trail permitted, passed over
the ridge and out of sight of the house. Immediately the
solitudes shut down about them with titanic walls. They rode
down into a long, shadowy hollow, out through a tiny verdant
meadow fringed with the rusty brown of sunflower leaves, and
on up to the crest of the second ridge. Already they were alone
in the world, a man and his mate, with only infinity and its
concrete symbols embracing them, ancient and ageless trees,
limitless sky, mile after mile of ridge and precipice and barren
peak. And upon them and about them and within them the
utter serene hush of the Sierra.

With every swinging step of the horses taking them on, a new gladness blossomed in King's heart. For they were pushing ever further into the portion of the world which he knew best, loved best. The present left him nothing to wish for; he had Gloria, and Gloria had elected to come with him. Until high noon they would wind along, for the most part climbing pretty steadily with the old trail—Indian trail, miners' trail, trail which even to-day seems to lead from the first generation of the twentieth century straight back into the heart of 1850 and beyond. Here men did not penetrate save at long intervals; here was true solitude. And soon, when they should leave this trail to travel as straight a line as the broken country would allow toward Gus Ingle's caves, they would enter a region given over entirely to the wild's own bright-eyed, shy inhabitants.

There were red spots in Gloria's cheeks when they started. King sought to guess at what might be the emotions of a young girl going on with Gloria's present emotional adventure—vain task of a mere man seeking to fathom those troubled feminine depths!—marking that she was a little nervous and distrait.

"I know the place Gus Ingle tried to describe," he said, "as well as I know my old hat. Or at least I'd have said so until he mentioned the third cave. I've been there dozens of times, too, but I've got to see more than two caves there yet."

Together they had read the crabbed lines in the Bible; they had been silent thereafter as to each came imagined pictures like ghosts from the past; ghosts of greed and envy and despair. Now Gloria mused aloud:

"I wonder—do you suppose we'll find it as he says?"

"At least we'll see about it. And whether there be heaps and piles of red, red gold, as the tale telleth, be sure our trip is going to be worth the two days' ride. I'll show you such chasms and gorges and crags as you've never turned those two lovely eyes of yours upon, Mrs. Gloria King." (He couldn't abstain absolutely from all love-making.) "And a little grove of sequoias which belongs to me. Or, at least, I believe I am the only man who knows where they are. Friends of mine, those big fellows are, five old noble-souled monarchs."

She looked interested and treated him to a fleeting smile, but asked curiously:

"How can a man speak of a tree that way? As though it were alive—" She broke off, laughing, and amended: "But they *are* alive, aren't they? I mean—human."

"Why, you poor little city-bred angel," he cried heartily. "You will answer your own question inside of two days. No doubt I'm going to grow jealous of old Vulcan and Thor and Majesty. Sure, I've named them," he chuckled. "And you'll come with me into their dim cathedral to-morrow at dusk and listen with me to their old sermon. A man ought to go to church to them at least once a year, to keep his soul cleaned out and growing properly."

Gloria appeared thoughtful; that she was interested just now less in that of which he spoke than in the man himself he did not suspect. She was noting how he spoke of trees as friends; how he was different from other men whom she knew in that he stood so much closer to the ancient mother, the wilderness now embracing them. Instinctively she knew that it behoved her to penetrate as deeply as she might into the inner nature of this man who, hardly more than a pleasant, attractive stranger yesterday, was to-day her husband.

"What is the oldest thing in the world?" he asked her abruptly.

She wrinkled her brows prettily at him.

"Church to-morrow evening and school now?" she countered lightly.

"Answer," insisted King. "Just at a rough guess what would

you say was the oldest thing in the world?"

Gloria cudgelled her brains. Finally, since he seemed quite serious, and she knew that wisdom lay in pleasing the male of the species in small and unimportant matters, she sought to reply.

"The Sphinx or the Pyramids, I'd guess," she offered.

"Naturally," he returned. "And what will you say when I introduce you to the Pharaoh who was a big, husky giant before Thebes was thought of?"

Again she looked to see a twinkle of jest in his eyes.

"Pharaoh?" she said. "Just a tree? Over two or three thousand years old!"

"By at least another thousand," he rejoined triumphantly. "And as staunch an old gentleman as you'll find."

Even Gloria, a poor little city-bred angel, must muse upon the statement. Having caught her interest he told her picturesquely of his old friends; how they had dwelt on serenely while peoples were born and empires rose and fell; while Rome smote Greece and both went down in the dust; while Columbus pushed his three boats across the seas; while the world itself passed from one phase to another; how they were all but co-eternal with eternity.

"When you think how these old fellows were a thousand years old when the Christ was a little boy," he ended simply, "you will begin to realize the sort of things they have a way of saying to you while you lie still and look up and up, and still up among their branches that seem at night to brush against the stars."

She let her fancies drift in the leash of his. But again they left the picturesque ancient trees and returned to him. A little smile touched her lips and was gone before he was sure of it; she was thinking that a man like King kept always in his heart something of the simplicity of a little child; she wondered if she herself, though so much younger in actual years, were not worlds more sophisticated. For his part King noted that she displayed to-day none of that chattering, singing gaiety of their former rides together; he remembered, sympathetically, that she had had very little sleep last night, and that she had endured a wearisome twenty-four hours before, and that the long, nervous strain under which she had struggled must certainly have told upon her, both physically and mentally. So, believing that she would be grateful for silence, he grew silent with her.

Further and ever further into the heart of the solitudes they rode through the quiet hours of the forenoon, with Gloria ever more abstracted and Mark King holding apart from her, doing her reverence, drinking always deep of that soft, sweet beauty which was hers. They forsook the creeks where the yellow-leaved aspens fluttered their myriad little gleaming banners; they made slow, zigzag work of climbing a flinty-sided mountain; they looked back upon green meadow and gay poplar grove far below; they galloped their horses across a wide table-land over which shrilled the wind, already sharpened by the season for the work it had to do before many weeks passed. Though there were some few level spaces, though now and then as King sought for her the easier way they rode down short slopes, with every mile put behind them they had climbed perceptibly. Already Gloria had the sensation of being by the world forgotten—though for her the world could not be forgot. A ridge from which they looked out across the peaks and valleys seemed to her like an island, lost, remote, eternally set apart from other people whom she knew, from all her life as she had lived it. She went on and on and felt like one in a dream, journeying into a fierce, rugged land over which lay a spell of enchantment, a spell that had been cast over it before King's all but immortal trees had burst from the seeds, so that now, while the outside world pulsed and beat with life, and swung back and forth with its pendulous progress, here all was unchanged, changeless.

King led her, well before midday, to the spot in which from the first he had planned that they would noon. A forest pool ringed with boulders, which were green with moss under the splashing of the water from above, where the swaying pines mirrored themselves and shivered in the little breeze which ruffled the clear, cold water. Here was a tiny upland meadow and much rich grass; here a sheltered spot where Gloria might sit in the sun and be protected from the colder air.

He was quick to help her to dismount and noted that she came down stiffly; the eyes which she turned to him were heavy with fatigue; some of the rose flush had faded from her cheeks.

"Maybe I shouldn't have let you come after all, dear," he said contritely. "These are harder trails than we've ridden before, and we've had to keep at it steadier."

There was an effort in her smile answering him.

"The last two days *have* been hard to get through with," she said as she yielded to his insistence and sat down on the sun-warmed pine-needles. "I am sorry I am so—so—"

He did not allow her to run down the elusive word.

"Nonsense," he told her heartily. "You've got a right to be tired. But when you've had some hot lunch and a cup of hot coffee you'll be tip-top again. You'll see."

King unsaddled and tethered the horses where they could browse and rest and roll; built his little fire and went about lunch-getting with a joy he had never known in the old accustomed routine before. Now and then he glanced toward Gloria; he could not help that. But he saw that she was lying back, her eyes closed, and while his heart went out to her he did not force his sympathy on her. She was tired and, what was more, she had every right and reason to be tired. He hoped that she might get three winks of sleep. When he came near her for the coffee-pot he tiptoed. She seemed to be asleep.

But Gloria was not asleep. Never had her mind raced so. It was done and she was Mark King's wife! Higher and higher loomed that fact above all other considerations. But there were other considerations; her father hurt, she did not know how badly; her mother mystified, by now perhaps informed of Gloria's marriage; Gratton with the poison extracted from his fangs had the fangs still; gold ahead somewhere, in caves where men long ago had laboured and fought and snarled at one another like starving wolves and died; Brodie somewhere, Brodie with the horrible face. She shivered and stirred restlessly, and King, who saw everything, thought that she had dreamed a bad dream. But lunch was ready; he came to her with plate and cup. And again Gloria did her best to smile gratefully.

"You are so good to me, Mark," she said. Her eyes were thoughtful; would he always be good to her? Even when—but she was too weary to think. It seemed to her that only now was she beginning to feel the effects of all she had been through.

"I want to learn how to be good to you, wife of mine," he said very gently. "That is all on earth I ask. Just to make you happy."

"You love me so much, Mark?" she asked, as one who wondered at what she had read in his low voice and glimpsed in his eyes.

"Gloria," he told her gently, "I don't understand this thing they call love yet; it is too new, too wonderful. But I do know that in all the world there is nothing else that matters."

"Not even Gus Ingle's red, red gold?" she said rather more lightly than she had spoken.

"Not even Gus Ingle's red, red gold."

She looked at him long and curiously.

"You would do anything you could to make me happy? Anything, Mark?"

"I pray with all my heart and soul that I always may!"

Gloria seemed to rest through the noon hour and to brighten. When she saw him the second time look at the sun she got up from the ground and said:

"Time to go on? I'm ready. And after that banquet I feel all *me* again!"

He laughed and went off after the horses, singing at the top of his voice. She stood very still, looking off after him, her brows puckering into a shadowy frown. Oh, if she could only read herself as he allowed her to read him; if she could only be as sure of Gloria as she was of Mark; if she could only look deep into her heart as she looked into his. But she could not! His heart was like the clear pool just yonder across which the sunshine lay and far down in which she could see the stones and pebbles as through so much clear glass; hers was like the rushing stream above, eddying and swirling and hiding itself under its own light spray. All day long she had tried to see what lay under the surface. *Did she love Mark King?* She had thrilled to him as she had thrilled to no other man; but that had been in the springtime. Twice then she had been sure that she loved him. But that was so long ago. And now that she had allowed him to carry her out of the quicksands? What now? She was so borne down by all that she had lived through; he was so much a part of the mountainous solitudes towering about them. And was she one to love the wilderness—for long? Or did it not begin to bear down upon her uncertain spirit? Did it not menace and frighten and, in the end, would it not repel? Oh, if she had only let him go on alone this morning; if she had remained where she could rest and think and thus come to see clearly, even into her own troubled heart!

Their first hour after lunch led them through a region which, given over to silence itself, denied them any considerable opportunity for conversation. King rode ahead, turning off to the left from their resting-place by the pool, and riding through a sea of grey brush, following a narrow trail made by deer. Then the mountain-side reared its barrier and made all forward and upward progress slow and toilsome. Three times they dismounted and King led the horses; here Gloria clung to the steep mountain-side, looking fearfully down into the monster gorge carved at its base, dwelling with fascinated fancies on the thought of slipping, losing handhold and foot-hold and plunging down among the jagged boulders strewing the lower levels. There was really no great danger, she told herself over and over; King's cheery calls reassured her; no danger so long as they went forward on foot. But now and then when a horse's foot slipped and a wild cascade of loose soil and rocks went hurtling downward, she grew rigid with apprehension.

But there was only an hour of this. Thereafter they rode down a long slope and into a long, narrow, twisting ravine, rocky cliffs on one hand and a noisy stream on the other, a fair trail underfoot. Nearly always now King rode ahead, finding the way for her; and Gloria, her spirits drooping again with the advancing afternoon, vaguely oppressed by the solemn stillness about her, was glad that she too could be silent. When he did call to her she needed only nod or smile; he turned to point out some rare view that appealed to him, a vista worth her seeing, a cascade or a fall of cliff, or a ferny nook, or perhaps a late ceanothus-blossom. He pointed out a scampering Douglas squirrel and had her hearken to a quail.

"We're already in the finest timber belt in the world," he told her, full of enthusiastic loyalty to his beloved mountains.

Thus, he leading the way, she following with head down and shoulders drooping, they came about four o'clock to a small meadow, cliff-ringed, studded with big yellow pines and here and there graced with an incense cedar. Stopping in the open, sitting sideways in the saddle, he waited for her.

"And what do you think of this, Miss Gloria?" he called gaily as her horse thrust his black nose through the alders down by the creek.

Gloria drew rein and looked at him with large eyes across the twenty paces separating them.

"I can't go any further," she said bleakly. "I'm tired out!"

He was quick to see a gathering of tears, and swung down from his horse and went to her with long strides, his own eyes filled with concern.

"Poor little kidlet," he said humbly. "I've let you do yourself up...."

And it was his duty, his privilege, and no one's else in the world, to shelter her, to stand between her and all hardship. He put out his arms to take her into them quite as he could have picked up a little maid of six, something stirring in the depths of him which in man is twin to the maternal instinct in woman. But Gloria said hurriedly: "Please, Mark, I am so tired ..." and drew back, and he let his hands fall to his side. For a second time her act hurt him; her gesture was akin to locking a door last night. But in a moment, his pity and loyalty and staunch faith in her crowding the small ache out of his heart, he was unrolling a pack, making a temporary couch for her and commanding her lovingly just to lie down and look up at the tree-tops above her, and rest while he staked out the horses. Sensing that perhaps the very bigness and majestic silence of these uplands might rest heavy upon her spirit and perhaps depress if not actually awake in her an emotion akin to fear, he strove to cheer her by his own blithe acceptance of the fortune of the hour. He told her heartily that she had earned a rest if any one ever had; that it was well, after all, to get an early start at pitching camp; that he was going to make his lady-love as cosy here in his big outdoor home as was ever princess in castle walls. Gloria shivered and threw herself face down on the blankets. Gloria did not know what possessed her; she fought for repression, hiding her face from him. Out of a hideously stern world a black spirit had leaped upon her; it clutched at her throat, it dragged at her heart. When King called a cheery word from beyond the thicket where he had gone with the horses, she could have screamed. She was so nervous that now and again a fierce tremor shook her from head to foot.

*   *   *   *   *

King was counting it fortunate that they were granted so likely a camp site for the night. He looked up at the tall black cliffs shutting in the little meadow; they would hold back the night winds from Gloria. He chose the spot, well back from the creek, where she would sleep. High overhead, like brooding giants, stood the upright pines. Where a little clump of mere youngsters, lusty fellows not a score of years old, had the air of pressing close together as though thus with their combined strength they sought to match the strength of their aloof parents, a compact grove to make a further shelter against the mountain air, Gloria would sleep. He stretched a strip of canvas from tree to tree, making a five-foot wall of it. Close by he started his fire, knowing from experience oft repeated how a cheery blaze in the forest may dispel shadows within even as it makes the sombrest of shadows dance gaily under the trees; to one side he laid many resinous faggots, planning on their crackling light later on when the dark came. He ringed his fire with rocks, lugging them as heavy as he could carry up from the creek side, making the rudest of fireplaces. But it had the merit that it threw the heat back toward his extended canvas, and there between it would be snug and warm. All about him, as he laboured, was the singing of water and, high in air, the singing of pine tops. They made merry music and King, gone down to the stream to fill his coffee-pot, sang with it from a full, brimming heart. Gloria was tired, but she was resting now. And in a little while, when dark came, he and she would sit by his fire and look into it and talk in hushed voices, hand locked in hand; they would watch for the first of the big blazing stars to come out—he and Gloria, alone in the wilderness.

He saw a trout swinging lazily in a quiet pool. Trout for Gloria! He glanced toward where she lay; he was glad that she was not looking. It would be a surprise for her. He hurried to his kit in his pack, got out hook and line, baited with a tiny bit of red flannel, and went back to the creek. For he knew that it was not likely that the trout here could have had any remembered encounters with man; they were plentiful and might, like many other sorts of beings, be lured to their undoing by curiosity and greed. He cut a willow pole, stood back and cast out his gay bit of bait, letting it drift with the riffles. There came a quick tug, another, sharp and vigorous, and he swung his prize out of the water, breaking the surface into scattering jewels, flashing in the sunlight as it struck against the grass along the creek's edge.

Dusk gathered while he worked over his fire. The aroma of boiling coffee rose, crept through the air, blended with the aromas of the woods. He had made toast, holding the bread to the coals upon a sharpened stick. There were strips of crisp bacon garnishing a trout browned to the last painstaking turn. There were fried potatoes, cut by King's pocket-knife into thin strips and turned into gold by the alchemy of cooking. He set out his dishes upon a flat-topped rock, replenished his fire, threw on some fresh-cut green cedar boughs for their delightful fragrance, and went to call Gloria.

* * * * *

Gloria, too tired bodily and mentally to wage a winning battle against those black vapours which flock so frequently about luckless youth, had suffered and yielded and gone down in misery. She had been crying, just why she knew not; crying because she could not help it. Hers was a state of overwrought nerves which forbade clear thinking, which distorted and warped and magnified. The babble of the water which had been music to King was to her a chorus of jeering voices; the wind in the pines an eerie moaning as of lost spirits wailing; the trees themselves, merging with the dusk, were brooding, shadowy giant things which she suddenly both feared and hated; the cliffs rising against the sky loomed so near and so gigantically tall that she felt as though they were pressing in upon her to suffocate her, to crush her, to annihilate her. The world was turning black with the night; the night rushed, treading out the last gleam of sunlight; even the one star which she had glimpsed through her tears impressed her only with its remoteness. She was frightened; not because of any physical violence, for Mark King stood between her and that. But of vague horrors. She thought of San Francisco; of her own bright room there; of the lights in the streets, of pedestrians and motors and street-cars filling that other steel-canoned wilderness with familiar noises. And somehow, San Francisco seemed further away, immeasurably further away, than that one remote star blazing through the vastness of space.

"A cup of coffee and a bit of supper," King said gently. "You'll feel a lot better."

She rose wearily and followed him. Without a word she dropped down beside his banquet, putting out a listless hand to her tin cup. The firelight upon her face showed him her thoughtful eyes; but they were turned not toward him but toward the bed of coals. He had anticipated her lively surprise at the trout; she pushed the brown morsel aside, saying absently:

"I am not hungry. It was good of you to go to all of this trouble. I am afraid I am not much of a camper." She forced the shadow of a smile with the admission.

"Tuckered out," he thought as he looked into her face across which light and shadow flickered as flame and smoke in the camp-fire came and went fitfully, twisted by the evening breeze. "Clean tuckered out."

Gloria, feeling his gaze so steady upon her, turned her eyes toward his, eyes heavy and sober with her drooping spirit. As the flames frolicked about the pitch-pine he had tossed to the coals, he saw the traces of tears. He said nothing, supposing that he understood; he but strove the harder to be good to her, to share with her some of that rare joy filling his own heart. He sought with unobtrusive tenderness to anticipate her slightest want; he jumped to his feet and brought her a cup of water; he shoved aside a burning branch which rolled impudently too near the divine foot; he removed the offending fish from under her nostrils hastily and half apologetically; he piled the fire high when he saw her shiver. And finally when she pushed her cup away and let her two hands drop into her lap he gathered the dishes and carried them away to the nearest pool to wash them, leaving Gloria silent and thoughtful, brooding over his fire.

When he came back to her in the hush of the first hour of night, he thought that he understood her need for silence, and spoke only infrequently and briefly, and very, very softly, calling her attention now to the last lingering light upon the piney ridge behind them or to the liquid music of the creek, which, with the coming of night, seemed to grow clearer and finer and sweeter, or finally to the big star burning gloriously in the perfect deep-blue sky.

"And now," he said, taking up his short-handled axe, "I am going to make for my lady-love the finest couch for tranquil, restful sleep that mortal ever had."

As he strode away toward a grove of firs he was lost to her eyes before he had gone a hundred paces. The night came so swiftly it seemed to her feverish fancies that in the dark the big tree trunks were huddling closer together. In a moment she heard the sound of his axe, striking softly through green juicy branches. He worked swiftly, grudging every minute away from her. And then, with his arms full of the fragrant, balsamy boughs, he stopped and let them slip down to the ground and himself sat down upon a log and filled his pipe with slow fingers. He'd force himself to smoke one pipe before he went back to her, thinking that she would be grateful for a few moments alone.

Almost with the first puff of smoke there came to him Gloria's piercing scream. His heart stopping, he jumped up and ran through the trees to her, shouting: "Gloria I Gloria! I'm coming. What is it?"

Gloria was cowering against the nearest tree, her face showing frightened in the firelight, her eyes wide with nervous horror.

"There is something there ... in the bushes!" she cried excitedly. "I heard it moving...."

He looked where she pointed. Down by the creek, just waddling back into the alders, was a fat old porcupine, dimly seen in the fringe of the camp-fire. But King did not laugh. His first impulse upon him, strengthened by Gloria's helplessness, he took her into his arms, holding her close to him.

"Why did you leave me?" asked Gloria petulantly. "So long."

He had been away from her fifteen minutes while he cut an armful of fir-boughs, and thereafter filled and lighted his pipe—and to Gloria the time had seemed long! Little enough of love's confession, surely, but a golden crumb to a man's starving love. He drew her closer; their faces, ruddy with fire-glow, each tense with its own emotion, were close together.

"Oh!" cried Gloria. She wrenched away from him violently. "You—you hurt me. Let me go!" She buried her face in her hands; he saw her shoulders lift and droop; he heard her sob: "Oh, I was a fool—"

His arms had dropped to his sides and he stood for a moment speechless, staring at her as across a chasm shadow-filled.

"Gloria," he said, bewildered.

But now her hands, too, were at her sides, clenched and nervous; her white face was lifted and she broke out passionately into hot words; he saw her breast heaving and sensed that she was stirred to depths never until now plumbed. What he could not glimpse were the vague, unreasonable reasons, the distorted horrors grinning at her among the spaces of black gloom into which her spirit had sunk; had he been a fancy-sick poet, a pale-blooded creature given to blue devils and nightmare conjecture, he might have come somewhere near an understanding. But being plain Mark King, a straightforward, healthy, and unjaundiced man, his comprehension found never a clue to a condition which in Gloria was hardly other than an inevitable result of all that had gone before.

"I was half-mad last night," she panted. "There was no way to turn. That beast of a man drove me to desperation. Then you came, and—and—Oh, I wish that I were dead!"

Incredulous, amazed, near stupefied, he stood rooted to the ground.

"I don't understand," he said dully after a long silence broken only by a tumble and frolic of the water and Gloria's quick, hard breathing. He strove to be very gentle with her. "Just what is it? Can you tell me, dear?"

"Don't call me dear ... like that," she cried sharply. "Just as though I were your ... *property*." He saw the roundness of her eyes. She shuddered. "You knew that I was driven to it, to save my name, to stop hideous gossip...."

In her disordered mind she had been flung, as upon shoals, to many bleak points of view; she had blamed fate for her undoing, she had blamed Gratton, she had laid the responsibility upon her mother for having allowed her to drift; but always she had looked upon herself as the victim. Now, in her agitation, which had risen close to hysteria, it was suddenly

Mark King whom she blamed for everything; he, in the guise of fate, had betrayed her!

"You saw that I was half dead with terror; that I hardly knew what I was doing; that all I could think of was escape from the horrible trap that had been set for me; you—"

"So that was it?" But still his tone was utterly devoid of any emotion save that of incredulity. "You mean you didn't love me, Gloria?"

"When did you ever ask me if I loved you?"

"But you ... you married me.... Great God!" He ran his hand across his brow as though to brush away an obsession. "Not loving me, you married me just to save yourself from possible scandal?"

"What girl wouldn't?" she cried wildly. "Driven as I was?"

He tried to think with all of that calm deliberation which this moment so plainly required. In mind he went back stage by stage through all of last night's events. And so he came in retrospect in due time to the moment when he had come to the porch and had looked in through the window to take his last farewell of her; when he had seen her standing at Gratton's side. She had drooped so like a figure of despondency; she had lifted her head slowly at the "judge's" question. And then there had occurred that sudden change in her bearing and in her voice alike, when abruptly she had cried out: "No. No and no and no!"

"Tell me," said King heavily, "when you refused to marry Gratton last night—did you know that I was outside?"

"Yes," she answered. She wondered why he asked. "There was a mirror; I saw your reflection in it."

"If I had not come—would you have gone on with the thing?"

He hesitated, then said harshly: "Would you have married him?"

"I don't know. Oh," she exclaimed, twisting at her hands, "how can I tell what I would have done? driven one way, torn another—"

"You might have married him? You but chose me as the lesser of two evils? Was that it?"

"I tell you I don't know! I only know that I was hideously compromised; I would never have dared show my face again in San Francisco—anywhere—it would have killed me—"

And even yet there was in King's face only a queer tortured incredulity. For a long time neither moved nor spoke. His eyes were on her, hers intently on him. When he answered it was in a voice from which all of to-day's joyousness had fled.

"I'm going to make your bed, Gloria," he said evenly. "Near the fire, which I'll keep going. I'll make mine on the outside, so you need not be afraid of any prowling animal. Then in the morning we will talk."

She watched him go back for his scattered fir-boughs. And even Gloria noted how heavy was his walk. But she could not guess how when he was alone with his trees, and the darkness dropped curtainwise between him and her he went down on both knees and buried his face in one of those same fallen sprays from the fir.

CHAPTER XVIII

Flat on his back lay Mark King, his hands under his head, his eyes upon the slow procession of the stars. Just so had he lain many a night in the forest-land—but life then and now were as two distinct existences which had nothing in common, but were set apart in two separate worlds, remote one from the other. Now he saw the stars, as it were, with the physical eye alone, merely because they blazed so bright against the darkness above him; he was scarcely conscious of their gleam and sparkle. Of old he had been wont to commune with them; through the long years they had woven themselves into his rough-and-ready religion. Countless times had he watched them and mused and hearkened to the message which, as with a still voice, infinitely calming, travelled to him across the limitless vastitude of the universe. Countless times that voice had called him away from the toils and victories and defeats of the day, up into a place of quiet from which a man might look about him with a somewhat truer perspective; he glimpsed futility in much of human strife and striving; he saw nobility enshrined in a "small" act; he marked how, set in the scales of the eternal balances of scope and eternity, a copper penny set against a million dollars were as two feathers; they rode light, and there was little choice between them. He had known that firefly cluster of lights above to be the majestic processional of worlds. He saw himself as small; the universe as big. And the knowledge did not crush; it elevated. Throughout the whole of creation ran the fine chain of divine ordinance, of a law that flowered in beauty. There was God's work above him, about him, within him. And God stood back of it all, vouching for it, making it good. The spinning of worlds, the pulses of tides, the course of the blood in his veins—these were kindred phenomena; the law of God bound about with its fine chain of divine will and love the greater and the lesser bodies moving through the universe. Upon such a comprehension, brotherhood of man and tree and sun and flower, had been raised Mark King's haphazard edifice of a theory of life. The stars reminded him that through the eons all had been right with the world of worlds; they sang of hope and happiness and beauty. They showed a man the way to rich, full contentment. They lighted the path to generous dealings with other men. They threw their searchlight upon the day a man had just done with and set him thinking; they led his thoughts ahead to the day soon to dawn, making him wish to make a better job of things.

But to-night between him and his beloved stars stretched a region of shadows through which the eyes of his soul did not look. Something within him had been stricken; sorely wounded; beaten to its knees; chilled with death. He sought to think quite calmly, and for a long time clear consecutive thought was beyond his reach. A moment had come when he could only *feel*. He was swept this way and that. He had given to Gloria his love without stint, without reservation, without limit. The love which no other woman had ever awakened had poured itself out before Gloria like a flood of clear swift water breaking free. He loved after the only fashion possible to him, with his whole heart and soul, with his whole being. He adored. He made of his beloved a princess, a goddess. He saw her upon a plane where no woman ever lived, in an atmosphere too rare for flesh-and-blood humanity. A man does not love through human reason; rather through a reason, hidden even to him, deeper than humanity. Then Gloria had put her hand into his; Gloria had married him; Gloria had elected to come with him. After that he had seen nothing in its true light; Gloria had remade the world into paradise ineffable.

He had been on the heights, lifted among the stars. And without warning, without mercy, the world had crashed about him. From the zenith to the nadir. Small wonder that thoughts did not come logically! He floundered, lost, crushed, bewildered.

Just yonder, on the bed of fir-boughs he had made for her, lay Gloria. He did not look that way. The wind was rising; he heard it go rushing through the tree-tops; it struck with sudden, relentless impact; it set the shivering needles to shrill whistling; it made the staunch old trunks shudder. He heard the canvas flap-flapping by Gloria's bed; above him tossing boughs scraped and creaked.

One thing only seemed clear to him: the time had come when a man must seek to hold himself in check, when he must not leap, when he must strive with all the stubborn will in him to reserve judgment. His own life's crisis had come to him, revealing itself with the blinding swiftness of a flash of lightning. A step forward or back now would be one step toward which his entire destiny, from the hour of birth until now, had led him; there would be no retracing it; it would be final; and everything—everything—was at stake. He must think; he must try to understand all that Gloria had experienced; to see what impulses had moved her; to make allowances for her; to come to read aright what lay in her heart. He must see clearly into two human hearts! Task for the gods! As though the wilderness about him were a colossal malevolent entity endowed with the power to look into human breasts, it jeered at him with its voice of the wind.

He had but half a mind to give to physical senses. Though the wind howled all night long, he scarce was conscious of it; though the cold increased, he did not know that he was cold before he had grown numb. He had given to Gloria all of their bedding, save alone the one blanket he had wrapped about him; he had kept on all his clothing, buttoned up his coat, and forgotten that he was not warmly covered. Now he got up and walked up and down; he made the fire blaze up; he sat huddled over it until it burned down to a bed of glowing red coals.

Once or twice he heard Gloria stir restlessly upon her fir-bough bed. But he did not speak. There was nothing to be said between them now; they would wait until she had rested, until morning. Then there would be no more delay. They would understand each other then as few men and women had understood; there would be plain words and but few of them. He grew impatient for morning and sat looking forward to its coming with a face set and hard, growing as stern as death.

Gloria, exhausted, had gone to sleep, snuggled warmly into her blankets. It was the wind that awoke her; she started wide awake, her heart in her throat, startled by the flapping of the canvas at her head. She lay still and looked up; the pines were black and swayed dismally; the wind among them made shuddersome music; the cold began to drive through her blankets, through her clothing. Her body was stiff and sore; the branches of fir under her hurt her through the canvas and one blanket which covered them. She turned, twisting into a position of less discomfort. The creek babbled and splashed; its voice merged with the wilds into a bleak, cheerless duet.

She lifted her head a little; the fire was dying out and King had gone! The darkness bore down upon her; she heard everywhere vague sounds, noises as of stealthy feet. She knew a moment of blind terror; she tried to cry out but only a little choking gasp resulted. She saw something moving, a vague, formless, dreadful something, and lay back, chilled with fright. It was King; he was bringing fresh fuel. She sank back and again looked up at the pines swaying against the field of stars. She began to shiver; a nervous chill. She felt the slow tears form and spill over and trickle down her cheeks. She gathered her nether lip between her teeth and lay very still, shaken now and then by a noiseless sob.

She existed through a period of suppressed excitement. If King found cool logic eluding him, Gloria's mind was an orgy of nervous imaginings. She was back with her mother, weeping, sobbing out upon a comforting breast all of her hideous adventures; she was reading the tall headlines in the newspapers; she was commenting on them with simulated flippancy to Georgia and Ernestine; she was meeting Mr. Gratton for the first time again, treating him to such haughty disdain as put hot blood into his white face; she was standing erect in the morning, confronting Mark King fearlessly, demanding her rights, commanding that he take her home. And, piteously lonely and frightened, she was longing to have him come to her now, to put his arms about her, to hold her tight, to set his fearless body between hers and the vague and terrible menaces of the night and the jeering night voices. She heard a twig snap; her heart beat wildly; she wondered what she would do when he came—and she saw that he sat motionless by the fire.

The night wore on. She dozed now and then, fitfully, awakened always rudely by unaccustomed noises or by the cold or the discomfort of her bed. She put her hand to her cheek, wondering if she were going to be feverish; her face was cold. She saw that King had lighted his pipe. She wanted to scream at him. How she hated him for that. That he could smoke while she lay here in such wretchedness made her briefly hot with anger. He was a man, and sweepingly she told herself that she loathed all mankind. She accused him of heartlessness, of lack of understanding, of brutal lack of sympathy. He and he alone was responsible for everything—that vague, terrible *everything*. He sat there as still as a rooted tree; he bulked big through the gloom like a rugged boulder; he was a part of this wild land, as indifferent, as cold, as merciless. The thought now that he might come to her made her quake with fear; she was afraid of him.

If she could only sleep! No sleep to-night, little the night before, less the night before that. No wonder her brain swirled. If all this had happened at any other time—She was a bundle of nerves—nerves that vibrated at the slightest suggestion. She was going to be ill. Perhaps the end of it would be that she would die. All of the misshapen, monstrous fancies which are bred of a sleepless and nervous night made for her a period of such stress that as the hours wore on they blanched her cheeks and put dark shadows under her eyes and taunted her with longings for a rest which they denied her.

Thus, in the stern grips of their destinies, Mark King and Gloria lived through the night, two uncertain spirits awaiting the light of day. And thus their brains, those finite organs upon which mankind entrusts the ordering of great events, prepared themselves for the moment when they must grapple with and decide a matter of supreme moment. And all night the wind, like a hateful voice, jeered.

*   *   *   *   *

At four o'clock that chill, wind-blown morning King began the day. He saw that Gloria was awake and sitting up, looking straight ahead of her. He gave no sign of having noted her, but busied himself in a swift, silent sort of way with fire-building and breakfast preparation. Gloria, in turn, saw him; she experienced aloof wonder at the look on his face. He was haggard; his mouth was set and hard.

She had thought to be thankful when daylight came. Now she got up and went to the fire, rubbing her cold hands together, looking at an awakened world with dull, lack-lustre eyes. It was not yet full day; what light filtered down here into this sheltered spot was cheerless; as it drew forest details out of the thinning shadows it seemed to be painting them in cold grey monotones upon a cold grey world.

He and she, when he came back with an arm-load of wood, looked straight into each other's eyes, long and soberly, searchingly and hopelessly. After that they did not again look into each other's faces; no good-morning had passed between them since both sensed that any time for empty civilities had gone. There could be no conventional pretence at harmony even in small things; they must be in each other's arms or worlds apart.

Out of a night's grappling with chimeras, King had come to one and only one determination: he would go slowly, he would hold an iron check upon himself, he would throttle down a temper which more than once in his life, at moments of tempest, had blazed out uncontrollably. He would smother within himself that passion which in forthright men is so prone to burst into violence. Were Gloria to show herself to be this or that, were she to say this word or another, he would speak with her coolly, he would listen to her calmly, and in the end, since judge he must, he would judge with his heart ordered to beat steadily and not with a wild rush of blood. He had set a guard in his own breast as he might have set a guard over a camp of treacherous enemies.

Yet, from the outset, nothing was more unlikely than that these two should advance by smooth paths to a clear and utter understanding. His one glimpse of her face dethroned his cold logic and moved him very deeply; she was so white, so pitifully sad-looking. She, too, had suffered; God knew that she had battled through hours of anguish. He wanted her in his arms; he wanted to batter at the world with his fists to save her from its flings of grief and pain. He bit savagely at his lip and turned away. And she, seeing his haggard eyes, his drawn face, knew that she had been unjust last night when she had hated him for seeming a soulless man, who could smoke his pipe in all serenity and feel nothing of the unhappiness of the night. He did not look like the Mark King of yesterday; the glad gleam of joy had died in his eyes; the quick resiliency had gone out of his step. He, too, had lived through slow hours of torture. He did love her—she could never doubt that—

Had he suddenly caught her to him then, had he crushed her close in his arms, had he cried out in headlong passion that she *must* love him, that he would make her love him, that she was his, that he would not give her up—would she have wrenched away from him, hot with anger—or would she have crept close and known at last whether or not she loved him? But here was something else she could not know; he turned and went off for his wood; she crouched shivering by the fire.

They breakfasted in silence, the fire between them. Neither did much more than drink the strong coffee. Gloria sat tossing bits of bread into the fire. It was on his lips to tell her not to do that; waste in the wilderness is a crime. But he held his words back. He went methodically about camp work; cleaned the plates and cups and pans; remade the two packs. All this time she did not stir. At last he came back to her and stood by the dying fire, ominously silent. She grew nervously restive, wishing that he would say something.

"There's a day's work to be done," he said at last. His voice, meant to be impersonal, was only stern. "That means an early start. And—"

"Is it very much further to the caves?" she asked.

He had paused; she had to say something.

"It will take a long day getting there. You see, we didn't come very far yesterday."

This, she supposed, was a fling at her, and she stiffened under it. But when she spoke it was to ignore the innuendo, intended or not. For, wherever they might be led, she hoped it would not be into sordid quarrelling.

"It begins to be rather obvious that I should not have come. Doesn't it?" she asked.

"Well?"

"Now, if I turn back—"

"To the house?"

"And then to mamma and papa, in Coloma. And then to San Francisco."

"And I?"

"If you would go with me as far as the house—"

She saw how his body straightened, how his broad shoulders squared. There was something eloquent in the gesture; Mark King, with no toleration of a clutter of side issues, came straight to the main barrier, which must be swept aside for good and all, or which must be skirted and so passed and relegated to the limbo of dead hopes.

"Do you love me, Gloria?" he demanded. "As lovers love? As I have loved you? As a wife should love her husband?"

"Didn't I explain all of that last night?" she said petulantly. "Must we go over it all again? If I have ... have pained you, I am sorry. I can't say any more than that, can I? I thought I made you see how I was placed, how there was but the one thing for me to do...."

"Marry Gratton or me? And you chose me?"

She hesitated. She knew that he was angry, though he gave so little outward sign. Nor did she fail to recognize that he had grounds for anger. But none the less she resented his insistent questionings. She stood looking blankly at him. If she had only obeyed her straightforward impulse at the house to go to him and explain her predicament!

"I intended," she began in a low, strange voice, "to go to you, to tell you—"

"Answer me," he said sternly. "Yes or no. Did you marry me without love and just to save yourself from possible gossip of being alone all night with a man? Is that why you married me? Yes or no?"

To Gloria, as to King, the issue was clear and not to be clouded; to her credit be it said that she wasted no time in fruitless evasion. This matter would demand settlement, as well now as later. There was wisdom in ending all unpleasantness once and for ever.

"Yes," she answered defiantly.

Then suddenly it was given her to see a Mark King she had never dreamed of, a Mark King of blazing wrath thrusting aside the man whom she knew and who had held himself in check and throttled down his emotion until she spoke that quiet "Yes." The word was like a spark to a train of gunpowder. His determination to beat down his temper, no matter what came, was gone; his memory of her ordeals was wiped out; from his whole tense being there flashed out upon her a hot, heady anger, like stabbing lightning from an ominous cloud. His few words seared and scorched a place in her memory to endure always.

He clenched his hands and raised them; for an instant she thought he was going to strike her down.

"You are utterly contemptible!" he shouted at her. "And I am done with you!"

He turned and left her. Gloria stared after him in amazement. She saw how he walked swiftly, his big boots crunching through the gravel down by the creek bed, splashing through the water, carrying him up the timbered slope toward the horses. She could not know that he was almost running because he was telling himself in his fierce white passion that unless he left her thus he would lose the last power of restraint, and set his hands to her pink-and-white throat and choke her. Until the last second he had sought not to condemn too soon. Now, after his fashion, he condemned sweepingly. For the moment he held that she was less to him than the grime upon his boots.

When he came to the horses he was white with anger; he lifted his hand and looked at his fingers queerly; they were trembling. He cursed himself for a fool, shut the hand into a hard fist as steady as rock, and for an instant glared at it blackly. Then he opened the fingers slowly; a hard smile made his mouth ugly and left it cruel; the fingers had hearkened to a superb will, and gave no greater hint of trembling than did the nigged hole of the giant cedar under which he stood.

He coiled his horse's tie-rope and led him back to camp. As he drew near, Gloria promptly turned her back and studied her nails; she had had encounters with men before now and had not yet gauged the profundity of this man's emotion. She counted fully on bringing him to a full and contrite sense of his crime before she condescended so much as to look at him. But when she flashed him a quick, furtive glance she saw that he had his back upon her, and that he gave neither hint of softening nor yet of knowledge of her presence. He bridled the buckskin, saddled, tied his rope at the saddle-horn, and began making his pack. She watched, uneasy and concerned but not yet fully understanding. But when she noted how he took from their breakfast-table one cup, one plate, one knife and fork, only; how he did not appear interested in the marmalade-jar which she knew had been brought for her; how he left half of the coffee and bacon and sugar; a strange alarm came over her. She glanced wildly around. The forest glowered darkly; the silence was overpowering; the loneliness bewildering. He was going to leave her—she had not the faintest idea in the world where the trail lay.

King went swiftly about his preparations. He did not even see her; he studiously kept his eyes aloof. Within his soul he swore that he would never look at her again....He took up his rifle.

Gloria stirred uneasily. She did not like to yield to him even to the extent of saying a stiff word. But she felt that the man was not playing a part, and that in another moment she would be alone.

"You are not going to leave me here alone, are you?" she demanded coldly.

"I am going on," was his curt rejoinder.

"And I?" she persisted.

"What you please."

He went on with his preparations. Terror sprang up into the girl's heart.

"I would never find my way out," she cried, jumping to her feet and coming toward him. "I am not used to the mountains ...I don't know which way ...I would die...."

"To be rid of you the easiest way," he returned bluntly, "I would turn back with you until we got within striking distance of the open. But you have made me waste time as it is, and I promised Ben that I'd be in Gus Ingle's caves with no time lost. So I am going on."

"But," and all of her surging terror trembled in her rushing words, "I would die, I tell you...."

"And I tell you," he snapped back at her, "that I don't care a damn if you do. Must I tell you twice that I am through with you?"

He set his foot to the stirrup. Gloria, pride lost in panic, ran to him and grasped his arm, crying to him:

"You mustn't leave me this way! It's brutal ... it's murder."

"I gave my promise to Ben," he said. "You are not worth breaking a promise."

"If you won't take me back, then let me go with you."

"Worthless and selfish and cowardly! Useless and vain and brainless! Good God! am I, a man full grown, to loiter on the trail with the like of you? Let go!" He shook her hand off roughly and swung up into the saddle, sending his horse with a boot-heel in the flank down to the ford. But Gloria screamed after him, and ran after him, down to the creek and through it, calling out:

"Mark! Mark! For God's sake don't leave me. I am afraid; I will die of fear. Take me with you...."

He did not look back at her, but he did pause. After all, she was the daughter of his old friend.

"The woods are free and open," he said slowly. "To even such as you. For the third time and for the last I tell you this: I am done with you. But if you like you may follow behind me. I will wait for you ten minutes. Not here, but on the ridge up there. And if you have not come, I will go on at the end of that time. That is my solemn word, Gloria Gaynor."

He rode from her, straight and massive in the saddle, up the slope among the big-boled trees, and in a trice out of sight. She stood like one in a sudden trance. Then, with an inarticulate moan, she ran into the grove and grasped Blackie's rope, and dragged at him trying to make him run with her to her saddle and few belongings. The saddle nearly overmastered her; it was heavy, and she knew as little of it as did any city girl. But her need was sore and her young body not without supple strength. In half of the allotted time Gloria came riding up the ridge. Now King glanced toward her briefly. But less at her than at her pack.

"You had better go back for the rest of the grub," he said to her. "And for your blanket-roll. That would be my advice to the devil himself.... You can do it in the five minutes left to you."

Gloria flung up her head, opened her lips for a stinging reply, and then held for a moment in silence and hesitation.

"You hideous brute!" she flung at him. But none the less she hastened back for her outfit. Five minutes later they rode on into the ever-deepening wilderness, she just keeping his form in sight, he never turning nor speaking.

CHAPTER XIX

For his brutal treatment of her Gloria fully meant that in the ripeness of time he should pay to the uttermost. After that first panic she felt toward King only such anger as she had never experienced before, never having cause for it. Perhaps the emotion was the beginning of a new soul-life for her; certainly here was a moment of reversion to a condition of unplumbed progenital influences; the scorching anger arising from such a primitive situation was in itself primal. Hence the emotion no less that the experience itself was novel; clean, searing anger.

Following this emotion which rode her and sapped her nervous strength came a period of faintness and nausea. She closed her eyes and dropped her head and clung to the horn of her saddle with hands which went cold and shook. In this mood she called out once to King. But he was far ahead and did not turn. She did not know whether he had heard her. Gradually the weakness passed; they topped the ridge and the sun wanned her. Coolly and collectedly she turned her thoughts upon the insufferable insult and came back through a sort of circle to her first intention. Now the decision was cold and stubborn: he would pay and in full.

King led the way unfalteringly. Time and again she saw no hint of a trail underfoot or ahead; they broke through brush or made a difficult way through a thicket of alders or willows and invariably came again upon a trail. It was evident that the man thought only of his journey's end and was hastening; hence he took all the short cuts which he knew. In one of these pathless places, where the scrub-trees and tangle of brush were above her head, where it seemed that she must smother, she lost all sight of him. Her horse came to a dead halt. She listened and could not hear the hoofs of his horse. Again panic mastered her, and she cried out wildly. But just ahead was a mad mountain stream filling the gorge with its thunder. She knew that King could not hear her; she felt the desperate certainty that he would not heed could he hear. Then she struck her horse frantically with her bare hands, and pounded him with her heels, longing for the sight of King as one athirst in the bad lands longs for water. The horse snorted, and whirling and plunging went ripping through the bushes which whipped at her and tore the skin of hands and face. But in three minutes he brought her into the open and into full sight of King, riding up a gentle slope through big red-boled cedars. When her fear died, as it did swiftly after the way of fear, it left not the old, hot anger, but a new elemental emotion—cold hatred.

Thus upon their second morning the honeymoon entered upon its second phase. Every moment brought some new discomfort to her; the saddle hurt her: her clothes were torn, her tender skin bruised and scratched; pains came stabbingly with early fatigue As for King, he had come abruptly to look down upon her as utterly despicable; being a man of high honour he convicted her out of hand as one without honour; despising her, he despised himself for having linked his life in ever so little with hers. But yesterday he had knelt to her humbly in his innermost heart of hearts; now he sought to shut his mind against her quite as definitely as he turned his back on her.

What sombre, misshapen edifice they should build upon these corner-stones of hate and contempt was a matter into which no conjecture could enter even slightly had their compelling environment been different. In the city they would have turned their backs and walked away from each other. But two storm-driven men upon a raft don't separate until land is sighted. Gloria, at least, was in her present plight comparable to a shipwrecked sailor of little skill and less resource. Hence, what was to be, remained to be seen.

At ten o'clock the air was sun-warmed and sweet. Half an hour later the genial day was made over by the high wind trailing vapours into a chill bleak sky. They had climbed to fresh altitudes; the timber through which they progressed indicated that a height of at least seven thousand feet above sea-level had been passed. They passed through groves of the thin-barked tamaracks, came at the base of a rugged slope to scattering mountain pines, which reared into lusty perfection on bleak, wind-swept levels, where many of their companion growths were beginning to run out in dwarfed, twisted misery, and came to a rocky pass through the mountains where on all sides the red cedar, the juniper of the Sierra, throve hardily among bare boulders, crowning the lofty crests like a sparse, stiff, hirsute display upon the gigantic body of the world. The dwarf pine lingered here, straggling along the slopes, beaten down by many a winter of wind and heavy snow. But by noon they had made a slow, tedious way down a rocky ridge and were once more in the heart of the upper forest belt. In an upland meadow, through whose narrow boundaries a thin, cold stream trickled, they nooned. Long had Gloria hungered for the moment when she would see King swing down from the saddle; during the last half-hour she had begun to fear that his brutality knew no bounds and that he would spare neither the horses nor her but crowd on until nightfall. When he did dismount by the creek she drew rein fifty feet from him.

King slipped Buck's bridle, dropped the tie-rope, and let the animal forage along the fringes of the brook. To Gloria, in a voice which struck her as being as chill as the grey, overcast sky, he said:

"Better let your horse eat. We've got to go pretty steady to get anywhere to-day."

Gloria got down stiffly from her saddle. In all the days of her life she had never been so unutterably weary. Further, she was faint from hunger and her throat pained her; she went to the creek and threw herself down and put her face into the cool water, from which she rose with a long sigh. She had seen how King did with his tie-rope; she did similarly, but was too tired to trouble with removing the bit from her horse's mouth. Still Blackie accepted his handicapped opportunity and joined Buck in tearing and ripping at the lush grass. It was more inviting than the manzanita-bushes and occasional sunflower-leaves at which he had snatched during the day.

King made coffee and fried bacon; the horses had earned an hour of rest and fodder, and a man has the right to bacon and coffee even though hard miles lie before him. While he pottered with his fire he looked more than once at the sky in the south-west. With all of his heart he wished that he had turned back with Gloria this morning. By now he could have set her feet in a trail which even a fool could travel back to the log house, and he could be again hastening upon his errand. Gloria lay inert; she chewed slowly at a bit broken from a slab of hard chocolate and kept her eyes closed. Her face was very white; two big tears of distress slipped out from the shut lids. But King did not come close enough to see them.

When his coffee was ready he called to her, saying indifferently: "Better have a cup. It helps." But Gloria did not reply. King seemed not to notice whether she ate or not. But, when he had drunk his own coffee and she still lay quiet on the grass, he sweetened a cup for her, put some milk in it, and set it at her elbow. "Better drink it," he said coldly. And Gloria gathered her strength and sat up and drank. Thereafter she ate some bread and potted ham. Fragments of bread, the crust, and half of the ham she threw away. King opened his mouth to protest; then shrugged and remained silent. His back to a tree, he sat and smoked until the hour had passed.

Precisely at one o'clock they were on their way. Gloria caught her own horse, coiled the rope, and mounted. As King rode across the meadow and to the wooded slope beyond she followed. It seemed to her that this was all a dream; she was almost light-headed; the sternest of realities began to seem impalpable and distant and of scant moment. She knew that she was going forward because she must; that otherwise she would lie here in the lonely wilderness and die. In her exhaustion she noted, as one does note his own soul-play when overwrought, that the prospect of death seemed less terrible than that of utter desertion. The mountains were so big they stifled her. With every tortuous step forward this formidable land all about her had grown more severe, more lonely, more to her like the kingdom of desolation than she had ever dreamed existed. There were slope fields strewn with black lava rock where never a solitary blade of grass upthrust a thin spear; there were broken expanses across which the eye might travel wearily for what appeared endless miles. One could call out here with never a faint hope of being heard; one left alone here could die miserably, taunted only by the echoes of her own choking voice. This devil's land took on a vindictive personality; it was a hideous colossus, stooping over her, inspired with but one cruel desire, to crush her soft white body, to stamp out her life, to annihilate her and gloat over her shrieking despair. She felt like some hapless little princess in a fairy-tale who had wandered into a monstrous land of black sorcery.

By four o'clock, when it seemed to Gloria that she had reached and was passing the limits of her endurance, came two momentous occurrences. King, riding ahead as usual, was not quite so far in advance, and did not have his back turned square upon her. For the first time he had briefly mistaken the trail; they were on the steep flank of the mountain; he turned and rode back in her general direction but some hundred yards lower on the slope.

"The trail's down here," he announced shortly. He did not lift his eyes to her face, did not note the droop of the weary body. His look was all for her horse, and a new and unreasonable spurt of anger was in his heart Through her unbounded ignorance she had needlessly fatigued her mount, having no knowledge of the ways one employs to save his horse.

Gloria understood dully that she was too far up and must ride down to his level. She was beyond complaining or asking questions; with a sudden jerk upon the reins she brought Blackie about. King cursed under his breath.

"That's too steep!" he called to her. "Want to kill your horse?"

Blackie tried to swerve and sidle down. Gloria lifted her whip and struck him. Blackie snorted and obeyed her command. Some loose dirt gave way underfoot, the tired beast stumbled, a dead limb caught at his legs, tripping him, and Blackie lurched downward and fell. Through the grace of fortune Gloria rolled clear and unhurt. Blackie got up, tottering, with one quivering fore-leg lifted. King's face went black with rage.

But this time it was wordless rage. He dismounted and made his way up to the lamed horse; Gloria, from where she lay, thought at first that of course he was coming to her. But he kept his back to her as he lifted the horse's fore-leg and felt tenderly at the wrenched muscle. Gloria, without stirring, and without experiencing any poignant emotion, watched him listlessly, then shut her eyes. Her most clear sensation was one of relief; they would no doubt make camp here.

A cold drop of rain splashed on her cheek. She opened her eyes. King was removing Blackie's saddle. Gloria closed her eyes again and sighed. A sort of dreary thankfulness blossomed feebly in her heart that the torturous day was over. King would make some sort of a shelter; she would drink a cup of coffee and crawl into her blankets and go to sleep....

"Come on," called a voice as though from some great distance. "We've got to hurry as fast as God will let us."

Blackie was standing where King had led him, his saddle and bridle swung up into a tree, his foot still lifted, his nostrils close to the long grass but untempted. Gloria's canvas-rolled pack and the rifle were across King's back. As she sat up and stared at him she read his intentions. He was going on on foot, expecting her to take his horse.

"I can't," she said miserably.

He looked up into the sky and not at her.

"You can do what you please," he retorted curtly. "I am going on."

She rose and went stumbling down the slope. She swayed as she tried to mount, but he did not offer his hand. When she was in the saddle he strode on ahead. Blackie looked after them wistfully.

"The leg's not broken," King told her gruffly. "Just a bad sprain. Not your fault it isn't worse, though. He'll take care of himself; God knows he's got as good a chance as we have."

"What do you mean?" she asked quickly.

He merely swung up his arm toward the sky by way of answer and went on. The second big rain-drop hit Gloria's cheek. It was chill; its dullness seemed to drive straight to her heart.

CHAPTER XX

The storm caught them as it has caught so many a wayfarer before and since. The wintry season was not due for a full four weeks, but the winter had thrust sign and season aside and made his regal entry after his own ancient fashion. There came a crash of reverberating thunder, a scurry in the thickening mass of black clouds, a drenching downpour of rain. For twenty minutes they crouched in what scant shelter was afforded them by a squat, wide-limbed cedar. Then the wind went ripping off through the tree-tops, exacting its toll of flying twigs and leaving in its wake a brief, hushed calm. Through the still air fell scattering flakes of snow, big and unbroken and feathery. King's eyes were filled with concern; his face was ominous like the face of the world about him.

Again Gloria's tired body was assured of rest; again King said expressionlessly: "Come on." This time he helped her into the saddle, being in haste and of no mind to wait for trifles. He hurried on ahead; she followed on Buck listlessly, clinging to the saddle, her eyes often shut.

For an hour it snowed. Though there was no sun it was not dark save in the deeper canons. Nor was it as cold as Gloria had thought it must be—or else she was too tired to feel the pinch of the sharp air. But presently the flakes grew fewer and then ceased utterly. Those that lay on the ground or clung to branches melted swiftly; and with their departure the last light of the day was gone. Now King led the horse and Gloria rode through a gathering darkness. She wanted to ask why they did not stop; why they did not turn back, but lacked the spirit. Now and then she half dozed.

At last it was pitch dark and the rain was beginning again. King had stopped and was helping her down. She was numb now in body; her brain was numb. The rain hardened into a rattle of hail. Thereafter the air softened and filled with swirling snow. Gloria could not see if they were in an open valley or shut in by canon walls or upon the slope of a mountain. Nor did she greatly care. She waited until King prepared some kind of a shelter, and then went wordlessly to it; she felt fir-boughs under her aching body and was, in pure animal fashion, conscious of blanket and canvas over her and of a grateful warmth. Through a tangle of bushes she saw the flicker of a small fire; she smelled coffee; she drank half of the hot cup which he brought to her. Then she let go her grip upon a wretched world and passed like a child into a heavy sleep.

By his fire of little cheer Mark King sat, with his canvas drawn over his slumping shoulders, his head down, his heart as black as the night, his soul possessed by ravaging blue demons. At the end of a fool's day came a fool's night. He should have paid heed to the first threat of a thin film across the sky; he should have turned back with Gloria the first thing this morning; he should have done anything in the world save exactly what he had done. He should not have married her; he should not have brought her with him; it was even sheer idiocy to come after this blind fashion into the mountains in the late fall. Though the season was early the hour was ominous. The storm might pass before dawn. There remained the equal likelihood that it would not. Were he alone, or had he a man, or, yes, by heaven! a real woman with him, things would not be so bad. The wind jeered at him through the trees; the storm drenched his fire; he cursed back at both.

"One thing," he thought when his pipe brought him a solitary instant of peace, "I won't be worried with Gratton and Brodie and his double-dealing crowd. If they ever started they would have sense enough to turn back long ago."

After the cold, wet night came a sodden morning. King stood up and looked about him curiously; his first thought was to make sure that they had really camped upon the edge of that particular upland valley which he had striven for. And a glint of satisfaction came into his eyes; it is something to have followed such a trail aright upon such a night. Down yonder, a crooked black line in a white field, was the stream which many miles further on flowed into the American. Rising abrupt beyond it were the broken, precipitous cliffs of granite such as beetle above the mountain tributaries of the American. The rocks, like the river, were black, and looked far colder than the white world which extended in all directions.

If, in truth, there existed heaps of raw red gold somewhere in a cave in these mountains, and there had been any exactness in the description in Gus Ingle's Bible, then the spot was not more than three or four miles away. That was one consideration. It was still snowing. Here was a second consideration. King turned moody eyes to Gloria's canvas-and-fir shelter in the lee of a little bit of cliff. There lay the third. He prepared breakfast without delay but without enthusiasm. He felt a tired man with shackled limbs dragging a dead weight.

When he went to wake Gloria he first stood over her, looking queerly down upon her sleep. She showed less trace of the hard day and wild night than he had expected to see; his preparations for her comfort, instinctive and thorough, had been made with the cunning skill of a man familiar with situations like the present. She had rested; she lay curled up, snug and warm, under the covers, upon which a thin layer of fluffy snow had gathered. Her face was against a curved arm, and the sweetness of it in its tranquil repose was a bitter sweet to him. Her lashes against her cheek stirred and flew apart under his steady gaze. He looked into Gloria's eyes, sweet and soft, heavy with sleep.

"Time to be up," he said. He turned on his heel and went back in haste to his fire.

Gloria, awake, was ravenously hungry. She came sooner than he had expected, setting the wild disarray of her hair in some hurried order. Her eyes were quick and curious as she looked up at him. She shrugged her shoulders behind his back and extended her hands to the small, wind-blown blaze.

"Are we going back?" she asked colourlessly.

"No," he returned as indifferently. "It's about four miles to the caves. We'll be there in a couple of hours. Then we'll see what we see."

Gloria sent a long, searching, and awe-struck look across the broken country. Yonder, then, she realized dismally, lay their destination; bleak, black, rocky heights, at so great an altitude and in a region so barren that but few wind-broken trees grew, and the brutal face of the world was unmasked. She saw bare peaks, steep slopes, a tremendous gorge like an ugly gash; on the far side of the gorge sheer cliffs. Toward them King looked. Was it there that Gus Ingle's caves awaited them? Was that journey's end? She shivered and drew closer to the fire, closer to her companion, shrinking from the menace of the mountains.

"Is it going to keep on snowing?" she asked.

This time he shrugged. That was his only answer. She stared at him, a slow flush came into her cheeks, her eyes hardened.

"Oh, very well," she said coldly.

That was the whole of their conversation save for one curt remark and an impudent laugh in answer at the end of the scanty meal. Gloria tossed a piece of bacon into the fire. King looked at her sternly and said:

"Young lady, we may be up against the real thing right now.

Nobody but a fool will do a trick like that."

The laugh was Gloria's.

*   *   *   *   *

Once on their way they climbed almost steadily. The air grew rarer and colder. The snowflakes became smaller, at last a fine sifting like sand particles that cut at hands and face viciously. No longer were there groves to shelter them; on all sides bare, hostile rocks, and only occasionally a sparse growth of sprawling, earth-hugging dwarf pine and cedar, over which King strode as over so much low, tangled brush. Then came a long ridge, a spine from which the world dropped almost sheer on both sides, with the wind raging so that it seemed Buck must be blown off his feet, or the girl torn from the saddle and borne far out like a thistledown. With frightened eyes, which she strove vainly to keep closed, she saw long, broken slopes; occasionally when the air cleared, a frothing torrent; and once, at the end of a couple of hours, far down in a distant level land, a growth of giant timber. She thought that King was making his way down there. But his purpose soon became plain even to her; he was keeping high on the ridges, going about the head of the ravine which lower down cut like a knife across the timbered tract, headed for what he took to be Gus Ingle's cave. A mile away she saw it; a great, ragged, black hole in a high mass of rock, close to the crest of the next ridge.

She was wrapped warmly and yet here the icy breath of the wind pierced the fabric of her wrappings and hurt her to the bone. She watched King wonderingly as he hastened on; did the man have no sense of bodily discomfort? Certainly he gave no sign. He was like an animal; she found room for a flash of scorn in the thought. For so she was pleased to consider him lower in the scale than herself.

At another time she might have seen the world about her clothed in grandeur; now its sublimity was lost I upon her. It was a ravening beast, an ugly thing, big and brutal, and ... like

King. Oh, how she hated it and him!

When at last he waited for her and told her to get down she had the suspicion that he had gone mad. Certainly here was no spot to tarry; it was on her lips to demur. But she looked at his face and slipped stiffly from the saddle. They were high up on the ridge; Gloria, on foot beside him, clutched at the wind-twisted branch of one of the sprawling cliff growths, in sudden panic that she was being swept from her feet. Just below them was the deepening cleft in the mountain-side which, further down, widened and descended into the steep-walled gorge. Through it shot a mad, frothy stream. A hundred yards further on, high up in the cliffs, was the yawning hole in the rocks. King, holding Buck's bridle, looked about him and at the sky. Gloria read in his manner a hint of uncertainty. Hoping to influence his decision, she said quickly:

"Hadn't we better turn back now?"

He looked at her steadily before answering.

"In what," he replied in that impersonal way which maddened her, "have you so altered as to be worth a man's broken promise?" And then she knew that no thought of going back had had any part in his brief indecision. He was going forward, would go forward in anything he undertook; that was a part of his make-up. He was merely seeking the best place to unpack and a convenient spot to tether Buck. They were going to make camp either right here or nearer the cave, perhaps in it. She looked at the uninviting hole and shivered. She would know his decision when King saw fit to enlighten her.

Now he merely dumped at her feet the roll from the horse's back, setting his rifle down against it. Then he led Buck away, zigzagging tediously, at last passing from sight beyond an out jutting monster crag. Gloria crouched, seeking to shield herself from the whiplashes of the wind. She listened to it as it shrieked about the slabs and boulders of granite; the sound was indescribably eerie, filled with unrest, eloquent of the brutal contempt of the eternal for the feeble and transient. The universe grew utterly lonely; the wind was a whining thing cutting through the silence. And King was so long in coming back....

The terrifying thought electrified her: "What if he had deserted her? What if he had no intention of coming back?" She should have known better; perhaps, deep down within her, she did know better. But the suspicion brought its wild flutter; she sprang up and grew rigid in tense fright; she felt a strange, glad rush of joy as she saw his hat bobbing up and toward her along the mountain flank. When he rejoined her she was staring off at nothingness, her back to him.

He lashed the two canvas rolls together, swung them up to his shoulders, took frying-pan, coffee-pot, and rifle in his free hand, and nodded toward the small pack of provisions which had been left over from lunch. "Better bring those," he advised briefly. "There's no telling what may be in the cards." He went on along the knife-edge of the ridge, down into a little depression, up beyond. She hesitated, saw that he had not looked, bit her lip angrily, and snatched up the parcel. Then she followed him, stooping against the wind.

When she came up with him he had thrown down his pack at the very edge of the gorge. She came to his side, leaned forward, and looked down. Far below plunged the wildest torrent she had ever seen; it hurled itself in mad haste between boulders; it shot down over dizzy falls; it made for itself a white mantle of frothing waters; it looked as black as ebony in sections of smoother channel and as cold as death; it spun in whirlpools, it filled the air with its din. And King meant to go down to it; to cross it; to climb the dizzy cliff upon the further side! She knew from his look, without asking. For just across the chasm from them in the highest of the cliffs was the yawning black-mouthed place of horrors. If one slipped on those bare rocks, clambering down or climbing on the further side! She sat down suddenly; now when her lip was caught between her teeth it was to fight back the tears. The world was so cold and stern and brutal; this man was so much like the environment; she was so woefully, desperately heart-sick. On this lofty crest of a devil-tossed land she felt the insignificance of a fly clinging to the brow of an abyss.

King went about his task methodically. Gloria watched him rather than look across the rocky gorges. Slowly and with difficulty he made his way down the steep wall of rocks, dragging and pulling the roll of bedding and provisions after him. It required perhaps twenty minutes for him to get to the bottom. She wondered where he would attempt a crossing; the water looked so black in the pools, so violent over the rapids. He went up-stream; there lay an old cedar log so that it spanned the current, its sturdy old trunk ten feet above the water. For a moment King disappeared under an out-thrust ledge; then she saw him again, the pack on his shoulders. He had climbed up to the top of the log; he was crossing. Where he went now she must follow!

Fascinated, she watched him. Once she thought he was going to fall. But unerringly he trod the rude bridge underfoot, gained the other side without mishap, tossed down his bundle, and lowered himself from the log after it. Gloria marvelled at him; she could see his face and it was impassive. Could he not hear the hostile voices of the raging waters? Could he not feel the ominous threat of the bleak day and the monster cliffs? Was he a man without imagination as he seemed to be without fear?

On he went, down-stream again, clinging to the steep pitch of the gorge, until he was almost under the mouth of the cavern. He put back his head and looked up; it was a hundred feet above him and the cliffs, from where Gloria sat numb with cold and dread, looked unsurmountable. Yet he was going up them!

"And where he goes you will follow." It was as though the wild waters below were chanting it into her ears and thereafter filling the gorge with the mockery of derisive laughter.

Slowly, tediously, but with never a sign of hesitation, King made his way up the cliff. He had been here before; he knew and remembered every foothold and handhold. Nor was the task the impossible one it looked from a distance. There were cracks and crevices; there were seams of a harder material which, better withstanding the attacks of time, were thrust out beyond the general level; on them a man might stand. There were spots of softer material, scooped out into pockets by wind and water; there were flinty splinters; there were places where the wall, looking from across the canon to be sheer and perpendicular, sloped more gently, and a man might crawl up them.

King had drawn up after him, stage after stage, the roll of bedding, using Blackie's tie-rope to haul it up and to moor it briefly. Gloria saw it swing at times like a huge, misshapen pendulum; watched it crawl up after him. She saw the wind snatch at it and set it scraping back and forth when he let it dangle at rope's end; she saw King's coat flap in the wind. Once she cried out aloud, thinking a second time that King was falling. If he fell from that height—if he were killed—what then would be the fate of Gloria Gaynor!

But at length he came safely to the cave's mouth. He stood upright and looked about him. Then he drew up to his feet the dangling roll; with it in his arms he was gone into that yawning hole. She waited breathlessly for his return. She saw him come again into the light; he had the rope in his hand, was coiling it. He began to come down. He was returning for her.

She did not stir while he made the slow descent, nor while he recrossed on the log and climbed the steep bank to her.

"I am going to spend the day up there," he told her in his studied aloof manner. "I'll know soon enough now what truth there is in the story of Gus Ingle's gold. There's room in the cave to sleep, and there's shelter of a sort. To-morrow morning, if I find nothing, I'll start back with you. If you care to come up now I'll help you."

"What else is there to do?" cried Gloria, with the first flash of passion. "What else do you leave me?"

He slipped a loop of the rope about her waist, taking slow pains not to touch her with his hands, and turned downward again. She followed, filled with sudden fear when they had climbed down ten feet, obeying him hastily when he commanded her to stand still or to move on, feeling her fear grow mightily as they progressed. The wind, strengthening abruptly, tore at her in angry gusts. She was panting and shaking visibly when finally she reached the log spanning the stream. He was up before her, offering her his hand. How she hated to touch it! How she feared to follow him! But her hand went into his, her steps followed his, and without hesitation; for there was nothing left now to choice. She looked down and saw the water raging below; it was like a monster leaping at her, snatching at her. She wanted to look away and could not. Like one moving through the fearsome steps of a nightmare she went on, clinging to King's hand, his hand tight upon hers, cold hands which met because they must. At last the torrent was behind her; she came down into King's arms from the log; she was faint and would have sat down. But he urged her on.

It was another nightmare climbing up the cliffs to the cave. He went ahead; he stopped and braced himself; he tautened the rope about her waist and said: "Come on. Slow and careful does it." She clutched with her cold, sore fingers at the rocks, felt the rope tighten, and went up and up. The wind, as though in a fury at losing its quarry, shrieked in her ears, and in mighty gusts strove to drag her hands from the rocks and to set her swinging as it had swung the roll of bedding. She climbed on. King ordered and she obeyed; she waited for him to go up, further ahead; for him to call to her and draw in on the rope. Stage by stage, weary stages fraught with terror, she toiled up and up and up. And so at last, when it seemed to her that no strength remained in her, she came to King's side at the gloomy entrance of Gus Ingle's cave. The formless black void before her which under other circumstances would have repelled, now invited. It offered shelter and rest and protection. She crept by King with never a backward glance, and threw herself face down on the uneven floor.

CHAPTER XXI

A long time King stood at the mouth of the cave, looking forth upon the newly whitened world. The look of the thickening sky, the wintry sting of the rushing air, the businesslike way in which the snow swirled and fell created a condition upon which he had not counted and for which he had no relish. This was more like a mid-winter blizzard than any storm had any business being so early in the season. For many hours already the snow had been falling, piling up in the mountain passes; if it kept on at this rate through another day and night—well, he and Gloria had best be getting out without any loitering.

He looked at his watch; not yet eleven o'clock. Need for haste; the day would be short. Before darkness shut down he had half a dozen hours, hours for methodical search. Here was one of Gus Ingle's caves; another, he knew, was directly below and at the base of the cliffs; the third should be near. It was the third that he was chiefly interested in. He recalled the words in the old Bible: "We come to the First Caive and then we come to Caive number three and two!" There lay significance in the order of Ingle's numerals; first, three, and two. Two of the caves were for any one to see; before now King had been in both of them. Hence it must be that Gus Ingle's treasure lay in the third. That one King must locate. And without too much delay. He looked down at Gloria. She lay motionless just as she had thrown herself down.

Taking his rope with him King made what haste he could

going down the cliffs. The sides of the ravine were littered with dead wood, drift and limbs that had broken off the few battered trees above. He gathered as heavy a load of dry branches as he could handle, bound them about with his rope, and, fighting his way all the way up, clambered again to the upper cave. Gloria had not stirred. He moved about her, went a dozen paces deeper into the great cavern, and threw down his wood. Breaking branches into short lengths he quickly got a fire going. The flames spurted up eagerly, bright and cheery, and threw dancing light among the wavering shadows. He brought the bedding-roll closer and opened it into a rough-and-ready bed. Then he called to Gloria.

"You'd better lie here by the fire," he told her. "You're apt to catch cold there."

She was sitting up, watching him. Now she rose listlessly and came forward, dropping down into a sitting position upon the blankets, her chilled hands out toward the blaze.

"I don't like the look of this storm," he told her. "It is up to us to hurry. I am going to look around now. I think you had better rest all you can so as to be ready to make a start back as soon as I find out whether we are on a wild-goose chase or not."

"You mean—we may start back to-day?"

"I don't know what I am going to find, of course; whether I am going to find anything. But if we can get only a couple of hours on our way to-day, it's just that much gained."

"You are going to leave me here?"

"I won't be far." With that he set fire to a dry pine faggot, the best torch available, and left her, going deeper into the cave. She watched him, marvelling at the size of the cavern. He went on a score of paces; he seemed to be ascending a steepening slant floor and then to have gone over a sort of ridge and to be descending again. But still going further from her. Presently she knew that the tunnel had turned sharply to the right; she could hear the thud of his boots and for a little while could see the flare of his torch against a wall of rock; he himself had passed out of her sight.

But she knew that he had not gone a great deal further. For he was not so far away that she could not hear him; he was going back and forth; at irregular intervals she saw a dim, ghostly light playing upon the dark cavern walls. And, despite the weary ache of a hardship-tortured body, she began to be interested in his search. If there were, in truth, such gold here somewhere as he and her father with him had dreamed of— gold for which seven men had died sixty years ago, for which old Loony Honeycutt had hungered all these years, for which Brodie and his following and even a city man like Gratton were like so many ravening wolves on the trail—gold in quantity to make even toughened old gold-seekers delirious with the dreams of it—why, then, that gold was half Mark King's and half Ben Gaynor's! And it might be that now, at this very instant, Mark King was finding it; was standing over it, staring down at it by the ghostly flare of a smoking torch. She sat, tense and still, listening, trying to probe with tired but suddenly bright eyes through the dark.

She started, realizing that no longer could she hear King searching back and forth. It was very silent about her, only the crackle of the flames making a sound to be heard against the rush of air outside. It seemed to her that King had been gone a long time. She rose to her feet, tempted to follow him. She was curious to know what he was doing; why he was so silent; where he had gone. But in the end pride restrained her and she sat down again to wait in an attitude of indifference.

But the minutes dragged on and never a sound came back from the far, dark depths of the cavern; fifteen minutes, half an hour. She grew restless and walked up and down; she went to the mouth of the cave and stood looking out into the swirling snow-storm; she returned to the fire, throwing on more wood.

She felt sure that an hour had passed—two hours—she began to grow alarmed. Always that dread thought was ready to spring out upon her: "If something had happened to him!" She went a little way in the direction he had taken; stood peering into the dark, listening breathless and rigid. Never a sound. She went back to the front of the cave, looking down, staring out into the grey sky, across the ridge....

Gloria, trembling with a new excitement, was down on her knees before the pack when King returned. She sprang up to face him. And each, with the other's emotions and experiences of the past two or three hours unknown to him, marvelled at what was to be read in the other's face. Gloria was excited; King's excitement was no less. Where she had at least the clue to his altered expression, he had none to hers.

"It's here!" he burst out. "And I've found it. Tons and tons of it, such knobs and nuggets of pure gold as never man laid eyes on! We have here the Magic Lamp to rub: a castle in Spain and an ocean-going yacht and the newest thing in motor-cars and a trip around the world and a presentation to royalty—a fragment of heaven and a very large slice of hell. Ambition fulfilled and love consumed and hate born. We have old Ben made whole and full of power again. And here we have all that is left of Gus Ingle and his friends—except for a pile of bones back yonder!"

She saw that in each hand he carried what looked like a big rough stone; she saw from the way he carried them that they were heavy. The fires leaped higher, brighter in her eyes. Now she saw the way to make Mark King pay for all of his brutality to her; to pay to the uttermost!

"I have nothing to say to you," she said as stiffly as she knew the way. "I care to hear nothing you have to say. I have tolerated all that I mean to tolerate from you."

Her bearing, no less than her words, astonished him. For the first time he saw what it was that she held in her hands. She had been gathering up her own little personal effects; a tiny parcel of silken things, comb and brush, trifling feminine odds and ends. He stared at her wonderingly.

"I don't understand—"

Gloria treated him to cool laughter.

"You will in a minute. I am going."

"Going? You? In God's name, *where?*"

Deep silence answered him. He frowned at her in puzzled fashion a moment; then, suspecting the truth, since his racing mind could hit on no other possible explanation of her manner, he dropped to the fireside the things in his hands and went swiftly to the cave's mouth. He looked out into the storm, his eyes questing in all directions. Nothing. Only the thickening storm, the ridges dim beyond the swirl of snow—

Then he saw. For a long time he stood, studying it, seeking to make sure. What he saw was beaten down by the falling snow, dissipated by the wind, gone entirely over and again only to rise like a shapeless ghost of disaster. It was a column of smoke. Some one had encamped no great distance away; on the same stream, hidden only by the windings of the gorge. Some one? Why, then, Gratton and Brodie and their crowd, after all! He glowered angrily toward the faint smudge of smoke. Then he swung about and came back to Gloria's side.

"You saw that smoke?" he demanded. "You plan on going to them?"

"Yes," cried Gloria. She sprang up and confronted him angrily. "Yes to both questions."

"You know who they are, then?"

"No; but that doesn't matter."

"Which means as plain as print," he said thoughtfully, "that you would go to any man to be rid of me." He laughed unpleasantly and Gloria's anger flared the higher.

"Do you know," he said presently, "that they are probably Gratton and Swen Brodie and their outfit?"

"What of it?" asked Gloria, erect and defiant.

"You know that Gratton has set out to ruin your father? That he's a double-dealing scoundrel? That Brodie is worse? That neither is hardly the sort for a girl to trust herself to in a place like this?"

"I am not given much choice," Gloria informed him with high insolence.

"That's a fact," he conceded with a grunt.

He'd give a thousand dollars right now to be well rid of her; yes, and have Gratton and Brodie and the rest of them come on looking for any sort of a row that suited their ilk. He told himself that with savage emphasis, but he asked: could he let her go?

"Before I go," said Gloria when she thought that he had nothing further to add, "I want to say just one thing: father has always considered you his best friend. I shall lose no time in telling him what you really are."

Gloria's remark, coming just when it did in King's perplexity, settled his decision firmly on him. The girl was a vicious little fool; so he was determined to think of her unequivocally. But she was, after all, Ben Gaynor's daughter and, furthermore, the apple of Ben's eye. She was in King's keeping; he had been eminently to blame for bringing her here, his was the responsibility. Gratton's eye was the sort that soils a woman.

"You are *not* going," he said suddenly, turning upon her. "I won't allow you to put yourself in Gratton's or Brodie's dirty hands."

A quick light was in her eyes, a quick spurt of satisfaction in her heart. In King's decision she read the assurance that he was still madly in love with her, that now his jealousy stirred him. She lifted her chin and with her little bundle under her arm came forward, walking confidently.

"Stand aside, please," she commanded. "I am going, I tell you."

Again sensing the familiarity of the battlefield she felt an almost serene confidence, believing herself easily mistress of the situation. So much must have been plain to King from that "Stand aside, please," which Miss Gloria Gaynor of last week might have addressed to a porter, were it not that just now King's thought was not bended to trifles. When she came to his side and he did not stir, she sought to brush by him. There was no hesitation in the way in which he put out his hand and held her back.

"There can be only one captain to an expedition in adventure," he told her seriously. "I have been elected to the job. You'll pardon me if I put matters into one-syllable words? Until we are well out of this, if we are ever out at all, you will have to do what I tell you. You are not going to desert ship."

She stared at him speechlessly. Then:

"By what right do *you* issue orders to *me*?" she cried.

"Let us say," he returned in the coin of her own harshness, "by the old right of a husband. If that isn't sufficient you can add to it: by the time-honoured right of the lord and master! For that is just precisely what I intend being until I can turn you over to your dawdling set in the city again. Wait a minute," he added sternly, as he saw her lips opening to a rush of words. "I would be glad to have you go were conditions less exacting.

Now I have thought matters over and it appears essential that certain of our marriage vows be remembered. You don't have to love or honour, but by thunder you are going to obey! Reversion to an ancient order of things, eh? Well, the world was better then, largely in that women were worth a man's while. Further, for my part, I fully intend to keep my obligation of protecting you against your own foolishness, the storm, Gratton, Brodie, and the devil himself. And, finally, I mean to keep my promise to your father. He sent me to get Gus Ingle's gold; it's here. So is Gratton with his cut-throat crowd. I will in all probability have my hands full. But, once and for all, you stick with me. Where," he concluded with the last jeer, "the wife's place should be!"

Gloria tried to stare him down, to wither him with the fire of her scorn, to brave by him. But the man, all emotion having receded from his eyes, was once more like so much rock, but rock endowed with dormant power of aggression. She felt as though she had to do with a great poised boulder which offered no menace so long as she let it alone, but which needed but an unwary step of hers to destroy its equilibrium and thus bring it crashing down upon her, crushing her. She began by wondering if she had mistaken his look just now when she had leaped to the triumphant decision that he loved her; she ended by feeling hopeless and tired and uncertain of all things. To keep him from noting how she was trembling she went hastily back to the roll of bedding and dropped down to it. On the instant it became clear to her that physically King was the master. To her, before whom difficulties had heretofore invariably melted, it seemed equally clear that there must be a way out of an unbearable situation. So now, for the first time, she began a certain logical line of thought, seeking to shape her own plans.

"Please listen to me seriously," King said quietly to her. "I won't talk long to you. Your father is on the edge of bankruptcy. He is temporarily out of the running—at the hands of the very men you want to go to. He counts on me for what is in Gus Ingle's caves. I have found at least a part of it and I honestly believe that it is in your hands and mine to pull Ben through and leave him a rich man on top of it. Gratton and Brodie are down there; they'll clean us out if they can. The stake is big enough for them to stop at nothing short of murder, and I am not oversure they'd stop there. Gus Ingle's crowd didn't, and I don't know that men have changed much in half a hundred years."

"I am listening," said Gloria coolly when he paused.

"Here's the point: this is treasure-trove; we got here first. It is up to us to hold it. Can I count on you? You don't happen to have any love for me; well, you shouldn't have any for Gratton or Brodie, either. And you know that you can trust yourself to me. Can I count on you sticking on the job, your father's and your own job as much as mine, until we make a go of it?"

Gloria's logical thinking had barely begun, and as yet had not had time to progress. Her spite was lively and bitter. In her distorted vision, blurred by passionate anger, she cried out quickly:

"So, now that the odds are against you, you come cringing to me, do you?" Again she was misled into fancying that she held a whip-hand over him. "Answering your question, I would trust Mr. Gratton any day rather than you. He, at least, is not quite the brute and bully that you are."

King was hardly disappointed.

"At least you have given a straight answer," he muttered. "That is something."

Now he shaped his plans swiftly and carefully, knowing where she stood. It was characteristic of him that, once having seen clearly his own responsibility toward a foolish girl, he did not seek to simplify his own difficulty by ridding himself of her. Henceforth he would merely consider her his chief handicap, with him but against him. He consoled himself with the whimsical thought that there was never a proper treasure-hunt that did not carry traitorous mutineers on the questing ship.

CHAPTER XXII

And so, after all, he and Gloria were not alone in the mountains; that other crowd was still to be reckoned with. King stood at the cave's mouth, frowning into the ever-thickening smother of the storm. Their smoke was gone again, beaten down, hidden behind the snow-curtain. But they were there, at no very great distance. Thus, then, they knew something. Just what? Here was the matter of his perplexity; did they know all that he did? Or had they merely such a hint as would lead them as close as this? Or had they followed his trail?

He grew impatient with seeking to speculate. It struck him clearly and forcefully that he had but one thing to do: to trust that they did not have such full information as had fallen into his hands and to see to it that he gave them no help. Though they should come close, very close, still that which he had found might remain hidden from them. There lay his work; to do all that he could to hide Gus Ingle's gold. First he would bring with him more than the two nuggets; all that he felt he could manage to carry with the rest of his necessary load. Enough to help Ben Gaynor over a crisis; enough raw gold to slam down before some San Francisco capitalist, together with a tale which would make any man eager to stake the owner to what loan he asked. With that he'd seek to get back to the open. He would get provisions, snow-shoes, a dog-team, if necessary, a couple of trusted men to come with him; he would be back here within the week. But first, before he went, he would strive to make as sure as a man could that Brodie's crowd did not find the golden hoard.

He went a second time far back into the darkness of the further cave, carrying a smoking torch as before, vanishing from Gloria's eyes. She was alone; nothing stood between her and the cave's mouth; she was free to go! He must have thought of that. He was giving her her chance. She had but to snatch up the few things she meant to take with her, to go out, to find her way down the cliffs—She shuddered. She was afraid! Did he know that, too? Had he thought of that? She moved back and forth restlessly; at one instant she was sure that she would go, only to be certain of nothing before another second passed. How soon would he return? Would he hurry after her, would he bring her back forcibly?... She went where she could look out; the column of smoke had disappeared; the wind tore at her in mighty gusts. She hesitated and time passed.

How long he was gone she did not know. She only knew that she had done nothing when at length he returned. There was a look of grim satisfaction on his face; whatever he had gone to do he had done in a manner to please him. She noted that his coat was off; that in it, as in a bag, he carried something heavy.

"This goes with us wherever we go," he announced triumphantly. "It's a big breathing spell for Ben Gaynor." He dumped it out; there were other lumps like the two he had brought back the first time. She wondered dully if that grimy stuff were gold! She watched him while he emptied a provision-bag and thereafter dropped into it the stuff he had brought in his coat. On top of it went the articles of food.

"If you can whip up enough endurance for the work ahead of us," he announced impersonally, "we stand a good chance of getting out of this. Otherwise, we stand a whole lot better show of being caught here and freezing and starving to death."

Gloria shook visibly. Nervousness and fear and the cold were combined and merciless. Her look sped from King's face to what she could see of the snow-storm.

"But we'll wait," she asked in utter, weary meekness, "until this horrible storm is over?"

"One never knows about a storm like this," he told her. "It may blow itself out soon and it may keep on for a long time. Now, it's beginning to pile up in the drifts, to hide the trails, to make going harder every minute. As it is we'll have our work cut out for us; if this keeps up all afternoon and all night ..." He shrugged.

"You mean that then we couldn't get out at all?" she asked sharply.

He looked down on her thoughtfully. "I don't know," he replied slowly, "whether you could make it then or not. I am more or less used to this sort of thing and you are not. I figure that we ought to take no more long shots than we have to. If we start right now and have any luck we can make several miles before night and camp in some of the thick timber. We'd be as well off there as we are here and just that much nearer the outside. If the weather allowed us to travel at all we could be back at your father's place in four or five days at the longest. And," he added significantly, "we have food to last us just about that long."

Gloria sprang up hastily. "Quick," she cried. "Let's hurry."

King nodded and began his preparations. Into the squares of canvas he rolled everything they were to take with them, and he took no single article which he judged was not absolutely necessary. One small frying-pan and one light aluminium pot, with single knife, fork, and spoon, constituted all in the way of cooking utensils. With jealous eye he judged the weight, bulk, and worth of every other article, whether it be a tin of fruit or a slab of bacon. Those delicacies, which his love for Gloria had prompted him to bring with them, he now placed at one side, to be left behind. Bacon, to the last small scrap and fat-lined rind, coffee, to the once-boiled dregs in the coffee-pot, he packed carefully. Then, his roll made and drawn tight, he took up the discarded articles and hid them under some loose dirt in a remote, black corner of the cave. Ten minutes later he had gotten first his pack, then Gloria, safely down the cliffs, and they started. Head down, silent, like two grotesque automatons, they trudged on. They crossed on the fallen cedar, they climbed out of the gorge on the far side, they fought their way on.

Several times King turned. But she soon saw it was not to look at her; his glance passed down the long canon toward the spot where they had seen the smudge of smoke. She had come near forgetting that other men were near; she had no interest in them now. King had brought her here; King must take her safely back to the world which she had forsaken so stupidly. The obligation was plainly his; the power seemed his no less.

As Gloria fought her way along she was upborne at every step by the expectation of coming presently to their horse, of being placed in the saddle, and of having nothing to do from then on but hold to the pommel and have King lead her on to an ultimate safety. The progress would be long and the way little less than an adventure in hell to her; but at least hers would have become a slightly more passive part and she would be moving on toward the luxury of four walls and a maid and warm comforts. So when they came to the spot where King had tethered his horse, and there was no horse there, Gloria looked her blank, stupefied bewilderment, and then simply collapsed. She dropped down in the snow, her face in her hands, too weary and heartbroken to sob aloud. King stared about him with an almost equal consternation.

Leaving Gloria where she lay inert in the snow, King put down rifle and pack and hurried down into the hollow where he had tethered his horse. Five minutes of reading the signs in the snow told him the story. He had been right; his venture from the beginning had been loaded to the guards with bad luck. There was the end of the broken tie-rope; there the tracks showing the way Buck had gone, in full, headlong flight. The rope was stout and would have broken only were the animal terrified. If frightened, then there had been something to cause fright. Again, since the horse fled straight down the slope, that something startling it would have been at some point directly above. King turned and mounted to the ridge top again. Here were other tracks, all but obliterated by the snow which had fallen since they were made. A bear had come up over the ridge; had frightened the horse into breaking its tether and running. And the equally startled bear had turned tail and raced off the other way. Both animals were probably a dozen miles off by now; the bear, perhaps, twice that distance.

King came back slowly and sat down on his pack. From Gloria's dejected figure he looked to his watch, from his watch again to the four points of the compass. His lips tightened. The afternoon was passing and the dark would come early.

"Are you up to crowding ahead on foot?" he called to Gloria. "If you have the nerve we can really make better time that way, anyhow, from now on. Can you do it?"

At first she did not try to answer. But when he shouted to her again, his voice hard with anger, she moaned miserably:

"I am sick; I am dying, I think. I can't go on."

King grunted disgustedly.

He let Gloria lie where she was until she had rested. Then he went to her and put his hands under her arms and lifted her to her feet. She was limp and pale, her eyes shut, her lashes looking unusually black against the pallor of her pinched cheeks.

"We'll go back to the cave for the night, after all," he told her quietly. "It's the inevitable, and that's one thing there's no sense bucking against. Stand up!"

But the slight figure in its boyish garb drooped against him; Gloria's head moved the slightest bit in sidewise negation; her pale lips stirred soundlessly.

"What?" asked King.

"I can't," came her whisper.

He judged that here was no time for foolishness, but rather the time for each one to do his part if the two of them lived to make all of this an unpleasant memory.

"You've got to," he informed her crisply. "I can't carry you and the pack and rifle and everything, can I? I am going back; the rest is up to you. Do you want to lie here and die to-night?"

"I don't care," said Gloria listlessly.

He looked at her curiously. As he drew his hands away she slipped down and lay as she had lain before. He turned away, took up his pack and gun, set his back square upon her, and trudged off toward the only shelter that was theirs. Along the ridge, buffeted by the wind, half blind with the flurries of stinging hail with which that wind lashed him as with countless bits of broken glass, he did not turn to look behind him; not until he had gone fully half of the way to the cave. Then he did turn. He could not see her following as he had pictured her. He dropped his burden and went back to her. She lay as he had left her, her face whiter than he had ever seen it, her eyes shut, certain small blue veins making a delicate tracery across the lids.

He had meant to storm at her, to stir her into activity by the lashings of his rage. But instead he stooped and gathered her up into his arms and carried her through the storm, shielding her body all that he could. And as he stooped and as he moved off he was growling deep down in his throat like a disgruntled old bear. When it came to clambering down and then up the cliffs Gloria obeyed his commands listlessly and as in a dream, lending the certain small aid that was necessary. Even so, the climb was hard and slow, and more than ever before filled with danger. But in the end it was done; again they were in Gus Ingle's cave. King built a fire, left Gloria lying by it, and went back for his pack. When he returned she had not moved. He made a bed for her, placed her on it so that her feet were toward the fire, and covered her with his own blanket. Then he boiled some coffee and made her drink it. She obeyed again, neither thanked him nor upbraided him, and drooped back upon her hard bed and shut her eyes. Here was a new Gloria, a Gloria who did not care whether she lived or died. With a quickening alarm in his eyes he stood by the smoky fire, staring at her. Uninured to hardship, her delicate body was already beaten; with still further hardship to come might she not—die? And what would Mark King say to Ben Gaynor, even if he brought back much raw red gold, if it had cost the life of Ben Gaynor's daughter?

She did not stir when he came to her and knelt and put his hand against her cheek. He was shocked to learn how cold she was. Lightly he set his fingers against her softly pulsing throat; it was cold, like ice. Plainly she was chilled through. As he began unlacing her boots a curiously bitter thought came to him. She was his; the marriage service had given her to him with her own willingness; his wife. And now he was doing for her the first intimate little thing. He drew off her boots and stockings and found that her feet were terribly cold. He wrapped them in a hot blanket and hastened to set a pot of water on the coals. While the water warmed he knelt and chafed her feet between his palms, afraid for a moment that they were frozen. Finally, while he bathed them in steaming water, the dead white began to give place to a faint pinkness, like a blush, and again he put the blanket about them.

She had not moved. When a second time he laid his hand against her throat the cold of it alarmed him. He hesitated a moment; then, the urgent need being more than evident, he began swiftly to undo her outer garments. The boyish shirt he unbuttoned and managed to remove; it was wet through, and stiff with frost. He noted her under-garments, silken and foolish little things, with amazement; she had known no better than to wear such nonsensical affairs on a trip like this! Good God, what *did* she know? But he did not pause in his labours until he had slipped off the wet clothing. Then he wrapped her in another warm blanket and placed her on her bed, her feet still to the blaze. All of the time she had seemed, and probably was, hardly conscious. Now only she opened her eyes.

"I can't have you playing the fool and getting pneumonia," he growled at her. "We've got our hands full as it is. Don't you know enough to ..."

But she was not listening. She stirred slightly, eased herself into a new position, cuddled her face against a bare arm, sighed, and went to sleep.

CHAPTER XXIII

All night King kept his fire blazing. With several long sticks and a piece of the canvas, drawing deeply upon his ingenuity and almost to the dregs of his patience, he contrived a rude barrier to the cold across the mouth of the cave. Countless times he rolled out of his own bunk, heavy-eyed and stiff, to readjust the screen when it had blown down, to put more wood on his fire, to make sure that Gloria was covered and warm, sleeping heavily, and not dead. His nerves were frayed. In the long night his fears grew, misshapen and grotesque. Within his soul he prayed mutely that when morning came Gloria would be alive. When with the first sickly streaks of dawn he went to put fresh fuel upon the dying embers he found that there was but a handful of wood left. He came to stoop over the girl and listen to her breathing. Then he descended the cliffs for more wood.

During the night winter had set the white seal of his sovereignty upon the world. The snarling wind had died in its own fierceness, giving over to a still, calm air, through which steadily the big flakes fell. Now they clung to bush and tree everywhere; the limbs had grown thick and heavy, drooping like countless plumes. Fat mats of snow lay on the level spaces, upon flat rocks, curling over and down at the edges. Where he stood King sank ankle-deep in the fluffy stuff. As he moved along the cliffs and down the slope toward a dead tree he stepped now and then into drifts where the snow was gathering swiftly. As he looked up, seeking to penetrate the skies above him and judge their import, he saw only myriads of grey particles high up, swirling but slightly in some softly stirring air-current, for the most part dropping, floating, falling almost vertically. Nowhere was there a hint or hope of cessation. The winter, a full four weeks early, had come.

In the noose of his rope he dragged up the cliff much dead wood, riven from a fallen pine. Throughout the noise of his comings and goings the girl slept heavily. He got a big fire blazing without waking her and set about getting breakfast. While he waited for the coffee to boil he took careful stock of provisions. For two people there was enough for some twenty meals, food for about a week. Time to conserve the grease from the frying-pan; to hoard the smallest bit of bacon rind. He even counted his rounds of ammunition; here alone he was affluent. He had in the neighbourhood of a hundred cartridges for the rifle. While he was setting the gun aside he felt Gloria's eyes upon him.

During the night and now, during this inventory, he had been granted both ample time and cause for his decision. He addressed her with prompt frankness.

"Inside fifteen minutes we've got to be on our way out. As we go we'll look for the horse. But, find it or not, we're going."

She lay looking up at him thoughtfully. She had rested; she resented his coolly assumed mastery; she had not forgotten that there were other men near by. But she merely said, by way of beginning:

"The storm is over, then?"

"No. But we are not going to wait. We have food for only six or seven days, at the most."

She let her eyes droop to the fire so that the lids hid them from him. It was not yet full day; it was still snowing. Gratton and the men with him would, of course, have ample supplies. She yearned feverishly to be rid of King and his intolerable domineering. She estimated swiftly that, paradoxically, her only power over him was that of powerlessness; while she lay here hers was, in a way, the advantage. On her feet, following him, he would be again to her the brute he had been coming in.

"I am tired out," she said faintly, still not looking up. "I am sick. I have a pain here." She moved her hand to her side where, in reality, she was conscious of a troublesome soreness. "I can't go on."

He stared at her. She was pale. Now that she lifted her eyes for a brief reading of his look, he remarked that they appeared unusually large and luminous. There was a flush on her cheeks. His old fear surged back on him: Gloria was going to die! So he did what Gloria had counted on having him do: put milk and sugar in her coffee and brought the cup to her; he hastened to serve her a piping-hot breakfast of crisp bacon, hot cakes and jam. He urged her to eat, and made his own meal of unsweetened black coffee and cakes without jam. Triumphantly and covertly Gloria observed all of this. Hers was the victory. Mark King was again waiting on her, hand and foot, sacrificing for her.

He allowed himself half a pipe of tobacco—tobacco, like food, was going to run out soon—and smoked sombrely. Here already was the thing to be dreaded more than aught else: Gloria threatened with illness. As Ben Gaynor's daughter, never as his own beloved wife, she had become his responsibility. She was a parcel marked "Fragile—Handle with Care," which he had undertaken to deliver safely to a friend.

"I am going to look for the horse," he told her. He got to his feet and took up his rifle. "But don't count too much on my success. All the chances are that Buck is a long way on the trail back to his stable. Blackie has probably limped back home by now. Another thing: if I don't get Buck to-day he'll be of no use to us; that is, if the snow keeps on. But I'll do what I can."

But, before leaving, he did what he could to make for her comfort during his absence. He brought up fir-boughs, making them into a bed for her. He readjusted his canvas screen, securing it more carefully, thereby making the cave somewhat more snug. And at the last he dropped a little, much-worn book at her side; she did not know he had it with him. She did not appear to note it until he had gone. Then she took it up curiously. A volume of Kipling's poems, compact and companionable, on India paper between worn covers. With a little sniff she put the book down; just the sort of thing for Mark King to read, she thought with fine scorn, and utterly stupid to Gloria. What had she to do with *The Explorer* and *Snarleyow* and *Boots* and *The Feet of the Young Men*? Less than nothing, in sheer, regrettable fact. She knew he had one other book with him, Gus Ingle's Bible! The profaned volume of a murderous, long-dead scoundrel. What a library for a dainty lady! Gloria suddenly found that she could have screamed.

She scrambled up and went to peer out around the canvas screen. No sound out there, for the wind was dead and the snow dropped noiselessly; the creek in the gorge, because what little draught there was in the air bore down the canon, sent no sound to her ears. The wilderness of crag and peak and distant forest was hostile, pitiless. She sought eagerly for some sign of Gratton. There was none; no smoke this morning denoted his camp, no longed-for figure toiled upward toward her. But he would come soon; he must. King had found the gold here; Gratton would know and come. She would wait, hoping for Gratton's coming before King's return.

Meanwhile King, making his way down the mountain slope, found that his estimate of the storm was cheerlessly correct; the fluffy stuff underfoot was in places already knee-deep and mounting steadily higher. He shook himself and growled in his throat and ploughed through it vigorously.

"A pair of webs would look like wings before long," he muttered. "Well, we'll make 'em, since we can't buy 'em."

Making his way back to the point where Buck had broken his tether, King overlooked no precaution; since he did not care to have his and Gloria's hiding-place known unnecessarily to Gratton and his following, he forsook the natural pathway and made slower, hard progress along the gorge where others would be less likely to chance upon his tracks and where the tracks themselves would soonest fill with drifting snow. Passing about many a stunted grove he came at last to the place whence Buck had fled. He knew that in the general direction indicated by the line of flight, beyond two ridges, was the valley of the giant sequoias. There a horse would find water, shelter, and grass. If he failed to find the animal there—well, then, Buck was well on the trail or lost to King in any one of a hundred places.

And always as he went, panting up and ploughing down, the steep slopes, his eyes were keen for meat, be it Douglas squirrel or bear. But the woods seemed deserted and empty; only those cheerful, impudent little bundles of feathers, the snowbirds, and an occasional, darting water-ouzel along the creeks. These he let alone, but with the mental reservation that the time might well be at hand when even such as they must be called on to keep life in him and Gloria.

He had taken on a man's-sized contract for his morning's work and drove his big body at it relentlessly. And he took his own sort of joy from it, the joy of a fight against odds, the joy of action in the open. His body was wet with sweat, but neither his ardour nor optimism were dampened; his foot came perilously near frost-bite after he slipped into the hidden water of a small stream, but he considered the accident but a part of the day's work. So, prepared by common sense for disappointment, he looked hopefully to finding the horse. And as he pushed on he pondered other likely spots to seek this afternoon or to-morrow if he did not find the animal in the sequoias.

When at last he came to the grove of big trees he was among old friends. But he knew almost as soon as he reached them that they had no word for him to-day. On his wedding morning he had planned how he would bring Gloria here, taking it for granted, in his blind infatuation, that they would mean to her what they had meant to him. Now he passed swiftly like a noiseless shadow between the gigantic boles; he did not lift his head to look at old Vulcan's lightning-blasted crest, two hundred feet in air, all but lost up there in the falling snow; he gave no thought to the thousands of years which were Majesty's and Thor's. He went with his eyes on the ground, seeking tracks of a horse. And as he had more than half expected, he found nothing. The magnificent vistas, carpeted in snow, gave him no view of anything but snow.

Later he must cudgel his brains and seek elsewhere. Now, with other work to be done, he should go back the shortest, quickest way. So he set his feet into the trail which they had made, and turned his back upon the grove. Where he crossed streams he took stock of pools; there were trout there if a man could take them. This was another matter to see about. Oh, he would be busy enough. And yet he did not loiter, and stopped only briefly and infrequently to rest.

Before returning to Gloria, King meant to look in on Brodie's camp, if only from a distance. As matters stood now there was no telling what bearing Gratton's and Brodie's actions might have later upon his own affairs. It would be well to note if the men were preparing to fight the storm out or to pack up and leave rather than take prolonged chances with the season. So, a mile below his own camp, he slipped into a grove of firs and made his unseen way toward the fringe whence he counted upon seeing what they were about. He was still moving on slowly and had had no glimpse of the men when he heard them. He stopped abruptly and listened.

They were down there, against the canon wall. Words came to him indistinctly, muffled by the thick air. The tones of the voices were unmistakable. Three voices there were, each with its own peculiarity, none of them Gratton's. First a big, booming voice; then a sharp, staccato-quick voice; thereafter a high-pitched, querulous utterance, nervous and irritable. Disagreement, if not out-and-out quarrel, had already come to camp. King moved a few paces nearer, pushed aside a low branch from which the snow dropped with little thuds, and saw the men.

There were four of them in an excited group, and slightly drawn apart, one hand at his mouth, was Gratton. The four paid no attention to him, but formed a group exclusively self-centred. Of these four one now held his own counsel, his attitude alert, his hands in his pockets, his head turning swiftly, so that his eyes were now on one speaker, now on another. Across the brief distance King could see the puffs of smoke from the pipe in his teeth. The man wore a red handkerchief knotted about his throat; its colour was as bright as fresh-spilled blood. Swen Brodie.

Now and then as a voice was lifted King caught a word; repeated several times he heard the word "bacon." Here, doubtless, was the matter under discussion. One man, he of the thin, querulous voice swung his nervous arm widely and fairly shrieked his message; it came in little puffs and was lost between. King heard him shout "bacon" and "snow" and "hell." The three expressions, so oddly connected and yet disjointed, were significant.

Gratton stood apart and gnawed at his hand; though he could not see the prominent eyes, King could imagine the look in them. Swen Brodie puffed regularly at his pipe and watched and listened intently.

Abruptly the wrangling knot of men resolved itself into two definite factions. His fellows had turned upon the shrill-voiced man, plainly in some sort of denunciation or accusation. He was the smallest of the lot, and drew back hastily, step after step, offering the knife-edge of his curses as the others clubbed their fists.

"... a lie!" he shrieked. "Fools...."

Gratton gnawed at his knuckles, Brodie puffed steadily, and the two aggressors accepted windy denial as sign of guilt. One of them sprang forward and struck; the little man whipped out a revolver and fired. The shot sounded dull and muffled; a puff of smoke hung for a moment like the smoke from the pipe, appearing methodically between the passive onlooker's teeth; the man who had struck stopped dead in his tracks. There came a second shot; then in sharp staccato succession four others, followed by the ugly little metallic click announcing that the gun had emptied itself. Before the last explosion the balancing body sagged limply and sprawled in the snow.

King's first natural impulse was to break through the brush and run forward. But his caution of the day commanded by circumstance, though never a part of the man's headlong nature, remained with him, counselling cool thought instead of hot haste. The man down was dead or as good as dead; him King could not help. So he held back and watched.

There fell a brief silence while the man who had done the shooting and the men about him, no less than the figure lying in the snow, were as motionless as so many carven statues. At last Brodie spoke heavily.

"Benny's right. Bates had it coming to him. Times like this stealing a side of bacon is worse'n murder. Bates stole it; he was going to try to double-cross us and beat it out of here. Now he's dead, and good riddance." He spat into the snow when he had done.

Benny, chattering wildly to himself now, began a hasty reloading of his revolver. The man whom he had shot, whom Brodie named Bates, lay not five steps from Benny's feet, his blood already congealing where it flushed the snow. Oddly enough, King knew personally or by repute each of the men before him with the single exception of the man who had paid in full for his own—or some one else's—crime of stealing food at a time when food meant a chance for life. To begin with, there was Swen Brodie and there was Gratton. There was

Benny, who had done the killing, a degenerate, a morphine addict, and a thorough-going scoundrel. Beyond him stood the burly ruffian of the big, awkward, bony frame, who had brought the "judge" to the log house the other night at Gratton's bidding, Steve Jarrold. Through the trees, coming up now, were two more of the ill-featured party, a swart, squat Italian, and just at his heels a ragged scarecrow of a man named Brail. It was Brail who came close enough to stoop over the fallen man.

"Dead, ain't he?" queried Benny, half-coughing over his words.

His fellows had drawn closer so that they stood in a ring about the body. One man alone held apart. Gratton's eyes were wild, void of purpose; the dead, chalky-white of his face turned a sickly greenish tinge. After a little, while no one paid any attention to him, he began a slow withdrawal, moving jerkily step by step, his dragging heels making long furrows in the snow. Then King, too, began to draw back, slipping quietly and swiftly through the screen of tree and bush, stepping in the tracks he had made coming hither, praying suddenly for further fast-falling snow to hide or obliterate the trail he had made. And for the moment he was not thinking of the gold which they, too, sought, and which he had meant to snatch away from under their noses. He thought only of Gloria. If that crowd, in its present temper, found the way to his camp— if, in one way or another, Gloria fell into their hands—then could she thank God for a clean bullet and a swift end of things.

CHAPTER XXIV

The mere fact of being absolutely alone from midday to dark would have been for Gloria an experience at any time and in any environment. Of her friends in the city there were many who had never in a lifetime known what it was to spend half a dozen consecutive daytime, waking hours in perfect solitude, catching not so much as a fleeting glimpse of a servant, a policeman, a nurse, or a street-car conductor in the echoing street. Solitude rendered rippleless by an absence of any familiar sound; neither the whisk of a maid's broom, the clang of a telephone bell, the buzz of motors, or the slamming of doors. At those intervals when King thought of her, it was to realize that she might quite naturally find discomfort in her bleak surroundings, being denied coal-grate and upholstered chair; it did not suggest itself to him that the chief discomfort would be a spirit-crushing, terrifying loneliness.

She told herself, when he had gone, that she was glad to be alone. Five minutes later she began to stir restlessly; another five minutes and already she was listening for his return. Never once during the day was there a sudden or unexpected sound, whether the snapping of a burning faggot or the scratching against the rock of a log rolling apart, or the flap of her canvas, that she did not look expectantly toward the rude door through which she thought to see him returning.

Once that her restlessness came upon her she could not remain quiet. She drew on her boots and walked up and down, casting fearsome glances toward the darkest portion of the cavern, shunning it, keeping the fire between it and herself. When she peered out across the desolate world she drew back from its bleak menace, shuddering, returning to crouch miserably by her fire, shut in between two frightful things, the black unknown of the bowels of the cave, the white horror of the brutal, insensate wilderness. And, in her almost hysterical emotional frenzy she saw back of each of them the man, Mark King, as though they were but the expressions of his own brutality.

After an hour she felt that she would go mad unless she found something to hold her mind back from those hideous channels into which it slipped so readily. She snatched up the book which King had left with her, and forced herself to read. Pages eluded her, but here and there single lines or words caught her attention as a thorny copse catches and plucks the garments of one going blindly through it. So she was arrested by the line: "*In simpleness and gentleness and honour and clean mirth.*" And this was one of the times when she threw the book down and got up and walked back and forth impatiently. It was almost as though King had left the wretched volume behind to be his spokesman in his absence; she told herself angrily that he was *not* like that, had never been like that. He was a mere brute of a man, not "*such as fought and sailed and ruled and loved and made our world.*" He was, rather, unthinkably crude and boorish and detestable.

But, rebelling at utter loneliness, she was forced again and again to the only companion at hand. She read *The Explorer*, fascinated in a shivery, uncanny way by the first line, as though a ghostly voice were whispering to her from the black corners of the cave: "*There's no sense in going further—it's the edge of cultivation.*" And later: "*I faced the sheer main-ranges, whipping up and leading down.*" Others than she had gone into the last solitudes. Others who had joyed in it and sung of it! It was as though the dead shades of those others squatted at the edges of her fire and mocked at her. Then she could fancy that it was King himself jeering, and that he cried: "*Then He chose me for His Whisper, and I've found it, and it's yours!*"

She snapped the book shut. Later she opened it to the tale of Tomlinson. She did not entirely grasp it, but she could not entirely miss what it said. She hurried on; she wondered vaguely at the call of the Red Gods; here again, seeking distraction, she was whipped back to reality. There were the lines, staring at her, as though King had rewritten Kipling:

> *"Who hath smelt wood-smoke at twilight?*
> *Who hath heard the birch log burning?*
> *Who is quick to read the noises of the night?"*

And the answer was: "Mark King." Even now it was a torturous twilight in the cave, even now she smelled wood-smoke; even now she was like one starting at the noises of the night....

"Man-stuff," she thought contemptuously. She had heard such an expression used in connection with the verses of this uncouth scribe. It did not strike her that man-stuff might well enough be woman-stuff also, being one or the other, or both, for the sheer reason that it was human. She chose to consider it merely the sort of coarse food for male mental digestion. A man's nature was not fine and intricate; rather his emotional qualities must be like stubby, blunt, callous fingers, unskilled and not highly sentient. A man lacked the psychical and spiritual and intellectual development which was that of a maid like Gloria; his joys were chiefly physical. So he cared to blaze trails like the explorer; the impact of a storm's buffeting and the low appreciation of a full stomach drew limits marking his possibilities of expansion. He was a beast, and she hated the whole sex sweepingly and superbly. In great surges of genuine sympathy her heart went out to herself.

But, after all, the moments in which her thoughts were snared away from her fears and the oppression of loneliness were few and short. From wondering what kept King she passed to bitter anger that he should desert her so; she concluded that he was doing it with malicious intent.

Repeatedly she was tempted to go forth and seek Gratton: to hunt up and down until at last she came to him. Again and again she went to the mouth of the cave and looked forth. But each time she drew back, terrified at the thought of making her way unaided down the sheer cliff wall. She sought to tell herself that she was not afraid of the snow, of being lost, of being unable to find Gratton. But she could not climb down the cliff; she knew that she would fall. Dizzy and sick, shivering with dread and cold, she turned back always.

She let her fire die down, not noticing it. Then the cold reminded her, and she worked long building another. She knew where a block of matches was; she had seen King set it carefully away. In her excitement she struck dozens of matches, dropping the burnt ends about her.

At last her fire blazed up and she warmed herself. Then she was conscious of a strange faintness and realized that she was hungry. She went to their food cache and ransacked it hastily. She opened a tin of sardines and came back to the fire with it in her hands. She had no clear conception of the deed when, half of the fish consumed, the smelly stuff revolted her and she hurled the remaining part into the bed of coals.

* * * * *

King stamped the loose snow from his boots and came in. Gloria stood confronting him, tense, rigid, white-faced, her hands stiff at her sides. She wanted to cry out, to upbraid him, all of her fear of the day turned into molten anger, but at the moment her strength failed strangely, her heart seemed to be stopping, she choked up. The surge of her relief, like a suddenly released current, impacting with that other current of her unleashed anger, made of her consciousness a sort of wild, fuming whirlpool. Nothing was clear to her just then save that Mark King had come back and that, no doubt, his heart was filled with jeers; she could not read the expression of his shadowed face, but fancied it one of mockery.

King was tired throughout every muscle of his body. He set down his rifle, tossed his hat aside, and slumped down by the fire. Coming in from the storm-cleansed open he sniffed at the closeness of the cave. It was not alone the smell of smoke; his first thought was that Gloria had been cooking something. Then he noted the sardine-can. With a stick he raked it out of the coals. And now Gloria could read his expression well enough as he jerked his head up.

"In God's name," he demanded, "what do you mean by a thing like that? Are you stark, raving mad?"

For a moment she was at a loss to understand what had enraged him. The act of tossing the distasteful food into the fire had been purely involuntary; her conscious mind had hardly taken cognizance of the fact. When it dawned upon her what he meant, her own anger was still greater than her sense of her act's folly. But she found no ready answer to his accusation. She was not without reason; in their present predicament she was a fool to have done a thing like that; she could hardly believe that she had done it. And so she stared impudently at him and held her silence, and finally, with an elaborate shrug of disdainful shoulders, she turned her back on him.

But King flung to his feet and set his hands on her two shoulders and swung her about. Her eyes opened widely.

"Listen to me," he said angrily. "I am going to talk plain to you. You are a fool, a downright, empty-headed silly fool. What you have destroyed in wanton carelessness would have kept the life in a man a whole day. Haven't you sense enough to see it's going to be nip and tuck if we ever get out of this? You've shown yourself, from start to finish, a miserable cheat; there's no trust to be put in either your judgment or your intentions. Be still," he commanded, as she sought to wriggle out of his grasp, to avoid the direct blaze of his eyes. "I am going to do what I can for you; to see you safe through this, if I can. Not because you are anything to me, but just because you are Ben Gaynor's, and he is my friend. Understand?"

"You are hurting me," she said in defiance. "Take your dirty hands off."

"When I am done," he returned curtly. "I am going to stick to you and see you through, I tell you. But I am not going to have you throw all of our chances away by dumping grub into the fire. If you do one other brainless thing like that, and I catch you at it, I am going to tie you up, hand and foot, and keep you out of mischief."

"You wouldn't dare—"

But she knew better; he would dare anything. He *was* of the type that fought and sailed and ruled. Now, when having spoken his mind he turned away from her, she stared after him and watched him as he dropped back by the fire. Then she went slowly to her bed to hide her trembling, and lay down.

Presently she heard him stirring. She did not turn her head to look at him. But she knew that he was busied with supper. She smelt coffee, heard the clash of tin cup and plate, and realized that he was eating. She wondered if he had forgotten her. After a while she moved just a trifle and furtively; he had put away his dishes and was filling his pipe. And he knew that she was watching him.

"No," he said to her unspoken question. "I am not going to cook for you any more. I have had a hard day of it, doing the man's work. Had you done the woman's you would have had supper ready for me."

He lighted his pipe with a splinter of burning pine. Then for the first time he saw the waste of scattered matches on the floor. From them he looked to her in an amazement so sheer that it left him no word of expostulation. The suspicion actually came to him that the girl was mad. It was scarcely conceivable that a perfectly sane individual could do the things which she had done.

She saw him get up and begin gathering up all of the foodstuff. He carried it to the back of the cave, where he passed out of her sight in the dark. He was gone ten minutes and came back empty-handed. He made the second trip, after which there was left on a shelf of rock only half a dozen matches and enough food for one scanty meal. This Gloria ignored.

"Do you think," she said contemptuously, "that what you have hidden back there I couldn't find?"

"You could find it but you won't," he returned with quiet assurance that jerked the question from her:

"Why?"

"Because," he grunted contemptuously, "you are too much of a coward to go back there to look for it."

And in her heart she knew that here was but the mere truth. For, why was she not already in Gratton's camp? Her opportunity had come and gone—because she had been afraid.

CHAPTER XXV

King awoke filled with resolve and definite purpose. It was pitch dark, but he sensed the coming of wintry dawn. He drew on his boots and went to look out. It was still snowing, heavily, steadily, implacably. He kicked the loose fluffy stuff underfoot.

"The biggest storm in twenty years," he told himself. "And if any one of us in these mountains come out of them alive he'll have something to talk about. It's the real thing."

He went grimly about his fire-making, fixed purpose crystallizing to the smallest detail. Again he must seek immediately to locate his horse; one could eat horseflesh if driven to it. He must try to get game of some sort. And every lost hour meant lessened chances of his killing forest meat; deer and bear and the smaller folk, if they had been caught napping, would be scurrying out of the mountains long before now; soon the solitudes would be utterly barren and empty. He went to Gloria's bed.

"You'd better get up," he said briefly. "Time to start the day. While we eat I want to talk with you."

She awoke slowly, blinked at him, and only drew her blanket higher about her chin.

"I am tired," she answered petulantly. "Don't you realize that a girl..."

"I realize," he cut into her sleepy expostulation, "that you are weak and frightened and useless. And that those are three of the many things you've got to get over the shortest way if you don't want to die here."

"I don't know that I care to live," she began, turning with her old instinct toward an attitude which before now had robbed him of his harshness. But his plan was set in cold determination, and he cut her short again.

"If you don't care, I do. And I am going to pull you through with me, if for no other reason simply because I have set out to do it, and am not going to lie down on the job. What's more, you've got to do your share. I have built the fire; will you get up?"

"No," she flashed out at him, thoroughly awake now. "I won't!"

He stooped, caught the corner of her blankets, and whipped them off. Instinctively, she sought to draw the under-bedding over her, forgetting that she had not undressed.

"You brute!" she screamed at him.

"Get up," he told her sternly, "or, by heaven, I'll make you!"

She saw his face plainly now as his crackling fire burned higher. It was hard, his eyes were ominous. She hesitated and saw in his eyes and in a stir of his body that he was going to jerk her to her feet. She flung out of bed at that and upon the far side from him.

"Get your boots on," he ordered. "I don't want you catching cold from idiotic carelessness, and I won't have you going sick on my hands. For the first and last time I'll admit that I don't enjoy driving you like a cursed galley-slave. But I'll do it, and do a thorough job of it, if you force me to it."

She drew on her boots hastily and came to the fire and laced them. He was a new man this morning and relentless. She was afraid of him after a new, bewildered fashion.

"I never saw a storm worse than this," he told her. He had cooked the breakfast because he was in a hurry, and did not care to trust her wasteful fingers with their already precious food. "There must be two or three feet on the level places by now; ploughing through snow like that is killing work for a man, and you wouldn't last at it ten minutes." He had no intention of speaking contemptuously; she knew that his thought was not trifling with such matters as her feelings. He was merely indulging in plain talk. "We have enough food for a few days. After that, if we stuck on here and did not find more somehow, we'd die like dogs. Therefore we are going to get ready to beat it out the first chance we get."

"But if I wouldn't last ten minutes, as you so elegantly put it?"

"Not as you are; not as the snow is. But I'm hoping that before it's too late we'll get clear weather, a sun, a thaw, and freezing nights. Then we could tackle it on the crust. And your job now is to get yourself ready for that one chance."

Her anger at the indignity already done her whipped out the sarcasm:

"By getting ready, I suppose you mean for me to pack my trunk and order the expressman at the door?"

He looked at her with a long, impersonal stare which bewildered her; she was at utter loss to read its meaning until he spoke:

"You are to pack what endurance you've got into your muscles. You are to make up your mind to call up all of the grit that's in you. You'll need both. And you are to quit lying around and getting weaker every day; you've got little enough time to harden yourself, so you are going to take on the job right now."

She gasped, incredulous. He nodded sternly.

"Gloria," he said tersely, "I am going to do all that I can for both of us. You are going to do all that you can. That is final."

She bit her lips and gave him her scornful silence. The blood was red and hot in her cheeks.

She ignored him when he called crisply that breakfast was ready. There were limits to her obedience, she thought rebelliously. To be told do this, do that, to arise when this man's body was rested, to eat when his stomach was empty, was intolerable. King looked at her and had the understanding to grasp something of her thought. So he explained:

"I want you to come outside with me. You'll find it hard work. It would be a first-rate idea if you'd fortify your strength by the little bit of nourishment which we can afford to take. No? Well, I'm sorry.—Here." He offered her the pieces of a sack he had cut in two for her. "Tie those about your feet to keep them from freezing."

"When I want your advice, I'll ask for it," she retorted icily.

"Very well," he answered. "And I can't make you eat if you don't want to. After all, perhaps you are not hungry." He set aside her portion. "You'll have the appetite for that when we get back."

She had the appetite now. But she would prefer to starve, she honestly thought at the moment, than eat when he told her to eat. Now he finished in silence. She saw him glance at his watch. Her heart seemed scarcely to stir in her breast; then slowly it began to beat, swifter and swifter, hammering wildly. He had said that she was going out with him; what he promised to do, she realized again, he would do, if it were humanly possible. She wanted to run, run anywhere, just to be lost to him. And yet she stood stock-still and rigid, while her heart hastened and leaped and her mind sought to grasp the thing to do. She must go with him, do what he told her like a slave, as he had said, or he would make her. Her reason said directly: "You will go without a word." And yet, when he arose to his feet and knocked his pipe out and looked at her, her reason fled before the flood of the passionate wilfulness of the old Gloria, and she cried shrilly:

"I won't! I won't! I am not your slave and I am not going to jump at your bidding! You can't make me; you shan't make me. *I won't!*"

He had hoped for better than this. He came closer and looked intently into her eyes, seeking to measure what endurance and steadfastness and stubbornness were hers. But her eyes showed him only glimpses of a storm-tossed soul.

"I will make you," he said harshly. "So help me God, Gloria, I will make you. And I am through talking; I am sick of talk. Come with me."

She drew back and back in white-lipped fury.

"You don't *dare*...."

"Listen to me! We are down to bare elementals now; can't you see it? It is no question of what we'd like to do or dislike. It is a question of life and death. If to let you have your way were anything other than suicide, I'd let you have it. If I thought that you would listen to reason, I'd stop to reason with you. But as things are, I've got nothing left me but tell you what to do; and you've got to do as I say."

"My life is my own, to do with it as I please. I do not please to obey your commands."

Her tortured heart surged up in wild triumph as he turned; it sank sickly as he came back. He had a piece of rope in his hand, the heavy half-inch rope which had served to tie a horse.

"You would tie me!" she gasped. "Me!"

"No," he said tersely. "As though you were any other fractious animal refusing discipline when refusal means death, I am going to whip you!"

"God!" screamed Gloria. "Oh, my God!"

For again he but said simply the thing which he meant to do. And she knew. Yet the consummation was monstrous, unthinkable. She would not believe it; at the last minute his lifted arm would fail him; God Himself would wither it; undreamed rescuers would come; the earth would open ... *something* would save her from this humiliation which would kill her.

"While I count three," said King. And steadily, though there was a pallor on his own face, which should have told her the terrible relentlessness of his intention, he counted: "One, two, three."

She put her face into her hands and shivered, and felt the fear of one under the flashing guillotine. She willed to move, to obey, at this tardy second, but something within her, stronger than herself, held her back. "*I won't!*" she screamed. The blow fell swiftly. The rope cut through the air with vicious sibilance and fell across the stooped shoulders. The pain was immediate, hot and searing, and Gloria shrieked—once only—and grew still. She dropped her hands and looked at him, her face as white as a dead girl's, her eyes as unfathomable as a maniac's. She who had never been whipped in all of her life, she whose soft white body had been held inviolate by idolizing parents, she who had come to hold her own person as sacred as that of a high princess—to be beaten by a man! To be lashed across her shoulders with a horse's tie-rope. She, Gloria Gaynor, to have her bedding ripped off her, to be commanded to do a man's bidding—and to be whipped!

She had known fear, blind, paralysing terror. She had suffered indignity and experienced an insulted resentment that seared through her like a hot iron. She had known pain, merciless bodily pain. Now she was plunged into stupor. But that stupor was of only the fraction of a second in duration. A flash as of white fire flared through her brain. In a soul in torment something had happened. Something had been killed within her—or something had been born. A blow at a man's hand had seemed to cut through her being; it had separated body and spirit. She was conscious of the body as though she stood apart and looked down at it. He could beat that; he was stronger. The spirit rose above it—a spirit bathed in floods of fire. She was in the sudden fierce grip of such anger as kills, of such defiance as suffers death and does not yield.

"I won't go with you," she cried. "You may beat me; you may kill me if you like, unthinkable brute that you are. I will not follow you now; I will never follow one step ever. I have listened to you; now listen to me! I would rather die than be brought to safety by you. If I cannot find the way home without your help, I do not want ever to get home. I am not afraid of you or your rope. I had rather feel a clean rope across my shoulders until they were bloody than your vile hand on mine."

"You will do what I tell you to do," he said thickly. "It is the only way. I will make you."

Blazing eyes burning in a death-white face gave him his only answer. His own face now was no less white; iron-bodied as he was, he was trembling. Yet he lifted the rope. To strike the second blow. Not just to frighten her, but to strike. She read his purpose clearly, and she could not restrain a shudder of her flesh. But she did not draw back from him, and she did not cry out. She meant what she had said, or what some re-born Gloria had said for her; he might kill her, but she would not follow him.

And then Mark King, as he was about to strike, stayed his

hand at the last moment and hurled the rope far from him, and whirled about and left her.

CHAPTER XXVI

Someway he came to the base of the cliffs. He was outside; he was in the open. And yet he struggled blindly through a pit of gloom. He was conscious of but one fact in all the world; about it everything else turned and spun as sweep the bodies of the sky about the sun. He had lifted his hand against a woman. He, Mark King, had struck a woman. He had struck Gloria. His friend's daughter—Ben's daughter. He had struck her.... What had come over him? Had he gone mad? Stark, staring, raving mad? He knew all along that his nerves were on edge, raw and quivering. But no jangling nerves explained a thing like that. He, who had held himself a man, had struck a woman—a girl! A little, defenceless girl.

"My God!" he groaned.

He stumbled on. He did not know where he was going or why. He ran his hand across his eyes again and again. He didn't know why he did that; one couldn't thus wipe out a vision which persisted in his brain. He'd see her as she stood there every day and night until he died. In a sweeping revulsion of feeling he saw himself all that she had named him, a great, hulking brute. All along he had been brutal with her; he should have made due allowances; he should have been patient. He had plunged her into an existence of which she had no foreknowledge. He had looked to her for the sober sanity of maturity when he should have remembered how young she was, how little of real life she knew, how she had been driven to desperation by circumstances which crushed her; how she had gone sleepless, living on her nerves. He had held her weak and worthless and without spirit or character. And now he could only see her standing up before him, white but valiant, defying him, unafraid, welcoming death rather than yield to him. He would have given ten years off the span of his life to have the deed of one mad moment wiped clean.

It was a long time before consecutive thought returned to him. And it brought him only increased bitterness. Gloria had said that she would die here rather than have him lead her to safety. Well, he did not blame her for that. Rather, he told himself grimly, he honoured her for it. And yet, now more than ever, his and his alone was the responsibility of seeing that she went clear of this wretched existence into which he had stubbornly led her. He could not take her away against her will; he could not pick her up in his arms and carry her over a two or three days' journey! Nor could he entrust her to the only other human beings who were near enough for her to go to. What could he do? She would perish without help; hence he must help her. But how?

There was but one possible answer, and in due course of time he came to see it clearly. He must leave her, get back the shortest, quickest way to civilization, and send other men, trustworthy men, in for her. It could be done even though the storm continued. He could get a dog-team, Alaskan huskies, to be had in Truckee; he could load sledges with provisions; he could put the right man in charge and then lead the way. That would mean several days alone for Gloria; but what else was there?

And even that solution depended upon the consideration which by now was the elemental, all-essential thing; first he must find some sort of provisions with which to eke out their small supply. There was not enough in camp to sustain him while he battled with the storm for a way out and to sustain strength in her while she waited. He must first replenish the larder; otherwise they died. He must get fish in plenty or a bear or a deer. He looked at the grey, ominous sky, at the piling snow, and the chill of the wilderness struck to his heart. But at last his eyes grew hard again with determination.

In a distressed mental condition in which the only solid ground beneath him was his determination to do to the uttermost that lay within him for Gloria, he broke into mutterings, voicing aloud fragments of speech, forcing himself toward steadiness of forward-driving purpose.

"I've got to leave her.... She won't go with me. That means I've got to leave with her every scrap of food we have between us. I can go two days without eating.... I can! A man, if he's half a man, can finish his work before he buckles under.... Her one danger is Brodie. Otherwise she would be safe enough for four or five days. She's got to stick close to the cave; she must not dare to set foot outside....

"But that's not enough; they might come to the cave.... The way in is not overwide; would they see it from below? They don't know where it is or they would have done as I did; they would have come to it for shelter.... No, they don't know of it. Can I close up the entrance, somehow, so that they won't find it? There are loose rocks in there.... If they *do* come this way, up the gorge, it will be hard for them to see it from below.... Even if they should find it, I can show her where to hide. Way in the back. There's a place there.... I can get out in two days; back in two days. Somehow. Allow five days to cover accidents. Five days; she can stick it out five days. If I don't take a scrap of her food away from her.... Oh, I can make it; it is up to me to make it. I'll get a fish sooner or later—or a rabbit.... A man can eat his boots."

*   *   *   *   *

After a long time he went back to the cave. He knew now just what he would do, since it had become clear to him that there was but one thing to be done. Gloria faced him as he came in; she marked how he walked, like a very tired man. Her head was up, there were spots of colour in her cheeks; in her eyes was a new look. She had found herself. Or she was finding herself? Her spirit had risen undaunted in a crisis; in a clash of wills hers had not gone down before his. Rather it had been hers that had triumphed. She might know fear again, but the time was past and dead when she would bow meekly before a man's bidding. So she told herself, while with head erect she awaited his speech.

He began, saying very simply what he had decided must be said. He did not swerve for the useless words "I am sorry." He knew that she did not expect them, would not answer them. What he had done was monstrous and unpardonable; hence a man would not ask pardon. By his own act they were set as far apart as two beings inhabiting two widely separate worlds. It remained for him merely to instruct her concerning what she must do; then to find the way to bring her back safely to her father. Thereafter? There the haze crept in again; he would go away, far from the Sierra, far from California, to some corner of the world where no man who had ever known Mark King would see him again. At that moment he could have died very gladly, just to know that she was once more among her own people, and that so far as he was concerned life was a game played out and ended.

Now that he spoke again, his voice was no longer harsh and stern, but gentle rather. Gentle after a steady and matter-of-fact fashion that was infinitely aloof. He could not know how impersonal his utterance sounded in her ears, since he did not fully realize how at the moment he held himself less an individual addressing another than as the mouthpiece of fate.

"The first thing in the morning," he told her, "I am going over the ridge and to the headwaters of the other fork. I have been thinking of that country a good deal; it's a little far and hard going and I'll burn up a lot of fuel making the trip, but I've got a hunch a bear's in there. The one that stampeded Buck may have circled around that way. And I'm going to play every hunch I get, good and strong. It will probably be dark before I get back."

She thought that he had finished. But presently, in the same strangely quiet voice, he continued: "I may even be gone all night. If I am it will be because I am playing the last card.... You have said that you would rather be dead than go with me. I believe you meant that." Again he paused. Gloria did not again lift her eyes from the fire; did not speak. King sighed and did not know that he had done so. "If I don't get back to-morrow night it will be because I am trying to break through to civilization. I'll outfit a party and send them in for you. I'll get through some way in two days; I'll get help back to you in another two or three at latest. You have food here to keep you alive a week, if you spin it out."

Long before he had gotten to the end of his slow speech her heart was beating wildly. The old fears surged back on her, crushing her. To be left here alone four or five days—and nights! It was unendurable! She would be dead.

"You have your choice," he went on, his voice grown still more gentle. "If you will let me help you—"

But, even while in the silence that followed she heard the rapid beating of her own heart, something stronger, more stubborn, than the Gloria of another day kept her silent.

And still he had not finished.

"Before I go I am going to do all that I can to wall up the mouth of the cave. It will make it warmer in here and—and there will be less danger of any one finding the place. You threatened once to go to those other men; *no matter what happens, you must not do that.* You don't quite understand what some men are. These happen to be the worst of a bad crowd that ever got into these mountains. They respect neither God nor man—nor woman. They are in an ugly mood; they probably have more bootleg whiskey with them than food; I did not tell you, but I looked in on their camp and saw one of them, a dope fiend named Benny Rudge, shoot one of his own friends dead, suspecting him of having stolen a side of bacon.

You would be better dead, too, than in their hands. Never forget that. They don't know if they'll ever get out of this alive; they are desperate devils.

"But with the cave walled up, they won't find you. If the worst should happen and they came here, still you could hide. I'll show you the place, far back in the cave. You could run there with your blankets and food; you could stay there, never moving. No man could find you there. They would see where we had been here, but they would have to decide in the end that we had gone, both of us.

"I'll bring you plenty of wood; I am going to make a pair of snow-shoes of a sort for me; I'll make a pair for you. I hope you won't need them." He ran his hand across his brow but continued in a moment, his voice unchanged: "I'll go out before daylight in the morning; it will take me all that is left of to-day to do what must be done first."

He turned then and went about his work. She went back to the place by the fire, terribly moved, agitated to the depths of her soul, torn this way and that. But one steady fire burned in her bosom—the newly kindled white flame of her resentment. Just yonder, where he had hurled it, a grim reminder, lay the rope.

He brought fragments of rock to the cave's mouth, the biggest he could find, boulders which he rolled from the further dark, and with which he struggled mightily as he piled them one on the other. Higher and higher he built his rude wall, placing the smaller stones at the top. And in time, after hours of labour, he had hidden the great hole as best he could, leaving only at the side a way to pass in and out which could hardly be seen from below. Across this he fixed the canvas; were that glimpsed, its grimy-white would appear but a lighter-hued streak of granite.

"If you will come with me, I will show you your hiding-place."

She lifted her head and looked at him. No word had passed

between them during the back-breaking hours of his labouring. Again, she thought swiftly, he was seeking to command, to dictate. Doubtless, in the end she would have arisen and gone with him, since to refuse were madness. But he had not waited. He had gone alone into the depths of the cavern; she heard his slow, measured steps receding; she heard them again, slow and measured, as he came back.

"It's only about thirty paces, straight back," he was saying. "My steps, remember, but shortened so that it would be about the same for you. Say thirty-five. There I have made a little pile of rocks; you can't miss it. That marks the place, just at the side of the rock pile. That's where I found the gold. There is a blind cave back there, just under this one; there's only a small entrance to it, straight down, a ragged hole in the floor, hardly more than big enough for a man to drop down through. I had it hidden by dragging a boulder over it. Now I have shoved the boulder just far enough to one side to let you go through. Also, I have set bits of stone under its outside edge so that it is fairly balanced; if you go through, a quick tug at it will topple it over to cover the hole again. There's air down there, that comes up from below. And it's a better place to be than here—if any one should come."

She shuddered. But he had not seen. There remained much to do and the hours fled so swiftly. He set to work making the clumsy snow-shoes. He imitated a crude native shoe he had once seen in Alaska; he bent willow wands he had brought from along the edge of the stream, whipping them about with narrow strips of canvas, binding other wands crosswise, making, also of canvas strips, a sort of stirrup for each foot. The last of the weak daylight passed and died gloomily and he was still at his task, bending now by his fire, working on with infinite care. The sticks, brittle with the cold weather, broke under his strong fingers; patiently he inserted others or strengthened the cracking pieces with string. His face, ruddy in the firelight, was impassive; Gloria, looking at him, saw no mere man but a senseless thing of machine levers and steel coils; something tireless and hard and as determined as fate itself.

They had made their scanty suppers; after it both were hungry. They had been hungry thus for four days. There remained coffee and sugar enough for another half-dozen meagre meals; here the affluence ended. The bacon was down to a piece of fat two inches thick and seven inches long; there was bacon grease a couple of inches deep in a tomato-can; there was a teacup of flour; there was one small tin of sardines and a smaller one of devilled meat. To-day they were hungry, to-morrow they would be a great deal hungrier, the next day they would begin to starve.... King got up and went out, down the cliffs in the dark, for a last load of wood. When he came back she was lying on her bed, her face from the light. He stood a moment looking at her. Then for the last time he spoke to her:

"If I am long gone, you understand why. It would be best to save food all you can; not to stir about much, since exercise means burning up more strength, which must be renewed and by still more food.... There is not a chance in a thousand now that those men will find this place; if they do, there is not a chance in another thousand that they will find the middle cave. You will be safe enough.... And, if I do not get back to-morrow, you will know that within three days more, or four at most, there will be a party in here to bring you out."

CHAPTER XXVII

Gloria awoke with a start. She had not heard King go, yet she knew that she was alone in the cave. Alone! She sat up, clutching her blankets about her. Objects all around her were plunged into darkness, but where the canvas let in the morning she saw a patch of drear, chill light. Full morning. Then by now Mark King was far away.

Oh, the pitiless loneliness of the world as she sat there in the gloom of the cavern, her heart as cheerless as the drear light creeping in, as cold as the dead charred sticks where last night's fire had burnt itself out. And, oh, the terrible, merciless silence about her. She sat plunged into a despondency beyond the bourne of tears, a slim, white-bodied, gaunt-eyed girl crushed, beaten by a relentless destiny, lost to the world, shut in between two terrors—the black unknown of the deeper cavern, the white menace of a waste wilderness. And far more than pinch of cold or bite of hunger was her utter solitude unbearable.

She sprang up and built a fire. Less for the warmth, though she was cold to the bone, than for the sense of companionship. The homely flames were like flames in remembered fireplaces; their voices were as the voices of those other fires; their light, though showing only cold rock walls and rude camp equipment, was the closest thing she had to companionship. She came close to the fire and for a long time would not move from it.

She went to the wall King had built, moving the canvas aside just enough to look out, and stood there a long time. A dead hush lay over the world. There was no wind; the snow in great unbroken, feathery crystals fell softly, thick in the sky, dropping ceaselessly and soundlessly. It clung to the limbs of trees, making of each branch a thick white arm, stilling the pine-needles, binding them together in the sheath which forbade them to shiver and rustle. It lay in sludgy messes in the pools of the stream and curled over the edges of the steep banks and coated the boulders; it lay its white command for silence upon the racing water. A world dead-white and dead-still. That unbroken silence which exists nowhere else as it does in the wastes of snow and which lies upon the soul like a positive inhibition against the slightest human-made sound. No wind to stir a dry twig; no dry twig but was manacled and muffled; no dead leaves to rustle, since all dead leaves lay deeper than death under the snow. Gloria's sensation as she stood as still as the wilderness all about her and stared out across the ridges was that of one who had suddenly and without warning gone stone-deaf. The stillness was so absolute that it seemed to crush the soul within her. She went back hastily to her fire, glad to hear the crackle of the flames, grateful to have the emptiness made somewhat less the yawning void by the small sound of a bit of wood rolling apart on the rock floor.

She was hungry, but she had no heart for cooking. She ate little scraps of cold food left over from last night; she nibbled at a last bit of the slab chocolate; she filled a pot with snow gathered at the cave mouth and set it on the coals to get water to drink. And again, having nothing else to do and urged restlessly to some form of activity, she hurried back to the canvas flap and watched the falling snow, hearkening to the stillness. For in the spell of the snow country one is forced to the attitude of one who listens and who hears the great hush, and who, like the enchanted world about it, heeds and obeys, and when he moves goes with quiet footfalls.

Endlessly long were the minutes. Hours were eternities. She

stood by the rock wall until she was chilled; as noiselessly as a creeping shadow she went back to her fire and shivered before it and warmed herself, turning her head quickly to peer into the dark of the hidden tunnel, turning again as quickly to glance toward her rude door, her heart leaping at every crackle of her fire; she thawed some of the cold out of her and went to look out again. A hundred times she made the brief journey.

From being lightning-swift, thought became a laborious, drugged process; her excited mind had harboured throngs of vivid visions; she had known a period of over-active mental stimulation; she had seen, as in the actual flesh, Mark King ploughing through the snow, going over ridges, pushing on and on and on. Always further away, driving on through limitless distances. She had seen him fall, his body crashing down a sheer precipice; she had seen him lying, his face turned up, the snowflakes falling, falling, falling, covering it.... She had seen him going on again; she had seen him breaking his way to the open, getting back among other men, falling exhausted, but calling upon them to go back to her. She had seen men hurrying; dog-sleds harnessed; packs of provisions; men on snow-shoes. She had seen them coming toward her across the miles. Some one else was coming, too. It was big Swen Brodie, his face horrible. There was a rabble at his back. It was a race between these men and those other men. She had felt that Brodie was putting out a terrible hand toward her; she had seen other men leap upon him, dragging him back.... King had returned; King and Brodie were struggling.... Then again she saw King, fighting his way through the snow, going for help. She had tried to reason; he could be only a few miles away....

But at last a tired brain refused to create more of these swift pictures. She stared out and did not think. She merely felt the weight of the silence, the weight of utter loneliness. With dragging feet she returned to her fire and looked into the coals, and from them to the further dark, and from it back to the pale light about her canvas. She sank into a condition of lethargy. The silence had worked a sort of hypnosis in her.

Briefly, in her wide-opened eyes there was no light of interest. Vaguely, as though she had no great personal concern in the matter, she wondered how long it would be before one left alone here would go mad. And would the mad one shout shrieking defiance at the silence?—or go about on tip-toe, finger laid across his lips?

The morning wore on. At one moment she was plunged into a deep, chaotic abyss that was neither unconsciousness nor reverie, and yet which strangely partook of both. A moment later she was vaguely aware of a difference; it was as though a presence, though what sort she could not tell, had approached, were near her, all about her. That instant of uncertainty was brief, gone in a flash. She turned and a little glad cry broke from her lips. A streak of sunshine lay across the rocks at the cave's mouth.

It was like the visit of an angel. More than that, like the face of a beloved friend. She ran to her canvas and looked out. There was a rift in the sombre roofing of clouds; she saw a strip of clean blue sky through which a splendid sun shone. And yet the snow was falling on all hands, snow bright with a new shining whiteness. She watched that little strip of heaven's blue eagerly and anxiously; was it widening? Or were the clouds crowding over it again?

But though this seemed the one consideration of importance in all the world for her just now, in another instant it was swept from her mind, forgotten. Far below her, down in the gorge, she saw something moving! And that something, ploughing laboriously through depths and drifts of loose fluffy snow, was a man. Now her thoughts raced again. It was King. He was coming back to her.... No; it was not King; it was Swen Brodie! She began to tremble violently. She had barely strength to draw back, to pull the canvas closer to the rocks, to strive to hide. If Brodie came now, if Brodie found her here, alone—That fear which is in all female hearts, that boundless terror of the one creature who is her greatest protector, her vilest enemy, more dreaded than a wild beast, gripped her and shook her and swiftly beat the strength out of her. But, fascinated, she clung to the rocks and watched.

The man struggling weakly against the pitiless wilderness, wallowing in the snow, seemed to make his way along the gorge inch by inch. He carried something on his back, something white under the falling snow which whitened his hat and labouring shoulders. A sack with something in it, something to which he clung tenaciously. How he floundered and battled against the high-heaped white stuff about him which held him back, which mounted about his legs, up to his waist; at times, when he floundered he was all but lost in it. He lay still like a dead man; he struggled, and began crawling on again. He stopped and looked about him—how her heart pounded then! He was looking for something, seeking something! Her!

She was so certain it must be Brodie. Yet she remained motionless, powerless to move though she remembered King's word of the hiding-place where she would be safe; she peered out, fascinated.

In time the man came closer and the first suspicion entered her mind that, after all, it might not be Brodie. He stopped; he was exhausted; he pulled off his hat and ran his hand across his face. Then, still bareheaded, he looked up. It was Gratton!

Gratton alone; Gratton looking back over his shoulder more often than he quested far ahead; Gratton in a mad attempt to make haste where haste was impossible. Now his every gesture bespoke a frantic haste. He was escaping from something. Then, what? He had left the other men; he was running away from them. She knew it as well as if he had screamed it into her ears. A sudden spurt of pity for him entered her heart; he seemed so beaten and bewildered and frantic and terrified; who, better than she, could sympathize with one in Gratton's predicament? She looked far down the gorge; she could see, like a bluish crooked shadow, the trail which he had made after him. No one else in sight! Then she forgot everything saving that she and Gratton were alone, that they had been friends, that they were bound in a common fate. She leaned as far out as she could; he was just below now; she called to him.

He stopped dead in his tracks; he jerked his head up and stared wildly; his mouth dropped open, and in the shock of the moment speech was denied him. She called again.

"You!" Had not the silence been so complete his gasping voice would have failed to reach her; as it was she barely heard it. "You, Gloria? Here? My God—have I gone mad?"

The man's villainy of so few days ago appeared now, in the biassed light of circumstance, a pardonable, a forgettable offence. He had loved her; he had wanted to marry her; he had, with that in mind, tricked her. He had taken advantage of the universal admission that in love as in war all things were fair. The ugliness of what he had done was chiefly ugly because it had lain against a background of commonplace and convention; here, at the time when no considerations existed save the eternal and vital ones, all of Gratton's futile trickery was as though it had never been. She was calling to him again, urging him to clamber up the cliff, bidding him hurry before he was seen.

"How came you here?" was all that he could find words for. "You! And *here!*"

She would tell him everything! But he must not tarry down there. He must make haste—

Her words cleared his bewilderment away; he glanced again over his shoulder. The gorge was empty of other human presence. He looked back up at her. And then, before her eager eyes, he slumped down where he stood, lying in the snow.

"I can't." She heard his voice as across a distance ten times that which separated them. In it was bleak despair. "I've gone through hell already. I am—nearly dead. I couldn't climb up there. I—Oh, my God, why did I ever come into this inferno!"

She begged, she urged. But he only turned a white face up to her and lay where he had fallen, his body shaking visibly, what with the strain he had put upon it and the emotions which only his own soul knew.

"But it is so easy," she cried to him, forgetful of her now terror at mounting up here. "I have done it. Twice. I will show you just which way, where to set your feet."

"I can't," he said miserably. "It was all I could do to get this far. I—I think I am dying—"

Again and again she pleaded with him. But he had either reached the limit of his physical endurance or, shaken and unnerved, he had not the courage to attempt the steep climb. He lay still; his eyes were shut, and to Gloria, too, came the swift fear that the man might be dying.

"I am coming to you!" she called.

She began making the hazardous descent. She did not take time to ask herself if she could make it; she knew only that she must. She set foot on the narrow, sloping ledge outside, brushing off the snow with her boot, clinging with her hands to a splinter of granite, feeling her way cautiously, careful to move inch by inch along the way down which she had gone twice with Mark King. Her fingers, already cold when she started, went numb; they were at all times either in pits and pockets of snow or gripping the rough stone that was ice-cold. Painfully but steadily she climbed down and down. She strove not to look down; she had no eyes for Gratton, who now sat upright, his jaw still sagging, and marvelled at her. A dozen times he was prepared to see her slip and fall.

After a weary time she came to the base of the cliffs. Gratton was not a dozen paces from her. He looked to her like a sick man, gaunt, hollow-eyed; unkempt, unshaven, as she had never seen him before, he was like some caricature of the immaculate Gratton of San Francisco. He did not move but looked at her in a strange, bewildered fashion. Plainly he had had no knowledge of her being here; he could not explain her presence; he was every whit as dumbfounded as he would have been had she dropped down upon him out of the sky. Seeing that he made no attempt to move, she started to come to him. She was standing upon a rock; she stepped off into the snow, and in a flash had sunk to her breast. A cry broke from her as thus, for the first time in her life, she learned what it was to seek to force a way through deep, loose-drifted snow. Feather-light in its individual flakes, in mass it made haste impossible; to push on six inches through it was labour; to come a dozen paces to Gratton was hard work. She floundered as she had seen him flounder; she threw herself forward as he had done, and, sinking with every effort, at last reached his side.

"It's you—Gloria Gaynor!" he muttered. "But I don't understand."

"I came with Mark King. The storm caught us. Just as it caught you. But you must come with me; if you lie here you will be chilled; you will freeze. Later we can tell each other everything."

He shook his head. "I can't," he groaned. "I am more dead than alive, I tell you. I have been living through days and nights of hell; hell populated by raging demons. I have been since before dawn getting here." He cast a bleak look up along the cliffs and shuddered. "I'd rather lie here and die than attempt it."

Once more Gloria was urging and pleading. But in the end she gave over hopelessly, seeing that Gratton would not budge. And it was so clear to her that he would perish if he lay here.

"There's a hole in the cliffs just yonder," Gratton said drearily. "God knows what wild beasts may be in it. But I was going to crawl in there when you called."

Then Gloria saw for the first time the opening to that cave

which in Gus Ingle's Bible had been set down as Caive number one. It was almost directly under King's cave, at the base of the cliffs. The snow came close to concealing it entirely; as it was, just a ragged black hole showed a couple of feet above the snow-line.

"Come, then," she said. "Let's see if it's big enough for a shelter. It may do as well as the other."

Gratton heaved himself up with a groan. Gloria did not wait for him, but began the tedious breaking of a path the few feet to the hole, too earnest in the endeavour even to note how Gratton came along behind without suggesting that it was the man's place to break trail. Thus Gloria came first to the lower cave. She hesitated and listened, her fancies stimulated by his suggestion of storm-driven animals, and sought to peer into the dark. She could see nothing; she heard nothing. Nothing save Gratton's hard breathing close behind her. She got a grip upon herself and made a step forward, paused, extended her arms to grope for a wall, and made another step. There was still no sound; she breathed more freely, assuring herself that save for herself the cavern was empty. She stumbled over a rock, stopped again and called to Gratton. Only now was he entering.

"Light a match," she commanded.

"My hands are dead with cold," he muttered. "I don't know if I have a match. Wait a minute."

He began a slow search. Finally she knew that he had found a match; she heard it scratch against a rock. Then she heard Gratton curse nervously; the match had broken and his knuckles had scraped along the rock.

The second match he gave to her. She struck it carefully, cupped the tiny flame with her hands, and strove to see what lay about her. The little light gave but poor assistance to her straining eyes; but she did see that there was a litter of dead limbs about her feet. She began gathering up some of the smaller branches, groping for others as her match burned out. Again Gratton searched his pockets; he found more matches and some scraps of paper. It was Gloria's hands which started the fire and placed the bits of dry wood upon it. The flames crackled; the wood caught like tinder; the flickering light retrieved much of the cavern about them from the utter dark.

"Here I stay," said Gratton. He dropped down and began warming his shaking hands. A more abjectly miserable specimen of humanity Gloria had never looked upon. He was jaded, spiritless, cowed.

But he was a human being, and she was no longer alone! Across the empty desolation he had come to her, one who had lived as she had lived, who knew another world than this, who could understand what she suffered because he, too, suffered. There came a space of time, all too brief, during which her heart sang within her. She was lifted from despair to a realm bright with hope. King had gone for succour; she had a companion to share with her the dread hours of waiting. She began a swift planning; she caught up a burning brand as she had seen Mark King do, and holding it high made a quick survey, going timidly step by step further from the entrance, deeper into the cavern. It was much like the one so high above, of what shape she could hardly guess, so many were the hollows in floor, roof, and walls, so many were the tunnel-like arms reaching further than she dared go. Gratton could not, or would not, climb to the higher cave; then why should they not make this their shelter? She would have to climb the cliffs again; but she would have to do that in any case. Once up there it would be so simple a matter to toss down blankets and food and cooking utensils; a half-hour would see her camp moved from one cave to the other. Eager and excited, she began to tell Gratton what she meant to do.

"Wait a while," he urged her. "I am terribly shaken, Gloria. I have lived through experiences which a week ago I would have thought unbearable." He shuddered; she saw that when he said he was "terribly shaken" he had not exaggerated. And in the glare of his eyes she read that, utterly unnerved, he dreaded to be left alone even while she went up the cliffs. "I would say that a man would have died—or gone mad—with the strain that I have lived through."

"I know," she said gently. "I can guess. But when you get good and warm—and rest—I will make you a hot cup of coffee—"

"I have this. It's better than coffee for me now." He untied the mouth of the bag with shaking fingers, groped through its contents, and at last brought out a flask nearly full of an amber liquid. "It's the stuff Brodie's crowd makes," he explained, unstoppering the flask. "They've got more of it than food with them, curse their bestial hearts. Stuff which, way back in ancient history, ... which means a week ago!... I'd no more have thought of drinking than I'd drink poison. But it has saved the life in me."

He put the bottle to his lips and swallowed three or four times. He sat afterward making a wry face, his full eyes blinking. But gradually a faint bit of colour made his pasty cheeks something less dead-white, and the powerful raw corn whiskey injected into his blood a little reassurance.

"Let me rest a bit and get warm?" he asked of her. "I—I'd rather you didn't leave me just yet, Gloria."

Knowing so well what it was to have raw, quivering nerves, she tried to smile at him, and saying as lightly as she could, "Why, of course; there's no hurry," began to gather what bits of wood lay about, piling them on the fire. Thus she noted where, evidently long ago, there had been another fire kindled against the wall of rock; some one else had camped here, perhaps during summer-time, and this explained the fuel wood so conveniently placed.

Meanwhile Gratton took a second pull at his flask, set it carefully aside and stood up, swinging his arms to get the blood running, beating his hands against his thighs, stamping gingerly. He began looking at her curiously. Presently he said: "Do you think we are ever going to get out of this alive?"

"Yes." Her voice rang with assurance. "Mark King has gone for help. All we have to do is wait for a few days."

His pale brows flew up.

"King? He has gone? He has left you alone here?"

Again she said: "Yes." Gratton began plucking at his lip, striding up and down now. It became obvious to her that there had been nothing wrong within him beyond what his frantic terror had done to him. Perhaps, left alone, he would have died out there in the snow; now, having already leaned on her, having her company and the hope she held out, he began to look his old self.

"Now I'll go for the things in the other cave," she suggested. And as an afterthought: "Now that you are feeling better, perhaps you will go up with me and help?"

"Why," he said, "why—of course. Yes, we'll both go."

For in his new mood, warmed by the fire and the raw whiskey, and, further, having seen that she had done the thing with no mishap, he was willing to do what before he could not do.

"Come," he said. "Let's hurry."

Along the paths they had already made it was a much easier matter to make the return trip. At the cliffs Gratton allowed Gloria to go ahead, since she knew the way up and he did not. He followed her closely, and at first with little difficulty or hesitation. The higher they climbed, however, the slower he went; once he hesitated so long that she began to believe that dizziness had overcome him and that he was coming no further. But at length she came to the ledge and the wall King had made, and Gratton, looking up and seeing her above him, began climbing again.

Gloria held aside the canvas flap; he followed her into the cave. Her fire, though low, still burned. For the sake of more light she put on more dry wood from the great heap King had left for her. She began to look about, planning swiftly just how easiest to move the few belongings which must go with her. She could pile odds and ends into a blanket; she could remake the canvas roll as King had done so often; she and Gratton could drag the bundles to the front of the cave and push them over, down the cliffs.

"First, we'll get things together, all in a heap," she said aloud.

He came forward and stood warming his nervous hands at her fire, his eyes everywhere at once. He marked the shipshape air of the cavern, the parcels which were to-night's supper and to-morrow's three poor little meals, each set carefully apart from the others on the rock shelf. He saw how the firewood was piled in its place, not scattered; how Gloria's bed and King's looked almost comfortable because of the fir-boughs; how the clean pots and pans were in their places. Then he turned his full eyes like searchlights upon the girl.

"And you," he said, marvelling, "*you* actually came with a man like King into a place like this!"

"I was a fool," cried Gloria. "A pitiful little fool. Oh!"

Had she been thinking less of Gloria and more of this other man with whom she was now to cope she must have marked a certain swift change in his attitude. It became less furtive, more assured. His eyes left her to rove again, lingered with the two couches, and returned to her.

"You found King wasn't your kind," he announced. "You have quarrelled!"

290   Jackson Gregory

"From the very beginning," she replied quickly. "He is unthinkable. I would have left him long ago, only ..."

"Only there was no place to go," Gratton finished it for her. "And now," he continued slowly, studying her, "you are willing to come with me."

"Yes," she told him unhesitatingly.

"But," he offered musingly, "you refused me once and turned to him."

"Haven't I told you I was a fool? I didn't know then quite what men were ... some men."

She was not measuring every word now. She meant simply that she was determined to have done with Mark King, holding bitterly that she hated him; that she would go to any one to be definitely through with King. Yet he had time to weigh her words and draw from each one his own significance.

His eyes followed her as she gathered up her few personal and intimate possessions, comb, brush, little silken things of pale pink and blue. A faint colour seeped into the usually colourless lips at which his dead-white teeth were suddenly gnawing. When she saw the look in his eyes, she stared at him wonderingly.

"What is it?" she asked, her voice puzzled.

"What is what?" Gratton laughed, but the look was still there. His eyes did not laugh.

"What makes you look like that? What are you thinking?"

Now it was he who was vaguely puzzled. Then he shrugged.

"I was just thinking how superb you are," he replied, not entirely untruthfully. For his ulterior thought had been reared upon the vital fact of her triumphant beauty.

The compliment was too much like hundreds she had received in her life to alarm her. Rather, it pleased; what word of praise had she heard during these latter days?

His voice sounded queerly, as though his breath came with difficulty. Maybe it did, since he was no outdoors man, and to him the climb up the rocks and the brief journey along the mountain flank was a painful labour. Certain it was that the faint flush was still in the sallow cheeks. Suddenly he lifted his hands, putting them out toward her. She saw again the strange look in his eyes.

"Gloria!" he said hoarsely, "you are wonderful! And you have come to me!"

Gloria met his rather too ardent admiration with that cool little laugh which had been her weapon in other days. She was not afraid of Gratton. To-day she had led and he had followed. She had commanded and he had obeyed. Here was a pleasant change from King's masterfulness, and she fully intended to hold Gratton well in hand.

"I came to you," she said frankly, "because I was a woman in distress and had no alternative. That there has ever been any unpleasantness between us does not alter that fact. You understand me, don't you?"

He hardly heard her. To his mind the situation was clearness itself. Gloria had come alone into the forest with Mark King. She had been with him all these days and nights. But she and King had quarrelled; tired of each other already, perhaps. Gratton did not care what the reason was; he was gloatingly satisfied with the outcome. He had always coveted her; it took much to stir his pale blood, and only the superb beauty of Gloria Gaynor had ever fully done so. King had stolen her away, but she had left him and had come straight to Gratton!

He came a step closer and the firelight showed how the muscles of his throat were working. Gloria's eyes widened. But not yet did she fully understand and not yet did she fear.

"Mr. Gratton," she began.

"Gloria!" he cried out. "Gloria!"

His hands, suddenly flung out, were upon her. She tore them away, wrenched herself free from him, and started back. As she did so her little silken bundle dropped at her feet. Gratton caught it up and buried his face in it. Now as he looked up at her his eyes and all that she could see of his face were stamped with that which lay in his heart.

"Oh!" she cried, shrinking not so much from him as from the thing she read so plainly at last. "Surely, you do not think ... you do not misinterpret ... my being here at all, my being with Mr. King...."

"No," cried Gratton wildly. "I misinterpret nothing. You came alone with him into the mountains. What chance is there for two interpretations there? You gave yourself to him; you saw your mistake; you hated him. You have come to me. I have always loved you; I want you."

Her cheeks flamed red with hot anger. There was a flutter in her heart, a wild tremor in her blood. She drew back from him. He followed, his arms out. She was amazed, for the moment shocked into consternation. And yet she knew no such terror as had been hers when King had advanced on her, rope in hand. Her new contempt of Gratton was too high for that. Now she marked the small stature, little taller, little stronger, than her own; the pale face, the narrow chest, the slender body.

"You know what I mean, what I want," he was muttering. "That sweet young-thing innocence is all right in its place but that place is not here alone in the mountains with a man."

"Man!" she burst out scathingly. "You, *a man*! Why, you wretched little beast!"

But Gratton, his brain reeling with hot fancy, came on.

"You were afraid of King. You said that he made you do what he wanted. What about me? You are going to do what I tell you. I ...By God, I will make you! Beast, you call me? No more beast than any other man. I have wanted you all these years. You have wanted me, or you would not have been so glad to see me. Only a few days ago you were ready to marry me! And now ..."

His arms groped for her. Gloria swept up a dead pine limb that lay by the fire and swung it in both hands and struck him full across the face. He reeled back and stood, half in the shadow, his shoulders to the rock wall, his hands to his face.

"You beast!" she panted. "You cowardly, contemptible beast."

From the way in which he brought his hand down and looked at it and laid it back upon his lips she knew that his mouth was bleeding. And she read in the gesture and in the man's whole cringing attitude that the danger of any physical violence from him was past and done with. In the grip of his passion, ugly as it was, he had risen somewhat from his essential weakness; in the moment he had at least thought of himself as a conqueror. Now he was again what he always really was at heart, a contemptible coward.

An absolutely new sense of elation sang through Gloria's blood. She was fully mistress of the situation, and had found within her an unguessed strength. Physically superb at all times because nature had richly gifted her, now she was magnificent.

"Mr. Gratton," she said swiftly, "you have made a mistake. Mr. King has never offered me violence of that sort. Remember that, though we are alone, and in the mountains, I am the same Gloria Gaynor that you have known. And be sure that you treat me as such."

He nursed his battered lips and stared at her. The blow had dazed him. Slowly, as his mind cleared, there dawned in it the realization that he *had* made a mistake. The stick was still in her hands; a shiver ran through him. His desire went out of him.

"I wish to God I had never seen you," he groaned.

She had meant from the first to take the upper hand. Now she was almost glad that this had happened. For now she was very sure of herself; Gratton had merely been bold like other young men who had sought to presume; he had been cruder simply because the situation seemed to his mind to offer the opportunity; now a blow from her had accomplished the work of a haughty look in drawing-room encounters with those other young men. She dropped the stick and wiped her hands.

"We have other things to think of," she said. She might have been a young queen who had punished a subject and now from her exalted place condescended to consider that the indignity offered her royal person had never occurred. She began dragging the blankets from her bed, tumbling them to the floor. "Take these," she commanded.

"I was a fool for ever leaving San Francisco," he muttered bitterly. "You let me think that you cared for me, and now you treat me like a dog. I spent time and money trying to be the one to find gold in these infernal mountains, and I find nothing but storm and starvation. I don't believe there ever was gold here."

Gold! He stopped at his own words, his eyes flying wide open. During these later hours, fleeing from Brodie's men, stumbling upon Gloria, swirled away by mad longings, he had not thought of gold. But here was King's camp; straight here had King come after Gloria had brought him her father's message and old Honeycutt's secret. Then the gold was here! The cupidity which in the man never slept long was awake on the instant. He began looking about him eagerly. King was gone? Then not for men to bring help to Gloria but to aid him in carrying off the gold. Having brought Gloria here so that she could not tell others what she knew, he left her here with the same purpose; so Gratton would have done! King would have hidden it here; at least some of it. He began questing feverishly, shuffling about in the shadows while Gloria, busy with her plans for moving, wondered at him. He was striking matches, running back and forth; she could hear his mutterings. And presently, when Gloria had called and he had not heard, he came upon the bag which King had meant to take out with him that day the horse was lost. He hovered over it; he struck other matches, he came hastening back dragging it after him.

He went down on his knees by the sack, got a heavy lump in his hands, rubbed at it, held it closer to the firelight, rubbed again more excitedly, and finally sat back, staring up at her with new flames of another sort leaping in his eyes.

"It's next thing to solid gold!" he gasped. "There are thousands —thousands—Millions!"

She looked at him and marvelled. In his shallow soul no emotion lived long; greed of gold now obliterated the little ripples that another greed had fleetingly made. How had she thought well of him down in the city? How had she so much as tolerated him? On the instant it struck her that there was small justice in Gratton reaping any reward, having done nothing to earn it. "We have the things to move. Come; hurry."

"Why should we move, after all?" he demanded sharply. "Now that I have got up here, why not stay? There's wood here; everything is fixed up after a fashion. King would know where to send for us, and—and those cursed dogs of Brodie's would never think of looking up here, even if chance did lead them along the gorge."

Gloria, recalling King's warning, remembering Brodie's brute face, said hastily:

"Do you think there is any real danger that they will come this way?"

"I hope not," he groaned. "They couldn't follow my trail if they tried to. You see, I left them last night, as early as I dared; I struck out in a straight line down the slope; then I made a turn off to the side and along the ridge where there was but little snow. By now all those tracks are wiped out, what with wind and new snow. There's nothing to lead them this way."

"Then, if we go down quickly, if we get your bag of food and put out the fire down there, and come right back up, it won't be very long before our tracks will be gone. And we'll not budge from here until help comes. Come; let's hurry."

"Coming," said Gratton. "Yes; we must hurry."

She went ahead and began to clamber down the cliffs. Half-way down she wondered why he was not following. She found a place where she could cling and look up. Thus she was just in time to see him, standing at the mouth of the cave, clutching a heavy bag; he had been tying the mouth of it. Now he cast it outward so that it fell, striking against the cliff-side, and then rolling and dropping to disappear at last in the snow-bank below. And then he began, though hesitantly, to follow her.

"That's one thing Mark King won't get," he announced with emphasis. At last he stood beside her in the snow. "No matter how the game breaks, whether he comes back or not, and no matter who gets away with the rest, that bagful is mine! There's a fortune in it, and it's mine." He began tossing double handfuls of loose snow into the hole which the bag of gold had made. "When I get a chance," he muttered, "I'll move it somewhere else."

His avarice disgusted her. Just now the thought of

gold sickened.

"We are wasting time," she reminded him.

He followed her again, casting a last look behind him, then looking up at the sky, grey everywhere except for a long patch of blue.

"What we want is another three or four hours of steady snowing," he was saying when they slipped into the mouth of the lower cave. "Enough to hide that and to cover up our paths."

Gloria was already trying to put out the fire; if ill fortune should lead Brodie's crowd here, it would be just as well if they found no smouldering sticks to tell them that the fugitives had been here so short a time ago and could not be far off. She called to Gratton to help her. He stamped out burning brands while she hastened back and forth, bringing handfuls of snow with which to extinguish the last glowing coals. She worked vigorously and swiftly; he only half-heartedly, since his thoughts were elsewhere.

"Maybe," he said thoughtfully, "I'd better bring that bag in here and hide it somewhere—far back in the dark."

"No," she said. "Leave it where it is. We must hurry back to the other cave."

But he grew stubborn over it. The storm might end at any time; the sun might melt all this fluffy snow; the bag then would be for any one to see. Heedless of her expostulations, he left her extinguishing the fire and went back for the gold. He was gone several minutes, digging after it. She had finished her task when he reappeared, dragging the heavy sack after him. He disappeared swiftly, going into the deeper dark of the further end of the cave; she heard him moving with shuffling feet. What a treacherous, thieving, petty animal he was—

She started and whirled about. There was a new sound in the air, a low mumble, a vague murmur. Men's voices. Outside, coming nearer swiftly, were men. Her first thought was of King; then she knew that it was too soon for him to have gotten out of the mountains, found assistance, and returned. A deep, heavy bass voice drowned out the others; it was like a low-throated growl, ominous, sinister.

Gloria whirled again, this time toward the dark into which Gratton had gone. Blindly she hurried after him; she stumbled but kept on. She could hear him at work, hiding his gold. At last she was at his side; she clutched at his sleeve.

"Listen!" she whispered. "They are outside. They have followed you!"

She felt his arm stiffen as from head to foot he grew rigid. She heard his breath whistling through his nostrils. She could hear the beating of his heart—or was it her own? The voices came nearer, rose higher. Gratton began to shake as with a terrible chill.

"If they find me—oh, my God, if they find me—Benny killed a man he thought had the bacon—I had it all the time! My God, Gloria, if they find me—"

"Sh!" she commanded. "Be still! Maybe they will go by—"

The voices came nearer—passed on. Two or three men out there were speaking at once; then all were silent. The silence lasted so long that Gloria began to breathe again. Surely, surely Brodie and his men had gone—

Then again came Brodie's deep, sinister voice:

"Back this way, boys," he shouted. "He's gone in here. We've trapped the dirty white rat."

Gloria and Gratton clung to each other, too terrified to move.

CHAPTER XXVIII

Gratton, had he been left to his own devices, would have stood stock-still where he was, frozen to the ground in terror. Gloria tugged at him, whispering over and over: "They are coming! Don't you hear them? Quick! We must try to hide."

At last he seemed to awaken from a trance; he started and began hurrying with her, crowding by her, stumbling on ahead in the darkness, seeking the cave's unfathomed depths of darkness. She heard him stumble and fall; she ran blindly and caught him by the arm again, whispering fiercely:

"You must be silent! If they once hear us we have no chance. If we are still, maybe they won't find us."

After that he moved more guardedly. But still he crowded ahead; once in his excitement, when she brushed against him and he thought that she was going to get in his way, he shoved her violently aside. It was then that Gloria, looking back, saw Brodie's great bulk outlined against the snow outside. He came in; she saw his rifle; his figure was absorbed in the shadows. She saw other men following him; how many she did not know. One by one they bulked black against the daylight; one by one, as they entered, they were lost among the shadows. She had bumped into a wall of rock. Gratton was there, groping in all directions with his hands; she could hear his quick, dry breathing.

They could go no further. This was the end. Brodie called out loudly, his speech dripping with his habitual vileness; he shouted: "Gratton! Better step out lively like a man now. We got you anyway." Then he began to gather the scattered firewood; a match flared in his hand; his face leaped out of the dark like a devil's. Or a madman's, a man's mad with a rage which lusted for the killing of another man. Gloria's heart sank in despair; she felt as though she were going to faint.

But all the time her hands, like Gratton's, had been groping. At the moment when she felt that her knees were giving way under her, she found where an arm of the cave continued, narrow, slanting upward steeply, cluttered with blocks of stone. She tugged at Gratton's sleeve; she crept into this place and felt him close behind her, crowding, trying to press by her. She gave way briefly, felt him scrape past, and began crawling, following. Again only a few feet further on she came up with him again; once more he had come to the end of the tunnel. He was crouching, flattened against the rock wall. They were in a pocket with no outlet save the way they had come. She stood, turned toward the front of the cave, and waited.

"Get a fire going, boys," Brodie's rumbling bass was calling. Assured now of having run his quarry to earth, he took a wolfish joy from the moment. There was a horrible note in his laughter, booming out suddenly. "The little skunk's run to a hole; we'll smoke him out."

He spoke of Gratton as though he were a frightened animal, and like a frightened animal Gloria felt. She stooped and looked toward the pursuers; thus only could she see them, since when she stood erect the irregularities of the rocks above hid them from her.

Brodie lighted his fire. The other men—dully she counted them now; there were five of them all told—were gathering wood, heaping it on. The flames leaped, crackled, lifted their voices into a roar; volumes of white smoke shot out, thinned, were gone. The light flared higher, brighter. Dark corners and crevices were made palely fight. She could see the faces of the men now, their eyes reflecting the fire, looking like the eyes of wolves. Brodie carried his rifle as though he fully intended using it. At his side Benny Rudge fidgeted and blinked. By Benny stood that scarecrow of a man, Brail. Close by, interested spectators, were the squat Italian and the man who had brought the "judge" to marry her to Gratton, the leering Steve Jarrold.

"More fire, boys," called Brodie. Again his ugly laughter boomed out. "I think I see where he is."

Whether or not Brodie already saw them, it appeared clear that immediate discovery was inevitable. For there was no further hiding-place here to creep into; no such refuge as King had urged Gloria to hasten to if Brodie came. She remembered the caution all too late; she thought of King with wild longing, while Gratton cringed and pulled back and tried to screen his body with hers.

"Here's the grub he stole!" It was Benny's cracked, nervous voice, full of wrath.

She could feel Gratton shiver as he crouched against her. Sudden disgust filled her. They knew that he was here; they would take him in a minute; his seeking further to hide was so futile. And yet he was not man enough to stand forth at the end; he was the type who must be dragged whimpering and pulling back, pleading for mercy even when he knew so well that he deserved no mercy, and would have none meted out to him. Gratton had his one last chance to show if there was the spark of manhood in him; they did not yet know of Gloria's presence, and had he stepped out now, he might have given her a chance to remain unseen. But no such heroism suggested itself to Gratton.

"Come on, Gratton," shouted Brodie. "Or do you want me to begin shooting from here?"

The light of the fire flared higher, brighter. The eyes of the men who had just entered from the outside were growing accustomed to this place of shadows. Suddenly the man Jarrold called sharply:

"There's some one with him. There's two of 'em, Brodie. Go easy!"

Brodie cursed him for a fool.

"I don't care how many's with him or who they are," he bellowed. "The grub-stealing thief has got his coming to him. Step out, you lily-livered sneak, and take your medicine."

"That's all right," muttered Jarrold. "But it won't hurt to see who they are first, Brodie."

"Gratton's got no gun with him," cackled Benny Rudge. "Neither's that other guy. Come ahead, Steve. Me an' you'll pull 'em out."

Gloria pressed back against the rock, her flesh quivering. She saw two men and then another two coming toward her. The first sound broke from Gratton's lips now, a little gurgling moan. The men came on; one had heard and laughed. Then Gloria, with more shuddersome thought of rough hands upon her than of a rifle-ball, broke away from her cowering companion and came hastily to meet them.

"I'm coming out," she cried out to them.

It was all that she could do to hold herself erect and come back into the more open cave. Jarrold and Benny and the men after them came to a dead halt and stared at her. In the flickering half-light she looked a slim frightened boy.

"All of a sudden the woods is gettin' all cluttered up with folks," grunted Benny. "Who in blazes are you, kid? An' where's your mamma?"

His companions laughed; they laughed at anything. One of them, Steve Jarrold, came closer to look into her face. She saw that his steps were uncertain; she had heard how thick was his vocal utterance; now she smelled the whiskey with which he reeked.

A shout broke from Jarrold. He clutched her shoulder with a great claw of a hand and drew her closer to him, his face thrust down to hers.

"Let me go!" she cried, trying to jerk away from him.

"Easy does it," said Jarrold. "Easy—*kid*! I'm of a notion I've seen that face of yours somewheres."

"Never mind the kid," Brodie was growling savagely. "It's Gratton first. Out with him, Benny."

The others bore down upon Gratton. He had found his voice now; he shrieked at them; he begged shrilly; he battered them with his fists, striking weak, vain blows. Benny, though the smaller man, had him by the collar. The Italian caught an arm, and as they dragged him half-fainting toward the fire, Brail struck at him with a heavy boot.

"So," said Brodie heavily.

Gratton began an incoherent pleading, arrested impatiently by Brodie's great voice.

"Shut up! You've had your innings; it's mine now. You swiped grub when it's the same thing as slitting a man's gullet. You let another man be killed for what you done. Now you get yours!"

He jerked up his rifle. Benny and the Italian let Gratton go and jumped nimbly aside. Gratton stumbled and sagged, staggering like a drunken man. Brodie, with his rifle-barrel not six feet from Gratton's terror-stricken body, laughed again.

"Stop!" Gloria shrilled. She broke away from Jarrold's grasp and ran toward Brodie. "You don't know what you are doing. You—"

"Close your trap, kid," Brodie thundered at her. "Unless you want the second bullet."

Jarrold's big boots came clumping noisily across the rock floor.

"Easy does it, Brodie," he shouted. "She ain't no kid, I tell you. She's a girl. That's Ben Gaynor's girl, the one Gratton wanted to marry, the one King took away from him. Keep your eye peeled; King would be around somewhere!"

"Hidin' back there in the dark somewhere," muttered Benny.

Brodie, though his rifle had not swerved, was listening.

"No, not hiding in the dark corners," he said ponderously. "Not Mark King, rot him.... Ben Gaynor's girl, you say? Then we're red hot on the right trail, boys! You know what her and King would be after!"

Gratton's stunned brain began to function wildly.

"The gold is here, Brodie!" he cried out wildly. "King had got to it before us, but I've found it. I was coming back to tell you—"

Brodie had small liking for a coward and now his bull's voice cut Gratton's chatter short.

"No solid mountain of gold is going to save your hide—"

Benny began to jig up and down in a frenzy of excitement.

"Hold your hand, Brodie, you big fool," he shouted. He even jumped to Brodie's side and caught the rifle-barrel, shoving it downward. "If he does know where it is, give him a show to lead us to it. Ain't you got any sense? Before King gets back. If you popped him off now, how would we know where to look?"

Brodie snarled at Benny and whipped the rifle clear of the nervous clutch. But he understood what Benny had in mind and saw wisdom in obeying the command to hold his hand. His gross, heavy-muscled face, half in light, half in darkness, showed a look of hesitation. Gratton began a rapid, vehement talking, explaining, arguing, pleading; he had not meant to steal the food; he could lead them to the gold; he wanted none of it; all that he asked was to be allowed to live—

"Shut up!" Brodie cried again disgustedly. "You ain't dead yet, are you? So's you keep your lying face closed I'll give you one show. Step lively; *where is it?*"

Gratton, like a hound in leash suddenly freed, turned and sped toward the spot where he had hid the gold. Brodie, his rifle shifting in his hands, leaped after him, keeping close to him. Gratton was down on his hands and knees, scratching among the loose stones like a dog digging for a buried bone. Brodie put a heavy hand on his shoulder and jerked him back, hurling him to one side. Thus it was Brodie who found the bag and dragged it forward to the fire, dumping its contents on the ground. Benny was with him now, pawing over the heavy lumps. Brail, the Italian, Steve Jarrold—all rushed forward and snatched up bits of the ore that had rolled from the sack; one of them shouted in wonder; another seized the nugget from his hands; they all talked at once; Benny squealed in high rage as Jarrold shoved him backward; the Italian trod in the fire and cursed and kicked at it savagely, sending burning brands in all directions.

Gloria had stood powerless to move. Now she saw that in their flush of excitement no one was looking toward her. She began slowly, silently, edging toward the side of the cave, toward the way out. Her one thought was to slip away while none noted her; to dart out and hurry up the cliff to come to the hiding-place of which Mark King had told her.

"I never see such gold, and me an old-timer in the mines." It was Steve Jarrold muttering. "It's like they'd took clean gold down to the mint and rolled it and lumped it into nuggets. *This was broke off the mother lode.* Oh, my Gawd!"

Gloria made another quiet step—and another. Still no one saw her. If she could only make half a dozen more steps before these men awoke from the first moments of a spell that had made them oblivious of everything on earth except that little heap of rock! Another step; she went quicker; their backs were toward her. And still no one saw. Yes, Gratton alone had seen. She made a quick frightened gesture. His jaw sagged open; he watched her with bulging eyes. She could read his thought so plainly: he was thinking of his own ultimate chances for life, he was screwing up his courage to make a dash for the open himself. His eyes followed her step by step. Oh, if only he would look in some other direction! If any one of them saw Gratton's tell-tale face—

Then Gratton began a slow withdrawal from the others; he meant to do as he saw her doing.

"Heavy laka hell," the Italian was saying. "Justa da gold do that!"

"Give me that, Tony," snarled Brodie. He snatched the mass from the other's hands. "That's the biggest nugget any man living ever saw."

Gloria tasted the clean fresh outside air; she was within three paces of the line of snow. Then there was a sudden noise; Gratton, inching off backward, had stumbled over a dead stick. The men by the fire were startled out of their oblivion. Steve Jarrold, the one nearest Gloria, swung about, saw her, dropped what was in his hands, and lunged towards her. She made a dash for the exit. In two great strides Jarrold was upon her and had caught her by the shoulders, dragging her back.

And Gratton stood again, his feet glued to the ground; she could see the flash of his teeth gnawing at his fingers.

"Trying to make a sneak for it!" boomed Brodie. "I'll show you—"

"Not yet, Brodie, you big fool!" yelled Benny. "This is only a sackful, and not full at that. It's the rest of it we're after—the whole lousy mess. He's got to show us where this come from."

"I am not trying to get away," said Gratton, though his tone did not convince. "Haven't I made good already? Haven't I kept my promise? Am I not ready to do whatever I can?"

"Talk's cheap," retorted Brodie. "Get busy, then."

Gratton, struggling already in the meshes of the net drawing ever tighter about him, pointed to Gloria with shaking finger. He swallowed twice and moistened his lips to speak.

"King found it first. She was with him. I made her show me the sack of gold. I was going to go back to your camp, to tell you—"

"Cut it," commanded Brodie. "Leave out the lies and talk straight and fast. Where is the rest of it? Where did this come from?"

"I'm trying to tell you," said Gratton hurriedly. "There—there's another cave; up above. That's where King had his camp; that where's I got the sack. It's up there—"

"No wonder she wanted to skip out," jeered Steve Jarrold, his great bony hand locked about Gloria's shrinking shoulder. His ill-featured face, the small, pig eyes, always jeering, the black bristle of beard, not unlike a hog's bristles, were thrust close to her face. "Where's King all this time?" he demanded. "Up in the other cave, maybe?"

"No," she said dismally, seeking to jerk away from his evil glance and whiskey-laden breath. "He has gone—"

"That's good; let him go. We don't care, do we? Eh, girlie?" But again his hand tightened until the hard fingers hurt her. "But gone where?"

"We were short of food—he is hunting—maybe he has gone for help—"

"And you showed Gratton where he hid his gold? That's a nice little she-trick, ain't it? Well, while the showing's good, lead us to the rest of it."

"That's the eye, Steve," said Brodie. He stepped forward, shoved his rifle-muzzle against Gratton's body, and commanded: "You, too. Go ahead, you and her, and show us the way. And no monkey business, either of you, or I'll blow a hole square through you."

Gratton, grown nimble, darted ahead with Brodie always close at his heels. Gloria, forced on by Jarrold, came next, and after them the others. Benny was the last; he had taken time to put the gold back into the sack and set it aside among the shadows. For Benny believed in making sure of what they had, even while they quested better things. Then he caught up his rifle, the only other gun besides Brodie's, and came hurrying after them.

They went up the cliff in a long file, clawing their way, cursing the steepness, now and then one or another of them fumbling uncertainly, close to a slip and a fall. It was clear that, with the possible exception of Swen Brodie, not a man of them was entirely sober. But they made the climb safely and hastened into the upper cave eagerly.

"It's somewhere back there," said Gratton.

"More fire," shouted Brodie. His voice exulted; his blood

would be running now with the gold fever. He tossed on an armful of dry wood; the flames caught and roared; shadows quivered and danced. Already Benny was at the far end of the cave; the others ran after him. Even Jarrold relinquished Gloria's arm, eager to be in at the finding. But he called to her as he went:

"You stick where you are. I'm not forgetting you this time."

Fascinated, she watched them. They ran like blood-lusting dogs that had briefly lost their quarry, that were seeking everywhere, in every cranny, with slavering jaws. They turned aside into side-pockets of the main cavern; they got torches and looked high and low; they went back and forth, up and down; they stumbled against one another and cursed angrily; they caught up bits of stone, ran back to the fire to see if the fragments were shot with gold; cursed and hurled the useless things from them, and ran back again, to jostle and seek and be first; they were not so much like dogs now as human hogs, fighting to get first into the trough.

But they did not forget Gratton, and they did not forget Gloria. All the time both Brodie and Benny kept their guns in their hands; two significant looks had been all that was needed to keep their two prisoners in mind of the fact that no escape now was possible.

To Gloria it seemed inevitable that in this quest which over-looked nothing, and which as time wore on grew less frenzied and more systematic, they would find what King had found before them. She tried to think consecutively; she recalled all that King had told her of these men, all that Gratton had hinted at. She recalled with a shudder the look in the moist eyes of Steve Jarrold. It seemed to her that her only slim chance for safety lay in their finding the gold. For only gold, gold unlimited, could cause them to forget her.

For an hour they sought tirelessly. It appeared that there were many fingers to the further end of the cave, narrow, irregular channels into which they pressed. Their faggots burned out; the smoke choked them; they coughed and cursed, came out for fresh air, dived into the dark again. The short day was passing; the entering light, where they had torn the canvas aside, grew dimmer. And still they searched.

At last Brodie returned and stood looking from Gloria to Gratton.

"One of you knows," he said shortly. "Which one?"

"I swear to God—" began Gratton.

"Shut up! Then it's you?" The little, shiny blue eyes, never so coldly evil, drew her own frightened eyes, fascinated and held them. "You know"

"I don't know! All I know—"

"Don't lie to me! It'll do you no good." He lifted a hand and held it over her, the enormous fingers apart and rigid. "I'll make you tell!"

"Listen to me," she managed to cry out. "I don't know, I tell you. But I know where it might be. In a place you would never think of looking. Not in a thousand years—"

Blue fire sprang up in the gleaming eyes. The other men, drawn close, watched and listened, their eyes alive with many lights.

"What you know I'll know. I'll choke it out of you—"

"I'll tell you—if you will keep your hands off me! I'll make a bargain with you. I'll show you the place; if there's gold there, I don't care what happens to it—if you'll only agree to let me alone—to let me go—"

Brodie laughed at her. But Benny cried out:

"Of course we'll let you go! What do you suppose we want of you? Once we get our hands on it she can go, Brodie. Tell her so, you big—"

"Sure," said Brodie, with a wide grin. "It ain't women we're after this trick; it's something better. And—and it would be very nice of you to show us—Miss Gaynor." He treated her to a grinning mock respect, so obviously spurious that her fear of him rose higher, choking her. "Very nice, ain't it, boys?"

"I—I am not sure what you'll find," whispered Gloria. "I only know that—Oh, dear God, I hope you find all the gold in the world!"

Hastily she ran by Brodie toward the dark end of the cave. Then she stopped and tried to think; how many paces had King said? She came back to the fire; thirty, thirty-five? She began counting as she walked while they watched her wondering and following slowly after her. She found several boulders in her path; but she had not gone far enough. She kept on; thirty, thirty-two, thirty-three—She could hardly see about her. She stumbled against a rock in her way.

"Try here," she said. Already Brodie and Steve Jarrold were at her side. "This rock. See if it will move—"

They thrust her roughly aside. Brodie set down his rifle, laid his big hands on the boulder, and as if it had weighed only ten pounds, tossed it out of the way. He knelt, feeling along the ground. A sudden shout burst from him:

"Down here! There's a big hole; there's a dark cave underneath. That's where it is?"

They brought faggots; at the edge of the hole they hastily built another fire. They crowded round, peering down. Brodie tossed a brand through; it dropped a short distance, a few feet only, struck, and began to roll; it caught against a rock, smoked and smouldered, and went out. Brodie set his legs over the opening, called to the Italian to grab his rifle and keep an eye on Gloria and Gratton, and went down. The others crowded about the hole, waiting impatiently for him to go through, and then began piling down after him. Gloria could see their figures dimly; they went down and down along a long, steep, slanting passage-way; they had smoking torches and looked like so many fiends in the bottomless pit. She heard them calling back and forth excitedly; they went on, still downward; she heard their grinding boot-heels, but could no longer see them. Suddenly they were silent. Then there were swift mutterings. And then a great, triumphant, many-voiced shout. In Gus Ingle's treasure-cache they had at last come to Gus Ingle's treasure. And, among other things, to the skeleton of Gus Ingle himself, sprawling here for sixty years in the dark over a great heap of gold.

CHAPTER XXIX

Swen Brodie, whose will had at all times directed, was now absolute dictator. Big and brutal and fearless, drunken with gold, he loomed above his companions, driving them, commanding them, swearing violently that they would do what he told them to do or he'd dash their brains out.

"I led you to it," he reminded them in a great shouting voice. "But for me never a man of you would of smelled it. There's enough here to make a thousand men rich, and that's lucky for you! But we've got to hold what we got, and we got to get out of here with it—somehow. That somehow is for me to figure out. And, being as one man's got to run any job and the rest has got to take orders and take 'em on the jump, you're doing what I say! If any man jack of you don't like that, let him open his head right now!"

"There's no sense scrappin'," muttered Benny. "An' we're all satisfied, I'd say. But there's no call to start wavin' a red flag."

"We're going down to the lower cave," said Brodie. "Everything we can pry loose is going down with us. We'll pitch the loose chunks of gold over the cliff and we'll stow 'em away somewhere else—where King, if things break some way we don't look for, won't find 'em! We start right now, while there's daylight. What's more, we move our camp from down the canon to the cave below. Steve Jarrold, you and Tony are elected to that job, and you'd better get a move on. Bring up what grub's left, and the blankets and stuff. The rest of us will start in firing gold overboard and putting it somewhere more safe—all that's loose. And at that, think of the great, big, wide, yellow, rotten-soft seam of it down below!"

"Where are you goin' to put it?" demanded Jarrold.

"Not hiding it from you and Tony, Steve," cried Brodie sharply. "Put your suspicious ways in your pocket. And, if you're on the jump, you'll have our camp truck moved before we're done. Look alive, will you? A man never knows what's going to happen."

"Why not leave it here until we know—?"

"For one thing, because Mark King knows this place. Now, move! Come ahead, you other fellows. You, too, Gratton; we ain't forgot you." An uglier note crept into the harsh voice. "You can help. And so can you," whirling on Gloria. "Woman or no woman, you got hands and feet."

* * * * *

Night, pitch-black, had come when they had done. Gloria, scarcely able to stand from exhaustion, her body bruised, her hands and arms wounded from many a jagged rock as she had gone back and forth carrying heavy loads, went with the others into the lowest cave in which already the gold had been stowed away. She sank down wearily; she closed her eyes rather than watch the men about their fire, eating noisily, drinking noisily from the bottles which Steve and Tony had brought from their other camp. Trying to remain unnoticed in the shadows was Gratton. Brodie, having commanded that a rude rock wall like King's be built across the mouth of the cave to shut out the cold, and having laboured with the others at the task, came back to the fire. He took a long pull at a bottle, emptying it and smashing it to tinkling fragments as he hurled it behind him. He caught up a big piece of dried beef and gnawed at it like a dog; though Gloria kept her eyes away from him she could hear the tearing and grinding of the monstrous teeth.

"It's been a day's work, at that," he said with a full mouth. "But we ain't done. I noticed how no man has said a word about how we split what we found."

"There's five of us," said Benny quickly. "We split it five ways, even, like pardners."

Brodie turned on him slowly, still rending at his meat, still clutching his rifle and holding it so that no man might forget that he held it.

"Think so, Benny?" he said ponderously. "Being as I've worked on this lay a long time, since I let you others in on it, since I led you to it—think that's the fair way to split it? Now suppose you listen to me. You boys ain't mentioned a split because it was none of your say and you knew it. Say, in round numbers—but there's ten times that—that there's a million dollars tucked away here. Why, there's mines all through these mountains that never thought of stopping at a million; that was just a fair start! Well, to get going, say there's an even million. I get just half that; that leaves half a million, don't it? Now, shut up a minute!" he commanded truculently as more than one man stirred. "Listen to me. That's five hundred thousand to split between four of you; that's over a hundred thousand for every man jack of you. And that's what I call a fair split."

They growled in their throats at that, but no man took it upon himself to speak out definitely, though they glanced sidewise among themselves. Benny, who always had a thought of his own, said quietly:

"What are you doin' about Gratton? He'll claim his share, won't he? And, if you say him no, he'll shoot his face off, won't he?"

"No," said Brodie. "He won't." He paused, swallowed the last of his beef, caught up a bottle from Benny's side, and drank deeply. Benny, afraid that this bottle, too, still nearly full, would be broken, hastily snatched it back when Brodie had done.

"No," said Brodie heavily. "Gratton won't talk." He grew suddenly quick-spoken—he broke into a volley of accusation; his tongue lent itself to such a rush of vileness that Gloria, shrinking back, covered her ears with her hands. "Gratton stole grub. When grub-stealing was the same as slitting a man's throat. And what next does he plan? Why, to make trouble; to swear that Benny killed a man; that we was all in it; to get us all hung, if he can, or in the pen; then to grab what's ours. Look at him. You can see it in his frog eyes! He's done, that's what he is!" With a swift gesture his gun was at his shoulder.

Gratton scrambled to his feet with a choking cry. Gloria, too, had sprung up, sick with horror. She looked from Brodie to Gratton, who was not two feet from her. She saw that he was panic-stricken; his fear was choking him, stopping his heart, paralysing his muscles. He wanted to run and could not; he tried to speak but now not even a whisper came from between his writhing lips.

Slowly, an unshaken, senseless piece of machinery, Brodie raised his rifle. Now Gratton's voice returned to him; a strangling cry broke from his agonized soul. A hand, wildly outthrown, caught at Gloria's sleeve.

"You, there," called Brodie, "stand aside. Unless you're wanting yours too!"

Her own heart was stopping, her feet were leaded. She understood what he said—she knew that it was to her that he spoke—but she wouldn't believe, couldn't believe that he meant—*that*!

Gratton was pressing tight to Gloria, seeking futilely to get behind her. He began to articulate—to beg—to promise—

Brodie fired. A great reverberating roar filled the cavern.

Gloria, her brain gone suddenly numb, felt the grip on her arm tighten convulsively. Then it relaxed—slowly. Gratton, his eyes bulging, his mouth wide open, was sinking—

Gloria put her hands over her eyes and screamed. Again and again her scream broke from her. She tried to draw back, to run. But all her strength was gone. She crumpled and settled down almost as Gratton had done, and so close to him that she brushed him with her knee. She felt the body twitch. She leaped to her feet and ran blindly, screaming. She struck against the rock wall and sank down again.

The wonder was that she did not swoon outright. As it was, her soul seemed to float dizzily out of her body and through an utter dark. She thought that she was dying. As though across a vast distance she heard voices.

"Well?" It was the man who had done the shooting, his voice truculent. "Anybody got anything to say? Say it quick, if you have."

There was a silence. Then a shuffling of feet. Then an answering voice, thin and querulous. It was Benny; he, too, had killed his man.

"He had it coming," he said eagerly. "Any judge would say so. Stole every bit of grub when stealing grub is the same as cutting a man's throat, just like you said, Brodie. He had it coming. You done right."

"You, Jarrold," demanded Brodie. "Got anything to say?"

Again silence. Then again a voice, Jarrold's, saying hurriedly:

"No. Benny's right. He had it coming. Damn fool."

"And you, Brail? And you, Tony? Got anything to say? Talk lively!"

Brail and Tony, like the others before them, were quick to excuse Brodie's act. They spoke briefly and relapsed into silence. Then, beginning far away and coming closer with the speed of an onrushing hurricane, Gloria heard heavy feet crunching in the dirt and gravel. A hard hand gripped her shoulder, jerking her to her feet.

"You, friend," said Brodie. "What have you got to say about it?"

She hung limp in his powerful hand, speechless.

He dragged her closer to the firelight, peering at her with his red-flecked eyes.

"Don't forget who she is," another voice was saying. Steve Jarrold's. "Remember what I told you."

It was as though he prided himself on the fact that he alone knew her for Gaynor's daughter, and from it derived a sort of ownership of her; for while the others had never caught a glimpse of her until now, he had filled his eyes with her before. "We got to think this out. She came along with King. Got enough of him and switched to Gratton. That's like a woman."

Brodie let her slip down and turned away from her. His mood was not so soon for a woman.

"See she keeps her mouth shut," he said threateningly. "If she ain't got sense enough for that she ain't got sense to go on living."

Benny stooped and feasted his eyes on her. Then, straightening up, he turned to Jarrold with nodding approval.

"She skins anything *I* ever saw," he admitted.

In some strange way it seemed to Gloria that both Benny and Brodie had consigned her to Jarrold as though they admitted his prior claim; as though, among these three, she was looked upon as the property of one. She struggled to her feet.

"Don't let her go," said Brodie. "That's all I got to say about her right now."

She made an uncertain step toward the mouth of the cave. Jarrold moved at her side. She went faster. He put his hand on her.

"Didn't you hear what he said?" he asked.

She tried to break away and run. He held her One clear thought and only one formed in her mind. As she had never longed for anything in her life, she yearned for Mark King.

"Mark!" she screamed, "Mark King! Save me."

Jarrold clapped a big dirty hand over her mouth. He put a wiry arm about her and lifted her and carried her back to the fireside.

"None of that," he growled in her ear. She shrank away as she felt the tensing of his arm and was conscious of the contact of his rag-clothed body. She grew silent, cowering. She heard a sound of something dragging and could not hide her fascinated eyes. Thus she watched as Brodie gripped the slack of Gratton's coat shoulders and shoved the body out into the snow. She even marked how the living man spat after the dead.

"Go to the coyotes," he muttered. "They're your kind."

Gloria knew that if she took a step Jarrold would clutch her again. So she stood very still. Brodie came back and threw some wood on the fire and squatted down over the provisions, seeming to be taking stock of them. Perhaps he was but strengthening his heart, digesting the evidence of the case, assuring himself again after the accomplished fact that the deed was just. Still squatting, he drank again, this time from the bottle which had been Gratton's. As he tilted it up she saw that it was two-thirds full. When he put it down with a long sigh and wiped his wet mouth it was not over half-full. He brooded over the fire, he gave no sign of noticing her.

"Let me go," she said to Jarrold. "I am sick. I'd die here. Please let me go."

Jarrold shifted and looked to his companions. Benny shook his head.

"There ain't no hurry," he stated judicially. "What sort is she, Steve?"

"She come up to Gaynor's place along with Gratton," answered Jarrold as though he knew all about her. "He was crazy gone on her, crazy enough to want to marry her, even. Sent me for the judge. Then Mark King showed up. She fell for him and gave Gratton the go-by. Then she comes into the mountains with King, I guess. Next she gets tired of him and goes back to Gratton."

"'Frisco woman?" asked Benny.

Jarrold nodded. Benny clacked his tongue. Brodie still brooded at his fire, his eyes sullen upon the fitful flame and red embers.

"Where is King?" asked Brodie.

"Where is King?" repeated Jarrold to Gloria.

"I don't know," she answered, speaking with difficulty. "I ... Oh, for God's sake, let me go. I won't say anything about what I saw; I promise. If you will only let me go."

"They promise easy and break promises easier," said Jarrold.

Benny came up and touched Brodie on the shoulder. The squatting man started and scowled. Benny stooped and whispered. Brodie got up heavily and together the two withdrew, going further back in the cave. They talked, but Gloria could not catch the words. She saw the flare of one match after the other as they fell to smoking; the smell of strong tobacco came to her. She looked appealingly to Jarrold. He sidled closer, standing between her and the open.

"I'll pay you a thousand dollars when I get back to San Francisco," she whispered eagerly. "Ten thousand! If you'll let me go now."

Jarrold pondered, his stupid little eyes steady and unwinking on her.

"A thousand dollars," he returned slowly, "wouldn't do me any good if I never got it: as I wouldn't if none of us got clear of this damn' snow; neither would ten I And it wouldn't do me any good if Benny and Brodie shot me full of lead. And it wouldn't be much, anyhow, if we got away with what we found to-day! Everything being as it is, I ain't half as strong for a thousand dollars, nor yet ten, right now as I am for you! And you know it, don't you?"

He tried to ogle her, and her sick dread nearly overwhelmed her.

"And you got sense, too," went on Jarrold, leering meaningly. "It won't be bad to have a man stuck on you that's got all kind of kale, will it, girlie?"

As he poured out his wretched insinuations she was trembling; in her heart she thought that she had spoken truly and would die if they kept her here.

"I am married. To Mr. King," she said as steadily as she could. "I want to go to him. You have no right to keep me here."

"But you don't even know where he is," Jarrold reminded her slyly.

Brodie and Benny had given over their whispering and came back to the fire, where Brail and the Italian looked up at them sharply. Here was another guarded conference among the four; Gloria, though she could watch them, was unable to hear what they were saying. Jarrold began to grow uneasy, so soon is distrust bred amongst those who have found treasure.

Brodie made a last remark and laughed; the others laughed after him, and the four looked toward Jarrold and Gloria. Brodie, leaning back, caught up a bottle and drank, and thereafter passed the bottle to the man nearest him. Gloria was quick to see that he had set his rifle away somewhere against the rock wall in the shadows. Only Brail still clung to his gun; if he should set it aside—if there should come a moment when she could slip to the cave's mouth—in the outside dark, despite the deep snow, she would at least have a chance to escape from them. Even though she had nowhere to go, she longed wildly to be away from them. When their eyes roved toward her she thought that she would rather be dead, out in the clean, white snow, than here.

She wondered if these men were as utterly callous as they seemed. Gratton, so newly dead, appeared forgotten. They laughed and drank, they smoked and spat, they soiled her with their eyes and their talk, quite as though they had neither knowledge nor memory of manslaughter done. Benny alone, for a brief period, appeared nervous. She wondered what he was doing; he had rolled back his coat-sleeve; he was jabbing at his bare forearm with something which now and then caught and reflected the firelight. After a long time she heard a long sigh from Benny; he pulled down his coat-sleeve. The others laughed again.

"It's time we had a little talk," said Brodie out of a short silence. "Without anybody's skirt listening in. Leave her back there, further from the front door, Jarrold. Where she can't get an earful, and where she can't make a getaway; you come on over here a minute."

Gloria made no resistance but sank down limply where Jarrold left her and watched him as he slouched over to the fire. She sought to hear their words, to read the looks on their faces. But she caught only a monotonous mutter, unintelligible but evil, and saw only the bottle passing from one to the other. Brodie finished it and hurled it from him so that it broke noisily. A few times she heard them laugh; she could distinguish Brodie's throaty, bull tone and Benny's nervous cackle. Jarrold did not appear made for mirth, and him she feared most of all; yes, even more than Brodie, whom she had seen do murder, and Benny who, she knew, had done murder. Brail and the Italian said little; they were men to follow where other men led. She fancied that several times Steve Jarrold's little eyes left the bottle, the faces of his companions, and even the pile of gold to quest for her face in the dark.

"Come here," commanded Brodie.

She started. He was calling to her! She got up and moved forward slowly. It was obey or be dragged to him. In the pale light by the fire, standing so that the blaze was between the five men and herself, she stopped. Until now she had been very white; suddenly she knew that her face must be flooded with bright red; she could feel the burn of it. The eyes of the men seemed veritably to disregard her clothes, to make her feel another Lady Godiva.

"Gratton's, then King's, then Gratton's again?" Brodie chuckled. "I don't care whose before Gratton's the first time; but whose after Gratton's the last time, that's it! Who are you for, Bright-Eyes? Me or Steve?"

"No!" she cried, her hands at her breast. "No! I am not like that! I was not Gratton's; I am ... I am Mark King's wife!"

"So?" admitted Brodie good-humouredly. "Well, that cuts no ice; it's open and shut you'd gone back to Gratton. Now, come over here. Closer."

"I won't," she shuddered. "You don't dare make me! I ... Oh, won't you let me go? You have your gold there; you have gold and whiskey; you don't want me...."

"Whiskey, gold, and women," muttered Brodie. "They go together fine. And quit that little schoolgirl dodge; you make me sick. If you wasn't what you are, you wouldn't be where you are. Come over here and give us a kiss." He jerked from his pocket a dull lump, one of the smaller, richer nuggets. "I'm no pincher; come across and I'll give you a whole handful of gold!" His tone was playful.

But Jarrold cut in less playfully:

"Leave her alone, Brodie," he advised. "She don't cotton to you, and, what's more, whose gold is it, anyhow? We ain't divided yet. And she.... Well, if she belongs to anybody, she's mine!"

"So?" Brodie's monosyllable was expressionless. "Well, I was asking *her*. And she ain't answered yet."

Fast as the girl's heart beat, her thoughts sought to fly faster. These men were brutes; here she began, and, alas, here she ended. She had never known what brute meant; she had called Mark King that! And now, if only Mark King could hear her call, could come to her.... But that was less thought than prayer. These were brute beasts; their bestiality when they had first come upon her was terrifying; now, as the alcohol burned in their half-starved stomachs and the further intoxication of gold crept into their blood, her terror was boundless. In a moment she would feel upon her either the hands of Brodie or the hands of Jarrold. And she was helpless and hopeless. Until, since life connotes hope, there came a faint flicker of light. And with it came a sudden, compelling, swift longing. If she might set them to quarrelling over her, to send a snarling man at a snarling man's throat.... Her hands dropped to her sides, and were clenched; she lifted her chin; with all that strength that lay in the innermost soul of Gloria King she strove to drive her great fear out of her eyes, to hide it from their wolfish regard, to summon up in its stead a mocking inscrutability. There was but one thing left to do, but one part to play—Oh, God, if she could play the part! She stood motionless, silent; she battled with herself; she struggled mightily for a calm utterance. And in the end she said in a tone which she managed to make full of challenge:

"Which of you is the better man?"

They stared at her, all of them puzzled by her change of attitude as by her words. Then Brodie, with a noisy explosion of laughter, smote his thigh and, after him, Benny giggled foolishly.

"The better man!" Brodie shouted. "Hear her, Steve, old horse? The better man!" He lunged to his feet; he stood solidly, unswerving though more than ever slow and ponderous. "I'll go you, Steve. The lady's right; she goes to the man who's man enough to get her. That's big Swen Brodie, the best man in these mountains! I'll go you for her, Steve. By God, she's worth it, too."

But Steve Jarrold sat where he was, glaring.

"She's sly," he grunted, cursing before and after. "Can't you see what she's up to? She wants us to fight one another; she'd be glad if we both killed one another. You don't understand women, Brodie; they're sly like cats."

"Make a auction out'n it!" was Benny's mirthful suggestion. "Why just you two guys, anyway? Where do you get that stuff? Free for all, that's what I say!" He waved his bottle. "Auction her off, that's what I say! I'll give a bottle of whiskey for her; hey, Brodie?"

Brodie had laughed when Jarrold spoke; he laughed now. But he looked to Jarrold and not Benny as he spoke; he extended his great hands, the fingers crooked, curving slowly inward, like steel hooks.

"I can eat you alive, and you know it, Steve," he mocked. "What's more, *she* knows it! That's what she wants; she's picked me, Steve! That's just her way of letting you down easy; she don't aim to hurt your feelings. Will you come on and take a fall for her? Or is the lady mine? What's the word? Speak up, man!"

Gloria saw that Jarrold, though he sent a black, scowling look at the bigger man, was afraid. And yet they must fight—they must be driven to blows—she must somehow set them at each others' throats. It was so hard to think at all! Yet she could think forward to one occurrence only that could give her respite and a frail chance for freedom: if they would only fight as, in some dim instinctive way, it was given her to understand that such men would fight once a wrathful blow had been given and taken—if the others would only watch them and not her, if she could come to one of the rifles—or outside—

She turned to Jarrold. She gathered herself for the final supreme effort. She made her eyes grow bright through sheer force of will; she made her lips cease trembling and curve to a smile at the man; she even concealed her loathing and put a ringing note, almost of laughter, into her voice as she said softly:

"I know you are not afraid—and I think—yes, I am sure, that you could whip him!"

Steve Jarrold's eyes flashed. Then they left hers lingeringly; Brodie was stamping impatiently, calling to him.

"Take her!" snapped Jarrold. "Hell take both of you."

The laughter and challenge went out of Swen Brodie's bloodshot eyes; a new red surged all of a sudden into them. He turned and came slowly about the fire, his arms still uplifted, the crooking fingers toward Gloria.

CHAPTER XXX

Scream after scream burst from Gloria's lips; taut nerves seemed to snap all through her body like over-stressed violin strings. She ran, ran anywhere, ran blindly. She ran into Benny, who clutched at her; she fled away from him, back toward the darker end of the cave. The low rumble of a man's laughter answered her; drunken laughter from Brodie. Whether drunk with whiskey or with gold or with lust did not matter; drunk he was. Gloria's shriek rose like a madwoman's; Brodie's thick laughter was its sinister echo. Another man called out something; the slow, heavy feet of Swen Brodie were following, following. Boots scuffling, Brodie pursuing with a wide, patient grin; he was in no hurry, he was so sure of her!

His hands were almost on her. Gloria whipped aside and ran again. He kept between her and the front of the cave; with all of his grinning patience he was as watchful as a cat. She was driven back and back, deeper and deeper into the narrowing tunnel. He came on. He would be upon her in another half-dozen slow, ponderous strides. She could not pass him; she could not dart forward and out; his arms were widely extended on either side. He was expecting that. She could only save herself from him second by second—and the seconds were running out swiftly.

She prayed to God in wild passionate supplication. She prayed for sudden death, death before those horrid, crooked fingers touched her. But while she prayed to God it was of Mark King that she thought. And Mark King, because of her usage of him, was miles and miles away, so far that her despairing shrieks died without penetrating one-millionth part of the empty wastes across which he had trudged. And still she drew back and back and still she prayed for the miracle as she had done that day when she had seen King coming toward her with a rope in his hand, prayed for the earth to split asunder, for a flame to leap out and consume the beast crowding closer upon her—to consume him or herself.

At last she was at the end. The end of the passage-way, the end of hope. Brodie came on, his arms out. She could hear him breathing. She could smell the whiskey he reeked with.... Beyond him she saw Jarrold squatting by the fire; Brail leaning on his rifle, guarding the entrance; Benny and the Italian lounging in the shadows. Figures of hell, watching Brodie's actions with aloof interest ...Brodie made the last step; she felt his hand on her arm, closing, drawing her forward; the last agonized shriek burst from her....

"Oh, God—oh, dear God—"

She did not hear and Brodie did not hearken to a sudden new sound in the cave grown suddenly still; the sound of a cascade of loose stones. They came with a rush, they piled up near the middle of the open cave, dropping from the shadowy rock roof above. But Benny, always on nerve edge, shrilled:

"Look out! A cave-in"

She heard—God had heard—Better crushed under a falling mountain than in those brute arms.

And then she saw. From ten feet above, straight down dropped something else. Taut nerves of those who saw fancied it a great boulder falling. But no boulder this, which, striking the little pile of rocks, became animated, rose, whirled, and—

"Mark!" screamed Gloria. "Mark!"

Turned to stone, incredulous of their eyes, bewildered beyond the power to move, were those who saw. It was Brail who first understood, Brail the one man with a gun in his hands. He whipped it up and began firing, nervous and excited. It was after the second shot that King's rifle answered him; it roared out like the crash of doom in Gloria's ears; she saw the stabbing spurt of fire. Brail sagged where he stood, crumpled and pitched forward, his rifle clattering loudly against the rocks.

But by now the brief stupor that had locked the other men in staring inaction was gone. Gloria saw figures leaping forward; she knew that Brodie's hands had relinquished her; she saw Brodie bearing down on King, roaring inarticulately as he went; she saw Benny and Jarrold and the Italian bearing down upon him; King was in the midst of all that. They were upon him before Brail's head had struck the ground. They gave him no time, no space for another shot. He swept his clubbed rifle high over his head; she heard the blow when he struck, the hideous sound of a crushing skull. A man went down, she did not know which one. Only it was not Mark—thank God it was not Mark King!

And now King had a little room and an instant of his own as two other men swerved widely about the falling figure. He fired again, not putting the rifle to his shoulder. Another man fell, lay screaming, rolled aside—was forgotten.

"Where's my rifle?" Brodie was yelling.

He couldn't find it in the dark; he couldn't stop to grope for it. But Gloria knew; she remembered. She ran for it, found it, straightened up with it in her shaking hands.

Again King was using his weapon as a club, since they pressed him so closely. Again came that terrible sound; Steve Jarrold it was who went down. And with it another sound, that of hard wood splintering. The rifle was broken over his head, the stock whirled close to Gloria, King had only the short heavy steel barrel in his hands.

Benny had circled to the far side; Brodie had caught up a great thick limb of wood. They were coming at King from two sides at once.... Gloria tried to aim, pulled the trigger, tugging frantically. Only then she remembered to draw the hammer back; it was Brodie's ancient rifle and she struggled to get it cocked. She shuddered at the report. The bullet sang in front of Benny, and he stopped dead in his tracks. He was near the cave's mouth. Gloria pointed, forgot the hammer remembered, got the gun cocked and fired again. Benny plunged wildly forward; she did not know if she had hit him. He hurled himself headlong toward the narrow exit and through.

She had forgotten Brodie and King! She turned toward them. She did not dare shoot now; King was in the way. He moved aside as if he understood her trouble; Brodie, grown unthinkably quick of foot, moved with him. Brodie, too, understood. She saw him leap in and strike. The blow landed, a glancing blow. King seemed to have grown tired; he moved so slowly. But he did move and toward Brodie; he swung his clubbed rifle-barrel and beat at Brodie's great face with it. Beat and missed and almost fell forward. Again Brodie struck; again King beat at him. They moved up and down, back and forth; Brodie was cursing under his breath, and at last jeering. King was moving more and more slowly; his left arm swung as if it were useless; Brodie swept up his club in both hands, grunting audibly with every blow.... Oh, if she could only shoot ... if she only dared shoot! But Brodie, nimble on his feet that had been so patiently slow just now, kept King always in front of him, between him and Gloria's rifle.

"I'll get you, King. I'll get you," shouted Brodie, his voice exulting. "I always wanted to get you—right!"

There was a crash, the splintering of wood against steel. Both men had struck together; Brodie's club had broken to splinters. And the rifle-barrel in King's hands flew out of his grip and across the cave, ringing out as it struck. The two men, their hands empty, stood a moment staring at each other. Then Brodie shouted, a great shout of triumph, and sprang forward. And Mark King, steadying himself, ignoring the hot trickle of blood down his side where Benny's second bullet had torn his flesh, met him with a cry that was like Brodie's own. In his hot brain there was no thought of handicap, of odds, of Brodie's advantage. There was only the mad rage which had hurled him here, one man against five in a girl's defence, that and a raving, unleashed blood lust, the desire, overshadowing all else, to have Brodie's brute throat in his hands, to batter Brodie's brute face into the rocks. They met in their onrush like two bodies hurled from catapults; they struck and grappled and fell and rolled together, one now as they strove, locked in the embrace of death. An embrace in which Brodie's was the greater weight, the greater girth, the greater strength—and Mark King's the greater sheer, clean manhood.

Gloria ran toward them, the rifle shaking in her hands. Brodie feared her and strove to turn and twist so that she could not shoot. King saw her and shouted in a terrible voice which was not like Mark King's voice:

"Don't shoot—let me—"

She did not heed; she would shoot—if ever she could be sure that she would not shoot him. But she did not dare—they thrashed about so madly. They were like octopuses in mortal combat; their arms flailing seemed more than four arms—

Brodie had his hands at King's throat—King's hands were at Brodie's throat. She saw Brodie's bestial face gloating. He was so confident now. She saw his great hands shut down, sinking into the flesh. King's face, when she got one swift glimpse of it, was set, void of expression. King's hands, with tendons bursting, sank deeper and deeper. Then she understood that each man had the grip that he wanted; that it was a mere matter now of strength and endurance and will—and that glorious thing, sheer, clean manhood.

They were breathing terribly; they lay stiller, stiller. They did not thrash about so much. Their eyes were starting out of their sockets; their faces were turning purple—or was it the firelight? Men's faces could not look like that—not while the men lived. They gasped now; they did not breathe.

One of Brodie's hands came away hastily. He began battering at King's face, battering like a steam-piston. The blows sounded loudly; blood broke out under the terrific pounding. King's grip did not alter, did not shift. His eyes were shut but he clung on, grim, looking a dead man, but a man whose will lasted on after death. Brodie wrenched; they rolled over. Still King's hands did not leave their grip.

They were on their feet, staggering up and down, two men moulded together like one man. Brodie struck blow after blow, and with every thud Gloria winced and felt a pain through her own body. And still King held his grip, both hands sunk deep into the thick throat.

They were apart, two blind, staggering men. What parted them they did not know and Gloria could not see. Thus they stood for a second only. Brodie lifted his hands—weak hands rising slowly, slowly—uncertainly. King saw him through a gathering mist; Brodie opened his mouth to draw in great sobbing breaths of air. King, the primal rage upon him, saw the great double teeth bared, and thought that his enemy was laughing at him. It was King who gathered himself first and struck first. All of the will he had, all of the endurance left in his battered body, all of the strength God gave him, he put into that blow. He struck Brodie full in the face, between the little battered blue eyes. And Brodie fell. He rose; he got to his knees and sagged up and forward. King's shout then was to ring through Gloria's memory for days to come; he bore down on Swen Brodie, caught him about the great body, lifted him clear of the floor and hurled him downward. Brodie struck heavily, his head against the rocks. And where he fell he lay—stunned or dead.

"Come," said King to Gloria. "Come quick."

He turned toward the cave's mouth and with one hand began to drag away the stones so that they could go out. His other hand was pressed to his side. His work done, he picked up the rifle at his feet and went out. Gloria, swaying and stumbling, came after him. Neither spoke a word as they made a slow way through the snow. King went unsteadily with dragging feet. They climbed the cliff laboriously. They were in their cave—it was like home. She dropped down on the fir-boughs, stumbling to them in the dark.

CHAPTER XXXI

Gloria did not know if she had slept or fainted. When she regained consciousness, though it was pitch dark and dead still, there was no first puzzled moment of uncertainty. That last wonderfully glad thought which had filled brain and heart when she sank down on her fir-boughs had persisted throughout her moments or hours of unconsciousness, pervading her subconscious self gloriously, flowering spontaneously in an awakening mind: Mark King had come back to her in her moment of peril; he had battled for her like the great-hearted hero that he was, he had saved her and had brought her home. Back home! She had prayed to God when utter undoing seemed inevitable, when death had seemed more desirable than life, and He had answered. He had sent Mark King to her!

She was saved, and though it was cold and dark and still, she felt her heart singing within her. Having lived through all that she had endured, having been brought safely through it, she was as confident of the future as though never had evil menaced her. She felt new strength coursing through her blood, new hope rising within her, new certainty that all was right with her and Mark King, that all would be right eternally. Terror and anguish and despair that had surged over her in so many great flooding waves now receded and were gone; in their place shone the great flame of life triumphant; she thrilled through with the largeness of life.

Never, thank God, would she forget how Mark King, forgetful

of self, contemptuous of the frightful odds against him, had hurled himself into the midst of those drunken brutes; never would she forget how godlike he had stood forth in her eyes as those others leaped upon him and he beat them back. Forgetful of self—he had always been forgetful of self! She could not think of him as she had ever thought of any other man she had ever known—for what other man would have come to her as he had done, courting death gladly if only he could stand between her and the hideous thing that attacked her? The rush of great events had swept her mind clear of pettiness and prejudice; they bore her on from familiar viewpoints and to new levels; like roaring winds out of a tempestuous north they cleared away the wretched fogs that had enwrapped a self-centred girl; they made her see a man in the naked glory of his sheer, clean manhood.

To her now he stood forth clothed in magnificence. She could think upon him only in superlatives. He was fearless and he was unselfish; he was kind and generous and as honest-hearted as God's own clear sunshine. She knew now, suddenly and for the first time, because he had shown her, what the simple word *man* meant. How far apart he stood from such as Brodie, the beast! How high above such as Gratton!—And once, in the city, she had been ashamed of him and had turned to Gratton! Because he had appeared to her without just so much black cloth upon his back cut in just such a style! And now how bitterly she was ashamed of her shame. But for only an instant. Thereafter she forgot shame of any sort and exulted in her pride of him and in her pride that she was proud.

Yes, in glad defiance of a Gloria that had been, she was proud of the manhood of a man who had beaten her! He had been right; he had done that as the last argument with an empty-headed, selfish girl who deserved no better at his hands, a girl who had been like the Gratton whom she so abhorred and despised—despised even in death. She had been like Gratton the cowardly, contemptible, petty, selfish—dishonourable! All along Mark King had been right and she had been wrong, at every step. He had been gentle and patient after a fashion which now set her wondering and, in the end, lifted him to new heights in her esteem. When, without loving him, she had lied with her eyes and married him, that had been a Gratton sort of trick—like stealing his partners' food—

Without loving him! No, thank God; not that! She had always loved him; she loved him now with her whole heart and soul, with an adoration she had saved for him. When in the springtime she had ridden with him through the forest-lands, when their hands had touched, when he had held her in his arms—when she had seen him that first time from the stairway and had looked down into his clear eyes and through them into his heart—she had always loved him! She wanted suddenly to go to him, to slip into his arms, to make herself humble in pleading for his forgiveness. She was not afraid that he would not forgive; he was so big of heart that he would understand.

"Mark!" she called softly.

In the utter dark she could see nothing. The absolute stillness was unbroken. She called anxiously: "Mark, where are you?" There was no answer. She sprang up and called to him over and over. When still there was no reply she began a hurried search for a match; there were still some upon the rock shelf. Then it was that she stumbled over something sprawling on the floor.

"Mark!" she cried again. "Oh—Mark—"

She found a match; she got some dry twigs blazing. In their light she saw him. He lay on his back like a dead man, his arms outflung, his white face turned up toward hers. There was a great smear of blood across his brow, the track of a bloody hand as it had sought to wipe a gathering dimness out of his eyes. The fire burned brighter; she saw it glisten upon a little pool of blood at her side. She knelt and bent over him, scarcely breathing. If he were dead—if, after all this, Mark King were dead—His eyes were closed; his face was deathly white, looking the more ghastly from the dark stain across it. She lifted her own hand that had touched his side and looked at it with wide frightened eyes; it, too, was red. At that moment King's face was no ghastlier than hers.

For a little while she sat motionless, her brain reeling. But almost immediately her brain cleared and there stood forth as in a white light the one thought: *Mark King was about to die, and he must not die*! For he was Mark King, valiant and full of vigour and vitality, a man strong and hardy and lusty, a man who would not be beaten! He was the victor, not the vanquished. And, further, she, Gloria King, Mark King's wife, would not let him die! He was hers, her own; she would hold him back to her. Had he not come to her when she needed him, and done his uttermost for her? If now she was filled with life and the pulsating love of life, it was his doing. And now it was her task—her glorious, God-given privilege!—to do for him, to fight for him, ignoring the odds against her, to save him. She sprang up filled with stubborn, confident determination. He was hers and she would not let him die. She had learned to fight; she had fought against Gratton, against Brodie; she would fight as she had never done until now against death itself.

He was big and she little, yet she dragged his bed close to his side and got her arms about him and lifted him enough to get him upon the blankets. She ran to her fire and piled and piled wood on it until the flames roared noisily and brightened everything about her. She ran back to him and knelt again and slipped her hand inside his shirt, seeking his heart. The deep chest was barely warmer than death; the heart stirred only faintly. But it did beat. She sought the wound Brail's bullet had made and found it in his side. There was blood on her hands but she did not notice it now. She found where the bullet had entered and where it had torn its way out through his flesh. She did not know if any vital organ lay in that narrow span or if any major artery had been severed or if the rifle-ball had merely glanced along the ribs and been deflected by them; she only knew that he had lost much blood, that it must have gushed freely while he strove with Swen Brodie, and that now it must be stopped utterly. There seemed to be so little blood left in the pale, battered body! She did see how in the intense cold it had coagulated over the wounds, checking its own flow. But she did not mean for him to lose another precious drop. And then it was that Gloria's hands achieved the first really important work they had ever done in her life. She tore bits away from her own under-garments and made soft pads over each wound; with their butcher-knife she cut a long strip from a blanket. This she wound about his limp body, making a long, tight bandage. All this time he had not moved; she had to bend close to be sure that he still breathed. She got snow and wiped his face clean of blood, touching the closed eyelids gently.

When still the eyes remained shut and he looked like one already dead, she longed wildly for some stimulant. There was coffee; she would make hot coffee do. She got the coffee-pot among the coals, filled it with snow to melt, recklessly poured coffee into it. Then, while she awaited the slow heating, she returned to him and for the first time saw how wet his boots were.

She got the boots off and felt his feet; she stooped over them until for an instant she laid her cheek against a bare foot. It was like ice. She recalled how he had ministered to her. She heated a blanket and wrapped it about his feet and ankles. She heated other blankets and put them about him. The canvas at the cave's mouth had been torn down; she got it back into place to make it warmer for him. She put fresh wood on the fire. She hastened the coffee boiling all that she could by placing bits of dry wood close all about the pot.

She knelt at King's side; she got an arm under his shoulders and managed to lift him a little; she rolled up a blanket and put it under his head. Then she brought the cup of black coffee and with a spoon got some of it between his teeth. She spilled more than went into his mouth but she was rewarded by seeing the throat muscles contract as involuntarily he swallowed. Thus, patient and determined and very, very gentle with him, she got several spoonfuls of coffee down him. Thereafter she let him lie back again while she sought to plan cool-thoughtedly just how she must care for him, just what she could do for him. She knew little of nursing and yet knew instinctively that his condition was precarious, that he must be kept warm and still, that what strength remained in him must be saved by proper nourishment. *Proper nourishment!*

There were scraps of food left; Brodie and his men, in their gold fever, had not so much as thought to gather up the few bits of scanty provisions. She began taking careful stock; she found a scrap of bread that had been knocked to the floor and kicked aside; she picked it up and, carrying a torch with her, began seeking any other fallen morsels. In this search she came once to the hole in the floor through which Brodie and the others had gone down into Gus Ingle's treasure-chamber. And at its side she found something which at this moment was a thousand times more precious in her staring eyes than if it had been so much solid gold. It was a great hunk of fresh meat. Instantly she knew how it had come here. King had killed his bear! That was why he had returned to-night. He had brought it here; had missed her; had dropped it here. And then? She understood now, too, how he had come so unexpectedly into the lowest cave. He had gone down through this hole and had known a passage-way which led on down. She stood by the hole, bending over it, listening, wondering if any man stirred down there. But that was but for a moment. She caught up the bear meat, carrying it in both arms, and hurried back to her fire.

Though she knew little more of cookery than of nursing, she set about the very sensible task of making a strong broth. The proper nourishment that had seemed so impossible a moment ago was now ready at hand.

"God is good," she whispered, a sudden new gush of love and reverence in her heart. "He will help me now."

Jackson Gregory

For herself, since her own strength must be kept up, she cooked a strip of the meat on the coals. Then she went to King and for a long time sat at his side, her eyes upon his white face, her hand clasping his. Again and again she stooped and laid her cheek against the strong but now lax fingers; once she put her lips to his forehead; when she sat back her eyes were wet and the slow tears welled up and trickled unnoticed down her cheeks. But they were tears which left the heart sweetened, tears of tenderness, of gratitude, of sympathy and love.

As the night wore on, since she was determined that King should not be chilled, her fire consumed a great part of the wood. More wood must be brought; to-night or in the morning. She went to the canvas flap and looked out. There were clouds, but also there were wide rifts through which the stars blazed in all of that glorious crystalline beauty of the stars of the winter Sierra. While she stood looking out the moon, almost at the full, gilded a cloud edge, and after a moment broke through like an augury of joy. Stars and moon made the wilderness over into a land of fairy; at ten million points the snow caught the light, flashing it back as though the white robe spread over the solitudes were sewn with gems. Never had the world looked so white as now with a rare light shining upon its smooth purity; it was clean and fresh, gloriously spotless. Where black shadows lay they but accentuated the whiteness across which they fell.

Out of this sleeping, enchanted land, rising above it, sweeping across it, a low voice like a whisper came to her, a whisper in her ears that became a song in her heart. The snow that had, clung to the pines, muting their needles and stilling their branches, had dropped on during the day. Now the night wind which drove the clouds lingered through the pine tops and set them swaying gently in the vast, harmonic rhythm which is like the surging of a distant ocean. The everlasting whisper of the pines, that ancient hushed voice which through the countless centuries has never been still save when briefly silenced by the snow; which had borne its message to Gloria when on that first day she went with Mark King into the mountains; which many a time had mingled with her fancies, tingeing them, leading her to dream of another life than that of city streets; which now, suddenly, set chords vibrating softly in her own bosom. All these days it had been stilled; had it called her ears would have been deaf to it. But now insistently it bore a message to her, such a message as from now on she would hear in the quiet voices of her little camp-fire. To her, attuned by those varying emotions which latterly had had their wills with her, it was the ancient call; the summons back to the real things of his, to the bigness and the true meaning of life. Rising in response to it, awakening in her own breast, were the old human, instinctive influences, sprouting seeds in the blood of her forbears. It was the eternal call of the mother earth that one like Gloria must hear and hearken to and understand before she could set firm feet upon the ashes of a vanquished self to rise to the true things of womanhood. It was the

"... one everlasting Whisper day and night repeated—so: Something hidden. Go and find it. Go and look behind the Ranges—Something lost behind the Ranges. Lost and waiting for you. Go!"

Gloria understood. In her heart, lifting her eyes from the white glory of the earth to the bright glory of the sky, she thanked God that she understood.

Benny and the Italian were still alive and might be near? That did not in any way affect the fact that there must be wood brought for King's fire. She turned back for the rifle and the rope. She saw that King had not stirred; that he seemed plunged in a deep, quiet sleep. She stood over him, looking down at him with her love for him softening her eyes. He was going to get well—*if she did her part.* And her part was so clearly indicated; to give him broth and to keep his fire going. She did not hesitate and she was not afraid as she went down the cliffs. She meant to be Mark King's mate; she meant to be worthy of being his mate. He had not hesitated, he had not been afraid, when one man against five he dropped down into the lowest cave. She, like him, was of pioneer stock. She remembered that impressive monument to pioneer fortitude which stands in the mountains where the highway runs by Donner Lake; as in a vision she saw the little group that crowns the rugged pile. The woman, the pioneer mother, holding her baby to her breast, pressing on with her own mate, looking fearlessly ahead, daring what might come, not lagging behind the man, rather ready to lead the way should he falter. It was a glorious thing to have blood like that in her veins; it was the finest thing in the world to be a woman like that woman.

She stepped down into the packed snow at the base of the cliffs. Here she stood looking up and down the gorge for any sign of Benny or of the Italian or of any other of Brodie's crowd who might be alive and astir. But she saw no one; even Gratton's body, where it had been tumbled out into the snow, was hidden. She heard the deep, quiet breathing of the pines; the canon stream rushed and gurgled and babbled, shouting as it leaped over fails, flinging spray which the moonlight and starlight made over into jewels.

Gloria worked at her fuel-gathering, working in the snow until her hands and feet were nearly frozen. But her heart was warm. Though she made haste and was ever watchful and on the alert, her mind filled with such thoughts as had never come trooping into it before. Fragmentary, they were like bright bits spinning about a common centre. She looked up at the wide sky and it was borne in upon her that the universe was mighty and wonderful and infinite; she looked into her own heart and saw where she had been small and silly and finite. She saw that the snow-covered ridges stretching endlessly were like a concrete symbol of that infinity which extended above and about her; that they were clothed in beauty. She knew that when Mark King was made whole again and had forgiven her and they stood together, hand locked in hand, she would have no fear any more for his mountains, but rather a great, abiding love. She saw that her life had been empty; that only love could fill it, love and service such as she was rendering to-night. Pretty clothes, dress suits, did not matter, and strong, loyal hearts did matter. To-night she would rather have Mark King hold her in his arms and say "I love you" than to have all of the red gold in all of the world.

Three times that night she made the trip up and down the cliffs, bringing wood. At the end, though near exhaustion, she sank down by the fire for but a few minutes. The bear meat was boiling and bubbling; she poured off a little of the broth, cooled it, and then, as she had given King the coffee, she forced some of the strong soup between his teeth. She touched his cheek and dared hope that it was not so icy cold; she chafed his feet and wrapped them again in a not blanket. And then, with all of her covers given to him, she drew a coat about her shoulders and sat down at his side, on the edge of his blankets. And here, throughout the night, she sat, dozing and waking, rising again and again to keep the fire burning.

She started up to find it full day; she had been asleep, her head against his knee. The fire was dying down; she jumped up and replenished it, setting the broth back among the coals. King lay as he had lain last night; his continued coma was like a profound quiet sleep. He was very pale, and yet certainly not paler than when she had first looked upon his blood-smeared face.

She went to the canvas screen and looked out. The sun was shining. And oh, the glory of the sun after these long dark days! The sky was a deep, serene, perfect blue. The snow shone and glittered and sparkled everywhere. Down in the gorge she saw a little bird in quick flight. It skimmed the water; it Lighted on a rock in the spray; it put back its head and seemed to be bursting with a joy of song. A water-ouzel! A friend from out a happy past—To Gloria it seemed that the world was full of promise.

All day long she ministered to King, going back and forth tirelessly, since love and hope inspired every step she made. None of Brodie's men had come; she felt a strange confidence that they would not come. They were afraid of King as jackals are afraid of a lion; further, they did not know that he was wounded. She thought little of them, having much else to think of. She wound King's watch, guessing at the time; she judged it sensible to force a little nourishment upon him at regular intervals and brought him his broth every two hours.

At a little before noon Gloria, stooping over the fire, started erect and whirled about. King's eyes were open! She ran to him, dropping on her knees beside him, catching up his hand, whispering:

"Mark! Oh, Mark—thank God!"

He looked at her strangely. There was a puzzled, bewildered expression in his eyes. He strove to move and again looked at her with that strange bewilderment. She saw his lips move—he wanted to say something, to ask something and, deserted now by all of that magnificent strength on which he had always leaned, was as weak as a baby.

"Don't try to talk, Mark," she cried softly. "Please; not yet. You are better; everything is all right."

She gave his hand a last squeeze and hurried back to the fire; his eyes, still shadow-filled, followed her curiously. She came back to him with cup and spoon. This he could understand; he opened his lips for the spoon, he accepted what she gave him and when she had finished lay looking up at her wonderingly.

"You mustn't talk, Mark," she commanded him gently as, again, she knelt by him. "You are getting so much stronger! I'll tell you everything. It was last night; you have been unconscious ever since. None of the other men have been near; I haven't even seen one of them."

She saw his eyes clear.

"Mark," she whispered, "we are safe here because—because you are so wonderful! You were like a god—the bravest, noblest, best man in, all the world! You came in time; you saved me, Mark; they had not put hand upon me. And I am well and strong now; I am going to take care of you; you must just lie still and get well—*Oh, Mark*—"

His eyes closed again; he seemed very faint, very weary. Hushed, she sat tense, her eyes never moving from his face. After a long time he opened his eyes again; he tried again to speak; when the words did not come he managed a strange, shadowy smile with his bloodless lips and in another moment had sunk again into that heavy sleep that was so like death.

When next, two hours later, she again brought his broth, he stirred at her touch and awoke. This time his eyes cleared swiftly; he remembered the other awakening and her words. He looked at her long and searchingly and she understood what lay back of that look; he was wondering how she managed, how she endured to care for them both, how without his active aid she withstood hardship. And this time she smiled at him.

"I have been dining sumptuously on bear steaks," she told him lightly. "And I have slept and kept warm. There has been no one near. And the days are fine again. It was clear last night; the sun has been shining all day. Now, when you've had your own lunch, I'll tell you anything you want to know. Only you must not try to talk yet, Mark; not until to-morrow. I want you strong and well again, you know; it's lonesome without you."

She gave him, for the first time, a whole cup of broth, glorying in the certainty that already he was stronger. But even yet his weakness was so great that, before she had spoken a dozen sentences, he was asleep again. Clearly, even to Gloria, if but a little more blood had ebbed out of the wounded side, he would never have awakened; clearly to Gloria, triumphant, it had been she who had held him back from death. She, Gloria King, alone, had fought the great grim battle; hers was the victory. For at last she knew with her brain, as all along she had known in her heart, that it was to be victory.

So the hours passed. For the most part King slept, lapsing into the deep stupor of a drugged man. But at times he stirred restlessly; with slowly returning strength his wounds pained him; in his sleep he muttered; Gloria, watching him, winced as she saw his brow contract and saw how he tried to shift his body as though to pull away from something that hurt him.

*   *   *   *   *

King was awake. Awakening, he tried to move. His utter weakness, like a great weight bearing down upon him, held him powerless. But his mind, slowly freeing itself from the shadows of sleep, was suddenly very clear. He could turn his head a little. It was late afternoon; outside the sun was still shining, for a patch of light lay at the side of the canvas flap. At first he did not see Gloria; but his eyes quested until at last they found her. She lay by the fire, her head upon her arm, sleeping. The little huddled body looked weary beyond expression.

For a long time his haggard eyes remained with her. She lay on the rocks, without a blanket. His hand moved weakly; there were blankets under him, blankets covering him; his feet were wrapped in a blanket. He remembered that a long, long time ago she had said to him: "It was last night." All this long, long time he had had all the blankets.... He looked again at Gloria, at the fire; he saw wood piled near by. For many minutes he puzzled the matter; in the end it was obvious, even to a man as sick as King, that she must have gone for wood. Perhaps more than once. He closed his eyes and lay very still. He knew now that he had been desperately hurt; that, wounded, his fight with Brodie had brought him very near a weakness from blood loss that was pale twin to death. And yet he was alive and warm; he had had broth and blankets and the fire had been kept blazing. He managed to slip a hand inside his shirt; before his fingers found it he knew that the bandage was there. Gloria had done all this ... Gloria, whom he had struck ...

Ever since that blow, the one act of his life which he would have given so much to have undone, he had been ashamed. He had rejoiced in his battle with the men who had threatened Gloria with worse than death, rejoiced that in some way he might make reparation. But now, beginning to understand all that Gloria had done for him, how great were the sacrifices she had made for him, lying unconscious of all she did, it seemed to him that the thing that he had done was a very small thing set in the scales against her own acts. He wanted to get up and go to her; to put his blankets about her; to play the man's part and protect and shelter. But he could not so much as raise his voice to call her to him.... Ever since that blow, upbraiding himself, he had said: "She was only a little, terrified girl and you were a brute to her." And now he thought wonderingly: "After that, she has worked for you, has nursed you, has saved the worthless life in you when she should have let you die." Again his eyes flew open; now they clung to her with a strange look in them, born of many emotions.

Gloria, as though she felt his eyes upon her, stirred, rose, pushed the hair back from her eyes and came quickly to him. And as she came, she smiled. She went down on her knees beside him and took his hand in her two and held it tight. She had never seen in his eyes a look like the one now burning in them. She could not understand its mute message, but she spoke softly:

"Everything is all right, Mark. And you are better every time you wake."

His lips strove to frame words. She bent close to them and heard his wondering whisper:

"Every—thing—all right?"

"Yes, thank God," she whispered back to him. "Everything in all the wide, wide world!"

No, he could not understand that. She saw perplexity in his

eyes now. But she did not mean to let him talk yet and it was time for broth again. But again he was whispering:

"Blankets—yours—"

"Yes, Mark. After you have had your nourishment. When I need them."

But when he had taken his cup of hot broth he slipped off to sleep again and Gloria, smiling a tender smile, sat by her fire watching him as a mother watches a sick baby who, the doctor has just told her, will live.

CHAPTER XXXII

That night Gloria, listening now to King's breathing, now to the crackling of her fire, grew restless, restless. Again and again she went to look out into the quiet moonlight night, across the glittering expanses of pure white glistening snow. It was the restlessness of one who had taken a giant determination; who but awaited impatiently for the time to do what she was bent upon doing. In her heart was still that new-born gladness; in her bosom there was still something singing like the liquid voice of a bird. It had sung for the first time when first she had ministered to King, when she had understood what love's service was, when she had gone down the cliffs for firewood, when, because of her tireless nursing, she had been rewarded by his opening eyes; as the hours wore on it had grown into a chant triumphant. She, Gloria, had lived to do something that was noble and unselfish and brave; she, Gloria, had been unafraid and unswerving; she had saved a man's life. And that life was Mark King's! She had made amends; she had set her feet unfalteringly in a new trail; throughout her being she was aglow with the consciousness of one who had gladly done love's labour.

Now she waited only for the hour when again King must have his broth. She gave it to him, smiled at him, commanded him to go back to sleep, promising to talk with him in the morning. And then, when again he breathed with the quiet regularity of one sleeping, she went eagerly about her task.

Now, at her hour of need, she was buoyed up by a great and

wonderful confidence that she could not fail. Thus far she had accomplished each duty as it had stood before her, and from successes achieved grew the new faith that in to-night's task, perhaps the supreme and final labour, she would succeed again. They must have more meat; to-morrow or the next day, at latest, for the steaks which she had eaten and the strong broths to maintain and rebuild strength in. King had cut deeply into their supply. And she knew Mark King well enough to be very certain that, the moment he could summon strength enough to command his tottering body to stand on two legs, he would go. Now, while he was still too weak to observe greatly what went on about him and while he slept most of the time, it was for her to be before him. Fortunately—and were not all omens bright with hope?—it had not snowed since King made his kill; she could follow in the trail he had made and it would lead her unerringly to the spot where he had left the rest of the meat. She had everything ready, rifle, small packet of food, knife, even matches and strips torn from the sack for her feet. Down in the gorge, clutching her rifle, she stood looking, listening. Always the thought of Benny and the other man was on the rim of her consciousness, and fear is a basic and elemental emotion. But, though the moon set forth all details in clear relief against the snow, there was no man in sight, and, in the intense determination possessing her, she throttled down all fear-thoughts. She clung with a deep fervour to the thoughts that she and Mark King had put disaster behind them, that ahead lay hope and happiness, that God was with her and about her, and that all danger was gone. Down the canon she saw the broken, uneven snow where Brodie and his men had left their tracks, irregular trails up which Gratton had come, down which Benny and the Italian had fled. Upward along the gorge was one deep, straight path, wide and hard packed, the track of Mark King's crude snow-shoes. Into this she stepped, thinking even at the time how even Mark King's trail was characteristic of him and different from that of the other men; it looked purposeful and confident and, like the man himself, driving straight on. There was a sense of comfort in treading where he had trodden before her.

The world slept, but its quiet breathing she seemed to hear as the air drew through the pines. She turned up the gorge, a tiny dark figure in an immense white wilderness. The stars shone and she loved them; they were like bright companionable candles. The moon shed its soft lustre and she loved it; it thrust shadows back and drove out the dark. The night was all quiet splendour and peace and serenity. The snow was crisp, crunching underfoot; sunny days had thawed, clear, cold nights had frozen, and the crust had begun to form. Before she had gone a dozen feet she discovered this and its importance to her; where King's weight on the snow-shoes, along a twice-travelled trail, had packed the snow and where now the sun and cold had done their work, there was a crust which upbore her slight weight; she could walk swiftly; there was to be no more floundering. She could run!

And run she did, when she had crested the first ridge and had started down the far side. It was like flying! The crisp air cut her glowing cheeks; her blood leaped along her veins; she breathed deeply, a great, uplifting elation bore her along. Love—God is love—smoothed the way before her; the stars ran with her, the great blazing stars to which again and again she lifted her eyes. They spoke to her; they came close to her; when she stopped, resting, they were all about her, bending down, and she was lifted up among them. Fervour and the ecstasy of the hour in which was doing to the uttermost, forgetful of pettiness and selfishness and cowardice—she prayed mutely that she was done with them for ever, that never again would she be such a woman as Gratton had been a man—made her over into a radiant, glorious Gloria. The night stamped itself upon her for all time; out of the night she drew, as one draws air into his lungs, a new faith that was akin to the man's whom she served. For one cannot be alone with the stars and be unmoved by them; they are serene with eternity, refulgent with the perfect beauty of a perfect creation, eloquent to the heart of man and woman of true values. Under the fields of their vastitude, confronted by their infinity, Gloria, like thousands before, understood that man in fevered times is prone to turn to false gods. Gus Ingle's gold—her own gold, one day—was a thing to smile at. Or, at best, not a thing to expend wildly for gowns and gowns and shoes and stockings and limousines; to-night Gloria felt that she had had her fill of vanities like those, that she was done with them; that if, for every moan and agony and slow death and thought of envy Gus Ingle's gold had brought into the world, she could create a smile here and a hope fulfilled there and a glow yonder, she would ask nothing else of the yellow dirt. For dirt or rock or dross it was, and that was as clear as starlight. If her hand but lay in the hand of Mark King, what did gold matter? Or dresses—or what people thought or said of her or him? A strange little smile touched her lips.

"I love you," she whispered, as though Mark were with her—as in her soul he was.

Had there not been a great, glowing love in her heart she would have been afraid. But there was no room for fear. Had she not felt that he was with her and that God was with her she must have felt an unutterable, dreary loneliness; but she was upborne at every step and gloried in every exertion.

And exertion, until she came close to the limits of endurance, was to be hers that white night; hers the knowledge of supreme endeavour. On and on she went across the immense glistening smooth fields through which the trail ahead was the only scar, through groves of black pines whispering, whispering, whispering, down into shadow-filled canons, out into the open again, up and down and on and on, a tiny dot upon the endless wastes. Fatigue came upon her suddenly, when she had forgotten to save her strength and had gone over-fast. She rested, lying on her back, her eyes closed. She opened her eyes, she saw the stars, she rose and went on. She had gone miles; how many she could not guess. Always, after for a little while she had dropped down wearily, she rose again and went on; she learned that, though beaten down, one might rise again. That was Mark King's way; it would be her way. Despite the rags about her boots her feet were soon dangerously cold. She passed into the embrace of a forest of black trees casting blacker shadows. Their branches seemed motionless, but they sang to her with hushed voices. And always there was the trail King had made, leading her on; where he had gone before, she followed.

Where he had made slow progress, seeking game and breaking trail, she went swiftly on the packed snow. So, in the full splendour of the moon, she came at last to the final ridge, whence, looking down into the canon, she saw the end of her trail: hanging from a bent pine sapling was what she knew must be his bear. Down the steep slope she went, half sliding, half rolling. In the bed of the ravine she landed softly in the drift; here she rested, sitting in a nest of snow. And before she had stirred to begin the last short span of her journey, there came suddenly out of the silence a strange, quivering cry, bursting out upon her; a sobbing, throbbing scream.

"A woman!" cried Gloria, aghast.

A woman in an agony of terror, she thought. Or a lost soul, the wandering spirit of the dead, or God knew what impossible thing. Sudden terror leaped out upon her, striking like a knife into her heart. Fear, banished all this time, surprised her and clutched at her throat and paralysed her muscles. Blind panic gripped her. Then came the piercing scream again, and with it enlightenment, and Gloria sank back, seeming to melt into the snow about her. Yonder, just upon the next ridge where the moonlight carved in fine details the outline of a big bare boulder, stood the thing that had screamed; in this light its great body was weirdly magnified, so that the entire length of seven or eight feet appeared to Gloria's frightened eyes twice that. Long-bodied and lithe, small-headed and merciless, steel-muscled and chisel-clawed, the big cat in silhouette twitched its restless tail back and forth nervously, and from snarling jaws sent forth its almost human call to cut across vast, still distances.

Gloria drew back and back where she crouched, her body pressed into the snow-bank, in a panicky desire to hide. The big cat had smelled the meat, she guessed swiftly. When it leaped upward, seeking to snatch down the swinging weight, or clambered up the pine, then she must spring up and run, run as she had never run in her life, away from this terrible, murderous thing, back to King. Unconscious of cold and wet, she cowered and waited, scarce breathing. She saw how the big beast put up its head and sniffed; did it in reality smell the meat? Or had it sensed her presence?

For what seemed a very long time the gaunt-bodied animal stood as still as the rock beneath it; then, silent and swift, it turned and, like a cat at home leaping down from a table, dropped into the shadows at the base of the rock, and was lost to Gloria's sight in a little hollow. She waited, her eyes staring.

Again, all of a sudden, she saw it. Moving with the stealthy caution which is its birthright, it appeared fleetingly a score of feet lower on the steep slope, the body and its shadow, a twin for stealthy silence, gone in a flash, reappearing once more still lower on the slope and just beyond the pine sapling. It was coming on. Fascinated, Gloria sat like stone, with never a thought of the rifle lying across her knees.

The mountain-lion leaped downward softly from stage to stage of the canon-side, paused under the pine, lifted its head, and sent forth again its hunger-cry. All this time Gloria sat breathless; the fear-fascination still held her powerless. She watched the animal crouch and gather its strength and hurl its lean body upward. The lion fell back, the ripping claws having missed the meat by some two or three feet, and Gloria heard the low, rumbling growl. Again it sprang; again it missed. And then, for a weary time of silence it sat still, its head back, its eyes on the desired meal. In the moonlight Gloria saw the glistening saliva from the half-parted jaws.

But in the end feline craft found the way, and the cat set its paws against the tree trunk, and began to climb. Limbs broke under the two hundred pounds of weight; the bark was torn under slipping paws, but upward the sinuous body writhed.

Swiftly now it would come to King's kill.

King's! Gloria started; this was Mark's kill: he had stalked it, he had ploughed many miles through deep snow to get it. To get it for her as well as for him. To keep the life in her—now, without it, King would die. And now the lion was going to take it, while she watched and did nothing!

"Oh, God, help me!" She sprang to her feet, she jerked up her rifle and fired at the black bulk crawling upward in the pine. "It shall not have Mark's meat! It shall not!"

At the first shot the mountain-lion dropped through crashing branches. She had shot it—she had driven a bullet through its heart. God had heard her. That was her first wild thought. But in a flash she saw that it was on its feet again, and that with red mouth snarling it had swung about, facing her; she saw the cruel white teeth, wet and glistening.

Incoherently Gloria cried out, again sick and shaken with terror. In another moment she would have the lean powerful body leaping upon her. She fired again and again, taking no time for aim, as fast as she could work the lever and pull the trigger; she was trembling so that it was all that she could do to hold the gun at all. She prayed and called on Mark and fired, all at once.

Never did bullets fly wider of the mark, but never did the roar of exploding shells do better service. The lion, though ravenous, was not yet starved to the degree to whip it to the supreme desperation of attacking a human being and defying a rifle; it whirled and went flashing across the snow, seeking the shadows, gone in the drifts, vanishing.

Gloria gasped, stared after its wild flight a paralysed moment and then ran to the tree where the bear hung. She was shaking like a leaf in a storm; she was still terrified, filled with horror at the thought that at any second the lean body might come flashing back upon her. But through the emotions storming through her there lived on that one determination that would live while she lived: that was Mark's meat and she was going to save it for him. She began climbing the young pine; she fought wildly to get up into its branches; she was handicapped by the rifle which she clung to desperately. She got the gun in a crotch above her head; she pulled herself upward; she slipped, and tore the skin of hands and arms; but hastening frantically she climbed up and up. She got the rifle into her hands again, nearly dropped it, thrust it above her, jammed it into a fork of a limb and kept on climbing. At last she was where she could reach out and touch the swinging carcass. With King's keen-edged butcher knife she hacked and cut at the frozen meat, panting with every effort. The task seemed endless; the bear swung away from her; a branch broke under her foot and she almost fell; she was sobbing aloud brokenly before it was done, the tears rolling down her cheeks. But at last there was the thud of the falling meat; below her it lay on the snow crust. In wild haste she snatched her rifle; holding it in one hand, afraid to let it slip out of her grasp for a moment, casting a last fearful look in the direction whither the lion had gone, she began slipping down. And in another moment, with the precious burden caught up with the gun in her arms, she was running back up the ridge, her feet in King's trail. *The home trail!*

She looked behind her at every step, picturing the snarling cat springing out from every shadow, starting upward from every drift and snow-bank. But she clutched her meat tight and struggled on up the slope.

Her whole body was shaking; she closed her eyes, overcome with faintness. There was a faint wind stirring and it cut like a knife, probing through her garments where they were damp. She shivered and struggled on and on. She felt that she could run all night without stopping. She stumbled and fell and arose, panting and sobbing, and ran on. She no longer looked behind her: she had fallen when she did that. Again and again from far behind her came the clear, merciless scream of the mountain-lion. Time passed; half-hour or hour or two hours, she had little idea. Time itself was a nightmare of running, falling, rising, staggering, running again until the blood pounded in her temples, drummed in her ears. The cry came again, as near as before—nearer? Throughout the night as she struggled on she could always fancy the stealthy, silent feet following her, keeping time with her own. Cautious now, would its caution slowly subside as its hunger grew and as she always fled from it? The thought came to her that such a menace would follow one day after day; that it would wait and wait; that in the end it knew its time would come when sleep or exhaustion broke down its prey's guard. Then it would leap and strike.

Her rifle had grown a heart-breaking weight, until it seemed that it would drag her arms from their sockets to hold it up; the pack of meat on her back was like lead.

She wondered if King had missed her; if he were awake and wondering at her absence. She wondered if he would miss her soon; how soon? At the first glint of dawn? Would he begin to see, that she was at least, and at last, trying? Well, she had tried; though she died, still she had tried. She was cold to the bone; her teeth chattered, her body quaked. Yet she kept on. She fell; she lay with the tears of exhaustion rolling down her face; she struggled to get to her feet; she fell again. But always she rose and always she kept on. And so, in the fulness of time, after long frightful, hellish hours, Sec.he came to the last terror of the night.

The new day was bright on the mountain tops when she felt at first a dull sort of surprise and then a sudden, stimulating gladness, noting the familiar look of the ridge ahead. Yonder the cave would be. The cave and King, success and rest. She straightened up a little, brushing her hand across her straining eyes, making sure that she was right. She heard the insistent scream behind her, but now she did not heed it, for in front of her, stock-still in the trail, was a man. It was Benny.

To-night she had thrilled to an ecstasy descending from the stars, welling up in her own heart, and she had shivered with fear and had dropped with weariness akin to despair. Now suddenly all emotions were upgathered into searing anger. Her thought was: "He will take the meat from me! The meat I have brought for Mark." She grew rigid in her tracks. She jerked up her rifle in front of her; her tired eyes hardened. She had gone to the limits of endurance in a labour of love; she had succeeded; and now she would fight for what she had brought back.

Then she noted that Benny had not seen her. Though he was in full view on the ridge, he had had no eyes for her. He was stooping. She saw that he had a small pack on his back; food, no doubt. On the ground by him was a second pack, something in a crash sack; Benny was struggling to lift it to his shoulders. It must be very heavy. Gloria drew back hastily, glancing about her, found the only hiding-place offered, and slipped behind the big rock.

Presently Benny came on. She heard him from a distance; he was talking to himself excitedly, jabbering broken fragments of sentences, twice breaking into his hideous dry cackle of laughter. She shivered; his utterances sounded mad.

And mad they were. Perhaps his drug had run out; certainly for a nervous man there had been ample cause for jangling nerves. He jabbered constantly, his mutterings at last coming to her in jumbled words as Benny drew on.

He was talking about "gold," and he chuckled. He mentioned names, Brodie's and Jarrold's and Gratton's and another name, and he chuckled again. Gloria peered cautiously from the shelter of her rock. He was very near now, struggling with the smaller pack and his rifle and the heavy bundle in his sack. She thought that he was going to pass without seeing her. But just as he passed abreast of her hiding-place something prompted Benny to jerk up his head. He saw her and stopped suddenly; she saw his eyes. And she knew on the instant that if the man were not stark mad, at least he was not entirely sane. She lifted her rifle, cold all over; if he came another step nearer she would shoot....

"It's mine!" Benny shrieked at her. "Mine, I tell you!"

He broke into a run, passing her, leaving the trail, floundering down the ridge the shortest way. His rifle encumbered him; she saw it fall into the snow, while Benny, clutching his gunny-sack in both arms, stumbled on. He fell; he rose, shrieking curses. She watched, fascinated. The pack on his back slipped around in front of him; Benny tore at it and cursed it and hurled it from him. Still hugging his gold he was gone, far down the steep slope. Gloria shuddered and stepped back into her own trail. She could hear Benny cursing faintly. Like an echo came another cry across the ridges; the cry of a starving cat.

CHAPTER XXXIII

Mark King awakened to a sensation of piercing cold. In his weakened condition the chill struck deep, the pain of it sore in his wound. He moved a little to draw his blankets closer about him and, as an awaking impression, found that his strength, even though slowly, was surely returning to him. He was still terribly weak, but, thank God—and Gloria!—that hideous faintness in which he had been unable to stir hand or foot or to speak above a whisper had passed. He filled his lungs with a deep and grateful breath of satisfaction. In a day or two he would be able to carry on again, to do his part.

He turned his head, lifting it a trifle; already he had thought of Gloria, and now he sought her. The fire had burned down to a handful of glowing coals; Gloria, then, must be asleep. For that, too, he was grateful. He had but faint remembrance and dim knowledge of what tasks must have fallen to her lot, but his mind, active from the moment his eyes flew open, was quick to understand that the burdens had fallen upon her shoulders and that she must have been in dire need of rest and sleep.

He could not see her anywhere; no doubt she lay in the shadowy dark beyond the dying fire. He lay back, staring up into the gloom above him. It was thinning; day was coming or had come already. A day with sunshine! They could go out on the crust by the time that he was able to be about—

Then he remembered the blankets! Last night he had had all of them, Gloria's as well as his own. He had wanted to make her take her covers and she had put him off, and he had gone to sleep, forgetting! He stirred again, hastily, his hands groping, even his feet moving. He had them yet, his and hers. And she had slept through the cold night with no covering while he, never waking until now, had lain warm and comfortable. He struggled to turn on his side and got himself raised a little despite the pain from the exertion, seeking her. She must be frozen—

Gloria was not in the cave. He sank back, sure of that. For she should be sleeping close by the fire. Then she had gone down again for wood. He frowned and lay staring upward again. Gloria bringing wood while he lay here like a confounded log. He grew nervously restive at the thought; it was unthinkable that she should do work like that. He saw her in his mind, struggling with the unaccustomed labour. And always he saw her as he had first seen her, a fragile-looking girl, a girl with sweet little hands as soft as rose petals. He remembered her as he had seen her that first day, a vision of loveliness in her fluffy pink dress, her skin like the skin of a baby, her eyes the soft, tender grey eyes of the girl to whom he had given his heart without reservation. The glorious Gloria, all slender delicacy, like a little mountain flower, the Gloria for whom it had been his duty and his high privilege to labour. He must fight to get his strength back, to get on his feet again, to save her from such toil as was no woman's work in the world, certainly never the work for a girl like Gloria.

He heard a sound at the cave's mouth. Gloria was coming back. He found no words with which to greet her, but lay very still, waiting for her to come in. An emotion of which he was ashamed and yet which was infinitely sweet swept over him: it was so wonderful a thing to have Gloria come to him, nurse him, put her hand so tenderly on his. A thrill shot down his faintly stirring pulses as already he fancied her stealing softly to his side. So he waited and, when she came where he could at last see her, watched.

She set her gun down; at first he wondered at that. Poor little Gloria, he thought; taking her rifle with her when she went down for wood, frightened and yet strong-hearted enough to go in spite of fear. She came on, not to him but to the smouldering coals. She had turned toward him, but, no doubt, thought him still asleep. He watched her, still knowing that presently she would come, awaiting her coming. And again he was perplexed; he did not understand why Gloria walked like that. He had never seen her walk so before; she had always been so light of foot, so graceful—so like a fairy creature, scarcely touching the ground. Now her feet dragged; she groped uncertainly; she was like one gone suddenly dizzy.

She dropped down by the coals, her face in her hands. The light was bad; he could hardly see her now. He heard a sigh that ended in a sob. She rose, oh, so wearily. He saw her sway as she walked; she was throwing wood on the fire. It caught; a flame flared out; other flames followed with their merry crackling and leaping lights. And now he saw Gloria's face. It was drawn and haggard; it had been washed with tears; her eyes looked enormous and unnaturally bright. He saw her hair; it was in wild disarray, a tumble of disorder. He saw that she had sacks wrapped about her lagging feet; that her clothes were torn, that her sleeves were ragged, that her arms were covered with long scratches! His first thought, making his body tense with anger, was that he had not come in time to save her from Brodie's hands....

What was Gloria doing? Struggling with something on her back. Something which was tied across her shoulders. She got it free; it fell close to the fire, played over by the light of the flames. He craned his neck and saw; it was a great chunk of bear meat—he could see bits of the hide still on it!

He could not understand. Not yet. All that he could do was stare at her and wonder and grope confusedly for the explanation. It was clear that something was wrong with Gloria; she dropped down by the fire, she slumped forward, she lay her face upon her crossed arms. He could see the frail body shaking—he could hear her sudden wild sobbing.

The truth came upon him at last, dawning slowly, slowly.

"Gloria!" It was a gasp of more than amazement; consternation was in his heart. "*Gloria!*"

She lifted her head and sat up. He saw her great wide-open eyes and the tears gushing from them. She fought to control herself, a sob in her throat. She rose and came toward him in strange, wildly uncertain steps.

"Gloria! You—"

"Sh, Mark; you mustn't—"

But he couldn't lie still. He lifted himself upon his elbow and looked at her with wondering eyes. She stood over him, looking on the verge of collapse. Slowly she came down to him, half kneeling, half falling.

"My God," he cried hoarsely. "You went for my bear? *You did it.*"

She tried to smile at him, and into his own eyes there broke a sudden gush of tears.

"You wonderful, wonderful, wonderful Gloria!" he cried out. "There is no girl in all the world could have done that—there is no girl like you."

Her hand was questing his; he caught it and gripped it with all the strength in him; he hurt her, and at last, with the pain, her smile broke through.

"Gloria—"

"Mark?"

"Can you—not so soon, but some day—forgive me?"

She found only a faint whisper with which to answer him; her eyes were as hungry as his.

"Can you forgive, Mark?"

And now, when their eyes clung together as their hands were already clinging, each was marvelling that the other could forgive and love one who had erred so.

THE END

Choose from Thousands of 1stWorldLibrary Classics By

A. M. Barnard
Ada Leverson
Adolphus William Ward
Aesop
Agatha Christie
Alexander Aaronsohn
Alexander Kielland
Alexandre Dumas
Alfred Gatty
Alfred Ollivant
Alice Duer Miller
Alice Turner Curtis
Alice Dunbar
Allen Chapman
Alleyne Ireland
Ambrose Bierce
Amelia E. Barr
Amory H. Bradford
Andrew Lang
Andrew McFarland Davis
Andy Adams
Angela Brazil
Anna Alice Chapin
Anna Sewell
Annie Besant
Annie Hamilton Donnell
Annie Payson Call
Annie Roe Carr
Annonaymous
Anton Chekhov
Archibald Lee Fletcher
Arnold Bennett
Arthur C. Benson
Arthur Conan Doyle
Arthur M. Winfield
Arthur Ransome
Arthur Schnitzler
Arthur Train
Atticus
B.H. Baden-Powell
B. M. Bower
B. C. Chatterjee
Baroness Emmuska Orczy
Baroness Orczy
Basil King
Bayard Taylor
Ben Macomber
Bertha Muzzy Bower
Bjornstjerne Bjornson

Booth Tarkington
Boyd Cable
Bram Stoker
C. Collodi
C. E. Orr
C. M. Ingleby
Carolyn Wells
Catherine Parr Traill
Charles A. Eastman
Charles Amory Beach
Charles Dickens
Charles Dudley Warner
Charles Farrar Browne
Charles Ives
Charles Kingsley
Charles Klein
Charles Hanson Towne
Charles Lathrop Pack
Charles Romyn Dake
Charles Whibley
Charles Willing Beale
Charlotte M. Braeme
Charlotte M. Yonge
Charlotte Perkins Stetson
Clair W. Hayes
Clarence Day Jr.
Clarence E. Mulford
Clemence Housman
Confucius
Coningsby Dawson
Cornelis DeWitt Wilcox
Cyril Burleigh
D. H. Lawrence
Daniel Defoe
David Garnett
Dinah Craik
Don Carlos Janes
Donald Keyhoe
Dorothy Kilner
Dougan Clark
Douglas Fairbanks
E. Nesbit
E. P. Roe
E. Phillips Oppenheim
E. S. Brooks
Earl Barnes
Edgar Rice Burroughs
Edith Van Dyne
Edith Wharton

Edward Everett Hale
Edward J. O'Biren
Edward S. Ellis
Edwin L. Arnold
Eleanor Atkins
Eleanor Hallowell Abbott
Eliot Gregory
Elizabeth Gaskell
Elizabeth McCracken
Elizabeth Von Arnim
Ellem Key
Emerson Hough
Emilie F. Carlen
Emily Bronte
Emily Dickinson
Enid Bagnold
Enilor Macartney Lane
Erasmus W. Jones
Ernie Howard Pie
Ethel May Dell
Ethel Turner
Ethel Watts Mumford
Eugene Sue
Eugenie Foa
Eugene Wood
Eustace Hale Ball
Evelyn Everett-green
Everard Cotes
F. H. Cheley
F. J. Cross
F. Marion Crawford
Fannie E. Newberry
Federick Austin Ogg
Ferdinand Ossendowski
Fergus Hume
Florence A. Kilpatrick
Fremont B. Deering
Francis Bacon
Francis Darwin
Frances Hodgson Burnett
Frances Parkinson Keyes
Frank Gee Patchin
Frank Harris
Frank Jewett Mather
Frank L. Packard
Frank V. Webster
Frederic Stewart Isham
Frederick Trevor Hill
Frederick Winslow Taylor

Friedrich Kerst
Friedrich Nietzsche
Fyodor Dostoyevsky
G.A. Henty
G.K. Chesterton
Gabrielle E. Jackson
Garrett P. Serviss
Gaston Leroux
George A. Warren
George Ade
Geroge Bernard Shaw
George Cary Eggleston
George Durston
George Ebers
George Eliot
George Gissing
George MacDonald
George Meredith
George Orwell
George Sylvester Viereck
George Tucker
George W. Cable
George Wharton James
Gertrude Atherton
Gordon Casserly
Grace E. King
Grace Gallatin
Grace Greenwood
Grant Allen
Guillermo A. Sherwell
Gulielma Zollinger
Gustav Flaubert
H. A. Cody
H. B. Irving
H.C. Bailey
H. G. Wells
H. H. Munro
H. Irving Hancock
H. R. Naylor
H. Rider Haggard
H. W. C. Davis
Haldeman Julius
Hall Caine
Hamilton Wright Mabie
Hans Christian Andersen
Harold Avery
Harold McGrath
Harriet Beecher Stowe
Harry Castlemon
Harry Coghill
Harry Houidini

Hayden Carruth
Helent Hunt Jackson
Helen Nicolay
Hendrik Conscience
Hendy David Thoreau
Henri Barbusse
Henrik Ibsen
Henry Adams
Henry Ford
Henry Frost
Henry James
Henry Jones Ford
Henry Seton Merriman
Henry W Longfellow
Herbert A. Giles
Herbert Carter
Herbert N. Casson
Herman Hesse
Hildegard G. Frey
Homer
Honore De Balzac
Horace B. Day
Horace Walpole
Horatio Alger Jr.
Howard Pyle
Howard R. Garis
Hugh Lofting
Hugh Walpole
Humphry Ward
Ian Maclaren
Inez Haynes Gillmore
Irving Bacheller
Isabel Cecilia Williams
Isabel Hornibrook
Israel Abrahams
Ivan Turgenev
J.G.Austin
J. Henri Fabre
J. M. Barrie
J. M. Walsh
J. Macdonald Oxley
J. R. Miller
J. S. Fletcher
J. S. Knowles
J. Storer Clouston
J. W. Duffield
Jack London
Jacob Abbott
James Allen
James Andrews
James Baldwin

James Branch Cabell
James DeMille
James Joyce
James Lane Allen
James Lane Allen
James Oliver Curwood
James Oppenheim
James Otis
James R. Driscoll
Jane Abbott
Jane Austen
Jane L. Stewart
Janet Aldridge
Jens Peter Jacobsen
Jerome K. Jerome
Jessie Graham Flower
John Buchan
John Burroughs
John Cournos
John F. Kennedy
John Gay
John Glasworthy
John Habberton
John Joy Bell
John Kendrick Bangs
John Milton
John Philip Sousa
John Taintor Foote
Jonas Lauritz Idemil Lie
Jonathan Swift
Joseph A. Altsheler
Joseph Carey
Joseph Conrad
Joseph E. Badger Jr
Joseph Hergesheimer
Joseph Jacobs
Jules Vernes
Julian Hawthrone
Julie A Lippmann
Justin Huntly McCarthy
Kakuzo Okakura
Karle Wilson Baker
Kate Chopin
Kenneth Grahame
Kenneth McGaffey
Kate Langley Bosher
Kate Langley Bosher
Katherine Cecil Thurston
Katherine Stokes
L. A. Abbot
L. T. Meade

L. Frank Baum
Latta Griswold
Laura Dent Crane
Laura Lee Hope
Laurence Housman
Lawrence Beasley
Leo Tolstoy
Leonid Andreyev
Lewis Carroll
Lewis Sperry Chafer
Lilian Bell
Lloyd Osbourne
Louis Hughes
Louis Joseph Vance
Louis Tracy
Louisa May Alcott
Lucy Fitch Perkins
Lucy Maud Montgomery
Luther Benson
Lydia Miller Middleton
Lyndon Orr
M. Corvus
M. H. Adams
Margaret E. Sangster
Margret Howth
Margaret Vandercook
Margaret W. Hungerford
Margret Penrose
Maria Edgeworth
Maria Thompson Daviess
Mariano Azuela
Marion Polk Angellotti
Mark Overton
Mark Twain
Mary Austin
Mary Catherine Crowley
Mary Cole
Mary Hastings Bradley
Mary Roberts Rinehart
Mary Rowlandson
M. Wollstonecraft Shelley
Maud Lindsay
Max Beerbohm
Myra Kelly
Nathaniel Hawthrone
Nicolo Machiavelli
O. F. Walton
Oscar Wilde

Owen Johnson
P.G. Wodehouse
Paul and Mabel Thorne
Paul G. Tomlinson
Paul Severing
Percy Brebner
Percy Keese Fitzhugh
Peter B. Kyne
Plato
Quincy Allen
R. Derby Holmes
R. L. Stevenson
R. S. Ball
Rabindranath Tagore
Rahul Alvares
Ralph Bonehill
Ralph Henry Barbour
Ralph Victor
Ralph Waldo Emmerson
Rene Descartes
Ray Cummings
Rex Beach
Rex E. Beach
Richard Harding Davis
Richard Jefferies
Richard Le Gallienne
Robert Barr
Robert Frost
Robert Gordon Anderson
Robert L. Drake
Robert Lansing
Robert Lynd
Robert Michael Ballantyne
Robert W. Chambers
Rosa Nouchette Carey
Rudyard Kipling
Saint Augustine
Samuel B. Allison
Samuel Hopkins Adams
Sarah Bernhardt
Sarah C. Hallowell
Selma Lagerlof
Sherwood Anderson
Sigmund Freud
Standish O'Grady
Stanley Weyman
Stella Benson
Stella M. Francis

Stephen Crane
Stewart Edward White
Stijn Streuvels
Swami Abhedananda
Swami Parmananda
T. S. Ackland
T. S. Arthur
The Princess Der Ling
Thomas A. Janvier
Thomas A Kempis
Thomas Anderton
Thomas Bailey Aldrich
Thomas Bulfinch
Thomas De Quincey
Thomas Dixon
Thomas H. Huxley
Thomas Hardy
Thomas More
Thornton W. Burgess
U. S. Grant
Upton Sinclair
Valentine Williams
Various Authors
Vaughan Kester
Victor Appleton
Victor G. Durham
Victoria Cross
Virginia Woolf
Wadsworth Camp
Walter Camp
Walter Scott
Washington Irving
Wilbur Lawton
Wilkie Collins
Willa Cather
Willard F. Baker
William Dean Howells
William le Queux
W. Makepeace Thackeray
William W. Walter
William Shakespeare
Winston Churchill
Yei Theodora Ozaki
Yogi Ramacharaka
Young E. Allison
Zane Grey